# WITH NO *Regrets*

# WITH NO
## Regrets

# JULIE N. FORD

WHITE
STAR
PRESS

This is a work of fiction, and the views expressed herein are the sole responsibility of the author. Likewise, certain characters, places, and incidents are the product of the author's imagination, and any resemblance to actual persons, living or dead, or actual events or locales, is entirely coincidental.

*With No Regrets*

Published by White Star Press
P.O. Box 353
American Fork, Utah 84003

Cover and interior design by White Star Press

Print ISBN: 978-1-939203-65-6
Printed in the United States of America
Year of first printing: 2015

FOR CORY

# Acknowledgements

First, I want to thank my sister, Cory, for having a crush on her trainer, which planted the seed that grew to become this story. Next, a huge thank you to John Sutton and Chuck Poll for lending me their beautiful and inspired song lyrics. I also want to mention all of my beta readers, Christie Thompson, Sue Poll, and Breeann Allison. To my critique group, Braden Bell and Christi Minton, thank you for encouraging me when I so wanted to quit. You guys totally rock! Lastly, to Rachel Ann Nunes and all the folks at White Star Press for being such a dream to work with and for seeing the potential in this manuscript. All y'all totally rock too. :)

## Chapter 1

"Hello, my name is Finley."

Her name was all she'd been asked to share, and why she didn't stop there, she couldn't say for sure. Maybe it was the fact that she'd been forced into coming here today. Or possibly because somewhere in the uncharted regions of her soul, she knew she needed this. Whatever the reason, uninvited words continued to march across her lips.

"Well, most people just call me Finnie, except I hate that. I was named after my granny Opaline Finley-Taylor. I loved her very much." A tear pricked the corner of Finley's eye, her gaze sweeping the circle of questioning looks. "God rest her soul."

The woman sitting across from Finley—Burlie-Jean, the paper tag adhered to her lapel read—lifted one palm to the air, the hand of the other pressing to the center of her generous bosom. "Lord bless her poor, wretched soul," she echoed, eyes closed, face turned toward heaven.

Finley mustered a half smile in response. "So, Finley . . . My name is Finley."

"Hello, Finley!" chorused the group of three women and one man in return.

The echo of their greeting bounced from the rafters of the tired YMCA basketball court, falling in rivulets to shake Finley's tattered nerves. "Lord a'mighty," she said, pressing both palms against her chest to still the vibrations, "y'all give quite the welcome."

Careen, their group leader, shook back the curtain of strawberry-blonde hair that draped around her heart-shaped face, then settled her pebble-eyed gaze on Finley. "Now, just tell us why you're here?"

Dragging her fingertips nervously through the first traces of gray arching up from her widow's peak, Finley stalled, "Oh right," as she struggled against the memory, attempting to keep all the details, the sordid ones at least, corralled to the far corners of her mind. "Well, like I said before, I'm Finley," she repeated, knowing the blush reddening her cheeks would not go unnoticed. With raven hair, light blue eyes, and rosy cheeks and lips, it had never been a stretch for her to dress as Snow White on Halloween, and in situations such as this, next to impossible to hide even the smallest trace of embarrassment. "I'm forty. Just turned last week. Labor Day, as a matter of fact." She smiled as if sharing her birthday with a national holiday this year had been an exciting twist of events. It hadn't been. "They say forty is the new thirty, but with both my babies off to college and my home so quiet all of a sudden, it doesn't feel like . . ." If only she could define how she felt. "Well, someone should tell my mirror. Because somehow my reflection didn't get the memo," she said a little too brightly. "If you know what I mean," she added and then snorted. *Snorted!*

A subtle throat clearing, and then Careen leaned forward. "Yes, I think we all know what you mean, so why don't we get back to you telling us why you're here."

Finley crushed the folly from her voice. "Of course, I'm so sorry." She shared a brief apologetic smile with each of her fellow therapy victims—um, members. "I've forgotten my manners. My momma would hate that," she added on the trail of a sigh. "Momma. She's the *real* reason I'm here. Because she decided I needed help. That I wasn't handling my," she pursed her lips, searching for the right words, "my situation properly." In other words, the way *she* thought Finley should. "So here I am, in group therapy."

Careen's tiny bowed mouth pulled into a thin, condescending line. "That's right, Finley, and in group therapy we work as a *group* to help each other process and take steps to improve our lives. And, in *group* therapy, the very first step is for each member to admit, out loud, to the rest of the group, why he or she is here," she explained, carefully measuring each word. "So why don't you take a deep breath, start again, and tell us *exactly* why you're here today." She gave Finley a pointed look. "Okay?"

Finley gulped back on her chagrin. "All right." Threading her fingers through the thick layers of her hair, she re-deposited the bulk of it over her shoulders. Her hesitation had everyone leaning slightly forward, though she couldn't imagine why. They were all here for the same reason. "I'm divorced."

A quiet hush of relief that she'd finally said the d-word advanced around the small circle. The group members settled back in their seats.

Then Careen made a rolling motion with her miniature hand. "How long?" she prompted.

"Two weeks." Finley held up coinciding fingers. "It's been two weeks since I signed the papers, ending my twenty-one-year marriage." There, she'd said it—aloud. She was divorced. A divorcée. Single. Completely on her own. Alone.

Finley's heart rolled into a ball and beat against her throat.

For the first time since she'd signed the papers, the divorce felt real.

Final.

"Very good, Finley," Careen said, forcing the sort of smile that told Finley the worst was yet to come. "And here at 'Divorce Is Not an End But a New Beginning' we work to move forward by taking steps that will move us beyond the hurt where we can begin the healing." She flourished her delicate hands out to the group in an earnest plea. "Now, would you like to share with everyone why it is your momma insisted you come here today?"

Finley feigned thought for a moment. "It was nothing, really." She waved her hand, clearing the air of any notion to the contrary. "Just a minor altercation at last week's garden club luncheon."

"Small?" Careen pursed her lips, disbelieving. "Altercation?"

Finley rolled a shoulder in a nonchalant fashion. "Yes well, there may have been some name calling, a few deep, dark secrets revealed, and," she glanced around to see that everyone was leaning closer again, "a slap or two. But really, no one was hurt. Not seriously, at least."

"Hm-hmm," Burlie-Jean hummed with a sway of her head, her gaze sending a critical stare at Finley—a stare eerily similar to the one Macy Wallace had lobbed at Finley not five days ago. More specifically, the proverbial falling shoe that had sent Finley over the edge she hadn't even realized she'd been teetering on.

"It's okay, Finley," Careen said in a soothing voice. "Like I stated earlier, this is a safe zone." She made a sweeping motion with her hands, indicating the corner of the gymnasium they'd laid claim to. "Nothing said within this group is ever repeated or judged. We're all here to support one another."

Finley had known before coming here, she'd likely be

asked to recount the incident. But as the particulars of that day crowded their way to the forefront of her mind, she suddenly had the sensation she was falling, disappearing into an oblivion, only to reemerge and find herself, dreamlike, in a different time and place she'd wanted never to visit again . . .

The sunroom where her garden club held their meetings had been stuffed to capacity that day with tables full of warm-breathed women. Even with the wicker-paddled fans moving at high speed, and the air conditioning blowing incessantly, the room had felt stuffy. The ice in Finley's sweet tea had begun to melt, fanning a wet ring out onto the ivory tablecloth beneath. Conjectural whispers accosted her from all directions, circling her body like a python, squeezing until she could hardly draw a breath.

"When you're ready, Finley," Careen encouraged. "Just take your time."

Closing her eyes, Finley sunk deeper into her latest night-mare. "It was my garden club's monthly luncheon, and from the podium, Macy Wallace was talking about decorations for the autumn festival at Cheekwood gardens," she began, her voice vacant as if playing from a recording in her head. "Then, Macy glanced over at me with her trademark sympathetic look. You know, the kind that seems sincere though it's anything but, and said, 'Finnie, I'm so sorry you've been too preoccupied to be of much help this year, but we understand. Divorce proceedings can sometimes be such an emotional drain. And though we all know, and believe, that our Lord and Savior does not look kindly on the dissolution of any marriage, we want you to know that not one of your garden club sisters is judging you. Our hearts go out to you Finnie. And to your poor, broken-homed children . . .'"

"She said that?" the woman next to Finley scoffed. "She said, 'your poor, broken-homed children'?"

Finley's eyes fluttered, the here-and-now abruptly dropping around her like the changing backdrop of a play. "Well, those may not have been her *exact* words, but as I looked around at everyone, and the faked sympathy on their faces, I don't know—that was how it sounded to me," she admitted, then pressed her parched lips together. Taking a quick look around, she searched for a refreshment table, but saw none. Didn't these types of meetings generally include coffee and doughnuts? Ice water?

"And then?" Careen gently prompted, reminding Finley that she was nowhere near the end of her story.

Finley turned her attention back to the circle and all the eyes fixated on her with a weary interest. She hated herself for even considering the fact, but—how could she put this without sounding catty?—she and her fellow group members didn't exactly run in the same social circles. Normally, she wasn't one to air her laundry, especially that of the soiled variety, but it wasn't like she'd ever see any of these people outside of this smelly gym. So what could it hurt to simply go ahead and spill the rest?

Pulling in a breath tainted with the hint of sweaty socks, she pressed on. "Before I knew what was happening, my napkin was flying from my lap as I stood and hollered, 'Oh cut the crap, Macy, or should I say Kittlylou? You're one to talk! We all know about your past life and that pimp of a first husband who ran a gentleman's club outta that doublewide you crawled out from under. Or doesn't God consider a common-law marriage sinful to abandon?'"

Finley's fellow group members shared a hushed gasp, but she hastened on, desperate all of a sudden, to let it all out. "Then Macy smoothed a hand over that tacky yellow dye-job of hers and said, 'Why, Finnie, what on earth has gotten into you?' Momma was yanking on my skirt, telling me to sit down and shut my 'feral trap,' but I ignored her. 'Oh, I see how this is gonna go,' I said to Macy. 'And since we're *not* talkin' 'bout past transgressions, I guess we're just gonna pretend like I didn't catch you doing the white-trash two-step with my husband on my brand new Bernhardt sofa?'

"Macy's mouth fell open, and she covered the hole with her tawdry pink nails, and Suzanna, her minion-in-chief, got to her feet and said, 'Finnie Harrison, this is not the time or place for such talk!' She should have stayed out of it. 'Don't you 'Finnie Harrison' me, Suzanna! We all know the UPS man is delivering more than packages to your house every day. I mean, honestly, not even Molly does that much online shopping . . . Molly spends more hours watching the shopping channel than her husband does on that porn site he's addicted to, and an attic brimming over with the hidden evidence to prove it. But then who can blame her when her husband spends every free moment on that Internet porn site—Fifty Shades of Laid?"

Muffled snickers shook the shoulders of the woman sitting next to Finley, but she hardly noticed as she finished the rest.

"And then like Julia Roberts in the movie, *Something to Talk About*, more secrets came spilling from my mouth, and consequently the mouths of others. And by the time Momma and Cathyanne had drug me out, the skeletons of nearly every woman in that room had been exposed . . ." Finley let her words and the rest fade with what was left of her denial.

Though more than seventy-five women had witnessed her little hissy fit that day, up until this moment, Finley had worked hard to convince herself the incident had been nothing more than a bad dream—the kind you wake from, pinching yourself, thankful it wasn't real. Only now did she truly realize there would be no waking from this dream. It had been real— all too real—and she wasn't proud of her behavior or the lives turned on end by her outburst. But she hoped, in the very least, that releasing those women's secrets had somehow made them free. If what we kept hidden didn't fade from reality just because we refused to speak of it, why did Finley, like everybody else, try so hard to hide from who she really was?

Maybe if she didn't work so hard trying to be someone she wasn't, finding her true self wouldn't feel so impossible . . .

"Finley?" Careen was saying. "Are you all right?"

The group leader's question severed Finley from her musing. "Yes, fine," she whispered before reclaiming her voice. "Suffice it to say, I may have ruined a few marriages, not to mention friendships, that day."

"So this 'altercation,' as you called it, was about confronting the woman your husband was having an affair with?" Careen restated.

Finley shrugged. Truthfully, she'd been more concerned by Macy's insinuation that she'd ruined her life, shamed her family, and was headed straight for hell, than with provoking the woman she'd caught her husband with. "Yeah, I guess," she agreed, because doing so was easier than delving any further into the true cause behind her outburst. "But he and Macy were just a one-time fling. There were other affairs."

"Let's start with this business regarding Macy," Careen said. "How did it make you feel, walking in on your husband with another woman?"

Finley knew what Careen expected her to say. And sure, over the years she had struggled with the why-wasn't-I-good-enough question more times than she could count. Then one day, like a squeaky hinge or a picture frame that refused to hang straight, the vexation had grown insignificant with time and frequency until the "why" simply didn't matter anymore.

As for Careen's specific question, Finley thought back to the end of May. It was the day she'd dropped her daughter,

Royanne (named for Finley's husband and best friend—and yes, her daughter hated her name too), off at the Vanderbilt University dorms to attend a summer program, preparatory to her fall semester's classes. She'd planned to help Royanne settle in and then buy her a quick farewell lunch, but her daughter had circled Finley in a half-hearted hug and said: "Thanks, Momma. Love you. I can take it from here."

Finley had been dismissed. Rendered unnecessary.

Sniffing back a mounting wave of loss, she'd serpentined her way through parents and students, back the way she'd come, all while trying, unsuccessfully, to ignore a surging need for comfort in the form of red velvet cake balls. When her cravings only grew stronger, the closer she came to home, she'd dropped in at the market to pick up a few missing ingredients and headed for her big, empty kitchen.

Her mouth watering with anticipation of a little guilty pleasure, the very last thing she'd expected to see upon entering her family room was Roy's bare backside arching into view over the sofa, followed by a high-pitched squeak that was uncannily female. As Finley's grocery bag had floated in slow motion to the floor, she vaguely remembered a fleeting pinch of humiliation. But now that she was thinking back, she realized what had bothered her the most was not the sight of her husband tangled up with another woman, but how they were defiling her beloved new sofa.

"I felt . . . relieved," slipped from Finley's lips before she could come up with a more appropriate answer. Until that day, she'd obediently carried the burden of undeclared consent, drowning under the weight of an unfulfilling marriage. But this time, Roy's act of betrayal had been too blatant for even the most devout Christian to ignore, a clean slice through the tether that had bound her tongue, her first gasp of sweet breath upon breaching the water's surface.

Burlie-Jean pointed a curled acrylic nail in Finley's direction. "Girl, you done lost you're ever-lovin' mind," she called out with a tremor in her incredulous voice. "If I'd caught my Henry with his two-bit hussy, I-like-ta wrung both their necks right then and there. My man was just too darn sneaky is all."

The woman next to Burlie-Jean, the one who'd been chewing her nails the entire session, pulled her pinky finger out of her mouth long enough to say, "He abuse you?" then resumed her assault, but on her thumbnail this time. Painfully thin with stringy hair and big brown eyes that shifted anxiously around the room, the name on her tag read Sue.

Philandering behavior aside, and unless you counted never standing up to his mother whenever that spiteful woman spoke all manner of ill against Finley, Roy was a good man. "No," she answered, deciding that verbal abuse by proxy probably didn't count.

Sue tucked her now bleeding thumbnail into her palm and curled her fingers into a fist. "He a gambler?" she asked. "Lost all y'all's money?"

"No," Finley said. Money had always been Roy's number-one focus. He would never do anything to jeopardize his precious millions, or the social status his wealth had bought him. "He worked a lot though. He owns a car dealership down in Nashville. Three, actually."

The woman next to Finley piped up with, "A drinker then?" Finley had felt this woman's stare burning into her throughout the meeting, but hadn't yet addressed her directly. She turned to her now. If she looked past her surly expression, spiky jet-black hair, and pierced lip, she was actually quite pretty. From what was left of the nametag the young woman was painstakingly shredding, one impossibly thin strip at a time, her name was Nora. "He addicted to drugs?"

Roy was obsessed with having the biggest and the best of everything, but could his thirst to one-up the world be considered an addiction? "No." Finley shook her head and turned away.

Careen said, "Finley, then can you explain why it was you felt relief at catching your husband in the act of being unfaithful?"

Finley glanced around at the glum expressions of the women looking back at her and felt a twinge of guilt. These ladies had obviously fallen victim to heartache and possibly some terrible atrocities at the hands of their estranged husbands, and all she could come up with was that her husband had worked too much—which in all honesty, he hadn't. Not really. But does a woman have to have been a victim of the unthinkable to want out of her marriage?

"People always talk like it's such a tragedy when a twenty-year marriage falls apart, like if it had lasted *that* long then, surely, it should have lasted forever," said Finley. "Personally, I'm more surprised when couples who have only been married a little while split up."

"Statistics show the majority of marriages that end in demise do so within the first three years," Careen threw out. "So what makes you believe the opposite?"

Finley rolled her shoulders back and down, giving herself a moment to think, to look back to when she and Roy were barely more than teenagers. "Things were great—blissful even—between Roy and me at first, but then as we grew older and the years wore on, it became evident we had separate goals . . . always had, I suppose. Then, one day, I realized I couldn't remember what it was I'd ever loved about him," she said, though she knew full well what had driven her to marry at age nineteen. Her mother had deemed Roy a dangerous "loser" from the wrong side of town, and thus had forbidden her daughter to associate with him.

"Then as the anniversaries and birthdays came and went, he would repeatedly come home with milk chocolates when I prefer dark. Roses when daisies have always been my favorite . . . when I was mad, frustrated, sad, he never acted like he had a clue why. He ignored my tears. Finally, I realized that after all these years he didn't even know me." Finley swallowed back an uprising of acrid emotion. "I hear divorced couples say that they simply grew apart. But we never grew together in the first place."

Nora sucked in a spurt of air in detest. "You divorced your husband because he brought you the wrong flowers?"

Finley felt the sting of her teeth digging into her bottom lip. She'd entertained these thoughts in her head a thousand times before, but never had she felt her true feelings actually sliding over her tongue. The taste was bitter, the resonance petty, offensive even. No wonder she'd needed to use Roy's affair as an excuse for their divorce.

"Nora . . ." Careen warned in a stern voice. Then she softened her gaze and shifted it back to Finley. "So what are your plans for the future?" she asked. "What are you going to do now that you're single again?"

Finley rubbed a nonexistent chill from her shoulders. "I'm not entirely sure, but recently, I joined a gym with my friend, Cathyanne. I work out with a trainer twice a week." Her cheeks began to redden with a fresh blush at the mere mention of the hunky man who, bi-weekly, twisted her into more kinky positions under the guise of exercise than Roy had in two decades of marital relations. "His name is Josh," she added, like his name could possibly matter to the group.

"Is that a fact?" Burlie-Jean said, sending her gaze for an obvious once-over of Finley's fitted yoga pants. "Sounds like that tight little butt of yours ain't all he's had his hands on."

Fire leapt from Finley's cheeks, burning a trail down her

neck. "Oh, no, it's not like that," she said, though there was no denying she'd indulged in a fantasy or two—nightly.

Nora cocked a skeptical brow. "What's it like then?"

Suddenly, Finley couldn't breathe. "I . . . Well, he's . . ." Or speak.

"He's?" Nora persisted.

"He's at least ten years my junior," Finley choked out. "We're not . . ."

"Not what?" Burlie-Jean jumped in with a purse of her dark, fully lined lips.

Finley gave her head a good shake. "Not anything," she said, taking a firm mental hold on reality. "Josh is young and athletic. And I'm *forty!*—*and* the mother of two *grown* children. Good heavens. I'm not that kind of woman. I would never—"

"Date a man you're obviously attracted to?" Nora sneered. "I bet your husband wouldn't think twice 'bout screwin' a woman half his age."

Sue let out a soft yelp, her eyes seesawing between Nora and Finley.

Silence stretched thin between them, affording the only man in the group the opportunity to speak for the first time. "But then again, an eye for an eye"—Finley shifted her attention across the circle to the man with close-cropped hair and the steel-eyed look of a cop. Ford was his name—"a tooth for a tooth eventually just leaves folks blind and unable to chew properly," he said in a slow unaffected drawl.

Finley stared back at him. What was he saying? That just because it was acceptable for a man to date someone younger didn't mean that a woman had the right to do so as well? Or did he mean that we could never truly get back what had been taken from us? "I'm not like my ex, and I never want to be," she said. "And besides, Josh is not the least bit interested in the likes of me."

"How do you know unless you tell him how you feel?" Nora countered.

"Look, y'all, if I was going to date anyone it would be Quinton," Finley said before she had time to realize she'd wanted to say it.

"Who's Quinton?" Nora asked.

Finley waved the idea away. "No one," she said with a gulp. "He's just my neighbor. We're friends. I don't even know why I said that." Quinton was a country singer who had been living next door to Finley for a little over eight years now. He was sweet and sexy, and habitually single, but there had never been the slightest hint of romantic feelings between them.

"Maybe because you want to be more than just Quinton's friend," Ford suggested.

Did she? Finley didn't know for sure. She'd never thought of Quinton that way. Well, not seriously, and she'd certainly never say as much out loud. "Um, I don't . . . know." Finley looked to Careen for help, and thankfully the group leader came to her rescue.

"All right, I think we've given Finley enough food for thought on her first day." Careen waved her arms in a settle-down motion. "As I explained earlier, each week we focus on one step, and then at the following meeting report on the progress we've made toward completing that step," she explained. "So for the benefit of our newest member, how 'bout we recite the 'Five Steps to a New Beginning' before moving on." She pointed to a rolling chalkboard. "All together now."

"Number one: Subjugate fear," she started, and the rest of the group joined in. "Take chances. Learn from and consent to the unexpected."

"Number two: Defy the rules, embrace the guidelines. Rules emphasize the result. Guidelines focus on the journey.

"Number three: Smash th[...]
comfort zone for the best answers [...]
for growth.

"Number four: Brimful heart. [...]
actions are hollow.

"Number five: Letitgo. Leave t[...]

Following along with the words [...]
smeared chalkboard, Finley felt a [...]
her forehead. Only five goals, but ea[...] ... gaping
pit of quicksand after another.

Take chances and defy rules? Smash the box? Letitgo?
What did any of that even mean? Brimful heart. Finley pressed
the heel of her palm to the center of her chest and felt nothing,
nothing but an empty hole where her heart should be. Just
because she hadn't been particularly sad to see Roy pack his
things and go, didn't mean his absence hadn't left a gap in her
life. His leaving had been like pulling a random peg from a
Jenga tower, only to find that it was the last piece still holding
the structure together.

Careen said, "I know these goals can seem overwhelming
at first, but taking the first step is the hardest part."

"Amen to that," Burlie-Jean agreed.

"Though some of us are further along than others, we're
all on the same path," Careen went on. "Everyone progresses
at his or her own pace. One step at a time, one week at a time
until we find our new normal," she said, then zeroed in on
Finley. "So start with number one, only number one . . ."

Finley watched Careen's lips spill words of hope and
encouragement. If only she could bathe in the completeness
each syllable offered until the possibility adhered to her skin,
remolding her, body and soul, into the kind of woman who
knew what it meant to be happy, one who refused to settle for
anything less—

...en said, causing Finley to start. "This coming ...t task is to identify a fear and then make an ...vercome that fear. Do you think you can do that?"

...ing already put too much of herself on display for these ...gers' entertainment, what Finley really wanted to do was ...eave and never set foot inside this circle again. "I'll surely give it a try," she promised, though, obviously, she had no intention of doing any such thing.

"Good." Careen appeared cautiously optimistic. "Okay, who wants to share next?"

# Chapter 2

*C*click followed by the whirring sound of her engine's fan kicking up a notch had Cathyanne shifting in the seat of her Audi A5. Outside, the temperature had climbed above the ninety-degree mark. Inside, her air-conditioner struggled against the oppressive heat to keep up with her demand for a controlled environment. If only Finley would buy a decent car, Cathyanne wouldn't have to be her taxi every time that prehistoric Jeep she insisted on driving broke down. Today, however, she didn't mind so much that Finley needed a ride. She'd been concocting a scheme, a last checkmark, so to speak, off of her proverbial bucket list, involving Finley (without her knowledge, of course), and had been waiting for the perfect opportunity to make the first move. Swiftly running out of time, she needed her plan to fall into place, and soon.

Gliding her hands over the baby-soft leather encasing the steering wheel, she turned her thoughts to the day she'd first laid eyes on this car. It had been an anniversary present from husband-number-two only hours before her lawyer had served him with divorce papers. Her second marriage had ended much the same as her first. Both times she'd married a man who was too old, too rich, and ultimately, too two-timing. Cars, she'd decided, made for more loyal lovers than men.

Her eyes shifted to the YMCA's front door in hope of finally catching a glimpse of Finley. If it took much longer for her friend to finish up with her group therapy, Cathyanne might have to shut off the engine and roll down the windows. In this heat, the humidity would turn her hair from silky mane to frizzy poodle in a matter of seconds.

Lowering the visor, she threaded her fingers through her cascading waves of blonde curl; thankful once again she could do so. It was hard to believe that five years ago she'd lost every last strand to the treatments she'd been given to stave off ovarian cancer. Anyone who was of the opinion that, *it's only hair, it'll grow back*, obviously had never had to go a minute without theirs. The worst day of Cathyanne's life started the morning all of hers had fallen out. Sure, the moment her doctor had said there were tumors growing inside of her had been devastating, but she couldn't see them. Seeing the clumps of matted hair piled next to the drain on her shower floor, followed by her bald head staring back at her in the mirror, had been evidence she couldn't ignore.

And what was worse, neither could anyone else. Still, she'd donned the brave face of indifference, playing the role of a heroic warrior. Then, for every one person who had described her as "beautiful" and "brave," there were another two out there who would stare, turn away, or worse, show pity. As a stylist slash image consultant, Cathyanne should have known how to combat the outwardly mortifying effects of hair loss. But try as she might to gloss over her temporary imperfection with wigs and stylish scarves, for the first time in her life, she'd felt truly exposed, defenseless in a sense, unable to bury her insecurities beneath her beauty.

Lifting a tube of gloss from the middle console, Cathyanne swiped a thin layer over her lips. Scrunching her freckled nose, she was making smooching noises in the mirror when her passenger-side door jerked open.

Finley flung herself into the seat. "Drive!" she commanded like a rabid bear was hot on her trail.

Startled, Cathyanne slapped the visor back into place with a *thump*. "What's going on?" she asked, fumbling to slide the gearshift into drive.

Finley shot a look through the back window. "For the love of all that's merciful—just go!"

With a quick glance into the rearview mirror, Cathyanne saw nothing alarming except a mother struggling to corral three small children into a minivan. Disturbing on a certain level but, generally speaking, not a reason for hysterics.

"Okay. Keep your yoga pants on." Cathyanne locked the car into gear and pressed the gas, rocketing the Audi forward, evading Finley's unseen predator.

Once the YMCA was a safe distance behind them and they were rolling down Main Street toward Gold's Gym, Cathyanne stole a peek at her friend's white-knuckle grip on her seat. "What are we running from? Were there a bunch of creepy divorced guys? Were they trying to hit on you all at once?"

"No." Finley shook her head. "There was only one man, but he wasn't creepy," she said, then hesitated. "Well, not really."

"Then what?"

Finley loosened her grip on her seat and slumped back, dropping her head to the headrest. "It was awful," she whined. "They expected *me* to talk."

Cathyanne gasped. "That's outrageous," she said, mocking her friend's aversion to self-analysis.

"I know," Finley agreed in all seriousness. "The group leader, Careen, she had this perky strawberry-blonde bob and petite little face, like a sweet little elf or something. But I tell you what, that woman was *no* pixie. She was sneaky. Manipulative. Before I knew what was happening, she had me talking about the luncheon *and* the divorce," she explained in one breath and then still had enough air to add, "That woman is a true monster in sheep's clothing."

"You mean, wolf?"

"Whatever," Finley snapped.

Cathyanne's focus left the road, her head whipping toward her friend in disbelief. Being snippy was very uncharacteristic for Finley. She was a mediator, not a fighter. "Excuse me?"

"Sorry," Finley said, exasperated. "It was just all so awful. Before I knew what was happening, I was like-like . . . Oh, what does Lindsey Lohan call it in that movie *Mean Girls* when she says too much?" She snapped her fingers a couple of times. "'Word vomit!' I started 'vomiting' details uncontrollably. Upchucking everything."

Cathyanne sneaked another peek at her friend's panicked expression. Could it be this elfish, devil woman had gotten Finley to finally open up about her divorce? Sure, Cathyanne had known that Roy was selfish, not to mention a cheating bastard, and could see that underneath Finley's carefully crafted façade of wedded bliss that she wasn't happy. But she also knew from experience that ending a marriage was hard, painful, and disappointing no matter what the circumstances. Even so, she had yet to see Finley shed one tear over the break-up of her marriage, much less show any sign, other than her public meltdown, that she might be hurting inside.

Not that Cathyanne was surprised. Finley guarded her feelings with more efficiency than the Smithsonian did the Hope Diamond. Unfortunately, this tight-lipped tendency was currently Cathyanne's biggest obstacle. If her plan for Finley was going to work, she needed to know what Finley both loved and hated about Roy. What drove her to finally divorce him? What did she want, no, *need*, in a man?

Fighting the urge to lean closer, Cathyanne asked, "So, what did you say . . . I mean, about the divorce—Roy, and all?"

Finley huffed again. "That's not what's important here. I need you to focus," she insisted. "It was like I'd died and got sent to hell."

Now it was Cathyanne's turn to release an annoyed breath. Why did Finley insist on making this *so* hard? "Okay, let me see if I understand you correctly. You think that what makes hell— *hell*—is that when you go there, they make you talk . . . about your feelings?" Up ahead, the light turned yellow, then quickly to red. Cathyanne stopped behind a jacked-up truck with a Rebel flag flapping from the rusty bed, and turned to address Finley directly. "Feelings you really shouldn't keep bottled up anyway because it's not healthy?" Finley bobbed her head up and down. Cathyanne rolled her eyes. "I see what you mean. It's unimaginably cruel."

"Right," Finley agreed, as if Cathyanne's last comment hadn't been laced with sarcasm. "Don't you see? I can't just go throwing caution to the wind and start talking about stuff. After what happened at the luncheon, who knows what insanity I could unleash next if I'm not careful?" she said, her words now coming out in quick breathless spurts. "No way am I ever going back to that therapy group again." She gave her head an exaggerated shake. "No way!"

The light changed. The truck's tailpipe blew a puff of black smoke as it lurched forward. Cathyanne expelled a shallow cough. "Come on, Finnie—"

"And that's not even the worst part," Finley jumped back in.

"It gets worse?"

"Oh yeah," Finley said, her words now ripe with outrage. "They have these five steps to . . . a-a whole new you, or some other such nonsense."

"Nonsense?" Cathyanne punctuated her question with one raised eyebrow.

"Uh-huh. The first step is to subjugate fear," Finley shrieked. "F-e-a-r!"

Cathyanne pointed a stern finger at her friend. "Finnie, you need to simmer down before you hyperventilate. Don't make me slap you. You know I will," she warned. "All right. I hear what you're saying, and I get that you're nervous about being single and in uncharted water and all, but really, what harm could there be in just giving this therapy a chance?"

Finley groaned. "Have you *even* been listening to me? This has nothing to do with *me* being single again."

Cathyanne turned into the Gold's Gym parking lot, her eyes scanning the rows of cars looking for an open space as she spoke. "So *you* say." From what she could see, this therapy was just what Finley needed to move on, and Cathyanne wasn't about to let her drop out without a fight. "If that's the truth, then what do you have to be afraid of besides what other people might think of you?" From the corner of her eye, she saw Finley's mouth drop open in protest. "Oh, come on, admit it. You worry more about what other people think than pretty much anyone I know."

Finley crossed her arms over her chest. "You're just saying that because you don't give a darn what *anyone* thinks," she said, her curt attitude back at center stage. "My momma raised me to have a little decorum. So sue me."

Cathyanne spotted a space at the end of the lot and sped up a bit. "There's a difference between decorum and turning oneself into some sort of Stepford wife . . . daughter, whatever," she pointed out. "Maybe it's time you stopped being so afraid of *your* momma and do what *you* want for a change. Taking a few chances might be just what you need. You should give this 'subjugate fear' thing a whirl."

"First, I am not a robot," Finley shot back. "And second, I am *not* afraid of my momma."

Cathyanne cranked the steering wheel. The Audi curled with precision between two towering SUVs. "Oh, really?"

"What?" Finley grabbed her water bottle, unlatched the door, and slid out of the car. "I threw Roy out when Momma said I should turn a blind eye."

Cathyanne cut the engine and moved to get out. Her stiff bones protested as she straightened to standing. Wincing with the pain, she glanced across the hood of her car to see Finley's watchful gaze on her. "Marathon shopping at Green Hills yesterday. Guess I forgot to stretch," she joked, knowing her friend wouldn't press. As much as it bothered Cathyanne that Finley was so closed with her feelings, she appreciated the way Finley was equally unwilling to pry into the affairs of others. Right now she needed Finley to focus on solving *her own* problems. Since the divorce, Finley had seemed lost and confused, a state of being Cathyanne would have never equated with her best friend. Finley had always been Cathyanne's rock. Well, everyone's rock for that matter. Lately, however, whether Finley realized it or not, she was the one in need of help.

After sending Finley a halfhearted smile, Cathyanne pressed the key fob, locking the car doors as they both started toward the entrance to the gym. "Look, Finnie, all I'm saying is that it's about time you started talking instead of holding everything inside." She turned to her friend. "What are you so afraid of?"

Finley lifted a shoulder. "I suppose the same thing everyone else is."

Cathyanne caught Finley's gaze and held it tight. "And what is that?"

A sigh escaped Finley's lips along with, "The truth, I guess," before she pressed her lips together. Discussion over.

A renewed exhaustion settled into Cathyanne's weary bones. "Look, all I'm saying is that you're not dead yet."

Finley's gaze snapped back to Cathyanne. "Dead? What has that got to do with anything?"

Cathyanne had never been one for showing compassion, but she gave a caring smile a try. "Obviously God still thinks you have a few things to learn."

Stepping around Cathyanne, Finley yanked the door open. "Seriously?" she barked.

"Yeah," Cathyanne said. "And it doesn't matter how I know this, but I just do. God only grants each one of us a certain number of days. How we choose to spend, or squander, those days is up to us. But one thing I know for sure, if I had my life to do over again, I'd spend less time making excuses for why I can't be happy, and considerably more time grabbing hold of happiness and hanging on tight."

Finley threw her a doubtful look. "*You're* really bringing God into this," she said, sidestepping a couple of guys whose broad shoulders and trim waists made them look like human wedges. "You, Cathyanne Morrow, the one who, growing up, mocked every word our Sunday school teacher ever said? The girl whose only use for a Bible was to level her loft bed in the dorms at UT?"

Cathyanne caught up to Finley. "So?"

"When have you ever brought God into anything?" She pointed a finger at Cathyanne. "And taking the Lord's name in vain doesn't count."

A comeback sat poised and ready to leap from Cathyanne's tongue, but she told the snarky reply to stand down.

It appeared the opportunity she'd been waiting for had finally presented itself.

"Dang girl, you are in one sour mood today," Cathyanne teased and then pretended like what she said next had just occurred to her. "You know what you need? You need a night out on the town. Why don't you come down to Tootsie's with me tonight?"

Finley stopped at a rack of rolled-up towels and let out a scoffing laugh. "What possible reason could I have for wanting to go to Tootsie's?" She handed Cathyanne a towel and took one for herself. "Me at a bar." She tossed a towel over her shoulder and started toward a row of stationary bikes. "Tell me you're joking."

Cathyanne shrugged a shoulder. "What? We used to go downtown all the time . . ." she started to say when something strikingly handsome caught her attention.

Across the gym, Josh, their trainer, was curling a bar with what looked like a hundred pounds on each end. He nodded a hello to her. She and Finley had a few minutes before their appointment with him, so Cathyanne stepped up to a couple of the recently vacated bikes, slung a leg over one, and dropped down onto the seat.

Finley straddled the bike next to Cathyanne's. "That was a long time ago, and I only agreed back then because you'd just gotten divorced—for the first time—and I felt sorry for you."

Cathyanne secured her feet into the pedals and started pumping. "Well, now you're getting divorced—for the first time—and I'm returning the favor." Pressing the up arrows, she set the bike to her usual resistance while stealing a glance at Finley for any sign of suspicion. She couldn't exactly admit she was trying to set Finley up, and with her neighbor no less. Normally, Cathyanne didn't bother herself with other people's mental health. But over the years, Finley had always been there for her, both after Cathyanne's father took off and when her mother shut herself up in her room for weeks, leaving three young girls to fend for themselves.

At age twelve, Cathyanne had been afraid that children's services would eventually take them away, but Finley had snuck in food every day and helped Cathyanne after school with the cooking, cleaning, and caring for her sisters. Then there were the dark days after both divorces when a woman could only survive with the help of a best friend. Needless to say, Cathyanne had taken much more than she'd given back. So for once, she was determined to put her friend first by making sure there would always be someone there for Finley, someone who would truly love and care for her, and that man just so happened to be living, conveniently, next door to Finley.

"That's sweet," Finley said through a stiff smile. "But, no."

"Come on, you've been divorced for two weeks now and separated for what, three, four months?" Cathyanne recapped. "Time's a wastin'. 'Subjugate fear,' and all that. You gotta get back in the game and find husband number two."

Finley's eyebrows rose to form deep, arching wrinkles across her forehead. "Why? So I can find myself right back where I am now?" She shook her head. "Again, no thanks."

Lacing her fingers, Cathyanne pressed her conjoined hands to her heart. "But your true love could be out there waiting for you," she whined like a schoolgirl and added a dreamy look for affect.

Finley returned Cathyanne's dreamy look with a wooden one. "At Tootsie's?"

"Sure, why not?" Cathyanne dropped her hands to the bike handles. "Speaking of which, it just so happens that your neighbor, Quinton Townes, is playing down there tonight," she said, playfully singing out his name. "I know you have a thing for him."

"Good heavens," Finley exclaimed like nothing could be further from the truth. "Maybe you're the one who's lost her mind and needs therapy. Quinton is my nothing-more-than-a-friend, and I don't have a 'thing' for him—or anyone else, for that matter . . ." she was in the midst of insisting when her eyes briefly locked on something in the distance.

Cathyanne followed the trail of Finley's gaze over the rows of Nautilus equipment to see that it wasn't a something, but a someone who had caught her friend's attention. Josh, to be exact. Then she watched in utter bemusement as Finley's cynical expression eased, her cheeks coloring to a soft shade of pink.

*What in the world?* Cathyanne couldn't imagine.

Arching her back deeper than necessary, Finley subtly accentuated her generous cleavage as she finger-combed her hair away from her face and fastened it into a ponytail with a band. "Besides, I just divorced my cheating husband." She turned back to Cathyanne, her expression showing resolve, though her face held its heat. "I'm devastated."

Cathyanne stole another glance at Josh. Were her eyes deceiving her, or was *he* blushing too? "You're something, but devastated is *not* the word that springs to mind," she muttered.

Finley ignored Cathyanne's last comment and said, "Besides, we've both seen the women Quinton gets photographed with in the tabloids. Every year they get a little younger, their boobs a little bigger, and their stomachs a little flatter." She slapped her thighs with both hands. "Nature seems to be having the opposite effect on me."

Cathyanne turned her gaze over Finley, noting that with the help of only a few months of training, her friend was looking pretty good. Plus, she'd seen the affectionate way Finley and Quinton looked at each other. The way they spent an excessive amount of time together doing rather mundane tasks like gardening and bottling fruit. She'd even mused that

Quinton was the reason Finley had let Roy go so easily. Finley might not be ready to admit it yet, but she and Quinton had a shared affinity. Cathyanne was sure of it. "So?" Cathyanne challenged.

"So, a man like Quinton Townes ain't interested in a woman like me for anything other than her cooking," Finley said with another subtle glance in Josh's general direction.

Cathyanne looked back across the gym just in time to see Josh lean forward and drop the dumbbells to the ground. He had a very nice, very perfectly round backside. As a matter of fact, everything about Josh was rather pleasing to the eye. He was just the right height for a woman who wanted to wear heels, but not too tall if she was in the mood for flats. The bulk of his chest and arms was impressive but lean, noticeable under a T-shirt while not overly obvious. His brown hair was thick and cut short, but not so much so that he couldn't muss the top to make it look sexy. His eyes, not green or brown, but more of a chartreuse, were gentle, his demeanor confident while not conceited.

"In all the time Quinton has been living next door to me, he's never given me the tiniest of an inkling that he's interested in being anything more than friends," Finley continued. "I help him write songs from time to time, and he helps me around the house. That's it, and that's all it's ever gonna be," she insisted.

Cathyanne tore her eyes away from their trainer, turning her attention back to her friend. "'The Lady doth protest too much, methinks,'" she recited, her friend's denial adding ammunition to Cathyanne's theory that all Finley and Quinton needed was a little push. An evening out, away from where Finley had only ever been someone's wife and mother. They needed neutral ground. And maybe a few beers, just to lighten things up a bit.

Only just now, she'd definitely gotten a vibe that something was brewing between Finley and Josh, which might complicate her plan considerably. *Why didn't I notice this before today?*

Well, maybe because who'd have thought a young, beyond-gorgeous man like Josh could be attracted to a forty-year-old woman who chronically dressed in ratty shorts, an oversized T-shirt, and gardening clogs? One who refused to dye that god-forsaken gray streak growing out of her hairline because it matched the one her granny Opaline had sported during her twilight years? But then, Granny had been eccentric and sassy in that no-nonsense, Southern-woman kind of way, meaning she'd rocked the Cruella de Vil hairdo with attitude. Finley, on the other hand, leaned more toward the passive-aggressive side of Southern politeness.

Nonetheless, given Finley's classic, porcelain doll features, she was capable of pulling off just about any look, de Vil or otherwise, even without the sassy attitude. And since Josh had only ever seen Finley at the gym where she looked about as good in her workout clothes as the women half her age, why wouldn't he find her attractive?

As Cathyanne turned the idea over in her head, she thought about how, from day one, Finley and Josh had seemed rather comfortable in each other's company. They also tended to get caught up in chitchat regarding eighties music and old houses. The second of which invariably led to a drawn-out discussion regarding what kind of landscaping lent authenticity to what time period. In other words, all things Cathyanne found unin-teresting, and thus, more or less had tuned out. Now that she thought about it, hadn't Josh not-so-subtly mentioned a time or two that his last girlfriend had been a full eight years older than him? Finley had to be at least ten years his senior, but then what would a couple more years really matter if he was, indeed, attracted to more mature women?

*Hmm?*

Still, would Finley—conservative, sensible, only-ever-been-with-one-man Finley—really consider dating a guy a decade younger than she? And what about Quinton? Cathyanne had been so sure he was the one. Evidently, discovering what was in Finley's head, not to mention her heart, was going to be a little more complicated than she'd previously anticipated.

The cell phone tucked into the waistline of Finley's pants buzzed, calling Cathyanne back from her reverie.

Finley lifted the phone and frowned at the display before pressing it to her ear. "Hey, Momma," she said flatly, then, "No, I can't come over tonight."

Cathyanne couldn't make out a word coming from the other end, but she knew Finley's mother was not one to take no for an answer.

"The therapy meeting was fine. I'm feeling much better. In fact, I don't think I ever need to go back again—" Finley was explaining when another of her mother's endless rebuttals cut her off. "Chicken fried steak? Yum," she enthused while feigning a gag, the action giving Cathyanne an idea.

In a last-ditch effort at getting Finley to come with her tonight, Cathyanne offered her friend a way out of supper with the folks in the form of mimicking a dancing motion.

Finley's eyes narrowed in Cathyanne's direction. "Momma, I'd love to, but, um, I . . ." then flashed as she quickly caught on, "can't. I'm going out to Tootsie's with Cathyanne tonight." More argument from the other end, only this time Cathyanne heard her name along with a few unflattering expletives. "Right, Momma, over my dead body. Look, I'm about to start my training session, so I've got to let you go." Finley pressed her lips to the phone with an audible smooch. "Love you," she said, then hung up and dropped the phone to the padded gym floor like it had sprung eight legs and fangs.

"So what did your momma say about me this time?" she wanted to know.

Finley shrugged. "Not much, just something 'bout me becoming a trampy divorcée like my best friend, and how next I'll be wearing clothes from Forever 21, and going out every night of the week trawling for men, blah, blah, blah . . ."

Cathyanne's jaw dropped. "Your momma knows good and well that I would never be caught dead in the atrocities that discount retailer tries to pass off as fashionable attire. And as to the second offense, I do *not* trawl. All I have to do is show up and the men come a-runnin' to me," she said, flippantly striking a provocative pose. "So, you'll come with me tonight?"

Finley stopped pedaling and hopped from the bike. "Not even if you threatened my new baby rose of Sharon with a swarm of hungry Japanese beetles."

Cathyanne's heart sunk. "But you told your momma—"

"What momma doesn't know won't hurt her," Finley stated, her focus shifting toward Josh once more.

Cathyanne followed Finley's gaze to see that their trainer was in the process of making his way toward them. She had to persuade Finley to come out tonight, and fast. Without a swarm of hungry beetles, Japanese or otherwise (she shuddered at the thought), Cathyanne had no choice but to sucker punch Finley directly in her sorest of spots.

Sliding from her bike, Cathyanne threatened, "Well if that's the way you feel about it, the next time I run into your momma at the spa, I might accidentally let slip how disappointed I was that you stood me up tonight, and I had to brave Tootsie's all by my lonesome."

Finley slapped Cathyanne with a skeptical look. "You wouldn't."

Cathyanne pretended to study her freshly manicured fingernails. "Oh, I would," she assured her friend.

Finley made a sound akin to a snarl. "Fine." She shook a finger in Cathyanne's face. "But you better not take off with some no-good hunk of man-candy and leave me without an acceptable way of getting home. Do you know how much a cab ride from downtown all the way to Gallatin costs?"

Cathyanne launched into a victory dance . . . on the inside, of course. Her plan had taken a detour but was coming together nicely all the same. "As a matter of fact, I do." She didn't bother trying to deny she'd abandoned Finley a time or two over the years, choosing the company of a handsome man over her friend.

A quick glance at Josh's intense gaze, unmistakably trained on Finley, told her that tonight, however, she just might be forgiven.

Two options, as they say, are much better than one.

# Chapter 3

Packed like corralled cattle between four wood paneled walls, the riotous crowd filling the bar overwhelmed the echo of Finley's boots as she made her way through the darkened hallway. Built during the early days of Nashville, Tootsie's was rumored to have launched Willie Nelson's career as well as other famous performers like Kris Kristofferson, Patsy Cline, Waylon Jennings, and in more recent decades, Quinton Townes.

At the end of the hallway, and through an open door, Finley spied her neighbor.

Jagged locks of ashy-blond hair peeked out from under a worn cowboy hat to poke at the frayed edges of his western shirt. A dimple split his right cheek as he smiled, his head bent toward that of a young woman.

Finley moved closer, watching as the groupie handed Quinton a cocktail napkin. "Will you sign this for me?" she said, adding a coy smirk.

Quinton ran his smoky gray eyes over the woman's skin-tight T-shirt as he slipped the paper and pen from her hands, his fingers lingering a touch longer than necessary on hers. "Who should I make this out to?" he drawled in that slow, Texas way of his.

Gazing out from under a pair of mascara-laden lashes, she said, "McKenna," and then bit down on her plump bottom lip.

Finley rolled her eyes. This one was young, even by Quinton's standards. Likely, not much older than her daughter Royanne, or Quinton's own estranged daughter, Annie, for that matter. Because she hadn't known him back when he was married, it was hard for her to imagine him as anyone's daddy. But then he'd become a father long before the world had known his name. Before his solo career had taken off and he'd mistakenly boarded a high-speed train running on tequila and cocaine, barreling headlong into the blinding lights of one forgotten arena after another. Before he'd traded the unconditional love of a wife and three children for the fleeting admiration of his fans. Before the cheers of the crowds had echoed into a deafening abyss where there wasn't enough booze or blow in his empty hotel room to silence the void. And certainly before he'd woken up one morning a homeless, washed-up one-hit-wonder with nothing but a broken-down Mazerati to call his own. The very day he just so happened to have entered Finley's life.

It had been roughly eight years since the first time Finley and Quinton met face-to-face. She'd been trespassing in her neighbor's yard, but for a good reason. If the deadbeat owner even tried to have her arrested for pruning his overgrown flowerbeds, well then she'd take responsibility for the law she'd broken. After all, he could hardly have expected her to sit by one more day and do nothing while his flowerbeds grew out of control. Soon the plants would begin to die from overgrowth and insufficient water. A travesty in Finley's mind, a clear justification for her crime.

She had been completely unaware of his presence as she'd worked, her hands keeping a steady rhythm, clipping buds from a rose bush before dropping the faded blooms into a plastic bucket—*snip, plop, snip, plop.* The sun was warm on her back. She was humming as she worked to the tune of Elvis Costello's, *The Angels Wanna Wear My Red Shoes,* when she heard something. It sounded like mumbling at first, but then became louder, more distinct. Someone was singing.

"Now I'm standing on my own with no one to let go. I didn't miss you. I didn't miss you. Till you're gone . . ."

Stopping, she listened, but this time heard nothing. Assuming the sound must have come from a passing car or something, she'd continued to work, *plop, snip, plop, snip . . .* But then the singing had come again, only different this time.

"There were times when I would fall. You would catch me. I didn't feel a thing at all. There were days in this life you kept sorrow from coming into my mind . . ." The voice continued until the thunking sound of something hitting the porch interrupted the flow.

She'd stopped her work again and glanced out to the road. No cars had passed by that she could see. But now that she'd heard the voice twice, she was fairly certain it had come from her general vicinity.

Squinting against the noonday sun, she searched the yard and flowerbed but saw no one. Then she turned back to the front of the house. Looking up onto the porch and into the shadows beyond the hedge, she spied a bottle of pills teetering precariously over a gap between two splintered wood planks.

"Hello, is someone there?" she called out, but there was no answer. She deepened her gaze, and this time was able to zero in on a man sprawled across a weathered wicker chaise. Her head snapped back in surprise. "Oh, I'm sorry. I hope I didn't disturb you. I didn't realize anyone was living here," she said and then waited while he again neglected to respond. Her eyes now adjusted to the shaded light, she looked closer, this time noting his rumpled attire, greasy hair, and unshaven face.

Trepidation stirred with concern, hastening her heartbeat. "Sir, are . . . are you supposed to be here?" she asked, though she had no idea what she would do if he said he wasn't.

The man rotated his head toward her. He licked his dry lips. "Yes, this is my uncle's place. Buddy Townes. I'm staying here a while . . . with his permission." Slowly, he pulled his emaciated body up to standing. "Hi, ma'am. I'm Quinton Townes." He forced his lips into a smile, his hand to lift in a feeble wave. "It's nice to meet you."

Tenting her eyes, Finley studied the man towering above her. His gaze was sad—vacant. His skin, withered like the spent rose petals she'd been clipping, hung from protruding cheekbones. And still, underneath the shell of a man standing before her, she recognized the recently fallen country star.

"Nice to meet you too," she said, her attention lighting on the half-empty whiskey bottle he held in his hand. She knew it wasn't right to judge, but if his reputation for deca-dent behavior was well earned, she was none too pleased with the knowledge he'd be living right next door to her and her impressionable children. "I'm your neighbor." She pointed across the yard to the historic mansion that—at the time—was undergoing renovations. "I'm Finley, but everybody calls me Finnie." She dropped her hand, allowing the sun to flood her eyes again. The sight of him, pathetic and ruined, broke her heart. "I'm sorry. I didn't mean to trespass," she said. "It's just that . . . Well, if you're gonna live here, you might want to pay these Knockout roses a little attention. If you don't keep 'em pruned, they'll consume the entire flowerbed . . ."

She couldn't have known it then, but her humming along with the rhythm of her clipping had been the inspiration for one of Quinton's best-selling songs. Not long after, he'd taken to calling her his "Muse." A title she wore proudly to this day. They'd been close friends ever since—just friends, which meant she wasn't sure he would appreciate her barging in on him at this particular moment.

Finley stopped just prior to reaching the threshold of his dressing room.

"That sure is a pretty name," he was saying as he scribbled on the napkin before handing it back to McKenna. As he did, his gaze flitted over her shoulder to catch sight of Finley lurking just beyond the doorway.

"Enjoy the show." He dismissed the young woman with a tip of his hat.

A quick glance around to see Finley standing there brought a pout to McKenna's lips. "I'm sure I will," she said as she passed Finley on her way out. Then she offered Quinton one more come-get-me grin. "You could always find me after the show. I'll be around."

Finley watched Quinton's eyes follow the young groupie as she walked away. And to be fair, she'd given him a lot to look at. Dressed in designer jeans strategically ripped to show that she wasn't wearing anything underneath, her hips swayed with the mesmerizing rhythm of a hypnotist's watch. More often than not, Finley was certain, Quinton would have taken McKenna up on her offer. But these days she'd noticed he seemed less inclined toward the noncommittal hookup. Maybe it was his age, forty-four and counting, or maybe he was finally tiring of a life without permanent connections. Finley really had no clue. What she did know was that after nearly a decade of battling his demons as an occasional performer, a floundering father figure, and a reclusive artist, he'd slowly hammered out a narrow semblance of a normal life. Now a respected songwriter, he was the proud owner of fourteen gold records, which included three number-one hits released by artists who appeared to be handling their fame much better than he had.

"Did I come at a bad time?" Finley wondered aloud.

Quinton continued to stare down the hallway. "Is it just me or do they seem to get younger every year?" he asked in a shallow voice.

He sounded as if he was speaking more to himself than to Finley, but she answered anyway. "I was thinking the very same thing," she agreed. "Funny how that happens when we seem perfectly able to stay the exact same age."

Shifting his gaze to her, a wide grin stretched across his face. "Are my eyes deceiving me, or do I see Finnie Harrison all gussied up and out of the house after"—though he wasn't wearing a watch, he made a show of checking his bare wrist—"ten o'clock at night?"

"You're one to talk, Mr. 'I don't like to perform anymore.'" She made quotation marks with her fingers. "If I'm not mistaken, this makes twice you've been on stage since Labor Day."

Quinton's eyebrows pinched together, his jaw tightening the way it did when he was anxious about something. He'd once confessed to Finley how he feared the roar of the crowd, calling it intoxicating—an open gate back to his addictive ways. The battle he risked losing every time he stepped onto a stage. A simple roll of the dice he was about to throw again here tonight.

"Why didn't you tell me you were playing this evening?" she asked as she crossed into the dressing room and wrapped her arms loosely around his neck. "I'm always here for you. I hope you know that."

He closed his arms around her waist and pulled her body tight against his. A show of affection, or need for comfort, she wasn't sure which. But given his trepidation over performing, the former seemed more likely. Even still, a whirl of something she thought might be pleasure took her belly for a spin. It had been a while since a man's touch—more specifically, Roy's touch—had left her feeling anything other than cold. And she took courage in the knowledge that somewhere down deep there was a possibility she might feel something for someone again one day.

"Like you would have come?" he said into her ear. "You hardly leave the house anymore." Which was mostly true. Since the day she'd found Roy on the sofa with Macy, she just didn't have a desire anymore to socialize. Given the mess she'd made of the luncheon, keeping a low profile was probably best until she could get both feet back on solid ground.

Finley pulled back. "Well, surprise. Here I am."

He scanned her from the scooping tank she wore under a sheer floral blouse, to formfitting jeans, and on to her cowboy boots. "Yes you are. And just look at you too." He whistled through his teeth. "Finnie, as I live and breathe, you are looking mighty fine this evening," he said, and appeared to mean it too. But then he hardly ever saw her in anything other than her gardening clothes. It wasn't a stretch to assume that the sight of her dressed in just about anything else would be a noteworthy improvement.

She waved off his compliment. "You're such a flirt," she said, lowering her gaze to hide the embarrassment staining her cheeks. "I feel ridiculous."

"Well, you look like a breath of fresh spring air." His voice was warm, heady. "Thanks for coming out tonight. It means a lot, having you here."

Finley lifted her bashful eyes. "Well, I suppose you have Cathyanne to thank," she said. "She blackmailed me into coming."

"Ah, that explains the outfit . . ." he surmised while leaving out, *and why you're dressed like a woman for a change.* She much appreciated his restraint. "What's Cathyanne holding over your head this time?" he wanted to know.

Finley slid her fingers into the pockets of her jeans. "I was invited to chicken fried steak night at Mother and Daddy's," she explained, scuffing the square toe of her boot against the cement floor. "It was either come down here and listen to you play or suffer the wrath of my momma." She visibly shuddered for effect.

Quinton motioned low with his right hand. "So, what you're saying is that coming to hear Quinton Townes perform is only one step"—he positioned his hand one mark higher on his invisible scale—"above small talk with the folks over a fried piece of beef?"

Finley pursed her lips. "If it makes you feel any better, Momma's chicken fried steak has been the blue-ribbon winner at the Hendersonville Baptist cook-off, three years and counting." She gave him a timid smile. "Besides, it's not like I don't hear you sing 'bout every other day from the other side of my hedge."

"So you've had your fill?" Quinton returned her smile.

Finley gave his arm a playful shove. "You better hush now. You know I love the sound of your voice. And so does my garden for that matter. Ever since you moved in, the general state of my flowerbeds has improved dramatically."

Quinton threw his arms up in mock offense. "Perfect. I'll let my agent know to add a patch of one-eyed Susans to my short list of demographics."

"Black-eyed Susans," Finley corrected, jabbing an outstretched finger into his chest. "And don't you poke fun. Flowers are very discerning listeners. One wrong note will have them curling up faster than a potat'a bug in the palm of your sweaty hand. It's true, I've seen it happen—"

"Mr. Townes, we're ready for you," a voice interrupted.

Finley turned to see a stagehand leaning in through the door. The fingers of his right hand were pressed to the headset, horseshoeing his shaggy haircut.

"Be right there," Quinton called back, then wagged a finger at Finley. "It's a good thing you came tonight because I have a surprise for you as well."

There was a flicker of mischief in his eyes just now that sent a feeling of dread, like a million anxious feet, running down Finley's spine. To say she wasn't keen on maintaining complete control of every situation would be a miscalculation of gargantuan proportion.

"What kind of surprise?" she wanted—no, needed—to know.

The stagehand beckoned to Quinton again.

Quinton strapped his guitar over his shoulder. "You'll see," he said, and started for the door.

Finley grabbed his arm as he passed. "Quinton, you know I don't like surprises," she reminded him.

Quinton gently lifted her hand from his arm. "You're gonna like this one," he reassured her and kept moving. "I promise."

"We'll see," she called after him.

Quinton stopped and looked over his shoulder. "Finnie . . ."

"Yeah?"

"I'm glad you're here."

"Me too."

## Chapter 4

Finley pushed her way through the mass of bodies, heading as best she could straight for the tall blonde near the front by the stage. She could always pick Cathyanne out of a crowd. Not just because she often wore high heels so she could tower over everyone else, but because there was a light, a presence about Cathyanne that said, *I'm here. Look at me and feel free to be in awe.* Finley, on the other hand, felt more comfortable blending in. She hated the limelight, was uncomfortable with undue attention. Maybe these distinctions were one of the reasons their bond had always been so strong. Cathyanne could hoard all the attention she wanted, and Finley was all too happy to let her have it.

Once Finley had finally shoved her way through the last few bodies—most of which looked way too young to be out this late, at a bar, on a school night—Cathyanne turned to her and handed her another full bottle of beer. Though she'd already consumed two, which was two more than she'd drank in . . . well, however many years it had been since the last time she'd been to a bar with Cathyanne, she gladly accepted it.

"Thanks."

Finley had never been much of a drinker, but tonight it felt strange to be out and around other men without Roy. She'd already openly defied her mother by refusing a supper invitation *and* thrown caution to the wind by coming downtown with Cathyanne wearing an outfit no self-respecting mother of two college-age kids should be caught dead in, so what harm could a few beers do? Clearly, she was not herself this evening. Whatever being "herself" looked like these days. Lately, she felt less and less sure of what being Finley Harrison really meant.

Finley lifted her bottle high. "To subjugating fear!"

Cathyanne knocked her beer against Finley's. "No fear!" she echoed, to which a few random voices from the bar concurred.

As they both took healthy gulps from their bottles, Finley felt her eyes dancing over to Cathyanne again. Underneath her opposition to being here, a part of her was glad Cathyanne had blackmailed her into coming. They'd flirted with some guys at the bar, which in all honesty was mostly Cathyanne, but Finley had batted an eye or two while interjecting a witty comment here and there. They'd even danced a little. Why not? She didn't have anyone at home waiting on her.

On top of all that, Quinton was about to play.

Life in this moment was as good as it had been in a long, long time. A tightness she hadn't realized had been monopolizing her chest came loose, pulled away, and flittered, it seemed, into the wooden rafters overhead. It had been way too long since Finley had felt this free, and she had Cathyanne to thank.

What would she have done if Cathyanne's cancer had taken her from this earth? From Finley? How would Finley have made it through the divorce without her best friend? She knew the answer, and the truth was beyond pathetic. She wouldn't have, because she never would have divorced Roy. Without the knowledge that Cathyanne would always be there for her, she'd have stayed with him. No question. Arguably, Cathyanne could be described as a vain and self-absorbed person, but in her own way, she'd always seemed to be right where Finley needed her, ready to catch her at the very moment Finley was about to fall.

Cathyanne bounced her eyebrows. "How's Quinton doing?" she wanted to know.

"Quinton's good." Finley tipped her beer back again. Her head took a full turn with the motion. Maybe she should slow down a bit. "A little nervous, maybe."

Cathyanne sent her a knowing look. "How can you tell?"

Finley didn't like the way Cathyanne kept eying her. Why did it feel like she was trying to pull a hidden meaning out of everything Finley said these days—often implying that there was something more than simple friendship going on between Finley and Quinton? So what if Finley had helped Quinton through some rough times, especially while he was trying to get sober. And in return, Quinton had blessed Finley with his music. His friendship. But that didn't mean there was anything else, anything romantic, between them. And okay, so deep down she *did* find Quinton attractive, and even *deeper* down might have even fantasized about what it would be like to be with him. With those sad, tortured eyes and that Texas cowboy swagger, who wouldn't? But Finley had never taken her affection for him further than indulging the occasional lingering stare. Up until a few months ago, she'd been a married woman, for heaven's sake. She wasn't under any delusions that a man like Quinton—famous and sexy with a quiet charisma—wanted anything but friendship from a forty-year-old housewife with permanent dirt stains under her fingernails.

Finley shrugged Cathyanne's comment off. "I just can, that's all," she said, looking away.

"Yeah, I bet you can," Cathyanne said and took another swig from her beer.

Growing tired of Cathyanne's not-so-subtle insinuations, Finley pointed the neck of her bottle at her friend. "If you've got something to say, maybe you should stop tiptoeing around and just come out with it—" she was in the process of demanding when, out of the corner of her eye, she caught the sight of a familiar, yet very out-of-place, face. The mere possibility that *he* would be here sent her level of irritation spinning in a completely new direction. Squinting to be sure, her eyes then rounded. "Cathyanne! What is *Josh* doing here?"

Cathyanne rose up onto her tiptoes for a better look. "How should I know?" she said, her gaze lighting everywhere but directly on Finley. "Maybe he's a fan of Quinton's?"

Finley searched the uncharacteristically innocent look on Cathyanne's face. "Yeah, sure he is." Her friend was absolutely up to something. "And maybe he was like, in *kindergarten* when Quinton was popular."

Cathyanne pursed her lips in disagreement. "I'd say more like a teenager. But then, what difference does it make why he's here when he's headed straight for us? So stop questioning and simply enjoy the view?"

"What?" Finley's head whipped around to see Josh excusing his way through the crowd, beating a path straight for them.

Finley watched as Josh moved closer. He was dressed in a green button-down that made his eyes pop, and a nicely fitting pair of worn jeans. Understanding dawned. Her gaze snapped back to her friend. "You did this, *didn't* you?"

"Me?" Cathyanne's eyebrows shot up in mock surprise. "Why would I?" she denied, her lips twitching, holding back a devious grin.

*Cathyanne's trying to set me up with Josh!*

Finley wanted to disappear, to pull a wicked-witch-of-the-west and melt to the floor in a heap of too-tight jeans and swath of floral. "Because somehow, you . . . you know I have a . . . a . . ." Finley stammered, utterly inept at speaking her thoughts, her fantasies, aloud. Not that she needed to. Obviously, Cathyanne had developed the ability to read minds.

"A what?" Cathyanne put her hand to her ear. "A little crush on our trainer—"

"Good evening, ladies," Josh's friendly voice cut through Cathyanne's words, refastening that knot in Finley's chest.

"Hey, Josh," Cathyanne demurred. "Imagine running into you here."

A look of confusion wiped the smile from Josh's face. "Wait? Didn't you say—"

"Yeah, well, no matter," Cathyanne interrupted Josh like he was about to reveal a confidence Finley had already come to understand. Her friend was a deceitful meddler. "So, here we all are, and I owe you a drink." She handed him her half-empty bottle of beer. "And now, if you'll both excuse me, there's a little someone yummy over at the bar in need of my attention." She shared a sly glance with one of the guys they'd been flirting with earlier.

Finley dug her fingernails into Cathyanne's arm. "You promised," she warned through tight lips.

"Yes, I did." Cathyanne pulled out of Finley's grip and rubbed the pressure of Finley's fingertips from her arm. "I promised I wouldn't leave you here with no way to get home." She motioned to Josh. "And now that Josh is here, you have a way home. See, I'm a woman of my word." Then she leaned in to whisper in Finley's ear. "Unless you'd rather hitch a ride with Quinton."

Finley's eyes rounded to saucers before pulling into angry

slits. "I'm certain Quinton already has other plans," she said, remembering the young woman from his dressing room. Just because he'd dismissed that one didn't mean he hadn't made plans with another.

Cathyanne ignored the warning in Finley's voice. "Josh it is then." She quickly turned to address him before Finley could think, much less protest. "It's no problem for you to give Finnie a ride home." She poked out her bottom lip and fluttered her lashes. "Right, Josh?"

Josh swallowed what looked like a grapefruit. "No, I don't mind." His eyes volleyed between the two women, perplexed. "It's no problem at all."

"Great!" Cathyanne clapped her hands together. "Josh, you have a good night." She gave him a wry smile. Turning to Finley, she leaned in close again. "And Finnie, you can thank me in the morning." Then she winked as she backed away, and was swallowed by the crowd.

Finley stared helpless at the receding sight of her *ex*-best friend's blond head. "Yeah, *if* I ever speak to you again."

At her side, she could feel him there. Josh. He was staring at her, intently, if she wasn't mistaken—if all the beer she'd consumed earlier wasn't completely obscuring her peripheral vision. What in heaven's name was she supposed to do now? Sure, they'd shared an amicable enough, professional relationship, and occasionally discussed their common interest in historic homes, but chatting about plants and architecture, much less the proper way to perform a squat, seemed a bit out of place here at Tootsies. Nevertheless, it wasn't like she could pretend he wasn't in the bar, so what choice did she have but to attempt a conversation before fleeing to the safety of the closest exit.

Assuming a friendly smile, she turned to face Josh. "I'm so sorry about this," she said, her voice tripping over her forced composure. "I'm sure there are a dozen other girls in here you'd rather be driving home tonight, and now you're stuck with me. I can call a cab. Really, it's no problem."

"No." Josh shook his head with insistence, his unwavering gaze glued to Finley. "There's no other woman I would rather be taking home tonight besides you."

Finley's heartbeat kicked up a notch or two. *Taking home?* That sounded like a hook-up. Finley had never "hooked-up" with a man before. And didn't want to. The idea of *her* going home with some guy, hunky acquaintance or otherwise, for the sole purpose of noncommittal sex was preposterous.

A cynical laugh bubbled up from her gut, rolling from her lips before she could stop it. "Yeah, I don't think so."

Josh's expression turned confused. "I'm sorry, I don't understand. Did I say something funny?"

Finley reined in her nervous laughter and took a closer look at Josh's serious gaze. Deepened by the warmest shade of green she'd ever beheld, regardless of how young he was on the outside, behind those eyes she sensed his soul had been around for a lot longer than most. Still, what were the chances he genuinely wanted to spend time with a seasoned woman like her? That he wasn't bothered in the least about driving her home?

"No," she gave her head a stern shake, "I think maybe I've just had a little too much to drink." She forced a sweet smile. "I'm glad you're here."

He clicked his beer with hers. "Looks like it's just you and me, Miss Finley," he said and then tipped the bottle back, swigging down the remainder of Cathyanne's beer.

Finley watched the action of his throat carrying the liquid from his mouth to his stomach, musing before she could stop herself what it might feel like to press her lips to the tanned skin of his neck. The idea made her feel warm all over. Then

Josh's chin lowered, his perfect lips releasing a satisfied *ahh* that sent Finley's insides a twitter.

She promptly told her lustful thoughts to behave.

Spying a passing waitress, she dropped her half-empty bottle onto the woman's tray.

An instant later, a low roar began to rumble from the crowded dance floor.

Finley turned to the front just as Quinton's boots hit the stage. Cheers rose higher still. Next, arms, legs, and various other body parts swarmed against her as the crowd pushed forward, toward the stage. The increased mass of bodies slammed her into Josh. He circled a strong hand around each side of her waist to keep them from being separated. Finley tensed at the feel of a man other than Roy touching her. Josh's hands, his close proximity felt unnatural—wrong—but as her impaired balance fought the jostling bodies to keep steady, she was thankful for the security of Josh's presence.

She leaned back and inhaled. Generally she didn't like the smell of men's cologne—too synthetic—but Josh's was mild with a touch of citrus. The tantalizing scent reached out to her, reeling her the rest of the way in without a fight, and she relaxed into his solid chest.

Quinton stepped up to the mike, his heavy-lidded gaze scanning the crowd. "Is everyone feeling all right tonight?" he said, his voice low and gravely.

Shouts blasted Finley's ears from every direction, Josh's among them.

"I'll take that as a yes." Quinton chuckled. "Folks, I'm Quinton Townes, and the folks here at Tootsie's have been gracious enough to allow me to come down here and play for y'all tonight. I'm a mite rusty, so I hope you'll be patient with an old, wore out country star like me." He swept the crowd with a bashful grin.

"I'll show *you* some patience after the show," a woman yelled back.

Quinton squinted against the bright stage lights to see the woman behind the voice. When his gaze settled on someone in the distance, he released a shy laugh. "I appreciate the offer, darlin'," he said and left it at that. "All right, to start things off tonight, since y'all always want to hear it, and I never get tired of playing it, I thought I'd sing the song that launched my career."

The bar erupted once more in a roar of cheers punctuated by catcalls and earsplitting whistles. Quinton picked a few opening cords and then paused for the cheers to settle.

Resting his lips to the mike again, he said, "This one's called, 'Me, The Boys, The Bar, and the Band'."

The crowd went wild.

Quinton threw a glance over his shoulder to his band as the music hit the eager crowd like an atomic blast. "Well we work all week to earn a few bucks and another tank of gas in the pickup truck," he sang. "It's Friday night, time for some reckless fun . . ."

Finley felt Josh's body moving against hers, his hips swaying with the beat. Heat from his firm chest permeated the thin fabric of her blouse, bringing on a fit of desire, of fantasy come to life. Her head whirled.

Josh leaned in close as he sang along with Quinton and the rest of the bar. "'Me and the boys gonna tear up the town, get a little rowdy and shoot a few down . . .'" Josh's breath was moist on Finley's ear, and smelled of fresh mint with a hint of beer. His lips, his body, his hands were all so close—within her reach. The feeling was intoxicating.

Closing her eyes, she let her head fall back to rest on his shoulder. A smile pulled across her face when his grip tightened around her waist.

The music blasted from the stage, circled the room, and swelled until Finley worried the thundering bass would burst through the wood-paneled walls to shake the dark night beyond. Quinton pulled the strings of his guitar hard, galloping from one spot to another until he'd filled every inch of the small stage with his presence. Then he slid behind the drum kit and pounded out a short solo. Clearly in his element, Quinton was a born performer. Finley had never seen him like this. She could imagine how Lois Lane must have felt the first time she realized her mild-mannered co-worker was also a super hero, and a surreal feeling overcame her. She was in awe.

On the dance floor, the crowd went mad.

". . . It's just me, the boys, the bar, and the band. Honkey tonking people and this blue-collar man. Gonna go out, gonna get a little slammed. Jose, Jack, and Jim have the party planned. For me, the boys, the bar, and the band . . ."

Finley's head was spinning full force by the time Quinton plucked the final few cords. Josh let go of her, raising his hands high over his head to clap before dropping his fingers to his lips with a whistle that had Finley pulling away, her fingers stuffing protectively into her ears. Her distance from Josh brought her back to earth. She took another step away, giving herself a moment to plant both feet firmly to the ground. This, whatever it was, should not—could not—happen between them. She was not Jacqueline Bisset, and Josh, Andrew McCarthy, living some turn-of-the-century remake of that trashy eighties movie, *Class*.

Sucking in a long breath, she steadied her fanciful heart.

Quinton thanked the crowd, which only made them go crazy all over again. As he waited for the bar to settle, a stage-hand appeared with a stool. Quinton perched atop the haggard wooden seat and adjusted his guitar in his lap while the stage-hand lowered the mike to Quinton's new position. The dance floor quieted.

Quinton started strumming, slow and thoughtful. The lights on the stage went down one by one, leaving only a single spotlight over his head.

"This is a lullaby I wrote for my daughter when she was a baby. I used to sing it to her at night when she couldn't sleep—the nights I was home at least," he added along with a doleful laugh. "I told her it would chase the monsters away." He strummed a few more cords. "Any of y'all out there afraid of monsters?" Cheers, but more somber now, went up sporadically through the crowd. "Any of y'all planning to go home with a monster?" He gave the crowd another lopsided grin. "You know who you are." More shouts of admission.

Chuckling at his own joke, Quinton then spoke into the mike. "For my baby girl, Annie." With closed eyes, he lapsed into song: "Little star, shine so bright in the darkness. A ray of hope when the world seems so hopeless . . ."

Josh leaned his lips to Finley's ear. "Do you want to dance?" His breath reawakened her skin, reigniting the fire she'd try to squelch.

Finley looked around. "No one else is dancing."

Josh took her by the waist and spun her around to face him. "So what? I don't think anyone will mind." He seemed intent on dancing with her, but she wasn't sure it was a good idea.

"Come on, Miss Finley, what are you afraid of?" Josh persisted.

What was she afraid of? That people would think she was a cradle robber? A cougar? She stole another quick glance around, and to her surprise, no one appeared to be paying them the slightest bit of attention. Perhaps it was the beer talking, but she heard a voice in her head repeating, *Subjugate fear* . . . Her mantra for tonight. What harm could there be in sharing one little dance? And whom was she trying to fool, he was too cute to resist anyway.

Taking one of his hands in hers, she circled the other around his neck. "Sure, why not." Then her stomach leapt into her chest when the shadow of a grin crossed his perfect lips.

Josh pulled her body in tight to his, their hips moving together in perfect sync to the easy rhythm of Quinton's guitar. Another wave of longing, driven by a hunger for more, rolled up from where their hips met, and settled into the light drumming of her heart.

"You look very pretty tonight," Josh said, and she nearly swooned.

She knew she should shrug off his compliment, stop the fanning of this heat between them before it sparked, but she couldn't bring herself to do it. The sad longing of Quinton's heartfelt words mixing with the pleasing feel of Josh's body against hers were drowning down her reservations.

"Thank you. You look very handsome yourself," she said, lifting her eyes to his. The depth of the wanton look he gave her stole her breath away. No man had looked at her with that much passion—that much raw desire—in a long, long time. And like the birth of a new perspective, her belief that fantasies weren't meant to be lived evaporated into the stale moist air, becoming nothing more than a secret she would never repeat.

". . . Think of the things you'd like to see with your baby. Just one more star to count until you fall asleep." Quinton hummed into the microphone. "Little star . . ."

Josh's eyes fell to heavy slits, his lips moving to within a breath of Finley's. "I hope I'm not being too forward, but I really want to kiss you right now," he whispered. His gaze, his desire, his sweet breath falling on her lips, had her melting from the inside out.

Finley's heart, her skin, and everything in between slowly dissolved into Josh. What was the harm in one little kiss? Her head fell back, her lips parting, reaching for Josh's.

Quinton said. "Did y'all like that one?" His familiar voice thundered into Finley's ears, bringing her back to herself once again. She pulled away, her heart ticking like a metronome set on high. The particulars of her body, her mind, reappeared with each insistent tap. What had gotten into her? Allowing a man she hardly knew to kiss her right here, in front of all these people?

Quinton spoke again. "Okay, this next one I'm dedicating to my good friend and neighbor, Finnie Harrison," he said. At the sound of her name, Finley tore her gaze away from Josh's and spun toward the stage. "'Cause she helped me out with this one, and it just so happens that she's here tonight." Quinton squinted against the stage lights, searching the faces until his gaze met hers. When it did, Finley caught a hint of surprise and looked down to see that Josh's arms were still around her. "It's called 'Yard Sale Memories.'" His eyes locked with Finley's and held her gaze a beat. "This one's for you, Finnie."

Quinton closed his eyes. The lyrics to one of the songs Finley had helped him finish began to slip from his lips, descending over the crowd like a melancholic fog. "He pulled out of the drive with tears in his eyes," Quinton began. "This day was no different. Just another sunrise. When out of the corner, a sign he did see, written in black was, Yard Sale Memories . . ."

Josh's arms came around Finley again, pulling her against him, but this time his close proximity didn't have the same electrifying effect. This song, a ballad about an old man's memories—all that he had left in this world, enclosed in ten brown boxes—reached out to her, and grabbed hold of her heart. She'd been able to help Quinton finish this one mostly because it spoke of loss and regret, the moments we all want to pull back, redirect, and start anew with hindsight as our guide. The very words and actions that shaped our lives without forethought, rocked our existence, and sent us barreling into paths we never saw coming. Paths that led us to nothing but confusion and sorrow—a lost and broken end. And like Quinton, over the years, Finley had acquired plenty of those.

". . . I pointed to number ten, and he tipped his hat back and sort of smiled," Quinton sang. "And said that's the day she walked out the door, no longer could she put up with my foolishness anymore. Not because she didn't love me. Because I know that's not true. She had other things to work on. Other things to do . . ."

Bitter tears burrowed their way into the corners of Finley's eyes as she tried to sweep the painful images Quinton's lyrics conjured in her mind. She had wanted Roy to go, but watching as he backed out of the drive for the last time had been immeasurably harder than she could have imagined. Years of building a life together, crushed, one by one, under the receding tires of his car.

As Quinton droned on, box number five held the story of a child the Lord had taken too soon. Our fates are never really our own. And box number one, the day the old man had met the woman he'd love forever.

*Forever*, Finley repeated in her mind. Forever had been easy when she was young, when tomorrow was full of nothing but her dreams, and the idea of reaching middle-age as unimaginable as flying on a paper airplane to the moon.

When Finley was a teenager, she hadn't dreamed of being a CEO, a lawyer, or even a nurse. Unlike the other girls in high school who viewed college as a passage to something better, Finley had felt trapped by the myriad of possibilities that college offered. Terrified that a higher education meant she would have to fight her way up a ladder she had no desire to climb, always torn between career and family, feeling guilty because there wouldn't be enough of her to go around.

All she'd ever wanted was to be a wife and a mother, to move into her grandmother's home and make it her own, to cook and look after a family.

Finley had run headlong toward her dreams, and now at age forty had achieved them all.

Quinton's voice broke as he continued to sing ". . . He then looked me in the eye and said, son, now go back home, walk in and hug her, tell her she's the only girl you love. Learn from your stop today that you don't end up an old fool like me, sitting at a table, trying to sell . . . Yard Sale Memories . . ."

There was no one for Finley to go home to anymore. No one to hug and tell she was sorry. With a quick, no-fault divorce, her marriage had been divided, reorganized, and repurposed. She'd made sure of that.

So where did she go from here? With more than half her life left to live, who did she want to be now? What were her dreams? And where did a woman go in search of the happiness that had eluded her, her entire life?

Safely wrapped in Josh's strong embrace, she couldn't help but wonder whether or not indulging in a brief interlude, the playing out of a few tawdry fantasies, would get her any closer to the answers she sought.

There was only one way to find out.

Pulling out of Josh's grip, Finley turned to face him. "Take me home."

# Chapter 5

The floor of Cathyanne's sunroom was cool from the plummeting temperatures, lingering from the night before. September in middle Tennessee tended to yo-yo between balmy and downright cold. Overnight, the wind had pivoted from the southwest to the north, bringing a nip to the air, a whisper of the colder season that would soon come to stay.

Ignoring the cramp radiating out from her side, Cathyanne lowered her body down into plank pose before scooping her shoulders to the ceiling and settling into upward dog. This morning, she'd woken with an ache in nearly every bone of her body and had decided to forgo her training session at the gym, opting to practice yoga at home instead.

She turned her face to the warmth of the sun shining through the sheets of glass enclosing her porch, bright but apparently not yet strong enough to warm the room. With a glance down at the cell phone resting on the corner of her mat, her eyes betrayed her desire for focus, to leave the world behind and center. The screen was dark. A blank void. She was alone, and no one cared. But then the only person she really wanted to hear from today was Finley. It had been nearly a week since the night they'd gone to Tootsie's, and Finley had yet to return any of Cathyanne's texts or calls. While Finley had been angry with Cathyanne many times before, she'd never gone more than a few days without a call, and never a whole week.

Breathing in against her discontent, she blew the frustration out, raised her hips, and pushed back into downward-dog. Her hamstrings tightened momentarily before relaxing into the pose. Her rebellious body coerced into submission, a sigh escaped her lips, her mind relishing in a moment of peace. Lowering her knees to the mat, she settled back onto her heels, hands in prayer position in front of her heart. Her gaze drifted over to her phone again. Nothing. Irritation seeped its way back in. She didn't have time for all this foolishness. One more day. If Finley didn't call by tomorrow, Cathyanne was going to hunt her down and force her to talk.

Getting to her feet, she walked over to the window and pressed her palm against the glass. The heat from the other side bled into her cold skin and traveled up her arm. She closed her eyes, memorizing the feeling while savoring the breath moving in and out of her lungs. "Come on, Finnie, let me help you," she whispered. Beyond the window, birds actively called to one another. A dog barked. A golf cart whizzed to a stop.

She opened her eyes to see two of her neighbors setting up to putt on the 12th hole. Her 3,200 square-foot house backed up to the exclusive Bluegrass golf course. She'd played regularly when her second husband had still lived here.

Now, she only watched.

The couple spied her and gave a halfhearted wave. She waved back with matched enthusiasm. Cathyanne wasn't well acquainted with many of her neighbors. She'd never been good at polite chitchat. Plus, her ideas and opinions always seemed a bit too strong, lingering around the outside of normal. To put it plainly, people generally found her to be a smidge odd. As if there were a glass wall between her and everyone else, she could see them—watch their lips move—but an understanding, a real connection, couldn't be formed. The only time she didn't feel out of place was when she was working. She was good at transforming people, at making them into more acceptable versions of themselves, achieving for others what she'd never been able to do for herself.

She'd often wished that she could be more like Finley. Finley was a master at saying the right things at the proper times, at making conversation with even the dullest of people. Finley voted republican, attended church, and dressed in unassuming attire. People looked up to Finley, wanted to be like her. Sure, Cathyanne was attractive and always impeccably dressed. Men and women alike were consistently drawn to her, but with the exception of Finley, her relationships and friendships never lasted.

The couple turned back to their game. Cathyanne went in search of something to occupy her thoughts. Moving through her living room flanked with plush sofas and surrounded by tasteful art, she noticed that the couch cushions sat erect, the throw pillows perfectly plumped. The room appeared lonely, deserted as if it had never been used. How sad. On to the chef's kitchen, looking equally as idle, she stopped at the stainless steel, double doors of her refrigerator.

Her fingers circling the cool metal handle, she hesitated, her eyes taking a quick track down the front. Suspended with the help of a magnet in the shape of a happy yellow bumblebee, her bucket list, so to speak, hung there like a timer, ticking down to zero. Sand draining much too quickly from an hourglass bolted to the table.

One by one, she took inventory of the list, noting each item she'd been able to mark through. *Skydiving* (a little cliché, but still). *Get in shape* (after the treatments she'd wanted to feel healthy again, to be healthy again). *Learn yoga*—practice in Nepal. *Drive a racecar. Nordstrom*—buy every pair of shoes that caught her eye. *Eat a triple patty burger, fries, shake and full-sugar Coke*—without thinking once about fat or calories (sort of negated the being fit thing, but she'd only done it once, and it had been wonderful—liberating). *Ride a train up the east coast* (beautiful). *Walk the Great Wall* (hadn't been as awe-inspiring as she'd expected). *Swim with dolphins. Night shark fishing* (never again). *Ski the Alps*—have a torrid affair with a handsome, mysterious instructor who can't speak English. *Date a real cowboy* (not as sexy as it sounded—they tend to spit and speak with horrid grammar). *Eat an entire box of Godiva. Try on the Hope Diamond* (for obvious reasons, this one wasn't checked off. Yet). *Ring the bell at the stock exchange* (in an effort to show that he was not a complete selfish jerk, husband number one had come through on that one). And finally: *Do something completely selfless . . .*

She'd saved the most difficult for last.

Pulling the heavy metal door back, she reached in for her latest miracle juice. Some sort of exotic concoction of fruits she couldn't pronounce, marketed to those looking for a way to trick nature. For Cathyanne, it was a fraying lifeline. For the otherwise healthy, a way to avoid aging. *Everyone should have to face the possibility of a much-too-early, before-my-time death at least once in their lifetime,* she mused, *maybe then each birthday, each wrinkle and gray hair, would be a blessing, a cherished gift, instead of a curse cast by that foe, relentless time.*

She filled a shot glass with the purpley liquid and knocked it back. The bittersweet taste was raw against her throat, hitting her belly like a punch to the gut.

Down the hall and into her bedroom, she sidestepped a pair of size thirteen boots. They'd been sitting there since that night at Tootsie's. When she'd woken the next morning he—whatever his name was—had been gone. Rumpled sheets and those boots were the only evidence that he'd been there at all. How, or better yet, why, he'd left without his boots, she couldn't imagine, but there they sat all the same. She slumped down onto the end of the bed, her silent phone cradled in her hand, and gazed back down the deserted hallway. The silence was more than she could bear. It grew to a cavernous void that made her feel vulnerable and small. She could call her mother or sisters in Atlanta, but since they so rarely talked, if she called for no particular reason, surely they'd suspect that something was up and assume the worst. No, she'd made her decision. She would do this alone. It was the only way.

How long she'd been sitting there, gazing at nothing before the vibrations shook her back to life, she couldn't be sure. But the sudden quake in the stillness sent her heart rocketing into her throat.

She pressed the phone to her ear. "Finnie, finally. It's been a week," she said in a rush, like she didn't already know that Finley wouldn't stay mad at her for long. She never could. "I thought you'd dropped off the face of the earth or something. Why haven't you returned any of my calls?"

Finley tsked. "Do you really need to ask that question?"

"What? I was just trying to help," Cathyanne said, impatient. Of course she could see why Finley was mad, but Cathyanne's intentions had been genuine, and she didn't want to waste time with pointless theatrics. "I know you have a massive crush on Josh, and by the way he was pawing you with his eyes at our last workout, I figured all you two needed was a little encouragement. I want you to be happy. I thought I was being a good friend."

"You thought wrong," Finley shot back.

"Didn't I see him kiss you?"

Silence and then, "He tried. And so what if he did?" Finley said, only now it sounded as if her anger was rimmed in confusion.

*Uncertainty might be good*, Cathyanne considered, *it means Finley is questioning*. "It means I was right. He is interested in you."

"So. What does him trying to kiss me have to do with the fact that you blindsided me? And even if I might have the tiniest of crushes on the man, what makes you think I wanted to do anything about it?" She blew a frustrated growl into the phone. "Heaven above, Cathyanne, he's practically an adolescent. I could go to jail or something."

A crooked smile tugged at Cathyanne's lips. She'd been right. Finley had definitely been considering the possibility of dating Josh. "Stop being so dramatic," she said, doing her best to make it sound like dating a younger man was no big thing—because it wasn't. "He's thirty-one, and perfectly legal. Good heavens, Finnie, are you really so frigid that you'd walk away from a perfectly good man just because being with him might raise a few eyebrows?" She released a scoffing laugh. "There are a million other forty-something women out there who'd kill to be in your place."

"No there's not." Finley sounded like a spoiled child.

"Are too."

"Are not."

"Are . . ." Cathyanne stopped herself. What was up with Finley? She usually wasn't this juvenile. "Ugh! This is ridiculous," she said and then assumed a more authoritative tone. "Are you going to tell me what happened after Josh brought you home, or not?"

"Not," Finley huffed. "It's none of your business."

Finley was being her usual closed-lipped self, but Cathyanne wasn't giving up. Not this time. Hoping to draw the truth out, she decided to aim as far beyond the mark as she could. "Did he spend the night?" she asked. "You slept with him, didn't you?"

"For the love of Pete!" Finley yelped right before Cathyanne heard a jostling from the other end of the line, followed by a thump.

"Finley?"

More jostling and then, "There is something seriously wrong with you," Finley accused, her words becoming more audible as she readjusted the phone back to her ear. "You know that?"

Cathyanne let her body fall back onto the bed. She was getting nowhere in record time. "Come on, Finnie, dish," she said and hesitated only a second before upping the ante. "If you don't tell me, I'll be forced to use my imagination, and I don't think you want that." She held her tongue a heavy beat and watched a spider hobble across the ceiling. "You and I both know that when my imagination gets away with me, so does my mouth."

"Don't even go there. I'm not falling for your blackmail again," Finley said, and sounded as if she meant it. "Besides, everyone already thinks I've gone and lost my mind. Imagine all you want, but there's nothing to tell. He dropped me off. Simple as that."

*Right, simple,* Cathyanne doubted. "Then why'd you cancel your workout for today?"

"Why'd you cancel yours?" Finley called Cathyanne's bluff in a cool, calculated tone.

*Two could play this avoidance game.* "'Cause I'm not feeling up to it," Cathyanne said, nonchalant.

A short pause, then, "Why, what's wrong?" Finley's voice switched to concern.

Cathyanne smiled as the upper hand reached out to her. "You first. Tell me what happened with Josh," she said, then held her breath and prayed.

Finley's sigh was long and weary. "Cathyanne, if there's something going on with you, something I need to know . . ."

A wicked cackle sounded in Cathyanne's head. "Nope, you first." Finally, she had Finley right where she wanted her.

"Fine . . ." Cathyanne could hear the eye roll in Finley's voice. "But all of this is your fault. If you hadn't fed me all that beer—"

"Finnie, no one held a gun to your head and made you drink," Cathyanne cut in before something *else* became her fault.

"You as good as did," Finley interjected. "Dragging me out to that honky-tonk in my fragile condition."

Cathyanne closed her eyes against her mounting temper and slapped an arm over her throbbing forehead. "Just tell me what happened."

"Well, if you must know," Finley began, a heavy sigh bringing an end to her indignation. "The truth is . . . I was kind of into him at first—after I cursed you out in my head, and all—but then I just couldn't . . . I'm not ready."

"Oh," was all Cathyanne could muster. Why hadn't she considered that Finley might need to take things a bit slower? Perhaps it *was* her fault the night hadn't gone well after all. As usual, she'd swung at the pitch too early. The perfect metaphor for her life, a series of one strike-out after another. She should have started them out slow with a not-so-chance meeting at Starbucks, and then excused herself to take an important call, or something akin to that.

"And now, thanks to you, I feel really bad," Finley went on. "Josh was the perfect gentleman. He held the door open for me, let me go through first. Opened the car door for me too.

Roy never did that, at least not after we were married. But Josh . . ."—her voice took on a dreamy tenor—"even after he drove me all the way home and I informed him I wouldn't be inviting him in, he still walked me to the door to make sure I got in the house safe."

Cathyanne kept her voice low, cautious, as she asked, "Did he kiss you again?"

"No," Finley said, drawing out the word. "I think he wanted to. He kept jiggling his keys while going on about how 'cool' my house was, talking about the Doric pillars, how the echinus of the columns was figured in the egg and dart pattern. He really does know a lot about pre-civil war homes." She took a notice-able breath. "He moved here to Tennessee from Oklahoma just so he could work on restoring antebellum homes. It's his specialty. But then you already know that."

Cathyanne's body popped up to sitting. "No, I didn't. I don't usually pay attention to what y'all are yammering on about at the gym," Cathyanne confessed. "But don't you see, you two have something in common. You both like old houses, old . . . things."

"He wanted to see the inside. Seemed genuinely inter-ested," Finley offered.

Cathyanne felt the life returning to her withered hope. "And since he's so enamored with old stuff, and you keep droning on about how old you are, y'all are a match made in heaven."

"Really? Not helping," Finley scolded. "You know, you're so twisted, they'll have to screw you into the ground when you die."

Cathyanne's stomach flipped over on itself. Death was not a matter to be glib about. It came to all of us whether we were ready or not, twisted or straight, and what happened on the other side was even the most devout person's guess. She pulled her knees up to her chest to still the angst, and stayed her course.

"So did you invite him in?"

"Of course not," Finley said, as if Cathyanne had mentioned the unthinkable. "Maybe I've been out of the dating scene for a while, but I still know a few things. And I know if a lady invites a man in, he's assuming he's gonna get lucky."

Cathyanne fell back onto the bed again. Flopped over onto her stomach. "Right, and we can't have any of that, now can we?" She rapped her forehead against the mattress a few thwacks.

"Look, Cathyanne, that kind of sordid lifestyle might appeal to you, but I have two children and a reputation to protect," Finley said, then gave Cathyanne her standard answer for backing away from anything that might deviate from her carefully-walked path. "What would people think?"

"Who cares? Like you said, your reputation for being Miss Perfect, Miss Decorum, is already ruined. Remember the luncheon?" That was a low blow, reiterating Finley's fall from grace, but Cathyanne was running short on ammunition. And patience. "Besides, maybe they'd be thinking, 'Good for Finnie. She's finally loosening up and decided to have some fun, for a change.'"

"Be serious," Finley said. "I don't want to have any fun. Not that kind anyway."

*Thud. Thud. Thud.* Cathyanne's head hit the mattress a few more times. "Then what *do* you want?"

A shallow, staticy breath came through the phone. "I wish I knew."

For the first time since the divorce, Cathyanne could feel Finley's perplexity, her pain and confusion. It reached inside her, grabbed hold of her heart, and squeezed tight. Caught off guard, "Oh, honey . . ." was all she could think to say.

"Yeah, well." Finley brushed off her moment of transparency. "Look, I have to let you go. I've gotta have a few, choice, words with that no good whore of an orchard manager of mine," she said, which had Cathyanne pulling back on a gasp. She wasn't used to hearing Finley use such coarse language—well, coarse for Finley anyway. "Weeds are popping up all over the place and we've got borers."

Finley's house fronted a ten-acre peach orchard. Cathyanne knew that weeds were a breeding ground for pests. And borers? If she wasn't mistaken, they were destructive little insects that left oozy sores on the tree's trunk. Finley was a master gardener with a knack for making just about anything you could plant in the soil grow. But in the last decade of owning that house, she still had yet to conquer the mountain of issues associated with a massive orchard. Though Finley would never admit it, that orchard was bigger than her—a Goliath towering over a boy David. Except in this scenario, the David was armed with nothing more than a broken sling, and fresh out of rocks.

"Wait, do you need a ride to your meeting?" she asked, as if Finley hadn't vowed never to return to therapy group again.

"No, I got my car back two days ago," answered Finley, much too quickly.

"But you're going, right?"

Finley sighed again. She'd been doing a lot of that during this conversation. Only this time, her heavy exhale sounded angry. "Cathyanne, I love you like I would my own sister— you know I do—but maybe it's time you worried about your own life, and let me handle *mine!*"

"But—" An abrupt silence filled the space where Finley's voice had been.

Cathyanne scowled down at her phone. "She hung up on me!" she said, like the empty room around her was capable of sharing her outrage.

What now?

## Chapter 6

Shielding her eyes from the midday sun, Finley gazed long between the rows of peach trees that fanned out from behind her property, swept around the border of where Quinton's ended, and disappeared over the rise. The sky beyond stretched into the horizon in a clean slate of blue, a tempered ocean turned on end as far as the eye could see.

Through a gap in the nearby foliage, Finley heard the squeak of the porch-style swing that hung under a pergola at the back of Quinton's yard. The lyrics he'd been working on for a few days now drifted on the breeze over the divide. "At sixth and Broadway is where it all began, standing at the bar with a drink in my hand, when in walked a girl, can't mention her name. Because we met, life will never be the same," he sang, followed by his guitar twanging out the same cord over and over as he hummed, no doubt waiting for inspiration to come. "Legends Corner. Where it all started, where it all began . . ."

The soulful tenor of his voice reached out to Finley, calling for her to come, relax, and sit a spell, but she resisted. It was only a matter of time before he showed up on her side of the divide. On days when he was feeling especially blocked, he'd usually wander over, see what she was up to. Then he'd help her garden, can peaches, whatever it took to clear his mind and restore his focus. Only she didn't have time for music writing this morning. She had work to do, and besides, she was in a sour mood. Something dark had been hanging over her since that night at Tootsie's, and seemed to have settled in for a long stay.

Pointing to the mounds of fallen leaves bunched at the base of her peach trees, Finley spoke curtly to her orchard manager, Skylar. "Getting these leaves up is your first priority." In order to keep critters from making her orchard their home over the winter, the falling leaves needed to be raked up and hauled off. "I don't want any bugs settling in so they can do their business on my fresh crop and leave their offspring to feast, fat and happy on my fruit. Also, most of these rows still need to be re-graded to catch the rain run-off. It's supposed to be a dry winter."

"Yes, Miss Finley, I understand," Skylar agreed as she hooked her thumbs on the back pockets of her shorts and surveyed the immense job ahead.

It was two weeks past Labor Day, but the woman insisted on sporting her usual attire of white Daisy Duke shorts and tight tank top. Her glossy dark hair had been roped into a braid that rested between her globed breasts.

"No, I don't think you do," Finley lashed back. "Look, Skylar, I'm not losing half a harvest again next summer. One year in the red was bad enough."

Skylar said, "You're right, and I'm sorry about this year." She plucked the braid from her chest and tossed it over her shoulder as she spun away. "I'll take care of it." Her tone was respectful, but her blue eyes betrayed a look of impertinence as she sashayed off and disappeared between the trees.

Finley's eyes fired daggers of contempt at the back of young Skylar's head. "I bet you will," she mumbled and headed back for the house.

Kicking off her Wellingtons, Finley pushed through her back door where she wasn't a bit surprised to see there was a man in her kitchen. Leaning over the counter, Quinton was helping himself to a cup of coffee. Since Roy left, Quinton had fallen into the habit of letting himself into Finley's kitchen for a cup of her coffee, and if he was lucky, breakfast too. His feet were bare, he had holes in his jeans, paint staining his sweatshirt, and a mop of hair he hadn't bothered to comb, but even in her disagreeable state, the sight of him made her smile—on the inside, at least.

Quinton took a seat at the bar that separated the kitchen from the family room. "When are you going to fire that woman?"

Finley opened the refrigerator, took out a carton, and slid it across the counter to him. "By 'that woman,' I'm assuming you mean Skylar?" Quinton nodded as he added some to cream to his coffee. "I can't fire her," Finley growled as she lifted a plate from the cabinet. "Who would run the orchard if I did?"

"Oh, I don't know." Quinton sipped his coffee. "Someone who hasn't slept with your husband, maybe?"

Finley sent him a dour look. As if she needed reminding, had it really been necessary for him to bring up what a man-whore her husband had been? Roy couldn't have simply limited his scope of indiscretions to random strangers, or even to the tackiest of her garden club sisters. Oh, no, he'd had to go a few rounds with Finley's orchard manager as well. Skylar had been the one and only woman, however, in Roy's vast repertoire of mistresses who'd most closely resembled Finley—a much younger, tighter version, of course. A coincidence? Finley didn't want to go there.

"Ex-husband," Finley corrected. "And don't you think I'd throw that trampy little butt of hers to the curb if I could? It isn't easy to find a suitable replacement. And in the meantime, it's not like I can take care of this house, the garden and the orchard, *and* cook you breakfast everyday all by myself. Now can I?" She reached into the breadbox and palmed a homemade loaf.

"Well, no," Quinton agreed. "Hey, do you have any of that spice bread you made the other day?"

Finley wagged the loaf she'd already selected in his face. "I'm way ahead of you," she said, and dropped two pieces into the toaster.

Quinton hummed in anticipation, then said, "But, since you're considering a new orchard manager, might I suggest finding a tight-assed young man instead?" He bounced his eyebrows. "Might help improve your mood a bit."

Finley slapped him with a piqued stare.

Quinton held both hands up in surrender. "Whoa, Finnie, what crawled up your garden shorts today?"

Finley yanked open the refrigerator again and took out a jar of preserves. "What's in my shorts, or any other piece of my attire, is none of your concern."

Quinton hid a smile behind his mug as he took another sip. "Does this sour mood have something to do with that handsome young man who had his arms around you the other night at Tootsie's?"

Finley snatched the butter and a knife on her way back to the toaster, and set them down, a little harder than necessary, along with the jar in front of Quinton. First he had to go and bring up Roy, and now Josh too. Finley was already feeling out of sorts, she didn't need to be reminded of that night and what a disaster it had turned out to be. Well, disaster may be too strong a word, but given the fact she was too embarrassed to return to training, and thus likely never to enjoy the sight of Josh again, it sure felt that way to her.

"That's *also* none of your concern."

Quinton unscrewed the lid on the jar and sniffed. "Peach, my favorite." He set the preserves back down, and sent Finley a teasing look. "So, who is he?"

Quinton's toast popped up. Finley shook her head as she dropped it onto the plate. "Nobody. It was nothing," she said and moved the plate over in front of him. "And that's all you're gettin' today." She pointed to the toast.

Quinton lifted his knife. "With the way he was pawing you, it didn't look like nothing to me," he persisted while slathering his toast with butter first and then preserves.

Finley sent him a bothered look. "He's my trainer. His name is Josh. There's nothing more to it than that."

Taking a bite, Quinton studied Finley as he chewed. "I saw you leave with him."

Finley opened the dishwasher and began to unload. "Cathyanne ditched me, so he gave me a ride home," she said. "Nothing torrid about it."

"No?" Quinton questioned.

"No!"

Quinton eyed Finley as he took another bite. "All right, fine, so don't sleep with him, but why not give the poor guy a chance?" he said, though he didn't sound fully committed to the idea. "You know what your problem is, Finnie?"

"I don't have a problem."

"You worry too much about what other people think."

"Ugh!" she groaned and turned her back to him, stacking some plates onto a shelf. "Don't you start with that too."

"Did I ever tell you about the first song I wrote?"

Finley couldn't imagine what a song could possibly have to do with her alleged worries over what others might think of her, which was completely unfounded, by the way, but if discussing it took the focus off her, she'd happily indulge him a minute or two.

Crossing her arms, Finley spun back to face him. "Sure," she said, remembering how during one of his rough patches—an alcohol-induced relapse, to be exact—she vaguely remembered how he'd recounted something about a song, a church, and his father. "I think you mentioned it at one time or another," she said, though she couldn't recall the details. "You might need to refresh my memory."

"I was eleven, and the song was a nativity ballad for the South Austin Baptist church's Christmas pageant," he began, the words or memories, maybe both, thick in his throat. "My daddy disapproved of the song because he thought the melody was too crude, and the lyrics unconventional. But then, what did I expect from a man who'd never felt anything but a generous amount of contempt for everything I loved?" He lifted a shoulder and gazed into the far corner of the kitchen.

"When I'd finished my performance, all I remember is the way the sanctuary sat too long in silence. How my heart dropped to the pit of my stomach. And just when I thought my daddy was right, that I had no talent and my music wasn't any good, the pews erupted in an applause that quickly transitioned into a standing ovation." He shook his head and laughed without smiling. "That affirmation reached into my soul and took hold. That was the first time in my life I truly felt accepted," he admitted, his faraway gaze heavy with emotion. "As amazing as it was, those few beats of silence will forever be my worst enemy."

"Right, but what does all that have to do with me?" Finley asked.

Angst creased Quinton's brow. "Let me finish," he shushed her. "And even though everything turned out all right, every time I played after that, I was afraid, terrified that the crowd wouldn't cheer this time. That's why I drank so much, and did drugs—to ease my fear. It was easier to hide instead of face it. The problem with hiding, though, is that it makes a person stagnant, weak."

Worry for his sobriety softened Finley's brittle mood, a little. "So what's different now?" she asked, her mind rolling back to the first few years after he'd moved in next door. To the many times he'd fallen off the wagon, gone on a binge of alcohol, pills, or cocaine, and how he'd tried to detox on his own because there'd been no money for rehab. She'd scraped him off the bathroom floor and held a cool washrag to his head as he shook and hallucinated, more times than she wanted to count. "You played the other night without drinking. Didn't you?"

"With therapy, time, and good friends"—he sent a smile her way—"I finally figured out that it doesn't matter whether or not people like my music. I write and play what's in my heart. I do it for me, because I can. If folks embrace it, then that's great. If they don't, then that's okay too. I move on. What others think of me, of my music, doesn't change who I am. Doesn't make me less of a man or diminish the gift God gave me. Yes, the doubt and fear still creep in at times, but I've learned to move past the fear and allow my life to continue on. No matter what comes, it's what's meant to be, and I'll deal with it."

Finley went back to the dishwasher, busying herself with putting the silverware away. The reason behind his story was beginning to present itself, and she didn't appreciate his motives one bit. "That's great, Quinton. I'm proud of you," she said by way of polite brush-off.

"Thanks, but don't you see," he continued as if she'd missed the point, "our fears and insecurities hold us back, so it's up to us to keep moving forward, to keep from getting stuck in a rut."

Finley held her tongue a beat, allowing the clank of silver to fill the air instead. First Cathyanne and now Quinton? What was with everyone lately, feeling the need to offer unsolicited, completely unnecessary advice?

Finley pushed the silverware drawer shut. "Why are you telling me all this?" she asked, each word carefully placed directly behind the last, giving him one more chance to catch the intonation of back-off in her voice.

He didn't.

"Like me, only different, you're letting other people decide whether or not you're good enough," he soldiered on. "You keep yourself so busy with this house and everything that comes with it that you don't have time to think about what you're missing, limiting your possibilities to some unwritten list of expectations."

Finley kept her gaze fixed on him a long moment as she struggled to control the malice welling up inside her. The luncheon aside, she wasn't one to let her temper get the better of her, so she plastered on a winning smile and tried one more time to end this conversation before it turned ugly.

"Thanks, Quinton. I appreciate your concern. I *really* do. And I know you only have my best interest at heart . . ." she began, as if reading off a script inside her head, which in all honesty she was, since the words were flowing almost verbatim straight from her cotillion handbook. Unfortunately, the script seemed to suddenly run out of lines, and she had no choice but to improvise. "But there seems to be a problem with everything you just said because it's . . . well, it's the most asinine thing I've ever heard," she said, still trying but not succeeding at keeping the venom from her voice.

"Yes, I *am* a busy woman. I have responsibilities, but can't you see, I'm living my dream." She laughed ironically. "And what's *so* wrong with society having a few rules? Seems to me like this country was better off when folks had some decent standards to live by, when they cared a little more what others thought. Nowadays everyone's going around, hooking up without any regard for commitment, and"—her eyes darted around, her mind groping to punctuate her point—"and wearing white after Labor Day," she added, which was a valid, however completely irrelevant, example. Then the words, "And divorcing, ripping their families apart" spilled from her lips before she could stop them.

"Look, Finnie, I'm sorry, I didn't mean . . ." Quinton began but couldn't seem to find the words he needed to apologize for what had clearly been Finley's offense.

Embarrassed over her tirade, Finley dropped her eyes to the floor. The poised woman she'd always been didn't rant. Lunatics ranted. *What has gotten into me?* She was afraid to imagine. Regardless of whether or not she thought someone deserved her disapproval, she never said hurtful things to the people she cared about, to anyone for that matter, but there was no denying she'd yelled at Quinton just now, and hung up on Cathyanne earlier today.

Tears seeped into her eyes as a feeling she couldn't place swept over her, leaving a sense of unfamiliarity in its wake. "Forget about it." With her heel, she kicked the dishwasher door closed. "I have to change. Apparently, I have a therapy group I need to get to.

# Chapter 7

"'Glass ceiling,' my fat, black ass!" Burlie-Jean slapped a hand to her generous hip. Her rhinestone-encrusted fingernails reflected tiny flecks of light from the gym's skylight onto the circle of group members as if to accentuate her point. "More like a brick wall. And how am I supposed to defy it when I'm not just bumping up against it—it's closing down on me!"

"Have you tried meeting with a headhunter?" Ford offered. "Worked for me a time or two. Got me a step-up to senior management, benefits, and retirement."

Burlie-Jean swayed her head and pursed her maroon-lined lips. "Says the over-privileged white *man* to the poor black *woman*. I don't know which is worse, that I'm black, a woman, and a hearty one at that," she glided a hand down the curve of her rotund, hourglass figure, "or if it's 'cause I have babies and am a single momma too. I worked eight-hour days while going to night school to earn my accounting degree, and I sure don't appreciate being looked at like I'm some welfare case. Where

got that degree? They think the social workers
Family Services hand them things out to all the
ong with food stamp cards?"

_e a faint throat-clearing sound. "With all due
respect, ma'am, I am not over-privileged," he said, keeping
his voice level, even, though his cool gaze betrayed offense.
"I worked hard all my life. I spent twenty years in the military
serving this country. Received my training and education on
the job, fighting for your freedom."

"Well, good for you." Burlie-Jean whipped her hand up
and snapped her fingers. "Three-squares a day, a bed to sleep
in, all the health care my tax dollars can pay for, *and* a lifetime
of pension—"

"Burlie-Jean," Careen interrupted in a stern voice. "In this
group we do not disrespect one another. We all understand
that you're frustrated after being laid-off from the county, and
that your husband refuses to contribute, but—"

"*Ex*-husband," Burlie-Jean corrected with an attitude that
sounded very similar to when Finley, herself, had reinforced the
same distinction earlier today with Quinton. Why were divorced
individuals so adamant about clarifying this distinction?
Like specifying the *ex* gave them a leg up, a false sense of domi-
nance, of decisiveness. Obstinacy over culpability, an unnecessary chip weighing down one's shoulder they were too stubborn
to flick off.

"Right, of course," Careen apologized. "But we mustn't
degrade the service Ford, and other men and women in the
military like him, have given in the name of our freedom."

"Freedom? For who, exactly?" Burlie-Jean planted a fist
firmly on each hip. "Huh? Rich, white men who already have
more money than there are loose women to blow it on?" she
spat. "'Cause where I come from, we don't feel all that free.
Trapped is what we be feelin'."

A grin split Nora's dark purple lips. "Guess y'all are still waiting for that freedom to 'trickle down,'" she said, snorting out a laugh.

Like a dome of social incorrectness had closed around the group, the gym fell into an unnatural silence. A subtle reminder of the cuts a person's words were capable of inflicting. Wounds for which there was no balm.

Sue's eyes sliced back and forth, hacking through the silence. "I'm white and have a job, but I don't feel free either," she said around the middle finger she was chewing. "Working at Walmart don't pay enough for me to live on, now that I'm on my own. We was barely scraping before my . . ." She dropped her hand. "Before my husband left for good."

"I can see this is hard on most of you," Careen jumped in, her eyes lighting on everyone, it seemed, except Finley. "But resentment and name-calling doesn't help anyone. Remember what I said before about anger and grudges. They're like squeezing a hot coal in your palm"—she made a walnut-sized fist with her tiny hand—"and expecting it to burn the person you're angry at. The only people we hurt with our negative thoughts and words are ourselves. When we name-call, we're showing the world that we have insecurities we're trying to hide by pointing an accusing finger at others." Her gaze tracked around the circle, her mouth pressed shut, indicating it was time for the group to move on.

Finley thought about how she'd called Skyler a whore. Highlighting Skyler's bad judgment in bed-partners—specifically, Roy—hadn't made her feel any better about herself, about getting older, or about lusting after a younger man. The cloud that had been looming over her the last week or so, darkened. When had her life become about pointing a finger at someone else in order to keep others, and herself, from noticing her growing list of weaknesses?

After everyone had held his or her tongue a few more tense moments, Careen stilled her focus on Finley. "Finley, you've been pretty quiet today," she observed. "It's good to see you, though. To be honest, I'm surprised you're here at all. I didn't think you'd be back."

Finley smiled to hide her discomfort. "Not as surprised as I am to be here." Therapy group was the very last place she'd expected to be today. But then, she'd been feeling lost for quite some time now—which, after her conversation with Quinton this morning, she realized wasn't going unnoticed by the people around her. She'd been walking a slippery slope to a dark place that was obviously getting the better of her, and quickly tiring of the funk she'd slipped into. She wanted out. Fortunately, she wasn't so dysfunctional as to not see she needed help to do so. So what harm could there be in coming here today? If there was even the smallest chance this group might help, she had to give it a try.

Careen asked. "Do you want to talk about what brought you back?"

The group's focus shifted from Careen to Finley. Four pairs of eyes, all staring her down—waiting, probing, like eight annoying fingers poking her all at the same time, saying, *Tell me . . . tell me . . . tell me the answer to a question you can't even comprehend yourself.*

Finley swallowed against the pit of uncertainty hardening in her throat. "No, not really," she choked out. Wanting to get better and knowing she needed help were one thing. Being able to talk about it? Another issue all together.

Nora reached up to fiddle with the ring circling her lip. "Yes, you do. Or you wouldn't be here," she said, then rolled her eyes away.

"Nora," Careen cautioned. "Finley, we can't help you if you won't share." She cut another glance of warning at Nora.

"Though she needs to work on her method of delivery, Nora has a point. You're here, so you must have something on your mind."

Like setting a ball in motion that had picked up momentum before she'd realized an instant too late she couldn't keep up, Finley had unwittingly agreed to delve into whatever was bothering her the moment she'd settled her backside into this cold metal chair.

She heaved a weighty sigh. "Something's wrong with me," she said, forcing the belief from her lips. The words tasted bitter, but not as unsavory as she'd anticipated.

Pulling in a steadying breath, she gathered courage and started with her most obvious problem. "I've been snippy lately. I yelled at my best friend. I hung up on her. And then my neighbor was trying to give me some advice, and I hollered at him too. Poor Quinton. He didn't deserve that. I was rude twice in one morning, and that's not like me." It also wasn't like her to be a complete head-case, but she kept that to herself.

As if this therapy session was finally getting interesting, Careen leaned forward. "Can you identify what first set you off?" she asked and then held silent, the kind of quiet that told the group no one was allowed to speak except Finley.

Finley's mind zeroed in on Cathyanne, on the night at Tootsie's, and then again early this morning, and how her friend had suddenly decided she was entitled to meddle in Finley's love life. Like Finley wasn't capable of making those decisions on her own. Like she needed to be handled.

"I realized my best friend is a manipulative, underhanded, busybody," she said.

Careen edged a little closer. "Go on."

Finley glanced around the group. Was it her imagination, or had they all edged slightly forward as well? Why did it seem like everyone was much more enthralled by her problems than by anyone else's? But then maybe they weren't, and she would now have to add "self-absorbed" to her growing list of disagreeable new character traits.

"Because I was trying to do that 'subjugate fear' thing," she said. "I trusted her and did something, went somewhere I normally wouldn't. She told me we were going to Tootsie's to see Quinton Townes, and . . ." She hesitated. Where to go from here? The long version of how Cathyanne had attempted to push Finley on poor Josh, or the short? Would the *Reader's Digest* version of her night at Tootsie's properly convey the depth of Cathyanne's betrayal?

Ford stepped in to fill her pause. "You a fan?"

His question shook Finley from her stupor. "Sure. But he's also a good friend, and Cathyanne knew I'd want to see him play."

A high-pitched squeak had everyone looking to Sue. "I love Quinton Townes. He's *so* dreamy." She released a nervous giggle, then went back to work chewing her thumbnail. "You're really friends with him?"

"Yes, and neighbors," Finley clarified.

"Of course y'all are," Nora interjected with a scowl. "Why doesn't that surprise any of us?"

Careen sent Nora another pointed look before directing her attention back to Finley. "What happened at Tootsie's?"

Finley fought the urge to return Nora's sneer. What was her problem anyway? Was she jealous because she didn't have a famous friend like Quinton? Or did she harbor this amount of disdain for humanity in general?

"Well, as it turned out, it was all just a setup. I walked right into her trap."

"Trap?" Careen prompted.

Finley laced her fingers together. Twisted them one way and then the other. "She tried to fix me up with someone.

A man . . ." Heat blossomed onto Finley's cheeks. "It was awful. And embarrassing."

Careen nodded. "Is it possible she was just trying to help you move on?" She gave Finley one of those therapist's looks. The kind that said, *I can plainly see the answer to your problem. I'm just waiting for you to catch up.*

Finley wondered if they taught that look in psychology classes. Was perfecting a knowing gaze part of the curriculum? And if so, how long did Careen have to stand in front of the mirror practicing before she'd perfected said look?

"I s'pose," Finley half-heartedly relented. She wasn't ready to forgive Cathyanne just yet, but at the same time, didn't want Careen to think she was dim-witted.

Careen continued to eye Finley, this time incorporating the one-eyebrow lift. "And your neighbor, what did he do to set you off?" she asked. "What was so offensive about his advice?"

Careen's gaze burned through Finley, scrambling her thoughts with self-doubt, stirring her feelings until her most guarded emotions rose to the surface. She could still see Quinton's face and the uneasy look in his gray eyes, the way his bare feet shifted on the floor beneath his stool. He looked every bit the part of her aging, country star friend. Except that this morning, instead of being his normal, life-is-good self, he'd seemed worried. Concerned about her. But Finley had always been the one in control, the one who knew what to say, and had pearls of wisdom to bestow. Not Quinton, and for that matter, certainly not Cathyanne. Watching out for others had always been Finley's role, not the other way around. When had she allowed her divorce, something she'd ultimately wanted, to turn her life inside out and upside down?

Finley shifted her eyes away from Careen's. How could

someone as small as Careen be so adept at assuming such a menacing presence?

Consulting the far corner of the gym, Finley summoned up some of what Quinton had said. "He started saying some nonsense about how I'm too afraid of what others think to live the way I want."

"What does he think you're missing? What's this fear keeping you from doing?"

Finley gnawed her lip in thought. At the time, she'd been too busy protecting her ego to rationally consider the point Quinton was trying to make. "He thinks I should date the man my friend tried to fix me up with, I guess."

"But you don't want to?" Careen subtly prompted.

Before Finley could answer, Nora snuck in another comment. "What's wrong with him?" She rolled up the corner of her top lip. "He bring you the wrong flowers too?"

Finley felt the beginning of an insult readying itself on the tip of her tongue.

Recommitting herself to the avoidance of spewing any more ugliness today, she bit back her angry words and said, "No, there's nothing wrong with him, except"—she hesitated to take a breath before rushing on with the rest—"he's young—younger than me. That's all."

"You mean your trainer?" Nora filled in the blank. "The one you've been lusting after?"

Burlie-Jean pointed at Finley. "You go for it, girl." She sucked air through her teeth. "I would. I'd take me a little piece of young, tender man candy if I could." She closed her eyes. "Mmm-m-mm." Then she pointed a curl-tipped fingernail at each member of the group, ending with Finley. "It'd be nice to have the upper hand for once. You know that's why men date twenty-year-olds—so they can be in charge. Shoe's on the other foot now, baby. Time you walked in it."

The group murmured its concurrence.

Nora tossed out a challenge. "Unless she really is scared of what others will think."

Finley shot Nora a warring look to which Nora came back at Finley with a stare just as fierce.

Careen cut the tension with a judicious question. "Finley, do you want to date this man?" She laid a finger to her lips, her eyes consulting the ceiling. "What was his name again?"

"Josh," Sue volunteered.

Finley rubbed her shoulders, reliving the thrill of having Josh's arms around her. She could almost smell him, and feel his heart beating against her back, his warm breath on her cheek. "Ideally, I guess I do," she admitted. "But we don't live in an ideal world."

"Say this age difference disappeared," Ford proffered. "Take it completely off the table. How would you feel about dating him then?"

"Or," Nora cut in, "pretend you're like a pioneer, only you're going boldly where most women only dream of going." Her contribution might have sounded motivating had she not added what came next. "And why not? Why shouldn't the woman who has everything get more? It's the American way."

"Ahem!" Careen cleared her throat and sent Nora another reprimand with her eyes. Then she traded the glare for her usual supportive look and turned back to Finley. "A lot to consider." She bobbed her head encouragingly. "I think we should consult step number two again." She looked to the chalkboard and read, "Defy the rules, embrace the guidelines. Rules emphasize the result. Guidelines emphasize the journey."

Finley's heart pounded, beating against her ears, and then the back of her eyes. "Defy the rules . . ." she repeated as the gym seemed to fall away. An image of her and Josh walking arm in arm under a crisp autumn sky slid in where the dusty basketball court had been. In her vision, Josh leaned down to drop a kiss to her temple. How wonderful it would be to ignore their age difference, to forget all her worries about what others might think and just see what happened.

"Are you dense or something?" Nora's question wiped away Finley's daydream. "Defying society's rules means you should ask out your trainer." Pinching her thumb and finger together, she shook her hand real fast. "Ringing any bells?"

Ford said, "Sounds like a good place to start."

"Yes, it does," Careen agreed. "Remember our motto. Divorce is not an end, but a new beginning." She gave Finley another encouraging look. "All right, folks, time's up for today. Let's recite our Five Steps to a New Beginning."

The group began in obedient unison, "Subjugate fear, take chances, learn from and consent to the unexpected. Defy the rules. Embrace the guidelines. Rules emphasize the result. Guidelines focus on the journey . . ."

Finley's lips moved, her voice giving up the words while her mind drifted miles away. Could she really see herself defying the rules? Had she even made any progress with step number one yet? Learned from, and consented to, the unexpected? And what had she learned from subjugating fear, from her outing at Tootsie's? That after all these years of friendship, Cathyanne was not to be trusted? Or, as Careen had suggested, had Cathyanne simply been looking out for Finley and trying to help?

In hindsight, Finley had to admit that her friend's push toward Josh could be interpreted as being exactly what she needed. But she'd run from the unexpected—Josh—like a scared rabbit, assuming he was the complete wrong course for her to take. Then, she'd taken out the misgivings that had followed on the people who loved her most. Finley had found her dark side. But in the process, she'd come to understand that her lack of current direction was the source of her bewilderment, and now recognized how lost she'd really been. Adrift in a world familiar and also foreign, searching for answers to questions she couldn't ask because she didn't know where to begin.

"*A good place to start,*" Finley repeated Ford's words in her head. A spark of hope lit her breast, warmed her soul. Isn't that what she'd been searching for? A direction. A first step. Could she adopt Quinton's philosophy that if people didn't approve of her, or of her behavior, then that was . . . okay? Easier said than done. But as Quinton had proven, with practice and the help of good friends, being true to one's self was not impossible.

What if Josh was *her* place to start?

What if he wasn't?

It was scary, walking blindly into the unknown. But then, how hard could it be, inviting Josh over to see the house? He already said he wanted to see it. Maybe she could fix a little lunch too? No big deal. Not exactly a lifelong commitment—and really, no one had to know.

The thought of calling him terrified Finley, but she liked the idea of Josh being her starting place.

As good a place as any.

Plus, she had to admit the view was pretty amazing.

# Chapter 8

Reaching deep into the belly of her Grand Wagoneer, Finley tried not to muss her blouse as she rummaged around, looking for her favorite pair of pruners. She had a wayward dogwood branch obstructing the sizable placard the historical society had positioned in her yard after she'd completed the renovations a few years back. *Finley House, est. 1833*, it read. She wanted everything to look perfect when Josh arrived, but she couldn't seem to locate those dadgum clippers.

October had begun with more cool days than warm, which meant she probably should clean out and organize the gardening supplies she hauled around in the back of her Jeep during the spring and summer months. But lately she'd found most aspects of her "normal" routine simply more trouble than they were worth. For the rest of the south, fall decorating was in full-steam-ahead mode. But Finley had barely spared a thought on the subject. Other than a few pumpkins she'd harvested from her garden, she hadn't stockpiled a single bag of candy, hadn't swapped out the zinnias for pansies in her flowerbeds, nor had she baked a single batch of fresh apple muffins.

She knew what Careen would say. She'd equate Finley's lack of structure to situational depression or low self-esteem or some other overreaching diagnosis Finley felt fairly certain didn't apply to her. Her children were gone, her husband was too, which meant everything that had anchored her and dictated her schedule in the past had changed. She'd been left to stumble around, trying to figure out where she belonged now that she was on her own. What woman in her place wouldn't feel a touch disjointed?

Her hand had just closed around the familiar feel of the rubber grips when she heard a man's voice say, "Miss Finley?"

Startled, she jerked back and knocked her head on the hatch. "Josh." She dropped the pruners and quickly readjusted her course, easing her body through the opening without further incident. Straightening, she turned to see him making his way from the FJ Cruiser he'd parked at the other end of her horseshoe driveway. "Is it noon already?"

Josh increased his pace. "Are you all right?" he asked, stopping just shy of reaching out to her. "I didn't mean to startle you."

Finley winced, her fingertips massaging the crown of her head. "Don't worry about it." She dropped her hand and forced a smile as she proceeded to smooth the hitched-up hem of the white blouse she wore with a pair of pocketed jeans and simple, but stylish, sandals.

With the exception of that night at Tootsies, she'd never seen Josh outside of the gym. She hoped he approved of her everyday look—classic but simple. Cathyanne would have had her wearing something sexier, but the provocative look wasn't for Finley and never would be. Even if she didn't fully know who she was these days, she wanted Josh to accept the one part of her she knew would never change.

"It's always so quiet around here." She motioned out to the country road that ran in front of her home. Thinly dotted with a varying array of homes surrounded by acres of rolling fields, the road stretched through miles of ghostly quiet. The closest structure was the old farmhouse Quinton occupied just beyond a grouping of century-old oak trees. "I don't know why I didn't hear you drive up," she said, nervously chewing her bottom lip.

He offered her an easy smile. "Next time I'll honk twice," he said, his gaze lighting on the lip she was gnawing before shifting away, glancing instead over her shoulder and into the open hatch of her Jeep.

A look of repulsion, or shock—she couldn't tell which—darted across his face.

Remembering how clean and orderly his SUV had been the night he'd driven her home from Tootsie's, she saw her truck through his eyes.

The back compartment was littered with buckets, shovels, empty pots, bags of fertilizer, and who knew what else? The pungent scent of earth mixed with compost wafted out to tickle the senses.

Josh ran his index finger under his nose as if to stifle a sneeze. "What year is your Wagoneer, a nineteen-seventy-nine model?" he asked. "Eighty, maybe?"

Stepping back, Finley reached up and lowered the window, then lifted the tailgate, slamming it closed. "Nineteen-eighty-two," she corrected, her fingers fondly gliding over the rear wood panel. Sure it was old and void of all the "bells and whistles" newer Jeep models boasted, but it had four-wheel drive, comfortably held all her supplies, and emanated a timeless elegance she felt a kinship to.

"Good year." Josh held back a smile. "That's right about the year I was born."

Finley swallowed hard. "Is that a fact?"

Silence built a wall between them as Finley shifted her gaze anxiously over the ground around Josh's feet. It had taken her more than a week to work up the courage to invite him to lunch, and the call had been quick and to the point, which meant there were still things that needed to be said before they could move forward.

After a few too many uncomfortable beats, "I want to apologize—" shot from both their mouths, the words running atop each other, becoming jumbled in the space between them. Another instant of silence and then, "Go ahead" came out almost simultaneously as well.

Josh held a hand out to Finley. "Ladies first."

Finley swallowed against the awkwardness and trudged forward. "I'm sorry about the mixed signals I gave you that night at Tootsie's," she said, her gaze still avoiding his. "I've just never really been with anyone other than my husband. Not since I was a teenager anyway."

Josh took a step forward. "No, it was my fault. I know better than to down a beer on an empty stomach. I guess I got caught up in the moment is all."

Finley's eyes shot to his. "'The moment'?" she repeated. As in he hadn't meant to kiss her? Or he'd made a mistake?

When Finley failed miserably at keeping a mortified look from overtaking her face, he dashed to clarify, "What I mean is . . . Okay, it's just that . . ." But his tongue kept tripping over what he was trying unsuccessfully to say.

Hoping to make this easier for them both, Finley jumped in. "It's all right, I understand," she said, forcing out a chuckle that sounded more like she was being choked. "A guy like you would never want to, um, you know, someone like me."

Josh pushed his hand out in a stopping motion. "No, I *did*," he said in a rush. "It's just that I don't normally date clients."

Finley's humiliation hopped to the backseat. So he was apologizing for kissing her not because he found her unattractive, but because of a work-related, ethical dilemma? "That's understandable. You're a professional. I get that," she said, feeling a mixture of competing emotions. First, disappointed that her attempt at "defying the rules" had come down to nothing more than a benign lunch between friends. Pathetic. Second, relief because no physical relationship meant no need to be embarrassed or uncomfortable about dating a younger man. Third, frustrated. If inviting Josh to lunch wasn't to be the first step on her journey to finding her new path, then would she now have to find a new place to start? Ugh!

Josh's hand closed into a fist, which he then shoved into the pocket of his jeans, his greenish-brown eyes darkening to the color of mud.

Pressing his lips together tight, his gaze darted around before hitting an abrupt stop on the other car that occupied Finley's garage. "Is that a Porsche Panamera?" he asked. "Who does it belong to?"

"Me," Finley said with disinterest. "My husband bought it for me as a Mother's Day gift."

Stepping into the shadowy garage, he ran his fingertips through the layer of dust blanketing the car. "Don't you ever drive it?" he puzzled.

Finley crossed her arms over her chest and rolled a shoulder. "Why would I when my car drives just fine? I didn't want it, and he knew I didn't. I wanted an aerator. Been asking for a new one for years." The words twisted from her lips with a bad taste. "He hates my car, detests anything American made." She motioned toward the Porsche's trunk. "Look at it. I bet I couldn't even get more than two bags of mulch in there."

Josh's eyes rounded on her. "Miss Finley, who cares about trunk size when you can go from . . . like zero to sixty in like . . . five seconds?"

Finley gave him a dull look. "Obviously, I do." She re-crossed her arms.

They stood there a moment more, Josh's creased brow showing utter bemusement. "What's an aerator?" The pucker between his brows tightened. "You mean like for the lawn? Can you even drive one of those?"

*Why did it seem like all men lost the ability to think clearly when in the presence of a performance vehicle?* Finley ruminated as she fought the urge to roll her eyes.

"Of course not, but that's not the point, now is it?" Then before her annoyance with her ex-husband's blatant disregard for anything important to her could fully surface and lash out at Josh by default, she changed the subject. "Come on. I'll show you the house." She moved around him, heading across the drive.

Glancing back toward the garage, Josh shook his head one last time before falling into step beside her.

When they'd made their way to the porch, Josh stopped and shielded his eyes against the hazy, October sun. Finley watched him scan a discerning eye over her roof with four dormers, then down to the restored, original copper gutters, and on to the hand-cut limestone blocks of the outer façade. Her garden-style antebellum mansion was flanked on both sides by two stone chimneys, reaching high over the pitch of the roof—four fingers pointing toward heaven. Supported by a row of pillars, a deep porch shaded the front of the house. Below the porch, her perfectly manicured flowerbeds swept the length to either side like a bejeweled skirt.

Josh laid a hand reverently to his chest. "Hello, lovely lady," he greeted Finley's home.

A feeling of mutual admiration warmed Finley's heart. "I couldn't agree more," she said, and their gazes held long enough to form a connection, a first link in what she hoped was a growing friendship. "Wait until you see the inside."

Josh held out a hand, indicating that she lead the way. On light feet, Finley took to the stairs and swung the right screen door open. Stepping aside for Josh to enter first, she watched his feet hesitate as if reluctant to enter ahead of her—such a gentleman—but then something in the front entry caught his eye, pulling him forward, it seemed, against his will.

"Is that the original fleur-de-lis wallpaper?" he asked.

"Of course."

Stepping across the threshold, Josh's foot found a loose floorboard. A smile pulled across his face. "Music to my ears." He breathed in deep. "Nothing beats the smell of centuries–old dust."

"Don't I know it," Finley agreed.

He pointed to the cracked plaster ceiling above. "Fourteen-foot," he stated more than asked, then glanced up the cherrywood staircase. "What's the ceiling height upstairs, eight feet?"

Finley followed him in and let the screen door fall closed behind her. "At the peak, yes."

Josh pointed further down the hallway, out to a bank of open French doors at the back of the house. "East to west exposure follows the seasonal winds for cooling," he mused aloud.

Stepping to the wall just outside of her formal living room, he ran his fingers over the molding of one of many evenly spaced openings along the corridor. "Palladian," he called the niche by name. "Before electricity, they used these to hold lanterns."

Finley suppressed a smile. "Yes, I know."

They shared a knowing look. "Right. Of course you do," he said, then crossed the entry. "Poplar doors, faux painted to look like English oak," he observed, his gaze running over the open doors that led into a narrow dining room. "They used poplar and cedar to keep the bugs and termites away . . ."

"Crazy how we think we're so advanced with all our fancy chemicals and pesticides, when all that's required is the proper building materials," Finley said, finishing his thought.

Josh looked down at her with eyes the color of nature. She beamed a grin back at him. It would have been so easy, felt so normal, for him to lean in and brush a kiss across her lips. But he didn't, and she found herself immeasurably disappointed at that. Further proof he wanted to keep their relationship platonic. A feeling Finley couldn't define settled into the pit of her stomach, and started to ache.

He pointed to the portrait over the fireplace. "Who's the surly looking gentleman?"

Finley moved deeper into her grand dining room. "That's my great-great granddaddy Finley. He built this place before the war," she explained, knowing they both understood that, though the US had been in a half dozen or more significant military conflicts since, any mention made of "the war" by a Southerner was a reference to the Civil War.

Finley gazed up at her grandfather with admiration. "Granddaddy Finley was one of Sam Davis's scouts—the Colman Scouts they called them."

Josh joined her at the fireplace. "That's pretty cool," he said, his eyes running along the mantle and over the framed pictures situated there. He picked one up, taking it in his hands for a closer look. "Your kids, I presume."

A feeling of pride ballooned in Finley's chest. She pointed to the young man, looking dapper in his dress-blue naval uniform. Tall and slim like Roy, he gazed back at the camera through the bright blue eyes he'd inherited from Finley. "Yes, that's Shep. He's at the Naval Academy studying economics.

He has a keen mind for business like his daddy, and a quiet authority like my father. He wants to be a fighter pilot and then do something in politics." She shifted her finger over Roy, who stood between them in hopes of avoiding any conversation regarding her ex, and stopped at the teenage girl. A crooked smile grinning deviously for camera, she had sharp features much like Roy's and a thick mane of dark hair like Finley's. "And that's Royanne. She's a freshman at Vanderbilt, also studying economics but with a minor in design, and no idea what she wants to do with either one. She got her creativity from me, her outgoing personality from her daddy, and her feistiness from my granny Opaline."

Josh studied the picture, and in his confounded gaze, Finley presumed to read his thoughts. Prior to this instant, he'd known she had grown children, but seeing two young adults who resembled her smiling back at him must have made it all very real. If he'd entertained even the slightest fantasy of being more than a friend to her, she doubted he did now.

Then she watched as his focus settled on the dark-haired man in the middle. A look akin to protectiveness, or jealousy—she couldn't tell which—wiped the pensive expression from his face. "Is this him?" Josh tapped the center of the frame with his finger. "Your ex-husband?"

Finley gave the man in the photo a cursory glance. She still felt a pang of regret at the sight of him. "Yes. Roy," she simplified. She should have thought to put away any remaining pictures of Roy. Most women in her position would have burned every last image of their ex. But even with the way things had turned out between them, she hadn't been able to convince herself to truly hate him. Besides, Finley loved her children, and her children loved their daddy. What kind of mother would she be if she'd tried to erase every last trace of their father from their childhood home?

Josh studied the man in the picture a moment more. "I've seen him before," he thought aloud. "Roy Harrison? He owns Porsche of Nashville, right?"

Finley confirmed with a slow nod.

"Yeah, I read an article about him in some car magazine," he recalled. "He started out with only a few small car lots, slowly buying up until he now owns a handful of successful luxury car dealerships?"

"Yes." Finley had seen that article too and was grateful to Josh for leaving out the part where Roy had been photographed with his arm slung around a young, leggy redhead.

Josh threw out one more detail. "He lives in Franklin now."

Finley flipped a few strands of hair over her shoulder. "That's right, down south of town with all the other self-important citizens of this fine city," she said, choosing sarcasm to mask the pain as she spun away, her sandals clacking over the wood-planked floor that led through a small butler's pantry.

Josh set the picture back where he'd found it and hurried after her.

Finley stopped next to the kitchen's center island and turned to face him. "Of course, this kitchen area was originally the informal living room," she explained. "The cooking, as you know, in the old days was done out-of-doors. And what we call the family room now"—she looked to the area beyond the kitchen where plush sofas, bookshelves stuffed with books along with Finley's massive movie collection, and a flat-screen TV consumed the space—"used to be the master bedroom." Then she pointed to an arched doorway in the far wall. "We added a new master suite through there."

Josh turned his gaze over the two rooms. "You've done a beautiful job here, Miss Finley," he said. "Restoring the front of the house to its original form while making this back area comfortable for everyday living. I wouldn't change a thing."

A bashful smile tinted Finley's face. "I thought we could have lunch out back." She led him through the set of French doors. "It's such a nice day."

Josh followed her to where she'd set up lunch on a round table at the far end of the veranda, next to a rock fireplace. The pleasing aroma of fried chicken wafted on the breeze. His gaze swept over his surroundings, his focus stopping not on Finley or the table heaping with food, but on the garden beyond the back porch.

Finley broke from her current path, turning to look over the landscape in search of what had captured his attention so fully. Weeping willows, wild roses, butterfly bushes, a variety of daisies, an apple tree arbor, and every species of plant in between—and all on the verge of falling dormant, fanned out between meandering pebbled paths. Six log cabin-style slave houses, three to each side, flanked the property. Stretching out far beyond, her peach orchard touched the horizon.

When Josh finally spoke, it was with awe. "It's like a Van Gogh painting," he said. "Chaotic, but then the longer I look at it, the more interesting it becomes." He turned to her with what appeared a puzzling question. "Why the contrast between this and the manicured landscaping out front?"

Finley shrugged. "Being a member of the historical society means the front must remain formal. But back here," she opened her arms to the view, "I can be as creative as I want."

Josh looked back to the garden. "It's awesome," he said. "I can't wait to see it come spring."

Despite their newly established friendship status, the way he'd insinuated he planned on being around two seasons from now to enjoy her garden brought a pleased smile to her face.

Finley motioned over to the table. "Shall we?"

As she started toward their lunch, Josh caught her by the

arm and spun her back to face him. Gripping a strong hand to each of Finley's shoulders, he pulled her to his chest.

"What are you—" she started, but before she had the chance to even consider what he could possibly be doing, he'd crushed a kiss to her lips.

Her body and mouth went rigid, but she didn't pull away. Feeling his heartbeat thumping, keeping pace with hers— faster, then faster still—sent her head spinning, not so much off-balance as with a sense of immense pleasure. Not having been kissed with this kind of urgency in a long, long time, she wouldn't have pulled away even if her brain had been able to tell her muscles to move.

His grip on her arms tightened, and their kiss sunk deeper.

A gasp vibrated up her throat, escaped their intertwined lips. "Josh . . ." Her shoulders relaxed, her hands traveling up his arms to circle his neck.

"Miss Finley . . ." he echoed as he shifted his grip to her waist and pulled her closer still. Her hips melted into his. Feeling his body pressed against hers released months of pent-up desire so fierce it stole the breath from her lungs. But instead of feeling exhilarated, she was suddenly overcome with the feeling that she was drowning.

Panicked, she pulled out of his grasp.

Pressing a hand to her heaving chest, she took a large step away. "I can't breathe." Only then did she take an instant to wonder what had gotten into him, and more importantly, into her.

Passion tangled with fervor in Josh's eyes. "That's the point." He made a move to reclaim her.

Finley stumbled further back, out of his reach. "But just now, in the driveway, y-you said you wanted to keep this professional, that you don't date clients."

Pulling a breath in through his nose, Josh then released the air in a forced stream. "I know I did, but that's not what I meant," he said. "It came out wrong."

Aggravated by his failure to properly articulate his intentions earlier, not to mention the tornado of yearning whipping through her blood, Finley stabbed a fist to her waist and held her ground. "Then maybe you should start explaining exactly whatever it was you *meant* to say?"

Josh heaved another weighted breath. "I'm attracted to you, Miss Finley. I have been for a long time. I want to *date* you."

"Date?" She eyed him with a critical stare. "What do you mean by date?"

Josh raked his fingers through his hair. "I don't know," he stalled as if making sure to use the right words this time. "Maybe we go out a few times a week, see where things go?"

"Hmm," Finley mulled the idea. As she did, that red arrow on the corner of her Monopoly board under the word "Go" popped into her head. She never could understand why a symbol meant to encourage forward motion was colored red instead of green. It was almost as if it intended to say, "proceed with caution," instead of, "this is definitely the place you want to start."

"Well then, tell me this." She gave him a cool, no-nonsense stare. "Say things between us are going well, and sometime down the road I find myself up early one morning and decide to bake a batch of fresh apple muffins. I bring some over to you and knock on your door, unannounced?" She paused for effect. "Will I have to worry about some woman answering the door in nothing but your T-shirt?"

Josh held up both hands. "When have I ever given you the impression I was some sort of player?" he puzzled aloud. "Look, Miss Finley, I know a little about your husband, but you must know that not *all* men are like . . . well, your ex. So, let's just take things slow for now? No pressure."

Finley studied the sincere gaze peeking out from under Josh's dark lashes. *What to do?* she considered. Remain stagnant because half of her wanted what the other half feared, or roll the dice and proceed with caution?

*A good place to start . . .*

Taking a step, then another, and then one more, she closed the distance between them. "Slow, huh?" she repeated. "Well then, if you're wanting to be more than just my friend, you should probably stop calling me 'Miss Finley.'"

Josh slid his hands around her hips and pulled her, gently this time, against him. "What should I call you then?"

Finley rose up onto her toes and pressed her lips to his.

"Plain 'ole Finley, I expect, will work just fine."

## Chapter 9

Finley's heart was full of sunshine as she plopped another of the hearty pumpkins she'd harvested from her garden down on the last of her front porch steps and stood back to survey her efforts. Gourds along with pumpkins in all shapes, sizes, and colors ascended the stairs before littering the porch in both directions. On each of her front doors she'd hung a simple wreath she'd constructed of berries and fresh evergreen sprigs and then twined with a dark crimson ribbon. Along her flowerbeds, she'd planted alternating pansies of yellow, orange, and white that stretched out in both directions like a candy corn chain. Come Easter, purple and red would be added to create a spring rainbow of flowers.

Breathing in deep, she savored the crisp feel of the mid-October air, mixed with a smoky hit of burning leaves. Vibrations from the back pocket of her favorite work jeans had her pulling her cell phone out to see a bright yellow emoticon, blowing a red heart-shaped kiss to her. *Josh.* Her grin broadened, the heat on her cheeks spreading all the way to her toes. A moist breath of cool wind lifted her hair and tossed it against her flushed face.

She'd begun last week's lunch date in a fit of nerves and second-guesses. Ended that same date in a dreamy fog. She couldn't remember the last time she'd felt this hopeful—giddy, even. So much so, she worried she might burst open with happiness, a waterfall of infatuation spilling out. An occasion such as this called for a powwow with a best girlfriend. Only the last time she'd spoken to Cathyanne, Finley had hung up without even saying good-bye. Now Cathyanne wasn't returning *Finley's* calls—a treacherous shoe, switching to the opposite foot.

Searching her contacts, Finley again found Cathyanne's cell number. With the phone pressed to her ear, her toe tapped the wood planks of her porch as she waited while one ring after the last went unanswered. Voicemail picked up, and Finley launched into yet another message.

"I know I'm the worst friend in the world for hanging up on you, but could you, just this once, put off holding a grudge long enough for me to tell you something? *Please.*" She held quiet a pitiful beat. "It's super important, and exciting—" she was adding when a black Mercedes swung into her driveway.

Finley swore under her breath and quickly summed up her message. "So, call me . . . I'm sorry. I need you." She pressed *end* and slid her phone back into her pocket.

The Mercedes rolled to a dusty stop. The passenger side window crawled down.

Finley leaned forward to greet an empty seat. Glancing further in, she could see that the smile on her father's face was tighter than usual, his strong jaw tense.

"Morning, sugar beet," Preston said.

Finley sent him a weak smile. "Hey, Daddy, where's Momma?"

Preston opened his mouth to answer, but the words that came next shot from the back seat instead. "Good heavens, child, I'm right here."

Finley peered through the two-inch slit in the rear window. "Momma?" she said. "What in the world are you doing back there?"

"Hiding," Preston interjected.

Finley frowned. "From who?"

Preston shook his head. "More like what," he said, his bright blue eyes sliding a quick glance to the back seat. "She doesn't want anyone to see her vanity bruises."

Finley squinted against the darkly tinted window. Her mother sat, back erect, in the seat. The wavy brim of a straw hat drooped to shade a bandaged chin and jaw line. Large sunglasses hid most of what remained of her face. The petite upturn of her nose, the purse of her ruddy lips, were her only exposed, defining features. On her best day, Adeline Dalton was a vain, socially conscious woman, but Finley had never known her mother to take her narcissism to this measure of extreme.

"Are you serious?" She tapped her knuckles on the back window. "Momma, roll the window all the way down."

Through the tint, Finley caught the shadow of her mother's arms knitting tightly across her chest. "I will not," she huffed.

A laugh rolled up from Finley's gut. "Lord-a-mercy, Momma." She pulled her fingers through the gray arching from the peak of her forehead. "What happened to the Finley-women tradition of growing old gracefully?" she scoffed. "What would Granny say?"

"Oh, Finnie." Adeline sighed. "I never told you this, because I know you loved her so, but it's time you knew. Your granny Opaline was as crazy as a Betsy bug."

Preston swiveled his body to the side, lobbing a severe look over his shoulder. "Missus Dalton. Don't you dare go there," he warned. He'd taken to calling his wife Missus years ago after she'd forced him to suffer through a showing of *Pride and Prejudice*—the extended BBC version. The resemblance between Elizabeth Bennet's parents and his own marriage had not been lost on Finley's dad.

He turned his attention back to Finley. "Your granny was no such thing," he disagreed. "Your mother and I are going on a cruise over Christmas. She says she doesn't want me to be the only man over sixty without a trophy wife on his arm." His tone indicated that what he'd just said was perfectly normal. The slight roll of his eyes told Finley he thought the idea was beyond preposterous.

Finley had to agree. But even more alarming, a thought occurred to her. "Over Christmas?" she asked. "Momma, you can't be gone over the holidays. What about all our traditions?" She leaned closer, trying to capture her mother's gaze through the shield of her glasses. "Christmas Eve supper at your place? Breakfast here? Granny Opaline will rise from the grave to curse us all if we break the Finley family holiday break-fast tradition." She gave her mother's bandaged face a grave look. "A crazy granny is one thing, but a vindictive ghost?" she added jokingly, while inside she was panicking—the holidays without her parents? This year more than ever, she needed them. "I don't think any of us want that."

"Finley, don't be so dramatic," Adeline came back. Though Finley couldn't make out her expression, she could hear a patronizing look in her mother's voice. "It'll just be one year. Besides, you weren't so concerned with breaking tradition when you went and *publically* divorced your husband."

Finley lowered her brow in mock confusion. "Is there any other way?" she asked. "With Roy living way down in Franklin, sooner or later folks would have figured it out."

Adeline ignored her daughter's snark and said, "Traditionally, we Finleys handle these types of marital issues *within* the family, in private where they belong. Divorce is bad for the family's reputation and a sin in the eyes of God." Even though they'd had this very conversation a half-dozen times over the last few months, her petulant tone again stabbed Finley's chest with guilt. "You should have considered how your decision to divorce Roy would affect us all." She held quiet a beat, allowing the knife to slide in and settle into Finley's heart. "Now, because of your selfishness and haste, the holidays will never be the same."

Adeline had skipped her usual subtle lead-up to heaping her unique brand of measured, withering guilt, striking instead directly at Finley's greatest weakness—her family. But what other choice had Finley had? Keep quiet and live the rest of her life trapped in a loveless marriage, sleeping every night next to a philandering man? It wasn't fair that the price of the rest of the family's happiness required Finley to sacrifice her own. Finley swallowed against the pain, against the sting of truth. She knew where this conversation was supposed to go from here. She'd be repentant on the outside, incensed with injustice underneath. Lately, the rules of this passive-aggressive game she'd been playing with her mother since birth were growing tiresome, and Finley, swiftly losing interest.

*Defy the rules.*

"What was I supposed to do, Momma?" Finley snapped in return. "Paste on a smile and invite all of Roy's girlfriends to Christmas dinner?" She pushed out a humorless laugh. "One big happy family. Is that what you think?"

Absolute silence seethed from beyond the crack in the window.

"No, sugar beet," Preston said, his words like honey. "Your momma's just mixed her pain meds with her morning gin again. She's not herself today." He stole a peek into the silence of the back seat. "What she means to say is that with the divorce and then the incident at the garden club, things are a bit tense this season is all. We thought it'd be easier for everyone if we broke tradition—just this once—and let all this unpleasantness settle. Next year, we'll get back on track." He flashed her his million-dollar smile. "Promise."

Her father, forever the mediator.

But Finley knew exactly what he *wasn't* saying. "I see," she said. "And by 'back on track' you mean, I eventually come to my senses, forgive Roy, invite him home, and life goes back to the way it's always been?" She raised a questioning eyebrow at him. "Is that what you're saying, Daddy?" she asked, then shot a look through the slit in the back window. "Momma?"

Another instant of angry silence ensued, followed by a quiet throat clearing. Adeline was steadying her temper. "No, what he's saying is that we all make mistakes," she began, her words a newly sharpened edge. "Marriage is hard. Being with one person for an entire lifetime takes the patience of Job." She paused. Through the slit in the window, Finley saw her mother's chest noticeably rise, then fall. "We have to forgive and forget. It's hard, but we do it for the sake of our children, and the ones we love," she added. "Take me for example—I forgave your daddy."

A growl rumbled from the driver's seat. "For-the-love-of-all-that-is-holy, *woman*. That was one time." Preston held up his first finger and shook it over the seat. "One time. And you still can't forgive." He sliced his hand through the air. "Will you *never* forget?"

"You're still alive ain't ya?" Adeline charged back. Then she turned to Finley, the ghost of a sweet smile straining against her bandaged chin. "Speaking of which . . . Listen, sweetheart, your daddy and I don't have much time, but I wanted to remind you about the garden club meeting on Tuesday."

Finley's eyes rolled to the sky. "Momma, I've been going to those meetings since I was a teenager. I know when they are."

"Of course you do, honey," Adeline said, her tone consoling now. "But you haven't been to one since the incident, and it's time you came back. You need to apologize for all the ugly things you said, and fix the friendships you all but ruined." She leaned forward, touched her fingertips to the glass between them. "The festival is coming soon, and our section of the garden is only half done. We need you. No one designs a haunted garden like you do."

The thought of being excluded from organizing the festival had been weighing heavily on Finley lately. Every year she looked forward to decorating, to being the center of the entire affair. This October would be the first in—she didn't know how many years—she wouldn't be involved.

An ache ran across Finley's shoulders. "Momma—"

"It's been more than six weeks now," Adeline cut in. "Most everyone is friends again and have gotten on with their lives. It's time you did the same," she said emphatically. "Is that support group helping you at all?"

Obviously her mother's idea of "moving on" had nothing to do with progression. *Back* to normal was what she wanted. "Momma, I'm pretty sure it takes more than a few sessions," Finley said. "I've only just begun the healing process."

Adeline's response was as expected: quick and with a pinch more of strategically placed guilt. "Isn't making amends one of the steps?"

Finley did miss the women at the club, needed the camaraderie and support of her friends, but she wasn't ready. Plus, she had yet to find the proper words needed to apologize, to convey the depth of her regret. Isolation wrapped its frigid arms around her and blew a bitter breath down her throat.

"You're thinking of addiction recovery, Momma," Finley corrected. "And besides, shouldn't Macy be the one to apologize to *me*? She's the one who had her scrawny legs wrapped around my husband's bare backside." She rested a fist to her hip. "Not the other way around."

Through the darkened glass, Finley caught the movement of her mother's hand sweeping the image away. "Oh, Finnie, don't be crass. You have no one to blame but yourself for not feeling welcome at the garden club. You're the one who shared your personal failures at the luncheon. What did you think was going to happen . . ." Adeline continued to prattle on. The woman was nothing if not relentless. "And what are you planning to do now? Hide out here, in this big old house—alone—for the rest of your life?" she asked. "You'll go stark-raving-mad just like Granny did."

Finley's granny Opaline was not crazy. Eccentric maybe, but not mad. Finley opened her mouth, readying to deflect her mother's blow, only nothing came. The image of Finley, old and alone, with no one to talk to but the spirits of her dead ancestors, traipsed across her brain. She'd be lying if she said that, over the last few months, the possibility hadn't occurred to her a time or two. Maybe she should get a dog. But then would talking to a four-legged creature that couldn't speak back really be any better?

Adeline continued. "There's no shame in owning to your mistakes," she said. "Folks are more forgiving than you think."

Finley crossed her arms defensively over her wounded heart. "You're probably right, but . . ." Her mother wasn't going to take what she had to say next very well. But then she didn't have to know her reason had to do with a little someone sexy named Josh, did she? "Even if I was ready to make amends, I can't be there on Tuesday—I have plans."

Adeline yanked the sunglasses from her face. Her hazel eyes were circled in charcoal bruises. "Break them!"

"No." Finley raised her chin in defiance, a contrary child. "I don't want to."

Adeline's gaze narrowed to match the slatted window. "Why?" she asked, suspicious. "What are you up to?" Finley could feel the probing nip of her mother's deft gaze. She shuffled a half-step back. "This is about a man, isn't it?" she accused, and as usual, her assumption was spot on.

If Finley was committed to defying the rules, then doing so meant maintaining a keen awareness of her limitations. This was the point where her mother would skillfully begin to wear Finley down with menacing scowls, more shame, and relentless interrogation. It wouldn't be easy, but Finley reaffirmed her right to make her own decisions—to find happiness—and held tight.

Adeline proceeded. "Mercy me, the ink on your divorce papers isn't even dry yet, and you're already catting about with a new man."

Finley kept her lips pressed shut, the staid look in her eyes unwavering.

"Who is this man?" her mother pressed. "He's one of Roy's associates, isn't he?" Her voice jumped an octave. "If it's revenge you want, there are better—quieter—ways of going about it."

From the front seat, Preston muttered, "For-the-love-of-heaven," his thumb and forefinger pinching the bridge of his nose.

Finley's inability to attend the meeting had nothing to do with Roy, and her mother's suggestion that it did touched tender places deep inside Finley she didn't want disturbed at the moment—or ever. She closed her eyes against the soreness.

"I'm not having this discussion with you today, Momma."

A red-painted nail jutted out from the window. "I will not allow you to embarrass this family again."

Of course her mother's visit this morning, her vacation plans for Christmas, and her invitation to come back to garden club had nothing to do with what Finley wanted—what she needed—or her happiness. As usual, their family's precious reputation was taking precedence over everything else.

Finley made her gaze incredulous and directed it at the back seat. "For once, could something be just about me? I'm hurting and you won't see it. You don't care about what I'm going through—" Her phone buzzed from her back pocket. She pulled it out and glanced at the display. Excitement rose up again, a fresh helping of sweetness to offset her souring mood.

Dropping her current train of reproof (like her mother would get what she was trying to say anyway) Finley shifted to a more appeasing tone. "Look, Momma, Daddy, I appreciate you stopping by, and for all y'alls concern, but I have to go. We can talk about this later." She wagged her cell phone at the car. "I need to take this call."

"What call?" Adeline's voice was frantic. "Who is that?"

"It's nobody, Momma."

"She says, 'It's nobody,'" her mother fussed. "Then why do you have to answer?"

Finley spun on her heal and headed for her front porch.

"Finley Dalton Harrison!" Adeline shrieked. "You do not walk away from your *momma!*"

Finley stopped, then pivoted to face the car again. "Fine, roll the window down then," she dared. "Look me in the eye and tell me that your cruise has nothing to do with punishing me for divorcing Roy. For me wanting to be happy. That apologizing to the club is for my own benefit, and not to repair *your* tarnished reputation."

No movement.

Finley pulled back on the hurt, the disappointment wringing her gut, and turned toward the steps again. As she moved away, her guilty side scolded her for being disrespectful—age forty or fourteen, a Southerner did not sass her mother—while her silently stubborn side, the part of her fascinated with the feeling of being in control for once, the one who rendered injustice instead of swallowing it—urged her to stay her course. Doing so felt good and then, somehow, not so much.

"Bye, Momma. Love you." Finley lifted her hand in a backward wave to the car. "Love you too, Daddy."

In the distance, Finley could hear the murmur of her father's farewell, the whoosh of the passenger side window winding up, and the evaporating sound of his chuckle. Then as the car tires slowly advanced around the rocky drive, Adeline's protests through the slit in her window.

"*What's gotten into that child? She's so secretive all of a sudden. Heaven help her, that house has already driven her insane . . .*" faded into the October air and disappeared.

# Chapter 10

Cathyanne dropped her luggage in the vaulted entryway. The smacking sound echoed a hollow welcome home. She should treat her Burberry bags with more respect. They cost a small fortune. Her next big journey, she feared, would not require baggage of any sort, so what did it matter how she cared for her things, when she would eventually leave it all behind anyway? When the only part of her that would last forever was what she carried deep inside, locked within her heart for an eternity? Apathy, integrity, malice, compassion . . . and the list went on. Every person's outlook on life was easy enough to overlook until it was too late. But she still had a little time left. What she took with her could still be her choice.

Her cell buzzed from her purse again. Lifting it out, she saw she'd received another message from Finley. This one had come in about fifteen minutes ago. How many did that make now? She'd lost count. A wistful smile cast a shadow across her lips. It was time she put an end to Finley's exile.

Tapping the screen over Finley's number, she pressed the phone to her ear.

Finley answered on the fifth ring. "Where have you been?" she said in a huff. "I've been calling you for days."

*Where have I been?* Cathyanne repeated in her head. In the middle-of-nowhere-Arizona, meditating and sucking down one unpalatable herbal remedy after another. Too little, too late. Hope was a funny thing. Even when reason and doubt told her to quit fighting, she persisted. Just a glimmer was all it took.

The moment she gave Finley even an inkling of a reason to be concerned about her health it would mean the end of Finley's fledgling interest in solving her own issues. Thus, Cathyanne had to keep the focus away from herself. And doing so meant remaining vague about where she'd been. "Don't you have something you want to say to me *first*?" Cathyanne deflected.

"For the record," Finley began, "*you* did go behind *my* back and bamboozle both me *and* Josh by trying to force us on each other."

Cathyanne lowered one eyebrow. "That sounds like a justification for hanging up on me. Not an apology."

"I already said I was sorry in my messages."

Cathyanne was more than ready to forgive Finley, but toying with her was more fun. "Umm," she disagreed. "Not the same as saying so in person."

"Fine, should we meet for lunch or something?"

Cathyanne thought for a moment. Seeing her friend would go a long way to staving off her loneliness. She took a quick glance into the mirror, noting the obvious slack in her jeans, the gray circling her eyes, her colorless lips, and she decided against a face-to-face meeting. Besides, she was too tired to endure the questioning looks, not to mention avoid the answers she wouldn't give.

"No, already ate," Cathyanne lied, her tone bothered. Underneath, tears of isolation and regret burned her throat. "Go ahead and apologize on the phone, but make it good."

Finley pulled in an audible breath. "I'm sorry," she said. Then emphasized, "I *mean* it Cathyanne. I don't know what got into me, but I'm better now. Please, you have to forgive me."

Cathyanne bit into her lip to suppress her tears. A hurt for a hurt. "Is that it?"

"No," Finley dragged out the word. "I'm sorry for being such a, you know, a . . ." she mumbled the expletive. "And for hanging up on you, and for getting mad because you were trying to help me."

Adoration flooded Cathyanne's breast. "Ah, honey." She didn't have it in her today to torture Finley any longer. "I just want you to be happy," she said, her words hiccupping with repressed emotion.

"I know you do." Finley sniffed, which brought a smile to Cathyanne's tears. As usual, the instant Cathyanne—or anyone else for that matter—had an emotion, Finley invariably felt it too. That was just the kind of person Finley was. "And you know I want the same for you," she said and then held her words, her silence preparatory to a shift in subject. "So, are you going to tell me where you've been?" Finley gave Cathyanne only a beat to consider before adding, "And don't lie to me. I drove over to your house. Your neighbor told me you went out of town."

*Stupid, nosey neighbors.* Cathyanne bit her lip again as she shuffled into the living room and looked around. Nothing was out of place. Everything was as it should be—almost. "I went to a spa . . . to pamper myself."

A short pause, then Finley asked, "And you didn't have your cell phone?"

She'd had her phone. There just hadn't been any cell service in *Timbuktu,* Arizona. But then the fewer details she divulged the better. "Nope," she simplified, popping the *p* playfully between her lips. "Who can relax with electronics going off all over the place? There was no technology allowed."

As if mulling the idea, Finley made a humming sound. Then after a few wordless beats she blurted out, "I have some news," her voice unusually bubbly all of a sudden.

"What's wrong with you?" Cathyanne asked. "You sound all twitterpated or something."

"Yes. Exactly!" Finley agreed. "Are you sitting down?"

Cathyanne plopped onto her sofa. "I am now," she said as she settled in. "Shoot."

Finley cleared her throat. "I invited Josh over for lunch." Her confession tumbled through the phone like a shower of hot sparks.

Cathyanne bolted up to standing. "You didn't!" Her head spun with the sudden motion. She pressed her palm to her forehead to restore balance. "When?"

"Last week. He came over last week," Finley repeated like she needed to say the words twice in order to believe them herself.

Cathyanne crushed the phone to her ear. "And?"

"And what?"

Cathyanne fell back onto the couch and draped her arm over her eyes. Had Finley really expected to spill something like that without sharing every intimate detail? "Well, did he like the house?" Cathyanne asked, starting with the information she knew she could get.

"He loved the house, and my garden," Finley began. "He said he has a client who's been looking for some slave houses."

Finley had a grouping of old slave homes on her land. Over the years, a few historical societies had made offers, but Finley had yet to part with them. She claimed to feel a strange kinship to those old log cabins. Festering nests for spiders and who knew what else was what they were. Cathyanne visibly shivered at the thought.

"Are you going to finally sell them?"

"No," Finley said reverently. "I can't, not yet. I feel like I need to hold onto them a little longer."

*Need?* Cathyanne considered arguing, but then what was the point? "So, did he enjoy the lunch?" she asked instead.

"Well, I couldn't tell for certain," Finley alluded, like she was hinting at something.

Cathyanne dropped her arm to the couch. "Why, he wouldn't eat it?"

Finley expelled a contented sigh. "What with the kissing and all, it was kind of hard to know for sure . . ."

Cathyanne sprang up to sitting. "Shut. Up!"

"Oh yeah, it was so romantic. Just like that scene in *Gone with the Wind* when Rhett grabs Scarlett by the arms and kisses her until she can't breathe," Finley said, her voice all throaty. "Except that we weren't at the top of any staircase and I wasn't wearing a hoop skirt of course, and well, you get the idea. Anyway, we really didn't take all that much time to eat." She breathed another sigh into the phone, only this one came out slow and tenuous, disappointed-like. "He couldn't stay long. He had to run off to some job site."

"Finnie, I'm so happy for you," Cathyanne gushed.

Finally, Cathyanne's plan was taking shape. Finley had started dating Josh, which hopefully meant Cathyanne was one step closer to that final checkmark off her list. She should sit back and take a moment to relax, contented in the impending completion of her mission. Only she couldn't seem to get comfortable. Something was amiss, but what?

Like the dread one felt when cresting a hill only to see a much larger slope waiting on the other side, she had the unmistakable feeling that her quest had only just begun, and that it would be all uphill from here.

⁓⁓⁓

Hugging a plump little pumpkin to her chest, Finley stepped across the invisible threshold between her yard and Quinton's. Glancing down at the please-forgive-me card she'd threaded through a fall-themed ribbon and tied around the stem, she prayed her neighbor would be half as forgiving as her best friend had been. In all the years they'd been neighbors, Finley had never lost her temper with Quinton, never needed to apologize, and so had no idea what to expect.

From his swing under the pergola, she could hear Quinton working on the same song he'd been struggling with the day she'd gone postal on him.

". . . At Sixth and Broadway is where it all began, standing at the bar with a drink in my hand. When in walked a girl, can't mention her name, because we met, life will never be the same . . ." he sang, unaware of her eavesdropping. "The door I opened would blow your mind. And I soon found out she wasn't my kind. Legends Corner. Where it all started, where it all began. Where I stepped in a boy, where I walked out a man . . ." He stopped singing, and Finley could tell by the tightness in his humming that he was having trouble figuring what should come next. Then he hit the strings hard, banging out a rock-inspired melody as if brute force alone would conjure the obstinate lyrics.

Clearing her throat, Finley stopped at the far corner of the pergola and sang out the line that had popped into her head as she'd watched him struggle. "What I thought was love was never to be . . ."

Following the sound of Finley's voice, he regarded her a

moment before finishing her thought. ". . . All that woman did was make a fool out of me."

Nodding his head in appreciation, he continued to strum as he asked, "To what do I owe this pleasure?"

Finley took a few tentative steps closer. "I need to apologize for the way I talked to you the other day." She lifted the pumpkin as a peace offering. "You were just trying to help, and I was being ugly." She rolled her lips together before letting them go again. "I am *so* sorry," she said, and when Quinton simply continued to strum, she tried again. "A-and I thought about what you said. You were right about me worrying too much over what others think, so I decided to take your advice and defy the rules like they say in my therapy group."

Quinton stopped strumming. "Wow." He whistled. "How does that crow taste?"

Finley swallowed hard. "Like a double-shot of Tabasco."

Setting his guitar off to the side, Quinton patted the empty space next to him on the swing. "Apology accepted."

Finley hesitated, but for only an instant before she dropped the pumpkin in Quinton's lap and slid in next to him. Quinton swung an arm around her back and Finley dropped her head to his shoulder. Inhaling, she breathed him in. He smelled fresh, like a cool gust of fall air, and she took a moment to enjoy the comfort of being this close to him.

"So, this defying of rules wouldn't have anything to do with that all-terrain vehicle I've seen parked in your driveway lately, would it?" Quinton asked.

Finley lifted her head. "Quinton Townes, are you spying on me?" she asked, her cheeks prickling with heat. "I swear you're worse than a nosey old woman."

Quinton chuckled. "Who's the lucky guy?"

Finley sat back against the swing. "Josh," she sighed out his name.

Quinton thought for a moment. "Your trainer?"

Finley nodded. "I invited him to lunch," she explained, her cheeks flooding with color, "and he's been back a time or two since."

"I see," Quinton said. "And has he stayed for breakfast?"

For reasons yet to be discovered, that question offended Finley. "First, one's sex life is not an appropriate subject for mixed company," she scolded, and though she'd done nothing to feel guilty about, her blush slid down her neck. "And second, have you seen his car parked in front of my house on any of the aforementioned mornings?"

Quinton pursed his plump lips in thought. "No, I don't reckon I have." Lifting his arm from the back of the swing, he then crossed his arms over his chest. "But, as you're well aware, I *am* a late riser."

"Well, he hasn't, and likely won't . . . at least not for a while. A *long* while." Finley felt the inexplicable need to clarify. "We're taking things slow."

"Slow," Quinton echoed, eyeing her as if she'd crossed some unforgivable line. "What does that mean?"

Self-conscious under his penetrating stare, Finley dropped her eyes. "You know, nothing serious, just going out once in a while, but exclusive like," she explained as she fiddled with the loose threads dangling from the rip in her gardening jeans.

Quinton gave the concept what appeared some serious thought. "So, I don't have to worry 'bout bumping into him the next time I'm up before ten and sneaking over to your house for my morning coffee?"

Though at times she feigned annoyance at his occasional appearances, she looked forward to the times he popped in, and didn't want anything to get in the way of their impromptu breakfasts just yet. "No," Finley said, decisively. She had no idea how far this thing with Josh would go, or how long it would last, but the image of Josh kissing more of her than just her lips lit a lustful spark to her eyes. "For now, anyway," she amended and looked away before Quinton could read her scandalous thoughts.

Quinton glanced away too. "Yeah, I bet," he said, the tendon in his jaw pulling tight. "We'll see how long y'all can hold out," he added. "A man can only be expected to be patient for so long, you know."

Finley whipped a derisive look his way. "Just because you can't stick with one woman longer than the time it takes for you to get your boots back on and scurry out the door"—she mimicked running with her fingers—"doesn't mean sex is all Josh wants from me," she said, though she knew perfectly well Quinton's aversion to relationships had more to do with a fear of reliving past mistakes than it did with an inability to commit. "Josh is a *real* gentleman."

"I bet he is," Quinton mumbled.

Was it her imagination or had Quinton's mood taken an unscheduled turn toward gruff? Well, two could play that game. Pushing her foot against the ground, Finley allowed the creak of the swing to fill their mutual silence.

A minute or two later, the quiet became unbearable, and Finley offered, "He's taking me rock climbing next week."

When Quinton's gaze swung back to Finley, the gray of his eyes had turned to dark billows of smoke. "Finnie, if I'm not mistaken, you *are* afraid of heights. In fact, you can barely scale a stepstool long enough to get a DVD from the top of that mammoth movie collection you own," he reminded her. Since over the years she'd called him to her house more times than she dared to count, needing him to climb the ladder for one reason or another, denial was not an option.

Finley rolled up one shoulder. "It's an inside rock wall,"

she said like a controlled environment made the height of no consequence.

Quinton snorted out a laugh.

"What?" She asked, defensive. "I'm trying here."

"To do what?" he came back. "Kill yourself?"

Finley's jaw dropped open in protest. "No, to defy the rules, like you wanted me to," she said, frustrated and quite frankly confused by his sour attitude. He should be happy she'd taken his advice to heart. What more did he want? "You're the one who told me I should date him so I wouldn't get stuck in a rut, or whatever."

Slowly, he pulled in a silent breath before letting the air go again, his gaze tracking the invisible stream. "I think you may have taken what I said a bit too literally," he said, and Finley didn't know if he was referring to her dating Josh, the scaling of a cliff, or both. Either way, Finley's brilliant idea of rock climbing with her new squeeze had unexpectedly flipped from her first big adventure to the worst idea she'd ever agreed to. "But I guess it doesn't matter now," Quinton added along with, "Good for you, Finnie, I'm proud of you." He smiled through eyes that appeared more resigned than pleased.

"Thanks." Finley accepted his complement but couldn't muster the enthusiasm that should have gone along with it.

*What have I gotten myself into?*

# Chapter 11

"I've fallen down a rabbit hole," Finley muttered, her eyes traveling foot by foot to the top of a vertical rock-encrusted wall. Above the peak, tufts of white clouds slid across the sky over a Plexiglas ceiling in need of a good washing. Was it her imagination or was she shrinking, growing smaller with each passing moment?

A pair of hands palmed her sides, then slid around her waist to form an x across her ribcage. Next, a firm chest and abs pressed solid against her back.

"Did you say something?" Josh whispered into her ear. His breath sent a stampede of delight through her senses, chasing her misgivings away.

She twisted around to face him and circled her arms around his neck. "Nothing that needs repeating," she said, rolling onto her toes for a quick taste of his lips.

Josh's hands traveled south to cup her hips and pull her closer. "Good, because it's much easier for me to do this when you're not talking." He touched his lips to hers in one of his gentle kisses. Like a whisper that screamed louder than words, his kiss claimed her full attention. He eased back. "Are you nervous?"

Finley's heart hummed, slowly returning the blood to her brain that had fled during their kiss. "Nervous about what?"

The right side of Josh's mouth lifted. "The climb." His eyes, greener than she'd ever seen them, grinned down at her.

Reality crept back in. Sadly, the heat from Josh's palms, his chest against hers, both faded as that shrinking feeling reemerged. Suddenly he was the treacherous rabbit, and she the foolish girl who had consented to follow him.

She wiggled some space between them. "Right, the climb," she repeated.

"I have something for you." He took her by the hand and led her over to a stack of cubbies. "Close your eyes."

Finley searched his excited expression, her nerves twitching with a different kind of dread. Though they'd both said they wanted to take things slow, they'd seen each other almost daily over the last few weeks. Still, she wished she knew him better, that she could read his thoughts and anticipate his next move.

"What are you up to?"

Over the years, she'd grown comfortable in her ability to foresee Roy's every intention. But then, her ex wasn't exactly a complicated man. Roy liked to hunt and watch SEC football, drive fast cars, drink beer, and eat just about anything that could be fried or barbequed. He liked his women a touch on the trashy side (why he'd married Finley was still a mystery to her and everyone who knew them both). He preferred she discuss her feelings with her friends and burden him with only the highlights—which he mostly ignored or dismissed anyway. Therefore, as one might imagine, his surprises tended to be equally as unimaginative.

Josh was a different sort of man all together. He liked to take long walks, ask questions, listen for answers, and then make follow-up inquiries, all while looking into her eyes as if there were a thrilling mystery there, waiting for him to discover.

Josh chuckled. "Just close them," he said again and then waited for her to comply.

Her eyes pressed shut, Finley held still in her own darkness. Josh's grip took hold beneath her arms, and in one swift motion, he lifted her feet from the floor, re-depositing her to sitting on the top of the cubbies. A breath later, Josh's lips had captured hers again, moist and hot. Like taking a rollercoaster ride blindfolded, the unexpected lifting coupled with the urgency of his mouth devouring hers, sent a wave of unabated exhilaration rolling from her stomach to her heart. The elation crested in her throat and then tumbled back down again.

When he pulled away, his voice was throaty. "Now remember, no peeking," he insisted.

Finley giggled. "Promise."

Josh fumbled around a minute and then she felt his hands slipping her tennis shoes off, dropping each one to the floor. A second later, he was tugging some sort of alternative foot apparel on in their place.

The temptation to look was unbearable. "Those better be Prada," she teased, though she didn't much care about designer shoes. That was more Cathyanne's thing.

"Just keep your eyes closed a minute longer." He secured the second shoe around her ankle, then said, "All set. Now you can look."

Finley's eyes popped open, her leg straightening to reveal a pair of curious-looking shoes. Black around the sole, a pink stripe followed next, and then gray where the laces hooked and crossed. *Rockstar* was embossed along the side. She wiggled her toes. The fabric was stretchy; the feel, feather light. "Climbing shoes?"

"Yep," he said, proud of himself. "You're official now."

Finley blinked down at her feet. "You bought these, for me?" she asked. Josh nodded. Why would he do that? She couldn't fathom but didn't dare venture to ask. "Good gracious, Josh, these must have cost you a fortune."

"Cost a fortune"—he tapped a finger to his temple—"or worth every penny?" He cupped her left heel in one hand and lifted it for a better view. "Look, they have microfiber lining for comfort and TRAX high friction rubber to keep you from slipping. We can't have you worrying about losing your footing when you're hanging from a fifty-foot cliff, now, can we?" he stated more than asked and let go of her foot.

A cliff? Hanging? Finley swallowed what felt like a dry ball of thistles. "No, I can't imagine we can," she croaked. Cold droplets of sweat popped up along her hairline. "But I'll have that pulley thing on, right?"

"Of course. You'll be perfectly safe," he soothed. "And don't worry. You're tougher than you think. I bet once you get through this first climb, you'll be wanting to do it all the time."

Finley gulped. "All the time?"

"Sure." Josh pointed up the ominous rock wall. "After you're comfortable in here, we can try climbing outside," he said and then his voice turned reflective. "There's nothing better than the hot sun on your shoulders . . . not a thing between you and the ground but whole a lot of fresh air."

The impulse to rip the shoes from her feet and toss them from sight tore through Finley like an Oklahoma twister. She'd agreed to one climb, and mostly because it had meant spending more time with Josh. But from the excited look on his face and the feel of the costly footwear he'd purchased to feed that enthusiasm, he had plans of turning this little outing into a regular occurrence.

Finley snuck another peek at the towering wall. Maybe she was losing her mind—well, obviously she was if she really thought to scale that thing—but had the top managed to stretch even a few yards higher? She was going to have to stop looking up because, at this rate, the next time she did, the apex was sure to have disappeared into the clouds.

Josh's hands grabbed hold of her waist, sliding her so close to him she had to wrap her legs around his torso. "Don't look so scared," he said against her lips. "I'll be right next to you the entire time." Then he was kissing her again, only this time her senses didn't evaporate as usual. Instead, she was trying first to figure out how she'd gotten herself into this mess. Second, how in the world she was going to get herself out of it. Clearly, she needed to reevaluate her priorities.

"Ah-ahem!"

The sound of exaggerated throat clearing pulled them apart.

Finley leaned around Josh's shoulder to see a young woman dressed in tight athletic shorts, scooping tank, and shoes similar to the ones Josh had just put on her. Her raven hair was pulled up into a high braid. Some sort of ropes and pulleys hung from her shoulders. She was smiling, but only in the sense that the corners of her lips were turned up. The rest of her, from glaring eyes to rigid stance, was clearly scowling.

Finley readjusted her position, blocking the woman from view. "Josh, what's my orchard manager doing here?" She tried to keep her voice low, but every word seemed to have echoed from the crest of that wretched cliff.

Josh sent Finley a quizzical look. "Your orchard manager?" he repeated as he swiveled around for a look. "No, that's Skylar, she's our climb instructor," he said, then patted Finley's thigh. "I'm just getting my girl ready for her first climb," he told Skylar.

Skylar eyed Finley from gray streak to climbing shoes. "Yes, so I see," she said merrily, though her stare continued to hold its frost. "Miss Finley, I never would have pegged you as an adrenaline junkie."

Finley coaxed a smile from her lips. "That's funny, because I was just thinking the very same thing about you," she said, the sunshine in her voice equally at odds with the fire in her gaze. "You have another job," she observed, only because she'd been raised better than to say anything else, such as: *That explains the general state of neglect plaguing my orchard.*

Skyler shared a demure look with Josh before forcing a less affectionate smile in Finley's general direction. "I've got bills to pay," she said with enough defiance to imply: *You can hardly expect me to make ends meet on the measly salary you pay me.*

A string of spiteful words lined up in Finley's head, falling into place something like this: *With what I pay you, plus payment for whatever services you perform on my ex-husband's behalf, I would expect you'd live quite well.* She felt a flicker of shame at her spiteful thoughts. Besides the fact that this was neither the time nor place to shine a spotlight on their dirty secrets, there had been something unexpected in Skylar's eyes just now, an emotion, and barely a flit of one at that. If Finley's interpretation were correct, she would define it as regret, or possibly even shame.

"Hard to believe you two know each other," Josh said.

The stiff smile on Skylar's lips softened as she turned the twinkle in her eye to Josh. "Small world, huh?"

"It sure is," Josh agreed before clapping his hands and rubbing them together. "Perfect. Now that we're all acquainted, I can't wait to smoke your skinny ass to the top." He pointed playfully at Skylar.

"In your dreams," she cajoled back while batting her sweeping lashes.

Was it Finley's imagination or was Skylar flirting with Josh? And right in front of her, no less? Like she wasn't even there? Anger lit a fire to her veins, the heat rising to form tiny bubbles in her blood. For years she'd turned a blind eye while Skylar and women like her wedged their way into the cracks of Finley and Roy's crumbling marriage. But that was Roy—their relationship had been more or less doomed from the start—and this was Josh. This thing between Josh and her, whatever it was, brimmed with potential—a tiny seed nestled under freshly tilled earth—and she wasn't about to look away while some vermin dug it up before it had a chance to sprout.

An invisible hand reached in and turned the dial on Finley's blood pressure to high. The Finley of two weeks ago might have cowered away, may have even chided herself for foolishly thinking she could compete with a young woman like Skylar for Josh's attention, but after a lifetime of doing exactly what was expected, she'd finally begun to muster enough courage to start living life on her own terms. Even though it hadn't quite been two months since she'd embraced this shift in perspective, she liked being in control, and wasn't about to give up her newfound freedom so soon. Or even take a step back. Especially now that she was starting to feel the first inklings of what it meant to be alive, to be in charge of her own destiny for once.

*No, not this time!*

Something dark and predatory clawed up her spine to cloud her self-doubting thoughts. Hopping from her perch atop the cubbies, she stepped around Josh and stared Skylar straight in the eye. "I guess we should get started then," Finley challenged more than suggested.

The cavernous space around them fell into an unnatural silence. The clank of hooks and pulleys from other climbers were the only sounds brave enough to defy the quiet rivalry vacillating between the two women.

Skylar was the first to breach the impasse. "Let's get you

two geared up, shall we?" She slid the ropes from her shoulder and handed a set to Josh, then one to Finley.

Finley studied the contraption, turning it over a few times before stepping into the harness and then back out. Readjusting, she tried again. Once she'd edged it up over each thigh, she fastened the closure the best she could around her waist. Done!

"Let me see what you have here," Josh said, pulling on the release then yanking it tighter. Finley glanced up from where he was working to see that he was already completely outfitted in a harness, helmet, and gloves. Re-securing the release, he said, "I think you're ready," and dropped a peck to her lips.

As Skylar began her tutorial, Josh kept an arm draped over Finley's shoulders while interjecting a comment here and there.

"These big holds are called jugs." Skylar pointed to a large grayish rock. "The small ones like this one," she gripped a smaller brown hold, "are called crimps." Then she ran her hand over a large, smooth protrusion. "This is a slopper. You can't grip these." She went on to demonstrate a few climbing techniques, including how foot placement was most important, and to always look down.

Finley hadn't planned on looking down at all, which meant that her strategy was defunct before she'd even touched the wall.

"Use your feet and legs," Skylar went on as she demonstrated. "Arms are just for support, and straight arms rather than flexed."

As Finley watched Skylar move easily from one position to the other, all she could focus on was how small and tight her backside looked framed in her harness. Like a cute little monkey, swinging effortlessly from one branch to another, she scaled up the wall then back down again. When Finley had dressed this morning, she'd felt confident in her choice of slimming black leggings, white tank, and black hoody with a white stripe down both arms. Now she worried that once *she* was up on the wall, the only mammal she'd resemble was a killer whale, vertically beached, and struggling back to the ocean.

Unzipping her hoody, she slipped it off and knotted the sleeves tightly around her waist.

"It's just like climbing a ladder," Skylar finished and hopped from the wall.

Josh stood facing Finley and lassoed her gaze with his. "Skylar and I are going to go first, give you some more tips on the way up," he said while carefully loosening her tied hoody. "Then you and I will go." He slipped her jacket from her waist and tossed it to the side. Finley watched, bemused, as her "shield" settled a few feet away on the dingy outdoor carpeting. "Make sure and watch me carefully," he added. "It's not as easy as it looks."

"Easy?" Finley gulped.

Two guys in baggy shorts and skullcaps appeared from nowhere and took hold of the ropes dangling from a pulley at each peak of the wall. The other end of the ropes were attached to Josh and Skylar's belts. A third took Josh's phone so he could record this momentous event. Finley hoped he wasn't planning to film her turn on the wall.

Standing a few feet back from the wall, hands gripping the rope, Josh looked to his opponent. "You ready?" he said, his voice teeming with the thrill of an impending contest.

Skylar gave him a look that was half contender, half seductress. "Whenever you are," she came back. "Last one to the top buys drinks tonight at Barefoot Charlie's."

Josh and Skylar stretched across the space dividing them and high-fived.

Rolling her eyes, Finley suppressed a jealous groan.

After a count of three, they climbed onto the wall. Well actually, leaped was more like it. One minute they were standing there looking up, the next they resembled a couple of tropical frogs, scaling the trunk of a tree.

Josh moved from one rock to the next, stopping every so often to show Finley a thing or two. "Using opposing hand and foot will get you a higher reach," he shouted down. "If you need to take a break, just balance like this." He stopped with his feet resting on two evenly spaced rocks and let his hands fall.

"You'd better stop talking, old man," Skylar hassled. "I'm feeling mighty thirsty."

Josh looked up. In his concern over instructing Finley, he'd allowed Skylar to gain a considerable lead. "In your dreams, little girl," he shouted back. Then as if his arms and legs had received an energetic shock, he began moving with considerable ease and quickness, crawling along the jutting stones, closing her lead.

Seconds later, he'd not only caught up to Skylar but had passed her.

Finley took the break in his tutelage to appreciate the pleasing view of his glutes from her angle and then the bulging ropes of muscle circling his arms, tightening then twisting as he ascended. Her fingers twitched with desire, counting the minutes until she could touch his taut skin again. If Skylar thought—even for an instant—that Finley was going to allow her to buy Josh a drink, or vice versa, she was sorely mistaken. But her musing barely had a chance to crest her lustful heart when Josh scaled the last few rocks and rang the bell at the peak.

Cupping her hands around her mouth, Finley yelled, "Way to go, Josh!" Her pride at her man having overtaken his opponent was short-lived, however, as he joined her at the bottom and she realized . . . now it was her turn to climb.

"Okay, babe, you can do this." Josh safety-checked her harness.

*He called me babe,* a voice in her head sighed. If she hadn't been about to willfully submit to her greatest fear, she might have noticed the flutter that had interrupted the steadily increasing banging of her heart. She might have even been flattered, or slipped an arrogant glance to Skylar, but she did none of the above. Fear had overridden any and all other possible emotions.

"Just look to me if you get stuck and don't know what to do next," Josh continued. "Take it one foothold at a time." He clipped on the rope that stretched to heaven from her waist. She looked down at the knot. Multiple loops circled the main lead, a noose at the end of a tortuously long drop. Josh touched her chin and lifted her gaze to his. "Don't forget to use your Pilates breathing."

All Finley could think about was that she was swiftly running out of time to admit she was terrified of heights and didn't want to do this. Not today, not *ever*.

She glanced over at the two guys who would hold her and Josh's leads, then to Skylar. She could see her own expression mirrored in their eyes, and knew that they knew she was seconds away from chickening out. Like a contestant on one of those reality dating shows, she was about to move forward with a feat she never would have considered had the affection of a handsome man, and the rivalry of another woman, not been driving her onward—or upward, as the case may be. But then was she really doing this only for Josh, to win his affection? Because doing so was important to him? Or had she come here in search of the first missing pieces to herself?

Cower verses courage? Finley weighed her options. "Okay, I got it." Steadying her gaze, she locked the helmet strap beneath her chin. "Let's just do it . . ." she said while leaving off the part about how she needed to hurry before her good sense had the chance to overpower her ego and jumpstart her brain into thinking rationally again.

A proud smile took hold of the concerned look on Josh's face, wiping the worry away. "That's what I'm talking about," he exclaimed, then pressed his lips to hers with a firm kiss.

The next ten minutes or so passed in a blur of heartbeat and breath, both chaotic and thrashing Finley's ears, consuming her chest. Somewhere in the distance she could hear Josh giving encouragement in the form of "That's it," "Grab hold there," and "You've got this . . ."

Her legs burned and her hands cramped, both shaking uncontrollably so much so she couldn't believe her limbs were continuing to drive her higher. Daring to stop for just a moment, she balanced on two evenly spaced rocks the way Josh had shown her and pressed her belly to the wall. Her arms relaxed, but only enough to rest without letting go completely. Not the best idea, she realized an instant too late, because now that she'd stopped, panic took advantage of her loss in focus to creep its way in.

Despite her best efforts to climb higher, the ground still remained within jumping distance. And the crest above? A million miles to go. Her stomach clenched and pin-balled between her chest and back. She couldn't breathe! Her head started to spin, the ability to distinguish between up and down growing more difficult with each thrash of her insides. Negative thoughts looped through her spinning head: *You can't do this. You're going to fall. They'll all laugh at you.*

"Finley," Josh was saying over and over. But Finley couldn't manage to lift her eyes to his, to zero her focus in on anyone or anything specific. Her gaze shifted aimlessly from the rocks to the ground below, then up to the dangling rope and the red button at the top, and back down again, finally stopping on Skylar.

Like she was trying to will Finley to fail, Skylar's blue gaze smirked up at Finley, as if to cast a subversive spell. Finley slammed her eyes shut. She knew what Skylar wanted, what she expected. Finley had seen it before. Beginning climbers who couldn't decide where to place their foot next, missed a step, or got scared and fell away from the wall, drifting shamefully to the ground by the good graces of the person at the other end of their rope. It would be so easy for Finley to let go. Because it happened all the time, no one would be surprised or even blame her for not making it to the top on her first attempt.

Snapshots from Finley's life flipped against the backdrop of her closed eyelids. Her marriage and all those wasted years, the fall festival she was missing, her mother's demanding glower, Roy's many conquests. Why *had* she allowed any of it? The answer was simple. Finley was a maintainer. A steadier. A smoother.

"But I'm so tired," she mumbled, referring neither to her pathetic life, nor the climb, but to both until she couldn't distinguish one from the other. Then the two became intermingled, one as equally important as the other.

She'd given up plenty of times in her life, allowed others to get the best of her, fallen in step, marched to the tune of what had been expected. Well, no more . . .

Subjugate Fear. Defy the rules.

Yes, she was a first-time climber, but did that give her permission to succumb to her fear of heights? To use her lack of experience as a crutch? *No!* She would not forfeit her victory to the demons from her past. *Not this time . . .*

Her eyes snapped open.

"Finley," Josh was still calling out to her. His face was ripe with encouragement while edged in concern. "You can do this. Just take a breath and regain your footing."

Of course he didn't give her the option to give up, to try again another day. Quitting wasn't in his nature, which was just what she needed. Right now, not just on this wall, but also with regards to the rest of her life, she needed to be pushed if she was ever going to exceed her limits.

Finley's lungs had shriveled into two ridged raisins, but she pulled the air harder, forcing them to expand. She sucked in one ragged breath after another until she felt she could breathe again.

In her mind's eye, she mapped a course to the next foothold.

Slicing Josh a tiny piece of her attention, she said, "I'm okay," then forgot he was there. Pulling her stomach to her back, she solidified her core. *Use your legs. Breathe.* Like Skylar had shown her, Finley gripped with her hands only as tight as she needed to keep herself steady. Her focus pinpointed the next rock, and she began to ascend again. Continuing this way, she directed her attention to the next foot placement, mapping and re-mapping her route as she put more of the wall behind her. Right foot, right hand. Left foot, left hand. Breathe.

Cheers rose up from the ground below. It sounded as if a small crowd had assembled. In the near distance, Josh continued to urge Finley on. Every joint and sinew in her body screamed out for her to stop, to let go, to free herself from this torture, but she would not relent. Sweat rained from her pores, drenching the skin of her arms, neck, and face. She ignored it all as she grabbed hold and pushed harder, higher.

Just a little further.

A few feet later, and she was slamming the palm of her right hand onto the red button at the top. A siren-type light whirled into action, its bright beam cutting across her gaze.

Only then did she heed her body's beckoning to let go, to release the wall, and take hold of the rope instead. She fell away, swinging from side to side. What once had been her lifeline had become the means of her victory dance. A shout of triumph rolled up her throat, vibrating over her lips. She looked to heaven first and thanked a higher being. Her second thought was for Cathyanne, and now she was hoping the guy down below with Josh's phone had captured every foothold of her climb, proof of Finley's bravery that her friend might otherwise disbelieve. Next, she thought of Quinton. Not to prove him wrong for mocking her, but because even though he'd seemed skeptical, she knew he'd be proud of her. Then her thoughts finally went to Shep and Royanne. What would her children say if they could see their mother now?

The light over Josh's wall ignited. Finley righted herself just in time to see him swinging toward her. "You were awesome!" he shouted. The adrenaline-fueled heat in his eyes met hers, and in that instant, she understood why he loved this sport so much. For the first time in her life, she felt empowered, capable, and completely free. Though her body was torn and ragged, her mind was open, uninhibited, and ready for anything.

Pushing off the wall, she met him halfway, their eager lips coming together, sharing in the thrill, the unabated fervor she couldn't have held back if she'd wanted to.

They stayed that way: legs, arms, and lips tangled together while the guys down below slowly lowered them back to earth.

Once Finley's feet hit solid ground, her legs threatened to betray her, to crumble to the floor, but she rallied her newfound strength and willed them to standing.

Next, high fives and fist bumps were shared along with congratulations, her perilous climb recounted from varying points of view. The consensus was that Finley needed to work on her technique, but overall she was a natural. Respect shined through smiling glances. For once in her life, Finley reveled under the glow of the spotlight. And it felt good.

A head bob along with a look that may have held the first inklings of respect was all Finley got from Skylar before she disappeared from sight, but that was all right. One conquest at a time.

After the well-wishers had peeled back, a chill worked its way over Finley's moist flesh. She glanced around for her hoody, moved a few paces out of Josh's grip, and swiped it from the floor.

Slipping her arms into the sleeves, she secured the zipper, and sensing Josh's absence, turned to find him standing a few yards away. He was intently watching a group of excited school children—who, by her estimation, were somewhere between eight and ten years old.

Standing amidst the fray, Skylar had reemerged and was chatting animatedly in a singsong voice, attempting to settle the group. By the light glowing from her expression, she was loving every minute of it.

As Finley rejoined Josh, she could see that his focus was not on the uncontrolled children, but on their leader. A clear showing of adoration beamed toward Skylar from his gaze.

What was left of the adrenaline high keeping Finley afloat, solidified, turning to dust in her veins. Her balance withered beneath her, and she grabbed hold of Josh's arm for support.

He reached out to steady her. "They're amazing, aren't they?"

Finley's head swam from side to side. "Who?"

Josh nodded toward Skylar. "Little kids." He circled his arm around Finley's shoulder. "So excited for adventure. Untainted by fear and self-doubt."

Finley turned her gaze from the pensive look on Josh's face to the pulsating group of children. "Uh-huh," she sputtered as the empty space inside her pelvis folded in on itself, forming tight perfect corners around mental images of her *grown* children.

"I used to think I didn't want any," he said, his eyes falling into Finley's with a sense of longing. "But lately I've been starting to . . . well, think that maybe I *do* want some, after all."

Finley's throat went Sahara dry. "What?"

"Kids," he said.

Finley mashed the doorbell once, then again for good measure. The excitement over her climb was going to burst right through her skin if she wasn't able to tell someone (besides Josh because he was there) about her accomplishment, and soon. Though she and Cathyanne still managed to talk on the phone almost daily as usual, it'd been about a month—the night at Tootsie's—since she'd laid eyes on her best friend. Guilt seeped into her conscience. She would have to try harder to carve out more time away from Josh, her home, and her garden, to spend with her best friend. Besides telling Cathyanne about the climb, Finley needed to make sense of Josh's confession to wanting kids of his own someday, and what that revelation meant to the future of their relationship.

However, tonight Cathyanne was nowhere to be found, so Finley had come in search of the next person on her list of people she couldn't wait to tell.

When Quinton finally swung the door open, he had a sleepy look on his face. He was dressed in an old pair of sweatpants and a rumpled Texas Tech T-shirt. Other than his Land Cruiser, there wasn't another car parked in his driveway, and given his casual attire, Finley was relieved to conclude that he was home alone.

Yanking the storm door open, she propelled herself over the threshold and straight into Quinton. "I did it! I made it all the way to the top." Her arms locked around his neck, her toes leaving the ground.

A sort of laugh choked from his throat. "Wow, Finnie, way to go." His arms came around her waist to support the weight of her dangling feet.

Tightening her grip on him, Finley buried her face in his neck. It felt good to be close to him—too good, she realized, and also borderline inappropriate. "Oh, sorry." She dropped her feet to the floor and stepped back. "I didn't mean to throw myself at you."

Quinton rubbed the back of his neck. "That's okay," he said. "I never tire of attractive women leaping into my arms."

Finley arched an eyebrow at him. "And that happens to you a lot, does it?"

"Not quite as often as I'd like." Quinton motioned for her to come inside. "I want to hear all about it."

All too happy to oblige, Finley made her way through the entry and into Quinton's great room. She looked around, appreciating the way he'd decorated this little farmhouse. Texas meets Pottery Barn meets bachelor pad, the space was one hundred percent Quinton, which made her feel right at home.

The far right cushion on his brown suede sofa had an indentation, evidence of a recent occupation. On the next cushion over sat a bowl of popcorn. The opening credits to a movie hovered frozen on his forty-inch TV screen. Prior to her intrusion, Quinton had been enjoying a relaxing evening at home, and Finley felt kind of bad for barging in on him.

"Am I interrupting something?"

Quinton made a don't-be-ridiculous face. "Nothing important."

Finley plopped down on the side of the sofa opposite from where Quinton evidentially liked to sit. How convenient, that he liked the right side when her preference had always been the left.

Anxious to tell her story, Finley got right down to business. "Climbing that wall was the most horrifying, most incredible thing I've ever done. You should have seen me, my legs and arms were shaking like crazy, but I got up there anyway."

Quinton settled into his seat. "I bet they were," he said, the glint in his eyes mirroring Finley's excitement. "So, start at the beginning."

Finley took a deep breath and began with how Josh had bought her those shoes. Next she moved on to Skylar being their climb instructor and then launched into an inch-by-treacherous-inch recount of her climb. By the time she'd finished, she was lying back against the arm of the sofa, her feet in Quinton's lap, munching on his popcorn while tossing him a kernel every now and again, which he would attempt to catch in his mouth. So far, he had about a fifty-percent success rate. Somewhere along the way, he'd taken off Finley's shoes and was in the process of rubbing her tired feet.

"Sounds like you had yourself one bad-ass adventure," he said, his gaze focused on his hands as his fingers worked Finley's foot muscles.

"Yes, I guess I did," said Finley with a sigh. "Come to think of it, I've never been on an adventure before."

"Sure you have," Quinton disagreed. "You raised two kids." He slid her a meaningful look. "Now, that's a true adventure. Remember the time Shep built a glider out of an old parachute, and he and Royanne tried to fly it off the garage roof?"

Yes, Finley would never forget that or any of the other shenanigans her two little darlings pulled while growing up. It was a wonder they all survived. Raising a family was nowhere near as glamorous or awe-inspiring as rock climbing, but kids could be just as unpredictable. A good parent had to be able to think fast on her feet. Finley smiled. She loved the way Quinton always seemed to find the magic in even the simplest of things.

"I've never thought about it that way," she was saying when Quinton's thumb found a tender spot on the arch of her foot. He then proceeded to apply the exact amount of pressure needed to make her entire body feel like it was melting. "Mmm, you are so good at that," she cooed, her eyes falling closed. "Roy was horrible at massages. He'd either rub too hard or too soft, and he never paid attention to what he was doing. I was always more tense after one of his rubdowns than I had been before."

"Good thing you have a new man to do your massaging."

Finley's eyes popped open. "I do?"

"Yeah, Mister Rock Climber Body Builder."

For some reason, Finley thought Quinton had been referring to himself. "Oh, right. Josh," she said, feeling a fraction of disappointment, though she wasn't sure why. She knew from experience that Josh was an expert at back rubbing.

"Where is Mister Adventure, anyway?"

"He's teaching one of those late-night, boot camp exercise classes at the gym," Finley said with a yawn. "He wanted me to come, but I've had more than enough exercise for one day. Plus, I don't like the loud music they play, nor do I appreciate someone yelling at me to punch the air harder, or whatever. I love my training sessions, but other than that I have no need for a gym. What's wrong with a good day's work out in the yard or around the house? At least then, at the end of the day, I've accomplished something tangible I can enjoy, and say, 'Look, I did that.'"

Quinton winked at her. "That's what I admire about you, Finnie. You don't waste time on things that don't really matter. You're beautiful, and not just on the outside, but because you know who you are."

Finley's cheeks heated under the affectionate look he gave her. Without warning, what began as two friends discussing their day had mutated into something considerably more intimate—heart-thumpingly so.

Setting the popcorn bowl off to the side, Finley lifted her feet from Quinton's lap. Apparently, she'd had more than enough foot rubbing for now. "I've got pictures from my climb," she said, her voice all strange and wobbly. She took her phone from her pocket and pulled up the pictures Josh had texted her. "You want to see them?"

Quinton moved one arm to the back of the sofa. "Of course."

Finley scooted over next to him, but not too close. "There I am when I first started." She held the phone out so they could both see and then began scrolling through the photos. "And that's me once I really got in the zone. See how high I am."

With the tip of his finger, Quinton tapped the screen over Finley's backside. "Looking pretty good in that harness," he said, lifting his eyebrows.

Finley elbowed him in the ribs. "Stop." She swiped her thumb across her phone to reveal the next shot. "Oh, and there I am at the top." But when she moved on to the next picture, her breath bunched up in her throat. It was one of her and Josh all tangled together, and lip-locked. "Um, yeah, you don't really need to see the rest." She hit the button on the side of her phone and the screen went black.

"Smart man," Quinton said. "Nothing like an adrenaline-fueled activity to get a woman's blood pumping, if you know what I mean."

Finley's jaw dropped, offended. "What are you saying, that Josh used rock climbing as some sort of aphrodisiac?"

Quinton raised a shoulder. "Every man has his tactics."

"I see. And what are yours?" Finley asked. "Your soulful voice and mysterious eyes?"

Quinton leaned closer. "You think my eyes are mysterious?"

His gaze landed on Finley's lips long enough to send her blood speeding off to places it had no business going.

"Uh-huh," she said, and just for an instant considered what might happen if she tilted her head a little closer to his. "Um, maybe we should . . ." she didn't know what.

The shadow of something Finley couldn't define raced across Quinton's face. "Watch a movie?" he suggested and fell back against his side of the sofa again.

Finley swallowed. "Right. A movie would be great."

Stretching over to the coffee table, Quinton snatched the remote. "I was just about to turn on *A Christmas Story* when you rang my doorbell," he said, as if a second ago, they hadn't almost kissed.

Finley breathed a subtle sigh of relief. Maybe she'd imagined the whole thing. "But, it's not even Halloween yet." She reached for the popcorn bowl again.

"So what? Every day's Christmas if you want it to be."

# Chapter 12

Finley's foot tapped the floor. She shifted in her chair. The warped metal listed to the left, but the slight deviation wasn't the only reason she couldn't manage to get comfortable. Across the circle, Ford related his attempt at Defying the Rules—something about rebelling against his ex-wife's expectations—only Finley was having an unusually difficult time paying attention. She wanted to listen, she *really* did, but her focus had been completely obliterated by a brimming need to share the story of her perilous journey to the crest of a faux rock-covered cliff with a group of fresh ears, ripe for the listening.

Ford finished his turn at sharing with a halfhearted shrug. Careen launched into her weekly lecture about how "no one can hurt you without your permission" and how they were all responsible for their own feelings, actions, and so on.

"Who hasn't shared yet?" Careen's gaze swept over the group. "Finley, do you have something you want to discuss?" she asked calmly, as if she hadn't noticed that Finley was about to pop.

Finley sucked in a half-breath before blurting, "I went on a date with my trainer. And I climbed a rock wall. All the way to the top. On. My. Own." Questioning looks ping-ponged around the circle, and she rushed to clarify. "Which I would never, *ever* normally do. I'm terrified of heights."

Careen did her bobble-head impression. "That's very inspiring, Finley. Good for you," she said, her tiny hands slapping together. "I think Finley deserves a round of applause." She motioned with her clapping hands to the group, who then joined in. "Finley not only defied a perceived societal rule by accepting a date with a younger man, but it appears she subjugated her fear of heights at the same time."

Sentiments of encouragement in the form of "Way to go," "So proud of you," and "You go, girl" reached out to Finley from around the circle, giving her a figurative pat on the back. As with the praise she'd received after her initial climb, she again found herself moderately comfortable with the group's attention here as well.

Finley's cheeks heated but then burst red. "Thanks everyone," she said. "I never could have done it without all y'all's encouragement." And she meant it too. For a brief disconcerting moment, she thought about where she might be right now without these near strangers. Frustrated and alone, stumbling along as she tried to keep pace with a life she had no idea how to live anymore was what first sprung to mind. Tears of gratitude threatened her eyes.

Careen asked, "Finley, why don't you share with us how you pushed through your fears?"

Finley steadied her emotions with a quick breath. "I'd be lying if I said I wasn't terrified, that I didn't want to back out," she admitted. "And I did, at one point, consider giving up. But then . . ."

"Then what?" Careen prompted.

"Skylar," Finley hissed the young woman's name. "She was below me with her tight bike shorts and smug expression." She frowned at the memory. "She was just waiting for me to fall or chicken out so she could prove to Josh that I'm too old, and that she's better suited—"

"Hold on a second," Burlie-Jean cut in, waving a plump palm in a stopping motion. "Who's Skylar?"

Finley noted Burlie-Jean's wrinkled brow, suddenly aware she'd gotten ahead of herself. "Our climb instructor," she back-pedaled, omitting the part about how Skylar also worked for her, and all the unfortunate details that went along with their past. "She has the hots for Josh, and is *so* obvious about it. Clearly, her momma never taught her a thing about being subtle with her affections for a gentleman." She swept an appalled look around the circle. "You know the type, your basic dark and sultry bombshell nightmare—"

"Right," Nora mumbled, but not so low that anyone missed it. "Kinda how you're *our* basic suburban-housewife nightmare?"

A word of caution for self-restraint sounded in Finley's head, but she was tired of Nora's habitual animosity toward her. To her recollection, she'd never done a thing to provoke such behavior. "Do you have a problem with me?" she asked, her voice tinged with a hint more anger than she'd intended.

"It's not just with you. It's *all* of the women who are like you," Nora lashed back. "With your fancy clothes and mono-grammed accessories." Her eyes darted to the initials sewn onto the cuff of Finley's Oxford shirt. "Drinking tea with your spoiled garden club cronies while whining, 'divorce is so hard,' then paying the bill with your husband's platinum card." She waved her hands mockingly in front of Finley's face. "News flash, no one feels sorry for *you*."

"Nora!" Careen jumped in. "That is enough." Her minia-ture arms circled the air, indicating the group's vicinity. "Need

I remind you that this is a safe zone? Everyone's feelings, no matter how varied, are both welcome and appropriate." Careen gave Nora a sharp look she then shared with the balance of the group. "Here, we do not judge."

For a moment, no one spoke. In fact, Finley was fairly certain by the tightness of Nora's jaw and the reddening of her face that Careen's admonishment had even the group's most derisive member holding her breath.

A few awkward beats passed before Ford bravely spoke. "Nora might have a point though," he said, his gaze lighting on Finley before moving on. "Whether we call attention to the fact or not, divorce can be harder, financially, for some of us, than for others." He rolled up a shoulder. "Take me for example. My wife earned twice what I do. Now that she's gone, I can barely make the mortgage on a house she insisted we buy. I'd sell it, but can't afford to until the market recovers a little more."

Burlie-Jean reached over and gave Ford's thigh a vigorous pat. "Hang in there Sweet th*ang*," she soothed. "God has a plan for all of us, a way of making things work out for the best." She turned her face to heaven and closed her eyes. "I wish He'd be quicker about it though," she said, then began to hum a pious tune. A good five seconds later, her eyes popped open again, only looking grave this time—beseeching. "If I don't get a job soon, me and my babies will be out on the street with nothing but the clothes on our backs."

Tongue tied by the images of Ford and Burlie-Jean along with two frightened children huddled in a dank homeless shelter, Finley's eyes bounced between the two group members. Her mind grasped for something—anything—encouraging to say.

Sue spoke next. "My husband's gambling left me with nothing but debt. And now, after years of working extra shifts to cover our bills, of trying to be what he wanted me to be, of taking the brunt of his"—she touched a light scar arching over her gaunt cheekbone—"frustration, I just found out he's having a baby with some dental assistant. He's gonna marry her." She pressed a matted tissue to her nose and sniffed. "Without what little bit of money he brought in, I've lost my apartment, and now my husband forever," she added as a sob escaped. Her tissue floated up like a tattered sheet billowing in the wind. "I feel like I don't have anything left, nothing to live for."

Finley's heart dropped to the pit of her stomach, dragging any possibility for an appropriate response along with it. Here she'd been preoccupied with something as trivial as a climbing date, going on about some silly rivalry, while the rest of the group had legitimate problems to deal with. "Y'all, I am so sorry . . . I had no idea."

Then to her dismay, from around the circle, she saw a handful of cold looks being tossed in her direction, and that was when she realized Nora wasn't the only group member who resented her presence here. As the frigid air settled in around Finley, what felt like a chasm of socioeconomic disparity fractured the circle, separating her from the rest of the group.

Finley's gaze veered away. Images of stuffy parties and grandiose cotillions where polite conversation was recited like carefully crafted scripts, limitless shopping trips, and lunches at the country club, flipped nickelodeon-style before her eyes. Obviously, her life had never been tragic by any means, but it hadn't exactly been fulfilling either. She'd been shaped and refined, tutored and put on display. And so it was no surprise that in adulthood she'd desired much of what had been expected—the beautiful home, the perfect family of four, the charity work. Only, what did her achievements matter when, in the end, her endeavors left her feeling insignificant, just another cultivated flower in a garden of pomp and circumstance?

Shep and Royanne aside, she wanted to mean something to someone in a way no one else could, to need that person just as fervently in return. She wanted her life to matter. And while it was true she wasn't fighting a battle of monetary survival like the rest of the group, she *was* at war against an unseen enemy, a threat to her soul deft at keeping at a safe distance ahead. Even so, she could now see that this distinction set her miles apart from the others.

Finley looked up at the group again, her eyes darting from one unfriendly face to another. Of course she was overreacting, but visions of the old South (nooses and burning crosses) flashed before her eyes. She gulped in a breath to steady her trepidation.

"I know what y'all are thinking, and I can't say I blame you for it. But if you'd just let me explain . . ." she began, but given the situation, couldn't seem to find the appropriate words. As if on cue, from the other side of the window, the sun sliced through the clouds and struck the gym floor with a flash of light—a spark of recollection—bumping something Cathyanne had said a while back against her brain. The memory nudged a little harder, and she gave it permission to step forward. "A friend of mine once told me, 'the things of this world are temporary,'" she managed to get out, but nothing more.

Careen rushed to fill the pause. "Meaning?" she encouraged, while her eyes conveyed caution.

"If any of you think money makes life easier, that growing up in a wealthy family, or having a rich husband, means a person's life is a fairytale, then you're mistaken." A tear leaked from Finley's eye and rolled down the side of her nose. "Unless your idea of a fairytale includes walking some invisible, socially acceptable line. Conforming to what's expected no matter what, even at the expense of your own happiness. If you dream of living a life where love is measured in purchases, and not in time, quality or otherwise, where a husband thinks all he has to do is provide for his family. That if he buys them the moon it won't matter he doesn't take the time to listen to them, to see them . . . then be my guest. And while it's true I have money in the bank and a nice home, if I died tomorrow, what difference would any of it make? With the exception of the love of my children, I'd leave this world more or less alone, the same as the rest of y'all." Finley's blurred focus reached out to the group for a thread of mutual understanding. "I mean, aren't we all here searching for the same thing? The answer to where we fit into this world now that we're all single again?"

Silence swelled between Finley and the others as all eyes actively avoided hers. She hoped against their averted stares that they could somehow reach a common ground.

But camaraderie wasn't destined for her near future.

"Oh, cry me a *golden* river," Nora spat out. "You underestimate the significance of having a roof over your head and food in your pantry. When you don't know where your next meal is coming from, where you'll sleep tonight, much less next week, because the price for even an ounce of the kind of security you so blatantly take for granted means there's a beating in your near future, that's when death becomes a welcome blessing. *That's* when you've pretty much figured out you *don't* 'fit' anywhere in this world." Then her menacing gaze took on a soft edge and skirted off in Sue's direction. A show of support or mutual understanding, Finley didn't know which. Likely both. "So in answer to your question, I guess you could say, *no,* we're *not* all here for the same reasons."

Nora's words whipped across the circle like a well-executed slap to Finley's face. She could feel the sting of fresh heat bleeding onto her cheeks. Her attention flew to her wringing hands, her mind turning to Roy, and how over the years his silence and veiled gaze had widened the division between them.

What if he'd been physically abusive instead—or in addition to? She couldn't imagine a life lived in constant fear of bodily harm, and that inability to conceive of such a horrific existence made her wonder, *Had my life with Roy really been that bad? The disconnect between us as unbridgeable as I'd thought?* Whatever the reason, misguided or otherwise, she'd chosen to end her marriage. The others here had been forced out by circumstances beyond their control. What if Nora was right and Finley didn't belong here? She'd been raised to know better than to remain somewhere she obviously wasn't welcome, but she was too stunned, too embarrassed to push to her feet and leave. Her only hope hung on an ability to fade into the lopsided chair beneath her. Highly unlikely, she was afraid. So it looked as if a peace offering was the only option she had left.

Fresh tears pricked Finley's eyes. "I guess y'all are right," she admitted, her focus tied to her tightly knotted hands. "And in more ways than one, I suppose I have it better than most." She looked up then and addressed the group's calloused expressions through a prism of tears. "If there's anything I can do for any of y'all, please don't hesitate to ask."

"You mean like write a check?" Nora bullied. "Organize a fundraiser?"

A defiant bristle sprang from Finley's contrition and worked its way into her spine. Here she was, trying so hard to find a common ground, to apologize and be helpful, while Nora, and the others too, seemed completely unwilling to allow her even an ounce of credit for her effort. How was *that* fair?

Burning with injustice, the bristle prodded further until the rebel inside Finley began to materialize. Metaphoric feet firmly planted, hands white-knuckle at the waist, she'd taken a complete about-face. "So what?" Finley challenged. "You want me to apologize because I come from money and the rest of y'all don't?"

Nora cocked her head with attitude. "For starters, yeah," she said, the *duh* implied. "Because the last thing any of us needs is one of your *bourgeoisie* guilt offerings."

Finley ignored Nora's insult and stayed her course. "Then what?" she said, throwing the question out to the group. "Most of you obviously need help, and so what are y'all gonna do about it? Sit around complaining while your lives, your futures, run through your fingers until there's nothing left?"

"Yes, Finley, thank you," Careen said, her tone of quiet control denoting, I've-let-this-go-on-long-enough-and-will-take-it-from-here. "As we've discussed in prior meetings, our fates—successes and failures—are up to us to decide. But do we have to go it alone? And just because we're experiencing a varying severity of trials, does that mean we're exempt from helping one another?" She dangled her questions like bait then closed her lips, waiting for someone to bite. When no one risked even a nibble, she tried again. "Any suggestions?" she asked, to which she received more silence. She sighed. "Nora, how 'bout let's start with you."

Nora fiddled with the tiny ring circling her lip, her eyes consulting her jiggling leg for an answer. "Well, for starters," she relented, "Sue, you're coming down to the salon so I can give you a complete makeover." She tucked the strand of purple hair framing her face behind her ear. "Haircut, mani-cure, make-up. Then you'll be ready to interview and find yourself a new job."

Sue's gaze hit the floor. "That's real nice and all," she muttered, "but I don't have nothin' suitable to wear with a fancy hair style and makeup."

Ford's face brightened with genius. "My wife was petite like you," he said. "When she ran off to Atlantic City with that Yankee carpetbagger, she left me with two closets full of designer clothes. And it don't look like she's coming back for any of it anytime soon." He gave Sue a determined look. "You're welcome to all of it." He sat back and crossed his arms with a faraway look. "I've always wanted a gun safe. One of her closets should suit just fine."

A bashful smile lit Sue's pale cheeks. "That's very kind, but what kind of job would I interview for?" she asked. "I've never done nothing except work at Walmart."

Burlie-Jean nearly blasted from her seat. "There are all kinds of retail jobs out there," she said, pointing her hooked fingernail toward the dingy windows lining the eaves of the gym. "I've been on Monster looking for a job myself. You just drag your little hopeless butt on over to my place, and I'll help you create a profile. We can job search together." Her rotund body quaked with enthusiasm. "I've already been out on a few interviews. No luck yet, but baby, these days it takes time." She raised her arms to the ceiling saying, "We'll lift each other up." Then fisting her hands, she flexed her muscles. "We'll be each other's strength."

Careen spoke next. "Now we're getting somewhere. See, we help ourselves when we help each other." Her gaze slid to Finley as if to say, feel-free-to-jump-in-at-any-time.

Finley's mind scrambled to come up with a brilliant offering of assistance like the others. She could invite Sue to stay in her guest room, but would that be weird? Inappropriate? Or, she could . . .? Good grief, wasn't she the queen of charitable service? But thinking back, in all those years of "helping" the community, had she ever done so on an individual basis? Actually looked someone in need straight in the eye and asked, "What can I do for *you*—personally?" and then, gone and made his or her wish a reality?

Never. Not once.

A brand-new sense of failure crept over Finley and called her a selfish fool. "I don't suppose you know anything about managing an orchard?" she said, regretting the absurdity of the question before the last syllable had cleared her lips.

Sue shook her head. "No, ma'am." She released a puny giggle. "I've never even been in one before."

Finley felt the fire of a dozen eyes, burning her to the bone. "I might have some friends with job connections," she pathetically tried again, leaving out the part about how none of said friends were speaking to her at the moment. "I'll make a few calls."

"Thank you, Finley," Careen said, a forced cheeriness to her words. "See, this is what the group is all about, working together to help one another, not separating ourselves or tearing each other down over differences." She brandished an outstretched arm over the group like a fairy godmother waving a magic wand. "Those were all great examples of how breaking the proverbial box can produce new possibilities."

*The box.* Finley cut her gaze to the chalkboard and the list of steps they were all presumably working toward completing.

*Smash the box: Look outside the box for the best answer and the greatest opportunity for growth.*

Step number three on the list, and the next phase in her progression. But what box did Finley need to break? Over the last few weeks, she'd slowly begun to loosen the chains of social correctness her upbringing had shackled her with. But there were still so many links, too many to count, holding her right where she'd always been. Futility flared inside her, gathered strength, and had begun to rake away her accomplishments thus far when something else Cathyanne had said broke free: *God still thinks you have a few things to do, to learn.*

A light switched on inside Finley's head. Yes, she could feel something there, the answer hiding in plain sight like that boy from her kid's puzzle books, the one who dressed in suspenders and a red-striped shirt. *Waldo.* Easy to spot for those adept at adjusting perspective, impossible for others who tried too hard to see what was right in front of them.

Though she hadn't come up with an appropriate offering for Sue, Finley couldn't help but feel that sometime during this group session, the next path she was meant to travel had been revealed—the box that needed breaking.

*What does God want from me?*

Finley closed her eyes and squeezed tight. She could feel it. In the space just beyond the shadowy images left by what her sight had last beheld, the answer awaited. All she needed was the inspiration to break through the darkness, to glimpse what lay on the other side of her limited vision.

So close. She pressed her mind to reach further. But not quite there.

## Chapter 13

*A* down comforter of clouds concealed the night sky, releasing its contents to earth in the form of millions of floating feathers. Feet pushing against the brick wall separating her covered terrace from the greenway beyond, the rhythmic motion of the patio swing lulled Cathyanne into a peaceful longing. The night was still, the sound of wet snowflakes splatting against nearly barren tree branches, rooftops, and stone being the only discernable sound. Closing her eyes, she inhaled a patch of frosty air. October thirty-first. The first snow of the season had come early by Nashville standards; Mother Nature's way of reminding grown-ups that this world, this life, still held a little magic.

"Tell me again why it is you can't come over?" Finley wanted to know.

A chill worked its way between the folds of Cathyanne's blanket. Shivering, she pulled the wool tighter around her shoulders and pressed the phone back to her ear. "Because I already told you," she sighed. "I'm way too tired to venture out tonight."

"But I haven't seen you in weeks. And I'm dying to watch a scary movie. You know I can't by myself, all alone, here in this big 'ole house," Finley moaned. "You have to come over."

Exhaustion seeped into Cathyanne's brittle bones. With each passing day, questions as to her chronic absence were becoming more difficult to answer. If it weren't for Josh and the mutual infatuation he and Finley shared, she never would have gotten away with being AWOL this long.

Laying a hand to her swollen belly, Cathyanne felt her heart beating against her boney ribcage. "I would but it's snowing, and my little sports car can't handle these slippery roads," she offered as an additional excuse, which just so happened to also be true.

Finley huffed into the phone. "And you say that *my* car is useless," she chided. "Wait. I have four-wheel drive," she said, as if stumbling upon a little-known fact for the first time. "I'll come over there."

Cathyanne glanced between the folds of her blanket, half-expecting to see her heart's rapid pulse lifting the Henley she wore with a pair of Halloween-themed pajama pants. Somewhere beneath the thin fabric, her enlarged liver was pressing against her diaphragm, making it difficult to breathe, especially in times of stress. Maintaining this ruse, knowing Finley couldn't be fooled for much longer, definitely constituted stress.

"Finley, it's not safe for either one of us to be out tonight," she reiterated. "Why don't we pick something from a movie channel? That way we can stay on the phone and watch it together from the safety of our own sofas."

"I would, but seeing as how Roy took the universal remote when he left, I'm afraid that won't be possible," Finley complained. "As it is, it takes three different remotes for me to watch cable alone. Four, if I want to watch one of my Blu-rays.

Besides, I haven't had time to figure out which of these stinkin' gadgets works my movie channels yet."

Steadying her nerves, Cathyanne pulled in as much extra air as she possibly could without being too obvious. "Well, maybe it's for the best. Even if you could start a movie, we both know that at some point, Josh is going to show up over there and then I'd plummet from B-F-F to third wheel in nothing flat," she said, deciding to incorporate one of Finley's favorite evasive tactics—a change in subject. "And why is it you're pestering me to come out on a snowy night anyway? Where's Mr. Perfect?"

Finley huffed a breath into the phone. "He's paintballing with some friends," she said, sounding as if fighting off a sudden onslaught of fatigue.

"Well, they can't play all night. I'm sure when he gets there he'll know how to work all of your . . . *gadgets.*" Even though Finley couldn't see her, Cathyanne bounced her eyebrows, giggling at her own pun. "Then he can stay and keep you safe from the boogyman."

"I'm sure he'd do a proper job of both . . ." Finley half-heartedly agreed, leaving the "but" hanging out there.

Cathyanne wasn't surprised at Finley's hesitance. Finley had always been old fashioned when it came to physical intimacy before marriage. What Cathyanne didn't understand, however, was how Finley could hold out on such an aesthetically pleasing man like Josh. Especially when she knew that Finley and Roy had been estranged long before he'd left for good. Even a conservative, traditional woman like Finley had needs. Unless . . .

"How long has it been since you, *you* know, with a man?" Cathyanne asked.

A perceived chill blew into Cathyanne's ear from the other end of the line. "I suppose however long it's been since Roy left," Finley said, as if stating the obvious.

Cathyanne's jaw dropped. "Y'all were still sheet-wrestling up until you threw him out?"

"We were still married, weren't we?" Finley asserted rather pointedly. "And anyway, Roy can be . . . well, you know, very persuasive."

*Persuasive?* Cathyanne repeated in her head while taking an instant to reflect. Pathologically charismatic, dangerously handsome, and persistent to a fault, Roy was a true salesman through and through.

"I guess it doesn't surprise me," she agreed. "That man could charm the stink off a polecat."

A beat of utter silence filled the line between them. "So am I the skunk in this scenario?" Finley wanted to know.

Cathyanne hurried to clarify. "No, I was referring to women like Skylar and Macy," she clarified, then corrected, "Or Kitty Lou. Whatever."

"Well then, it's official," Finley deadpanned. "I was married to a skunk charmer."

Rumbles of laughter rolled up from Cathyanne's diseased gut, joined by the sound of Finley's snickers popping through the line. As the laughter grew more intense, she wondered how something that hurt so much could feel so glorious at the same time. How long had it been since they'd laughed together? If she couldn't remember, then it had been much too long.

Once Cathyanne's chuckling had subsided enough for her lips to form coherent words again, she asked, "How did you know all that dirt you spilled at the luncheon about Macy anyway?"

A sigh wedged its way into Finley's laughter. "People just tell me things. I don't know why," she said, the folly holding firm to her voice. "It's a curse, I guess."

Cathyanne pulled back on her merriment. "No, people

trust you," she asserted, to which Finley lapsed into another round of laughter.

"Well I suppose they won't anymore," Finley said, her mirth taking on an ironic edge. "Not now that everyone has witnessed firsthand the lunacy I'm capable of unleashing."

The joviality in Cathyanne's chest lifted, leaving only sobriety behind. "Don't say that," she scolded. Even though recently Finley had lost her footing and stumbled, she'd always been a beacon of sorts to those around her. She was even-tempered and steady, always able to see a path where most only saw a curtain of fog. She simply needed to regain her balance again, that's all.

"You can't generalize your entire life, all the good you've done, to one unfortunate come-a-part," Cathyanne insisted. "You're a trustworthy person, a loyal friend, and good at taking care of people. It's important you remember that. God relies on us to use the talents He gave us to make this world a better place."

Finley sniffed back on her laughter. "What's with you lately?" she asked, though there was still a smile in her voice. "All wisdomy, like a sage dropping tiny seeds of enlightenment for wayward souls to follow."

Pressing the meat of her palm to the center of her chest, Cathyanne spoke a few mental words of comfort to a desperate heart fighting for each beat. "Yeah, right." If she was so wisdomy, then why was she having such a hard time figuring out what—or more accurately, whom—Finley needed in order to be happy? A fresh wave of exhaustion curled up inside her, laid its head to the pillow, and told her to pick up this fight another day.

"So . . . about the movie," Finley asked.

Cathyanne stifled a yawn. "How 'bout let's watch something we both already own? A holiday movie instead . . . *A Christmas*

*Story?"* she suggested. "I know you love it when I sing to you in my Asian accent."

"You know I do," Finley agreed. "But I just watched it last week with Quinton."

Like a window had magically opened in a room full of locked doors, Cathyanne felt the warm glow of possibility shining through. "Quinton, huh?" she asked, baiting her question with a hint of knowing.

"Oh, please," Finley balked. "Don't even go there."

"Why not?" Cathyanne feigned innocence. "We both know you're carrying a torch for that man."

"I'm doing no such thing."

"Then why does your voice peak a little whenever you say Quinton's name?" she asserted, then proceeded to demonstrate. "Qu-*In*-ton."

"It does not," Finley strongly disagreed. "Good gracious, woman, I . . . he . . ." she stammered, followed by a whole lot of quiet, which Cathyanne interpreted as denial.

And so she held her tongue, and her breath, waiting to see if Finley would finally admit there was something between Quinton and her. *Come on, Finnie, say it, say it,* Cathyanne chanted in her head, willing her thoughts to drift on the falling snowflakes from her mind to Finley's mouth. If there was ever a time they both could use a dusting of autumn's magic, it was right at this second.

A long moment or two rolled by before the tiniest of groans reached through the phone to grab Cathyanne's full attention. "And what difference could it make anyway when he's been living next door to me for what, like eight years, and has never once made the tiniest of passes at me?" Finley deflected—again.

Cathyanne decided she was going to have to work on her telepathic skills. But for now she'd have to rely on plain, old-fashioned reason. "Yes, but you're leaving out the part where you were married for all of those eight years," she countered. "Quinton may have become somewhat of a player after his wife and children left him, but going after a married woman? Not his style."

"Well, I'm not married now, am I?"

*Bingo!* Cathyanne thought. Close enough for a confirmation that Finley has, in the very least, entertained the idea of dating Quinton. "So, did your boyfriend know you were cuddled up on the couch the other night, watching a movie with your sexy, rock star neighbor?"

"Josh is hardly my boyfriend," Finley dismissed, while adding, "or not technically at least. But he knows he has nothing to worry about. What woman in her right mind would cheat on a sweet man like Josh?" she said in an ambiguous way that had Cathyanne wondering if Finley's question had been a reflection of her true feelings, or if it was meant to be rhetorical. "And besides, Josh doesn't like to watch movies. He can't sit still long enough. He gets restless. Gotta keep moving."

Again, Cathyanne was unable to attach a definitive meaning to Finley's words. Did Josh's disinterest in movies bother her? Or did she find his restless nature endearing? If the latter were true, why would she care about actually being able to *watch* said movie when she could make out with a hunky man instead? Was it possible she merely thought she *should* be into Josh because he was a sweetheart, and, well, hot? Or was she only dating Josh because Quinton had yet to show her any interest?

"Did I tell you he wants kids?" asked Finley.

"Who?" Cathyanne questioned because her ping-ponging thoughts had lost track of which guy held their current thread of discussion.

"Josh, of course," Finley said, impatient.

"Yeah, so?" Cathyanne said, deciding to give devil's

advocate a try. "What's the big deal? These days, women over forty are giving birth all the time."

"But what if that woman over forty doesn't *want* any more kids?"

"Well, does she?"

"I don't know."

Obviously, Finley didn't know what she wanted, which was exactly why Cathyanne was having such a hard time figuring out how to help her.

Cathyanne looked up at the bloated sky, shedding its moisture one flake at a time. "Just enjoy this thing with Josh while it lasts," she said, half losing herself in the prism of snow falling around her. "One day at a time." Closing her eyes, she listened through the phone to the sound of Finley's fireplace crackling in the background. She could almost feel the heat warming her cold cheeks—almost. A gloomy presence reached out from the sapphire night. The shadow hovered a moment, then cozied in around her. But she wouldn't allow it to stay. She refused to surrender to the darkness when the light still beckoned. The choice between resentment and acceptance was still hers to make.

Sure, death was gaining on her, and she had every right to fret, to be fearful even, to shake her fist and curse heaven for the unfairness of it all, but was that how she wanted to spend what little time she had left? Longing for what couldn't be? No, she'd be grateful for every second. This moment with Finley would never come again, and she'd be a fool to waste it. Mustering every available ounce of emotional control she had left, she shrugged off her fictional cloak of discontent and watched as it fell in a heap to the terrace.

"Stop trying to control every little thing," Cathyanne continued. "You can't make the most of today when you're so focused on tomorrow."

"There you go again," Finley teased. "Have you been reading one of those self-help books again? Because if you have, maybe you can help me process this." She paused for effect before adding, "My mother and daddy are going on a cruise over the holidays."

Cathyanne's feet hit the ground. "What?" She sat up straight. "Why?" Finley's mother and daddy never left town during Christmas. Their family traditions were more sacred than the Papal Conclave.

Finley said, "To get away from me and the mess I've made of our family, I suppose."

Cathyanne settled back into the swing again. It might seem crazy to an outsider, but knowing what she did about Finley's family, her friend's short explanation actually made sense.

"Your momma has always had a flare for the overly dramatic gesture."

"Yes, she has," Finley agreed, "but she's not my biggest problem."

"What could be worse than your folks punishing you by ditching out on the holidays?"

"Josh has been hinting that he wants to spend Thanksgiving together."

"So?"

"So?" Finley repeated, as if those two letters constituted a life or death question. "Per the divorce, Roy gets the kids this Thanksgiving, which leaves me alone with my folks. *So*, am I supposed to take my 'infant' boyfriend to Mother and Daddy's for what I'm sure will turn out to be the most awkward day of my life? The PTSD alone could ruin Thanksgiving—my favorite holiday, as you well know—forever. And what about Christmas? Are my kids supposed to spend the holidays with mommy's new special friend? And why do we have to split the holidays anyway?" she asked, stacking her questions until Cathyanne couldn't tell one from the other. "I don't want to give up any of them."

Cathyanne gave her head a shake. "I'm sorry to have to say this, honey, but that's just the way it goes," she said, mostly because it seemed to fit all of the above.

"Cathyanne?" Finley asked, her voice more solemn now than distraught. "Do you think I did the right thing, you know, by divorcing Roy and tearing my family apart?"

Her mind now buzzing with Finley's constant change in direction, Cathyanne knocked the back of her head against the swing a few thwacks to still the sensation. "Gee, I don't know," she said. "He was sleeping with the hired help, your friends, and who knows who else, so yeah, I do."

Finley *hummed*, mulling over the facts they were both already well acquainted with. "Right, and those weren't even his most offensive character flaws."

 "Agreed, so why are you questioning the divorce now?" Cathyanne asked, though she had a pretty good idea. "And don't you dare bring the Bible into this again. You and I both know that God doesn't expect a woman to stay with a man who refuses to keep up his end of the bargain."

Finley breathed a resigned breath. "Momma seems to think He does, and so do a whole lot of other folks down at the First Baptist Church."

Her patience growing thin with Finley's inability to state what was on her mind when they had more pressing topics to discuss—more specially, her future with Quinton or Josh—Cathyanne tried one more time to flesh out her friend's thoughts. "Finnie, can we just skip all this back and forth and cut straight to the reason you're second-guessing a decision we both know you desperately wanted to make, or you never would have gone through with it in the first place?"

Finley hesitated a beat or two before answering. "Some things were said in group the other day that have me thinking . . ."

"Thinking what?"

Finley sniffed. "That I've been blaming Roy for being selfish, for not paying attention to me, but what if the problem was me?" she asked, her voice thick with emotion. "What if I'd tried harder to reach him, to connect, to tell him outright what I wanted from him instead of expecting him to read my mind? If we'd been closer, then he may not have gone looking to hook up with all those someone-elses."

"Is that what you really believe, or are you just thinking out loud?" Cathyanne asked, to which she received only more sniffing. "Finnie, you can't blame yourself for Roy's wandering crotch."

Finley half-huffed, half-laughed. "Sure, everyone says that, but then in the same breath they're saying, 'It takes two to ruin a marriage.'" She choked a bit on the words. "All I'm asking is, don't I have to take some responsibility?"

Tears for her friend's confusion and her heartache leaked from the corners of Cathyanne's eyes. She, too, had asked herself this very question both times her marriages had fallen apart. A question she also had not been able to answer. What she knew for sure—infidelity was not the result of anything but selfishness and disrespect. If she and her husbands had loved each other the way they should have, then they'd have stayed together. That, or agreed on an amicable split before any cheating had occurred.

"Yes, I suppose that's true, but you can't go back to Roy just to save the holidays—"

"What if Roy and I tried again?" Finley rushed in. "I mean, knowing what I know now, we might have a chance. Right?" she asked without pausing for an answer. "When you said most everything on this earth is temporary? Doesn't that mean I should put the needs of my family above my own? After all, our families are the only things from this life that last forever, right?"

"I guess," Cathyanne agreed, then carefully added, "but only if being with Roy is what you want . . . *Forever.*"

"I don't know what I want." Finley sounded truly distraught. "How come I don't know what I want?"

"Hum?" Cathyanne wondered aloud. "Maybe because . . ."

*How come indeed?* Cathyanne could almost hear the rust scraping on the wheels in her brain as it worked to uncover the answer to Finley's quandary. We all had our lot in life—a vise, or a curse, for lack of a better word—an aspect of our personality that steadily held us back. Everyone had at least one obstacle—whether physical, emotional, or both—that got in the way of their progress, and more importantly, their happiness. For Finley, her curse had always been guilt. The fear of letting people down, especially when it came to her family. And right now that guilt just so happened to bear an uncanny resemblance to her ex-husband.

Josh, Quinton, and now Roy?

Somehow Cathyanne had to find a way to raise Finley's buried feelings to the surface. It wasn't going to be easy, might even get a bit messy, and was most certainly going to be painful, but it had to be done.

Suddenly, she knew just how to do it too.

The tricky part would be the timing.

# Chapter 14

"Higher?" Josh stated more than asked as he leaned in with all his might before releasing the rope swing, sending Finley soring once again into the branches of the beech tree overhead. The early November air whipping against her cheeks was a tolerable fifty-five degrees and heavy with moisture.

Her heart racing, she watched wide-eyed as the force of her plummet back to earth sent bunches of fallen leaves scrambling to get out of the way. "No. This is already too high," she shrieked as she whizzed past Josh again.

The plaid of his shirt blurred into a swish of red and blue stripes and then disappeared from sight.

"The ropes could break. I don't think this swing was meant to go this high," she pleaded, though she knew doing so was pointless. He had no intention of slowing her down just yet. He knew she'd always been one to err on the side of caution, and was constantly pushing her higher, faster, harder. With each additional challenge she accepted, she caught another glimpse of the woman she'd kept hidden behind pretense and expectation all these years. Like a bird coming out of its shell, one tiny peck at a time, she'd begun to look forward to seeing what hopped out once the final piece of shell had fallen.

Josh released a devious laugh as he stepped in to give her another shove.

"Are you listening to me? Don't you dare push me any harder," Finley warned even as a wide smile took hold of her face. She should have saved her breath. She was having the time of her life, and regardless, the upward force coupled with the fact that she was practically in the boughs of the tree again, had muffled her words anyway.

The distant sound of rumbling shook the air once more. Closer, by Finley's estimation, than it had been the last time. Much closer.

"What?" Josh put a hand playfully to his ear. "I can't hear you over the thunder," he said and then gave her swing another vigorous shove.

Finley invoked a serious look and aimed it at Josh over her shoulder. "You heard me just fine!"

"Don't worry, babe." He chuckled. "If you fall, I'll catch you."

Her insides went all tickly at his chivalrous offer. "Yeah, right," she pretended to be doubtful because swooning would have been too obnoxious.

"What, don't you trust me?"

A fork of lightning split the sky, illuminating Finley's garden like a strobe light. Turning back toward the thunderous sound, she gazed out across the orchard. The clouds looked like a stack of cannonballs, upended and rolling unabated across the sky. A silver curtain of rain closed over the hills in their wake.

Letting go of the rope just long enough to point before taking hold again, she hollered down to Josh, "Rain's coming."

Josh threw a glance over his shoulder. "What does a little rain got to do with anything?" he asked, then let out a maniacal sort of laugh.

Dropping her feet to the earth, Finley intended to put an end to this lunacy, but she was going too fast, and the swing soaring too high to stop that quickly. She yanked them back at the last minute.

"Stop pushing me this instant, or I swear, I'll jump," she said, and this time she meant it.

Josh moved out in front of her and sent her a daring look. "Go ahead."

Finley's fingers closed around the rope so tight her skin began to burn. He assumed she wouldn't jump, and quite frankly so did she, which was exactly why she did what came next. Without giving the possibility another thought, one moment her feet were passing the ground headed for another up-swing, her hands red against the ropes, and the next she was counting to three, her legs stretched out, feet ready to absorb the shock. Letting go, she held her breath, aimed square for Josh's chest, and launched her body from the swing.

Only then did she take an instant to consider what a bad idea jumping from a swing ten feet in the air might be.

A scream flew from her lips as she shot missile-style through the air, and right into the mixed look of shock and dread on Josh's face. Even still, she had to give him credit for not ducking out of the way. If Josh was anything, he was a man of his word. And though there was a strong possibility that this could end badly, he quickly shifted into a catching position. Except, he didn't so much as catch her as break her fall, and as their bodies collided and tumbled to the ground, she knew why she'd jumped. She'd needed to prove to herself that she could let go, that she could trust another person with her life. In that moment of uncertainty, she'd felt free. Not free of fear like after she'd climbed the wall, but free of the feeling that she had to maintain control of everything. All. The. Time.

Once they stopped rolling, Finley found herself with her back to the ground. Josh was sprawled across her, their arms and legs linked in a tangled mess. "Are you okay?" she asked.

Josh lifted his head. "Fine. You?" he asked, concern swiftly overtaking the dazed look in his eyes. When Finley couldn't keep the adrenaline smile from her face, his concern quickly shifted to a grin, too. "I *so* did *not* see that coming."

Finley lifted a shoulder from the ground. "Why not?" she asked haughtily. "You asked me if I trusted you to catch me. Guess you got your answer."

Readjusting his body so that his chest was even with hers, his green eyes gazed down at her. "Guess I did," he said, his lips forming the words one second, then closing over hers the next. His mouth was warm and firm with a hint of the dirt they'd kicked up during their tumble.

Normally, the taste of soil being introduced into Finley's mouth through another person's saliva would have put her off—not that she'd ever had this particular experience before—but ever since her talk with Cathyanne the other night, she'd been making an effort to enjoy whatever this was with Josh. To take every precious moment, one at a time. What she'd slowly begun to discover was that with all of the trepidation she felt over dating a younger man also came this sense of raw exhilaration she couldn't seem to get enough of. So what was a little dirt between more-than-friends when the man whose lips she'd presumed would only ever touch hers in her dreams were kissing her? In real life.

Threading her fingers through Josh's hair, she pulled him closer, her body arching into his with a voracious desire to feel more of him, to have all there was to take.

Josh's lips traveled down to explore her neck. "You're the most surprisingly unpredictable woman I've ever dated," he mumbled between kisses. "And gorgeous beyond all get out."

Another round of thunder boomed from overhead, closely followed by the crack of lightning. Finley's heart butted itself against her ribcage, as if insisting to be let out, but the incessant knocking had nothing to do with the advancing storm. To her recollection, she'd never heard the words "Finley" and "unpredictable" used simultaneously. Though she had no idea what the phrase "beyond all get out" really meant, "gorgeous" required no further explanation, and she hadn't been called that in a long time.

The idea that Josh found her both spontaneous and beautiful sent the blood pumping through her veins at a dangerously high rate of speed. "You're not so bad yourself," she was saying when the first drops of rain pelted her forehead and cheeks.

Josh's head snapped up, his eyes scanning the sky. "Come on, let's get you up and inside before this storm hits," he said, hopping to his feet with a surprisingly nimble deftness. Reaching down, he took Finley by the hand and pulled her up to standing. Her head, light from too much blood displacement, had her eyes feeling like they were rolling around in their sockets. In the few seconds it took for Josh to get her upright again and stable, the rain had begun falling in buckets, the thunder and lightning grumbling and flashing from what felt like all directions.

Finley held a hand up to shield her face from heaven's watery assault. "Too late," she yelled over the pounding, "it's already here."

Wrapping a strong arm around her shoulders, Josh steered Finley toward the house, but a bolt of white fire struck the garden between them and their destination, forcing him to pull back.

Glancing around for an alternate route, Finley pointed to an outbuilding sitting to the left of the garden, about half the distance to the house. "Potting shed."

Josh followed the direction of her outstretched finger. "Good enough," he said, and readjusted their direction.

Another flash of light cracked the sky close enough to them to have Finley's hair standing on end. She stumbled back, her heel catching on the uneven grass, knocking her feet out from under her. She would have fallen if Josh hadn't reacted, adjusting his grip an instant before she went down.

Reaching an arm under her legs, Josh lifted her feet from the muddy ground. "We're going to have to make a run for it."

Finley linked her arms around his neck and buried her face in his chest. In her periphery, she could see the wind bending the trees lining her property at nearly a right angle, but she'd never felt safer, more energized. The elements were waging a battle on the earth all around them, but somehow, with the way Josh had swept her up in his arms just now, determined to protect her from the storm, it all felt so tragically romantic.

His feet sloshing through puddles and covered in mud, Josh ducked his head under the awning covering the shed door. With Finley still cradled in his arms, he finessed the door open and slipped inside. Knocking the door closed with one shoulder, he leaned back and released a long, weary breath.

"Whew, that was close."

Finley pressed a grateful kiss to his wet lips. "My hero." She used a dreamy tone to go along with the gooey look she gave him. "Now put me down before you hurt that manly back of yours."

With a bashful smile, Josh lowered her feet to the dusty wood floor.

Her sopping wet sneakers had barely touched down when the roaring started. She'd heard people describe a tornado as sounding like a freight train barreling down, but the ear-piercing sound coming from outside of the shed walls was like no train she'd ever encountered before. Closing her eyes, she listened. Through the sound of her heart thumping in her ears, the only description she could come up with was . . . unearthly. What a large metal object moving at an enormous speed would sound like if it could scream.

Pulling Finley into his arms, Josh secured the door's bolt and then ushered them both to the middle of the room. Crouching down, he tucked Finley's trembling body beneath his and closed his eyes.

❧❧❧

"Wow! That was a close one," Josh called out once the wind settled down and the rain had begun to drum a steady beat on the tin roof. Speckled with mud from head to toe, he put his hands to his hips Paul Bunyan style and took in his surroundings. "This is one fancy potting shed," he said, his gaze scanning from the open-beamed ceiling to the dark wood trim, on to the oversized potting bench and shelving stacked with most everything Finley used to tend her garden.

Finley struck a match and held it to the wick of one of the oil lamps she kept out here with some of her other emergency supplies. "Originally, this was the kitchen." She blew out the match and added, "hence the massive hearth." She pointed to the stone fireplace consuming the center wall. "My granny Opaline added that wall," she motioned in the opposite direction, "to separate out a bedroom and bath, making it into the maid's quarters. The shower doesn't work anymore, but there might be a few towels."

She hung the lantern on an iron hook next to the door and then cupped her hands against the window, trying to get a glimpse at the state of her garden, home, and Quinton's next door, hoping all had survived the twister. But the rain was pounding the shed, falling in prismatic sheets over the glass, and she couldn't see a dadgum thing.

Josh sent her a sympathetic smile. "Looks like we're going to be here awhile." He pointed to the fireplace. "Is this thing safe?"

Finley rubbed a chill from her sopping-wet shoulders. "I had the guy sweep the chimney last fall when he did the ones in the main house," she explained. "How good are you at starting fires?'

Josh cocked his brow in a tricky fashion. "What do *you* think?"

Finley's heart fluttered in her chest. "I think I'll go rustle up some towels while you warm it up in here," she said, even though she was already starting to feel the heat.

❧❧❧

Fastening the last few buttons on an old pair of coveralls she'd found in what had once been the bedroom, Finley tucked a couple of threadbare towels and another pair of coveralls for Josh under her arm and made her way out into the main room. As she rounded the corner, she caught sight of Josh hovering over the beginnings of a roaring fire. He'd removed his flannel shirt along with the long-sleeved T-shirt he'd been wearing underneath, and had hung them on a couple of pegs to dry. With one arm resting on the mantle, he had the thumb of the other hand hooked in the front pocket of his jeans. The waistband sat low on his hips giving her a peek at the briefs he wore underneath. Apparently Jockey was his underclothing of choice. Something in her chest stuttered, pinged, stuttered, and then turned over again, this time settling into a metrical purring. Her eyes traveled from his jeans up, and on to the hills and valleys of his abs and chest. Baked to a perfect honey brown, his moist skin gleamed in the firelight, his perfectly toned muscles dancing with the flame.

Tearing her eyes from his chest, she took in the strong angles of his face, his serious gaze watching the fire as if anticipating an answer he'd been waiting a lifetime to hear.

"What are you thinking about?" she asked.

Josh's head whipped up like he'd forgotten she was there. A slow smile dragged up one side of his mouth. "You, and how . . ."—he surveyed her baggy coveralls, his eyes lighting on the name-patch that read, *Finnie*—"and how sexy you look in even the most unflattering outfit I'm pretty sure I've ever seen on a woman before."

Finley crossed over to him, a swarm of bees, butterflies, and pretty much anything else with tiny, fluttering wings, filling her chest. "You're an impossible flirt, but thank you," she said with a touch of false modesty. "I've got a pair for you too." She held out the coveralls and towels.

Josh kept his crooked grin aimed at her while he eased the towels and dry clothes from her hands. She tried not to drool as the muscles of his arms and shoulders tightened and rolled under his skin. "Thanks," he said, his gaze taking a quick side-trip from hers to look over her offering. Breezing over the patch, his eyes then made a quick U-turn to fixate momentarily on the name. He looked back to her under a questioning brow. "Roy?"

Finley's focus drifted off-center from his. "They'll likely be too long and a mite tight in the shoulders, but at least they're dry, and you won't freeze." She offered him a sheepish smile. "I think the temperature has dropped about ten degrees since the storm hit. At this rate, we could have snow again by morning."

Tossing the coveralls to the hearth, Josh then shook open one of the towels. "I bet I can come up with a way of keeping warm that doesn't include wearing your ex-husband's hand-me-downs," he said as he wiped the towel over his chest and shoulders.

Finley shifted her gaze from the heady look he was giving her. All of a sudden, instead of gently beating, those tiny wings in her chest felt as if they were desperate to escape a cage that had grown much too small. "I'm sure you can, but . . ."

Taking an end of the towel in each hand, Josh horseshoed it around his neck. "But?" he repeated.

Finley rolled her lips together and swallowed. Holding onto the towel the way he was only served to magnify the definition in his biceps, forearms, and chest. Part of her—the part currently siphoning off her blood supply—so wanted to get lost in those muscles, to forget about the storm, what may have become of her home and garden, and simply live in the moment. But the other half of her, the half that had yet to fully embrace her newly discovered surprisingly-unpredictable side, wanted nothing to do with any intimate activity she might come to regret once the sun reemerged. And that part of her was holding firm to the belief that love had everything to do with it.

"Look, it's not that I don't want to, or that I don't find you unbelievably attractive," she explained, her words coming out all breathy and rattled. "And you're just the sweetest guy and all—"

"Sweetest guy?" Josh interrupted, his mouth dropping open to match his rounded eyes. "Wow, Finley, way to kill the mood and my ego at the same time." He knocked a fist to the firm summit of muscle covering his heart.

"I meant that as a compliment," Finley apologized, the spontaneous side of her arguing for reconsideration. She commanded her hormones to stand down. Case closed. "And for your information, sweet is code for extremely-sexy, in my book."

Dejection, or possibly offense, rimmed Josh's gaze. "Then what's the problem?"

Finley's heart melted. Josh was the very last person on earth she wanted to hurt or make feel like he wasn't good enough. "I'm just old-fashioned, I guess." She pressed her palm to his warm cheek, felt the tickle of his scruff all the way to the pit of her stomach. "And truth be told, I've only ever been with Roy. And that was *after* I had his ring on my finger."

The green of his eyes grew thin as his pupils widened. "Not helping." He shook his head. "Knowing that only makes me want you more."

Finley pulled her hand away and stepped back. "Sorry, I didn't mean—"

He filled the gap she'd left between them and slipped his hands around her waist. "No, it's fine," he said, a moderate smile wiping the desire from his face. "I didn't mean to add extra pressure."

Finley gave him a curious look. "For the life of me, I'll never figure you men out."

Josh sent her a wry wink. "Right back at you, babe."

Her hip felt as though it was being crushed from underneath. Her mind, the fragment that was beginning to wake, told her to shift, to roll away. But the woody scent of a body, warm and solid beside her, was well worth the discomfort, so she stayed right where she was. Besides, she'd been having the most wonderful dream involving a man, someone who knew her, understood her, and still loved her, flaws and all. He was a best friend, a lover, her other half, and she never felt alone in his presence. The sensation was shear bliss, jubilant even—or was until what felt like a white-hot poker began to prod at her eyelids. She ignored the intrusion, choosing instead to slip back into her dream, back to where Quinton waited . . .

*Quinton?*

Finley's eyes popped open, a roller shade released with too much force, followed by her lungs pulling in more air than necessary. Gasping, she looked over at the sleeping man co-occupying her space. Her breath steadied as she enjoyed the pleasing outline of a strong chin, the curve of his perfect lips—Josh's perfect lips.

Settling back onto his outstretched arm, the one she'd been using as a pillow, she told her heart to calm the heck down. She hadn't been dreaming of her neighbor; the man in her dream had most likely been Josh. Yes, definitely Josh. Darned Cathyanne, and her incessant insinuations that Quinton had feelings for Finley. She was no doubt to blame for Finley's confusion. Her eyes fell closed again, searching the fading images for another peek at the elusive dream-man's face, just one more glimpse to be certain. Only, her subconscious had already closed a fist around the image, tucking the secret away for safekeeping.

Frustrated, and maybe even a smidge perplexed, her mind begged for more rest, but now she was feeling too out of sorts to sleep. *It was only a silly dream for goodness sake*, she scolded herself, even though she'd already given up and heeded her body's need to readjust.

Last night, when the storm appeared determined to linger, she and Josh had zipped a couple of sleeping bags together, added a few more logs to the fire, and crawled in for the night.

Unfortunately, the bag's limited space left little room for turning. She didn't want to wake Josh, so like a butterfly worming its way from a cocoon, she eased her body from the bag and out into the frigid air of freedom.

Stabilizing her cramped, unsteady legs beneath her, she pushed to standing and glanced back at the man who'd slept next to her. As she'd predicted, Roy's coveralls had been too tight through the shoulders for Josh so he'd tied the sleeves around his waist. The skin of his tan chest, soft but firm, like butter served at the perfect temperature, glowed in the morning sun.

Goosebumps started at her bare feet and rolled up to prick her hairline. Was it the cold morning air that had her skin taking a step back from her body, or the possibility that this glorious specimen of a man may not have been the same man consuming her dream? The uncertainty left a bittersweet taste in her mouth. Sure, she and Josh had things in common, not to mention an intense physical chemistry, but could their heat be enough to form a meaningful relationship? Would it grow into a love and friendship that would last forever? Or was their mutual attraction more like last night's storm—intense, but not meant to last . . .

"*Storm*," she repeated. "My garden."

Stepping lightly over to the window, Finley was almost afraid to look. There could be no denying the devastation such a violent deluge was capable of inflicting upon her unsuspecting home and garden.

Pulling the cuff of her sleeve over her hand, she wiped the condensation from the glass. The frost haloing the other side nipped at her skin through the fabric.

With a face-sized circle cleared away, she squinted through the paned window. Beyond the shed, puddles of water dotted the grass and pebbled walks. What was left of yesterday's warmth rose from the saturated earth in a white mist. Between the tufts of vanishing fog, she could see evidence of fallen tree limbs scattered over the maze of her flowerbeds all the way to the house, but to her pleasant surprise, all appeared more or less intact.

A sense of peace at knowing her garden and home had survived, circled a tight hug around Finley. What a temperamental creature Mother Nature could be. One minute she was all fight and fury, and the next, a serene child who'd fallen asleep amidst a floor strewn with toys. Then, like a mythical siren's song, the morning sunlight reflecting off the vanishing water crystals called to her with a sense of serenity, leaving her content to simply watch. The vapor twisted one way and then the other, swirling to form random images. As she continued to stare, she was drawn deeper into the mist's trance, the images becoming more distinct until a vision unfolded before her eyes.

Carrying wooden baskets of freshly picked peaches, modern women of varying ethnicity and age materialized amidst the fog. As she continued to watch them take shape, she somehow sensed that they were in one form of transition or another, much like those from her therapy group. Weaving their way through her garden, each individual stopped at one of the abandoned slave houses before disappearing inside. Only the small cabins she saw were no longer derelict as hers currently stood, but had porches that had been swept clean, and flowering baskets hanging from the eves.

A feeling of accomplishment—a calling of sorts—formed like a shell around her, seeping into her pores, and attaching itself until she felt at one with the impression.

Hands came around Finley's waist and pulled tight.

Startled, she pushed back from the window, a shallow yelp escaping her lips.

"Sorry, babe," Josh said, a chuckle in his voice. "I didn't mean to scare you."

Finley pressed a hand between her breasts to sooth her racing heart. "It's okay," she said, her stiff body relaxing, and falling back into his. "I was just . . ." *Just what exactly?* She looked through the window again, but on the other side, she saw only a garden this time, mussed by last night's storm. No women with peach baskets, or cozy cabins. What had just happened? Had she been hallucinating? Sleep walking? Had the women and the renovated slave homes been some sort of a dream?

Or had they been an epiphany?

"I mean, I was . . . just thinking," she said because she wasn't sure which.

Josh tightened his threaded arms around her waist. "Finley, are you okay?"

Her head reeled as further insight continued to flood her brain with possibilities, and epiphany slowly began to feel more likely. "I'm not sure." She pressed her fingertips to her temples. It felt as though she was back on the swing again, her feet reaching for the sky—higher, faster, harder. Prior to dating Josh, she'd never felt such a need to stretch, to extend far beyond the horizon. Now she knew there was something out there, something important, and what was even better, she knew what it was.

She'd found the box that needed breaking.

A crease pulled between Josh's eyebrows. "Babe, what's going on?"

Finley wiggled enough room between them to turn and face him. Then, closing her arms around his ribcage, her eyes searched his. She saw not only her boyfriend's eyes, but those of a renovation expert, a man she felt she could trust with her thoughts, her vision, and the new direction for her future—the one man who possessed both the heart and the knowhow to bring it to life. "Nothing, I'm perfectly fine. Everything is going to be just fine. But I have an idea I want to run past you."

# Chapter 15

"Thank you, Ford. Your new cat is . . . a-adorable," Careen said. Her words tripped over the wooden smile stretching thin across her lips.

Grinning like a man in love for the first time, Ford closed the photo app on his cell and slipped the phone into his shirt pocket.

Careen released a not-so-subtle sigh. "Well then, has everyone shared?" Her eyes swept the group as if taking inventory before stopping on Finley. "Finley, I don't think we've heard from you yet today," she said, adeptly adding an innocent look, though she knew full well that Finley had something pressing to talk about. After all, she and Finley had met the day before over a two-hour lunch where Finley had explained her vision, and detailed all the plans she'd made thus far to bring her foresight to life. Careen had been enthused to say the least, and had given Finley all the encouragement she needed to take her plan to the next level.

Today, Finley had been quietly waiting her turn, listening

patiently as the others related his or her efforts at moving forward with whichever step they were currently working on. Burlie-Jean had extended her job hunt to other states, and broadened her search parameters to fields other than accounting. Nora had started dating again, a history teacher from a local high school, and a "complete square," she seemed genuinely enamored with. Ford wasn't ready to trust another woman yet—hence the new cat. And Sue had enrolled in an online typing and computer course, something she'd previously believed herself "not bright enough" to consider. But much to Sue's surprise, she'd completed each course module thus far with unprecedented ease, and for the first time in her life, she appeared pretty darned confident.

And so it was Finley's turn to tell the group about the smashing of her box.

But now that it was her turn to share, her box felt very large by comparison, overwhelming even and quite capable of swallowing her whole. She'd spent the last five days with Josh brainstorming, drawing up plans, and meeting with inspectors. She'd tucked tail and groveled her way back into her garden club's good graces, which had been rather humbling, by the way. In addition, she'd paced the floor nightly, made copious notes during the day, and consequently felt exhausted and exhilarated at the same time. An intoxicating combination, she'd come to realize.

Now it was time to take the next step.

Her heart raced and dipped, rolling around in her chest, unable to decide if fear or excitement should accompany what she was about to reveal. "Yes, I suppose it is my turn to share," Finley agreed while unable to make eye contact with any of her fellow therapy mates. "It's been an interesting week, to say the least. So I guess I'll simply start by saying that I've found my box that needs smashing." The words tumbled from her mouth so quickly they dragged her breath along with. Clearing the angst from her throat, she took a moment to settle her nerves by allocating a glance to each group member. "And, I'm gonna need all y'all's help to do it."

Nora snorted. "Our help?" she asked, followed by another humorless laugh. "You wouldn't happen to be planning on being inside that box while we're obliterating it, would you?"

If Finley's nerves hadn't already been under siege by her emotions, she might have felt the urge to fight back, or more appropriately, reconsidered saying anything else. Since she had yet to speak a word of it, it wasn't too late to reconsider.

But before Finley had even a moment to rethink things, Burlie-Jean rushed to her rescue. "Hush, child," she shushed Nora while aiming an arched eyebrow at Finley. "I'm kinda interested in what Finley has to say," she said, though the steely look in her gaze held more contempt than curiosity.

Finley knew she had two choices. Keep to her plan, or come up with a less daunting box to smash—one that preferably didn't involve the group. However, since she'd more or less already mentioned needing their help, it looked like option one was the only way to go, and to do so she needed to tread lightly.

"I've decided to start a non-profit," she said as she reached underneath her chair and slipped a display board from the floor. Resting the board on her lap, she unfolded it, exposing a rendering of her garden, complete with a community of renovated slave homes and a freshened up potting shed sporting a sign that read *Office*, along with what used to be Roy's workshop appropriately dubbed, *Work Shop: Sorting and Canning*. "Using my home, orchard, and land, I want to help people. Women, to be specific, who have found themselves alone, and in need of a new start."

Ford squinted across the circle at the board. "'Finley's Garden: Growing Second Chances for Women,'" he read aloud the caption from the bottom of the board. "So, you're planning to let women live and work on your property?"

His question brought a smile to Finley's lips. Quinton had come up with the name for the non-profit. After Josh, he was the first person she'd wanted to tell, and unlike her plan to climb a rock, he'd been overwhelmingly supportive.

"Yes, they'll be working the orchard and cannery," she confirmed. "I'm planning to develop my own brand of peaches to be sold locally, and use the proceeds to provide free room and board to the women while they're getting back on their feet."

"So, you won't be paying them?" asked Ford.

"They'll make minimum wage."

Nora twisted her lips into her usual sneer. "So let me see if I've got this straight," she began. "You're taking in desperate women who obviously have no other options, and forcing them to work your land for nearly nothing?"

Of course Nora would try and spin this into something sinister. Again, Finley fought the urge to become defensive. "That's right," she said, choosing sarcasm instead.

Nora turned her eyes to the ceiling. "What is this, the fourteen hundreds all over again?" she balked. "Has Congress brought back indentured servitude or something?"

Finley could feel more skeptical looks being tossed her way, and she knew if she had any chance of making them see her plan for what it was, she would have to remain calm, decisive, neutral. "No, these women will be free to come and go as they please, so they can look for work and one day leave," she said, using even, measured words. "But while they're getting back on their feet, they'll need to help out a little."

Burlie-Jean leaned forward. "Right, and while they're 'helping out a bit,' they'll be living in what used to be *slave* homes?" She wagged a blood-red fingernail at Finley's rendering.

Finley turned her focus to Burlie-Jean, realizing for the first time how this might look to a person of Black-American descent, and she didn't like the sight of this new perspective one bit. Still, she had to hold her ground, or find a way to command the earth to swallow her whole. Needing a way to disappear was becoming a regular occurrence for her in these meetings. She needed to do something about that, and fast.

"Yes, but we're going to fix them up real nice with a living area, kitchenette, and bathroom." A cold sweat broke out along her hairline. Folding her rendering, she leaned it against her chair. "Why, what's the problem?"

Burlie-Jean's nostrils flared. "The problem is, *Little Missy*—"

"I'll do it," Sue broke in, raising her hand into the air as high as her arm would stretch. Her newly highlighted and styled hair shined and swayed against her neck with the momentum. "I don't care if it's a former slave home or a tent," she dashed on. "And I'll pick peaches and shove them in bottles, or clean your rain gutters. Whatever. It makes no never mind to me."

"Sue, you can't be serious," Nora chided.

Sue turned to Nora with an urgent look. "Why not? I'd have a place of my own—a safe place—while I finish up my training." Her tone turned desperate as she shifted her gaze to Finley. "Miss Finley, will you take me? I won't be a bother." She drew an x over her chest. "Cross my heart."

Having Sue come to work for her had been part of Finley's plan from the beginning, but with all the animosity freezing the air within the circle, she wasn't sure this was the right time to extend that offer.

"We can sure discuss the possibility," she evaded. She needed to win the others over first, but how?

Ford folded his arms, then rested his chin on one fist. "I don't really see what it matters what those little cabins used to be," he said, diplomatically. "It matters what they're going to be used for now. I would think the slaves that once called those four walls home would be glad to know they're being used for good in this century. Poetic justice is what this is."

"It's a lot of things," Burlie-Jean said with a scowl, "but poetic isn't one of 'em."

Careen had been sitting quietly, likely allowing the group time to work out their feelings organically, but apparently she felt a little modification was needed. "All right, I think we're all missing the point here." She waved her hands in the air like a referee. "Finley, why don't you skip to the part where you need everyone's help," she suggested along with a take-no-prisoners look. "But before Finley continues, I think this would be a good time to direct everyone's attention to the chalkboard and goal number four." She pointed to the list of goals and said, "All together now, '*Brimful heart: If one's heart is hollow, one's actions are hollow,*'" to which a handful of voices shuffled along behind.

Finley didn't have to press a hand to the center of her chest to know that the space between her ribs was still empty. Her heart had been hollow for so long, she'd almost grown accustomed to the weight an absence of purpose somehow left behind, and this was when the gravity of what she was doing took the opportunity to truly sink in.

What was she thinking, taking on a project of this magnitude without even a complete heart as her guide? How could she possibly know her own intentions were pure, much less be sure the sacrifices she would be required to make were prudent? But then, maybe that was point. Maybe this project was just what her heart needed to feel full again. Taking chances, enjoying the journey, and now, stepping out of her comfort zone, she'd done them all. If she stayed her course she'd have completed three of the five steps to a new beginning.

Fighting back tears of hope, of joy and anticipation, Finley marched on. "Right, well, while a woman stays at Finley's Garden, she'll be able to participate in group and individual counseling, provided by Careen," she held a hand out to their leader, "as well as job skills training, trade school options, resume writing, and the like. I also want to create a network within the local business community to form a consistently updated list of new career opportunities." Pausing to let all she'd said sink in and start to settle, she allowed the group time for objections. When none came, she continued. "In addition, some of these women might need a little sprucing up in the hair and makeup department. You know, to help them both feel better about themselves and be more presentable to potential employers." She took a breath to steady her nerves before addressing one individual group member directly. Finley was a firm believer in getting the hardest tasks over with first, a rip-the-Band-Aid-off-quick approach to unpleasant situations.

Adjusting her focus to the other side of the circle, she didn't even take a moment to breathe before diving in. Head first. Without a life preserver. "Nora, that's where you come in. You've done such a fine job with Sue here that I'd like to employ you as our resident image consultant. It wouldn't be a full-time position, just on an as-needed basis, but it would give you an additional source of income, and you'd be helping people at the same time," she said, stopping only long enough to tweak her tone a notch to teasing, a touch of humor to tame the angry beast. "Might even sweeten that sour attitude of yours a little."

Nora responded with a bored look. "There's nothing generally wrong with my attitude," she said, pulling the sleeves of her black sweater down over her hands. "It's just that some of the company I'm forced to keep, every now and then, brings out my unsavory side."

Sue circled both hands around Nora's arm and tugged a couple of times. "Come on, Nora," she pled. "Say you will. Say you'll help."

Nora pulled her arm out of Sue's grip, her eyes flitting to Sue with a look that was almost motherly. "Fine," she groaned more than enunciated. "I *might* be open to the idea." She jabbed a finger toward Finley. "*Might.*"

A smile tried to push its way onto Finley's face, but she told it to get lost. Nora would surely retract her "might" if she thought even for a second she'd said something that pleased Finley. "That's good enough for now," she said, allowing no discernable emotion whatsoever. "I'm sure I can find someone else if you decide you're not interested."

Nora watched as her sleeves swallowed her hands again. "I didn't say I wasn't interested, I just said . . ." she muttered, her gaze glancing up long enough to catch the beseeching expression on Sue's face. "Oh, forget it. All right, I'll do it." She sliced Finley a defiant stare. "You happy now?"

An ironic laugh popped from Finley's throat before she could swallow it back. "Happy or completely out of my mind," she said. "But for argument's sake, we'll go with happy."

"What about the rest of us?" Burlie-Jean wanted to know.

Finley adjusted in her seat so she was facing Burlie-Jean straight on. "Funny you should ask because as you know, every business needs a good office manager. Someone with an astute knowledge of accounting and bookkeeping," she said, and then added for effect, "Numbers have never been my strong suit."

Burlie-Jean knotted her arms atop her generous bosom. "Are you offering me a job?"

Her tone had Finley's insides shaking like a Jell-O mold in an earthquake, but she kept her voice steady. "What do you think?" she asked because if it wasn't, she could always rephrase, pretend like hiring Burlie-Jean was in no way a part of her master plan.

"I'm not pickin' no dadgum, worm-infested peaches," Burlie-Jean said by way of acquiesce.

Finley gave her head a shake. "Of course not."

"And the pay?" asked Burlie-Jean.

Finley could barely contain her excitement. First Nora, and now Burlie-Jean was as good as in. "Whatever you made at your last job, plus fifteen percent to start," she said without taking time to consider what that number might be. She'd planned on adding five percent but somehow managed to get caught up in the moment. So, just in case she'd already made her first big mistake, she said a quick prayer that she could afford it.

"Starting when?" Burlie-Jean asked. "I don't have time to pussyfoot around. I got bills to pay."

Finley heard words coming from her mouth, though she had no idea where they were coming from. "That's good because I'll be needing someone by the end of this month, if not sooner." She hadn't planned on making this up as she went along, but with her prospective accountant-slash-office-manager dangling by a thread, what choice did she have?

Burlie-Jean's eyes pulled thin, her head dropping to the side as she *hmm*-ed. "Looks like you've got yourself an office manager."

Finley forced a smile she hoped showed joy rather than insanity. "Happy to have you on board," she said, then turned to the next name on her mental list.

"And Ford." She adjusted her field of vision to him. "I would also like to offer the women a comprehensive course in self-defense. I think with your military background, you'd be perfect for this, and you can put the extra money you'll make toward building that gun safe."

Ford nodded in an amicable fashion. "I'd be happy to oblige in any way I can."

"What about me?" squeaked Sue.

Finley turned to the last group member with a smile. "Every business needs a lovely receptionist, and Burlie-Jean will need an assistant."

Sue rubbed her hands together like she'd gotten into something sticky. "I've never answered telephones before. Well, not all professional-like, anyway," she said, her words coming out all wobbly. "But I can learn. And with that online typing class, I'm getting right fast on the keyboard now too."

Tears bubbled up from the hollow place in Finley's chest. Here it was, the reason she'd been inspired to do this. For women like Sue. "Well, then, looks like I picked the right person for the job," she said, her voice thick with emotion. "And, if you still need a place to stay, you can live onsite as long as you need to. The potting shed, now office, currently has a small living space. It's nothing fancy, but we got the water and electricity working again, so you can move in whenever you'd like."

Sue's gaze hit her lap again. "Thank you, Miss Finley." She sniffed. "You're like an angel dropped from heaven."

Finley beamed with pride.

"Don't go nominating her for sainthood just yet," Burlie-Jean said, darkening the light mood. "How are you planning to pay for all this?"

Squaring her shoulders, Finley fingered away a stray tear. "I'm getting things started with my own money," she said, and when Burlie-Jean's eyes narrowed with skepticism, she hurried to add, "And don't worry, there's plenty to last us for a while." Tearing her gaze from Burlie-Jean's, she addressed the entire group. "But we'll need to start fundraising here real soon. As a matter of fact, I have our first fundraiser planned for the day after Thanksgiving," she added, thinking again about how awkward it had been when she'd stepped into her garden club meeting the other day.

The room had fallen into a silence deeper than the kind one often compared to a pin dropping. In fact, if it were possible for snow to fall indoors, she may have been able to hear a single flake hit the floor. Her dignity put aside for a greater cause, and knowing she needed the help of the women who had long been her friends and support, some for as long as she could remember, she'd groveled and then begged for help. To her pleasant surprise, even with the busy holiday season coming fast, her garden club sisters—yes, even Macy—had come to her aid.

"It's going to be a yard sale and silent auction at my home," she finished.

Nora tucked the orange stripe of hair framing her face behind her ear. "You're planning to fund a project this big on the proceeds from a yard sale?"

Finley ignored the cynicism in Nora's voice and foraged on. "To start, yes. And this isn't just any yard sale. My garden club members are a group of very connected women. We'll be selling some high-end antiques and auctioning off spa treatments, cosmetic procedures, pet grooming, and a car if I can muster the courage to ask my ex-husband," she said, mumbling that last part. Even though a car would bring in a nice chunk of money, with everything she had going on, she was pretty sure she didn't need the added complication of actually seeing her ex face-to-face.

"We're promoting this as a Black Friday yard sale, and last-chance for a charitable donation before the end of the year." Finley swept the group a confident look. "I have no doubt this will be a huge success." Because she was filled with more doubt than confidence, she added, "And this is only

the beginning. Like I said, some of my friends have connections in state and local government as well as in the business
community. There's plenty of money out there if one knows
where to go looking for it."

Questioning looks were shared between the group members,
but no one ventured a comment. Finley kept quiet too, feeling
more than hearing the sound of blood pumping at an alarming
rate through her veins as she waited to see if anyone was going
to back out. She needed this group, needed people who knew
what it was like to find themselves alone without warning and
looking for a fresh start, a new direction. Her plan, her vision,
lined up like a row of dominos, each one of these individuals
being a vital piece. Remove one, and all the work, all the success
she'd had thus far, would hit a standstill. Sure, there were
others out there who could do the work, but she wanted—no,
needed—these people (yes, the very individuals who just so
happened to mostly despise her) for her non-profit to succeed.

Careen turned a frustrated look over the circle. "For a
group of folks who generally have too much to say, y'all are
pretty quiet," she said, then paused, waiting a good fifteen
seconds more before speaking again. "So, what do y'all think?
Are you all-in, or are you all-out?"

Sue said, "I'm all-in. Definitely."

Ford concurred, "Me too."

Burlie-Jean conceded, "Well, since I don't exactly have any
other prospective employers beating down my door, I 'spose
I'm in too. But don't you think for one moment I won't be
keeping an eagle-eye on your books. And if I see a financial
disaster coming, I won't hesitate to take another position
without notice." She sent Finley a severe glare. "We straight?"

Finley choked on the magnitude of what she was agreeing
to. "I u-understand. C-completely," she sputtered before
regaining her voice. "Nora, are you still in?"

"Sure, why not?" She shrugged. "I'll jump on this insanity train with the rest of you freaks. But just so you know, I'm only going along with this because my morbid curiosity wants to stay tuned for the day this cockamamie scheme of Finley's crashes into a burning mass of blood and gore."

Finley blinked the grisly image from her mind. "Duly noted." She opened her arms to the group. "Well then, shall we get started?"

## Chapter 16

Hangers loaded with designer clothes, paintings encased in bubble wrap, antique furniture, and goods that spanned the imagination stretched from wall to wall, filling the living area of Finley's potting shed until she barely had room to side-step from one corner to the other. As she glanced around at all the donations for Finley's Garden, she felt overwhelmed by the outpouring of support. Who knew her garden club sisters would be so quick to forgive her and help out—not to mention, that they were all sitting on a mountain of valuable loot? Like she had so often in the recent past, she pressed a palm to the center of her chest. Only, unlike all the other times, this time she felt something. *Brimful Heart,* she mentally repeated the next goal in her progression. Her heart had been empty for so long, shriveled to half its capacity from insufficient nourishment. But working on Finley's Garden, knowing she would soon be helping women on an individual basis, had been like a well springing up inside her, bringing life to a withered soul and fullness to a cavernous breast.

Securing a price tag to the finger-hold of a Coclough china cup, she carefully replaced it back with the saucer into its specially designed crate. A bonneted Southern belle in a yellow hoop skirt and blue pinafore gazed off into the distance from its glossy surface, bringing an unexpected longing for a simpler time to Finley's overworked bones. As fulfilling as this project had become, it had also compounded her increasingly complicated life.

Setting aside the fact that she hadn't celebrated a holiday without both her kids in eighteen years, and all the depression that accompanied this being the first year in what would undoubtedly be many more, Thanksgiving dinner with her parents and Josh had turned out to be even more awkward than she'd previously dared to imagine. Even though, generally speaking, her concern over what others thought of her and Josh's relationship had dwindled to nothing more than a second thought, the way her folks' tight smiles had come nowhere near touching their eyes, their laughs a bit louder and more shrill than necessary, had clearly indicated that they felt the relationship inappropriate, and that had bothered her more than she wanted to admit. Then, once she and Josh were finally free of her family obligation, he'd asked her to go with him to a friend's house to watch football and play pool. But Finley didn't like to watch football or play pool, and the possibility of enduring more forced conversation and probing stares—being directed at *her* this time—was more than she could bear, which she knew was in no way fair to Josh.

In the few weeks since the tornado and her subsequent epiphany, he'd been her support, cheerleader, and partner. In fact, she was certain that without Josh at her side, her vision would have gone no further than this potting shed, but her relationship with him, nonetheless, remained complicated, to say the least. In other words, one moment she was thanking the powers that be for sending her a most agreeable companion, and the next, she worried that in time, outside of an interest in architecture, they would come to find that they had very little in common.

And so, even though she'd felt horribly ungrateful, she'd declined his invitation, insisting she had too much work left to do for the yard sale tomorrow. Plus, with Sue spending the holiday at Burlie-Jean's, she'd have the place all to herself.

Scootching her way over to the door, the toe of one of her Wellies caught on a couple of stacked boxes that had been shoved under a rolling rack of clothes. She stumbled, knocking the top box to the floor. A football, along with a few framed photos and what looked like a leather-bound journal, spilled to the floor.

"Dang it," Finley swore, this minor inconvenience tipping her from happily exhausted one second to overextended the very next.

Reaching for the ball, she noticed that *State Champions,* along with her high school crest, had been embossed over the nubby outer skin. Upon closer examination, she recognized some of the signatures of Roy's former teammates.

"Where in the world did this come from?" Spinning the box around, she saw that "Roy" had been written in Sharpie on not only the fallen box but the one underneath it as well. He must have forgotten these when he moved out and then they had been shuffled out here while Sue and Burlie-Jean were helping her clean out some of the closets in the main house.

Dropping the ball back to the box, she gathered the frames and journal, stacking them in the crook of her arm. The top picture was one of her and Roy at the senior prom. Faces thin and ruddy with a youthful glow, they both looked so young, so untainted by the heartache and disappointment their future together would soon bring.

The second frame held a photo Roy had taken of Finley

when she was pregnant with Shep. One hand resting atop her rotund belly, she smirked through the camera at the man on the other side as if she could never want anything more. An array of emotions ranging from joy to regret gathered to prick her eyes. Evidently, Roy had kept these photos all these years and had even meant to take them with him when he left.

Curious as to what else had been important enough for him to hold on to, she continued searching the contents of both boxes. There she found some board games, a ratty old teddy bear, a few leather-bound books, newspaper articles highlighting his athletic successes, jerseys, awards, and an array of other random items. In the twenty-plus years of savable memories, these two photos were the only evidence of Finley that had meant enough to Roy for him to keep. Early memories, the ones that bore no resemblance to what their life together, their marriage, had ultimately become.

Had he been just as miserable all those years as she?

Replacing the frames back into the box, she then turned her attention to the journal. She flipped through the first pages, her eyes scanning what equated to nothing more than a record of Roy's impressive high school athletic stats. Football, baseball, and basketball, complete with lists of assists, passes, touchdowns, RBIs, weight gain and losses, goals, and so on and so forth. Her fingers paused mid-flip, however, about halfway through when the endless posturing gave way to actual sentences and paragraphs.

Finley read the first sentence aloud, "Today I met the girl I'm going to marry," the very notion commanding the tiny hairs on her neck and arms to stand at attention. "Her name is Finnie. Funny name. Sometimes I can hardly say it with a straight face. But when she smiles at me—"

"That's private," a voice, husky with a rough edge, reached out from the doorway.

The unexpected presence of another person startled the book from Finley's hands. The journal tumbled through the air, landing spine-down at the squared toe of a man's boot. A piece of wax paper with a flower pressed between the fold dislodged itself from the pages and drifted to the floor.

Finley didn't need to look up to know whose feet occupied those boots. It had been nearly four months since she'd last seem him, which wasn't really all that long, but even if it had been twenty years, she'd have recognized the deep headiness of that voice anywhere. And honestly, she wasn't really all that surprised to see him. Somehow she'd sensed this day was coming for weeks now. Divorce meant the end of a promise, but no legal document could erase one person from another person's life completely. Nor could it stop his boots from finding their way to her shed again, even at the most inopportune of times.

Slowly she raised her eyes to meet his. Steel blue with a mischievous spark, Roy gazed down at her with a look she knew all too well. It was almost as if he were daring her not to find him irresistible. Scanning the breadth of his face, she took in his high cheekbones, growing more pronounced with age, and his dark hair, threaded with a touch more of gray than the last time she'd seen him. Then lastly to the rebellious swath of bangs that no amount of gel could keep from curling over his forehead.

"Why are you sneaking around?" she asked. But more important, "Are Shep and Royanne with you?" she added in a rush as she excitedly searched the patch of yard just beyond his shoulder.

"No, they're still with my mother and daddy, catching up, spending time with the grandparents . . . You know, holiday stuff." Then he gave her his trademark smile—half smirk, half sneer—his sharp features softening around lips that had touched Finley's more times than she cared to count. "I remember the day you gave that flower to me," he said, and even though she was well acquainted with that smile, and thus should be immune to its side effects, she experienced a slight weakening of the knees.

Stooping down, Roy plucked the wax paper from the floor. "You were elbow-deep in dirt, out in the school's greenhouse like always," he reminisced as he held the paper up for a closer look, gazing at the milky outline of a pink daisy. "You tucked this flower through the buttonhole in my polo shirt and said, 'This is the most perfect flower God ever created, and I want you to have it.'"

The instant of weakness that had threatened Finley's knees just seconds earlier reared its ugly head again, but she wouldn't allow it to intimidate her legs into submission. She'd almost forgotten how one hundred percent charming Roy could be when he wanted to. What she hadn't forgotten, however, was how she couldn't give him even the tiniest of hints that anything he said was having an effect on her—physically or otherwise.

"You remember all that, do you?" she asked, cocking an eyebrow in a doubtful fashion. Digging through her brain, she reconstructed the sight of Roy and Macy on her sofa. Holding tight to that repugnant image had gotten her through the divorce, and with any luck, it would get her through his short (fingers crossed) visit here this evening as well.

Roy reached out and fingered a strand of hair that had escaped Finley's clip. "What I remember is how your hair never stayed back in that bandana you used to tie around your head, and how the tips always got stuck in your lip gloss."

The light brush of his fingertips against her cheek raised another string of bumps along her back. Finley stepped back and out of his reach. "Yes, I remember. The day I gave you that flower was the first time you kissed me, blah, blah, blah," she said, hoping her dismissal of his visit to memory lane would squelch any indication that the recounting of their first kiss could possibly have an effect on her. "Again, what are you doing here?"

Roy ignored her question and studied the flower. "Gerber, like the baby food, right?" he said, referring to the type of daisy.

"Something like that," Finley conceded. "I'm surprised you remember."

Roy slipped the flower back between the pages of his journal and snapped the book shut with a *thump*. "What I remember is that those daisies were your favorite."

Finley eyed him a moment, trying to figure out if she believed him or not. "You remember all that, do you?" she asked. "Then why, in all the years we were married, did you insist on giving me roses, and just about every other cliché flower known to the pseudo-romantic, but never once a gerbera daisy?"

The effort Roy put into lifting one shoulder was barely enough to notice. "I suppose I was trying to be original, to show you that I'd put some thought into it," he said. "I wanted my wife to have the very best."

Finley's gaze spun to the ceiling. "Right, I forgot. Everything's about you . . ."

Roy let out a half-cough, half-choking sort of sound. "Ouch, sweetheart," he said, though the wry smile he gave her next held no expression of pain. "You could have just said you wanted something else."

As usual, he was turning this back on her. "Like last Mother's Day," she challenged, "when I asked for a new aerator and you brought me home a *car*?"

A look of genuine surprise joined the smirk on his face. "You were serious about that?" He chuckled. "I guess that explains the layer of dust covering the Porsche. Most women would kill for a husband who brought home extravagant gifts. Hell, if my daddy would have—"

"Well, I'm not most women," Finley lashed back before he could say another word. "And don't you dare go comparing me to *your* momma."

He held his hands up in a show of surrender. "Whoa, I was simply saying that—"

"Roy, just cut the crap and tell me why you're here?"

Leaving his hands raised, Roy moved a half-step closer. "Easy, darlin', you're acting like I'm up to something nefarious."

Finley clenched her fists at her waist. "Well?"

Shaking his head, Roy tossed the journal into one of his boxes, turned for the door, and motioned for her to follow. "Why don't you come with me and I'll show you."

Finley didn't budge. "No way."

Roy beckoned her on with an easy grin. "Come on now, stop acting so suspicious, and just humor me a moment," he said, forcing a sincerity they both knew she wouldn't trust. "If you don't, I might just change my mind about giving it to you."

Mildly curious as to what he could possibly think she would want from him, Finley found herself rather enjoying the feel of being in control for once. "Change it, or don't." She lifted a shoulder to her ear. "What you do with your mind is not *my* problem anymore."

Roy threw his head back and let out a deep laugh. "Good gracious, woman, when did you go and get so darned feisty? Either you come with me willingly, or I'll throw you over my shoulder and tote you out there like the caveman you believe I am. Either way, I got something I want to give you, and you're gonna see it. After that, it's up to you whether you accept it or not."

The idea of Roy throwing her over his shoulder equally excited and repulsed Finley. Holding tight to the repulsion, she leaned over to replace the lids atop his boxes and spoke as if she cared less either way. "What happened to you changing your mind?" she asked. "I like that option. It means we go our separate ways right now and forget you were ever here."

Roy's smile held firm while his eyes twitched like he really didn't know where to go from here, and Finley was pretty sure he didn't. In the past she would have simply indulged him in hopes of getting him out of her way faster. In his mind, her usual response had likely indicated that she enjoyed his annoying surprises, but she was a different person now. No longer the pleaser, the mollifier, she'd become surprisingly unpredictable, or so Josh had affectionately dubbed her.

"Come on. Finnie." Roy wiggled his eyebrows. "We both know you want to."

But this time he was right, and she hated her *new* self for being so dadgum curious. "No, *we* don't, but if it means you'll be on your way, let's get this over with."

Another grin pulling at one side of his mouth, Roy spun through the door and out into the shadows of a setting sun. Finley gathered up his boxes and followed along, the brisk November air stinging her flushed cheeks. As he led her around the house and out to the driveway, she tried—she really did—not to notice the agreeable way his jeans cupped his backside. Or how he still walked with a slight hitch, the same way he and all the other jocks back in high school used to strut across campus.

Glaring character flaws aside, her ex was a fine-looking man. No question.

Once they'd made it to the drive, Roy flourished a hand out to a sleek little royal blue sedan. "Voilà," he said, looking rather pleased with himself.

Dropping the boxes to the gravel drive, Finley scanned the car from bumper to bumper. Mid-priced by her estimation, the car was perfect for a young couple just starting out, or possibly a college kid, and also appeared to be brand new. He'd already given her one car she'd never driven, and their kids both had relatively new cars themselves, so "What is this?" she asked when she'd run out of possible recipients.

Roy looked at her like she was dense or something. "It's for you. For your charity auction."

Finley's eyes swung from Roy to the car and back again. Though she'd considered hitting him up for a donation, she'd decided against it, worried that opening even a professional line of communication with him would further complicate her already overcomplicated life a thousand times over.

"How? What? Why?" she sputtered.

A tricky smile thinned out Roy's lips. "What is it they say about second-guessing a gift horse?" He winked at her. "Don't question, baby doll, just say thank you."

A quick calculation of this car's five-figure price-tag coupled with her rapidly depleting bank account had Finley throwing her arms around his neck before she could stop herself. "Thank you!"

Roy's arms came around her waist, his hug lifting her feet from the ground. "You're very welcome, darlin'," he said into her ear.

His breath on her neck, the way his chest fit against hers, and the spicy scent of his cologne called up a flood of memories. Holidays, birthdays, and milestones both pleasant and then not so much—the former causing considerably more discomfort than the latter—and all of it screaming at her to retreat.

Her heart racing like it had caught fire, she dislodged herself from his grip. "That's more than enough thanks for now," she said, her words falling between labored breaths.

The frequency with which she'd been questioning the divorce lately, along with the stress that accompanied too many changes in a short period of time, had obviously left her feeling vulnerable and craving the familiar. Now was not the time for her to rehash her decision to divorce this man. She had way too many main-courses currently on her plate as it was. Reassessing the divorce would have to wait. It was time for him to leave, but as she grappled for a polite send off, her gaze traveled the driveway where she noticed something amiss.

"Wait, how did you get here?" she asked when the absence of an alternate form of transportation became apparent.

Roy pointed at the sedan. "I drove that. How else?"

Finley's brows rose in suspicion. "How are you getting home?" she was afraid to ask.

Roy stuffed his hands down into the pockets of his jeans. "I guess you'll have to take me."

Finley could see he was doing his best to sound apologetic, but she wasn't buying even an ounce of his humility. "All the way to Franklin? Roy, I don't have time for that," she said, exasperation drawing out her words. "Why don't you ever—"

"Ever what?" he broke in. "Think things all the way through?" he finished her thought like they were sharing an inside joke, but nothing about the last thirty seconds felt humorous to Finley. "You know me . . ." he added.

Finley smacked him with an impassive stare. "Yeah, I know you all right, well enough to know you only want people to think you're a step behind. Folks are easier to blindside that way," she said, finding him not the least bit charming at the moment. Manipulative. Opportunistic. Praying on others' weaknesses. Take your pick, Roy was a master at them all.

Roy dropped his head to the side. "Well then, I guess you shouldn't be acting so surprised that I purposefully stranded myself here so I could steal a little time with my . . . ex on the drive back, now should you?" He gave her that lopsided grin again.

Typical Roy. Here Finley was, on the eve of the most important fundraiser she'd ever hosted, and all he cared about was finagling some of her limited time for his own selfish devices. He didn't care about her or Finley's Garden. He had an agenda, and the fact that she couldn't even venture a guess as to what that agenda might entail ground at her very last nerve. How could she have entertained—even for an instant—the thought that kicking his sorry butt to the curb had been a bad idea?

"Ugh!" Finley growled. "Wait here, I'll get my keys."

⁊℮⁊℮⁊℮

Inside her kitchen, the welcoming scent of fresh coffee, brewed in anticipation of a long evening's work, mixed with spices and freshly baked apples, mercilessly teased Finley's haggard senses. Reaching for her Jeep keys, she cursed Roy for interrupting her solitude, her one chance in too many weeks to spend some time alone, planning, thinking, preparing.

"I'm not riding all the way to Franklin in that dusty old wagon," Roy said, snatching the keys from her hand. Hadn't she told him to wait outside? "We're taking the Porsche." He dropped the Jeep keys into his pocket, lifted the others from the hook, and handed them to her. "I'll give these back to you once we're on the road." He patted his pocket.

An insult started to take shape in Finley's mind but lost steam somewhere between her need to assert her independence and the fact that she was too exhausted at this point to care. "Fine. Whatever it takes to get you outta my kitchen," she said, though it already appeared Roy wasn't going anywhere—yet.

Sniffing the air, he headed straight for the counter next to the oven. "Is my nose deceiving me, or do I smell fresh apple muffins?"

Since she'd never known Roy's keen sense of smell to fail him—ever—especially when it came to baked goods, it was a rhetorical question, so she didn't bother to answer. "Take *one* for the road if you must."

She'd baked the muffins in anticipation of Shep and Royanne's visit and as a thank you to Josh. Only come to find out, Josh didn't actually want any. Not because sweets were bad for him, but because he genuinely didn't like muffins, or desserts of any kind, which was sort of a disappointment to Finley. She loved to bake. With too many muffins and not enough people to eat them, she was planning to take some over to Quinton once she'd finished up in the shed. As with her ex-husband and kids, her neighbor didn't have an aversion to her baking.

Roy took a muffin along with a seat at the counter. "Come on, Finnie, sit a spell," he said as he lifted a mug from the hook, reached over to the coffeemaker, and poured himself a cup. "Have some coffee. Relax." He sat back and began to peel the paper around his muffin. "Let's talk."

Shifting her weight to one foot, Finley knotted her arms at her waist. "Talk about what exactly?"

Roy opened his mouth wide and took a healthy bite. A satisfied smile turned up his lips. "For starters, are you dating anybody?" he asked around his chewing.

The impulse to tell him all about Josh and what a great guy he was while letting slip the fact he was also much younger and quite the catch washed over Finley, but then quickly receded when she realized she had way too much respect for Josh and what they had together to use him as sharpening a tool for her ego.

"That's none of your concern."

Roy slurped his coffee then swallowed with an *ahhh!* "Right, I didn't think so. Guess some things never change," he said like he was some kind of authority on all-things-Finley. "Good 'ole Finnie, always doing for others, never taking any for herself." He lifted the muffin for another bite. "Mother Theresa was celibate too, you know."

A bad taste geysered up from Finley's belly to burn her throat. "You're a pig."

With a swish of his wrist, Roy batted her insult away. "Nah, I just love your cookin', is all." He bit down on the muffin again. "And in case you're wondering, I'm not seeing anyone either."

Finley would have rolled her eyes but it wasn't worth the effort. "I really don't care one way or the other." She checked her watch. It was nearly seven. They needed to get going. A round trip to Franklin would take an hour and a half, even on a light traffic night like the Thanksgiving holiday. The sooner she got this drive over with, and was rid of Roy, the better.

"So, tell me all about this new charity of yours," Roy asked.

Surprise stirred with weariness inside Finley to form a delighted sort of caution. She dropped her wrist and the ticking watch to her side. In all the years they were married, she couldn't recall Roy ever having asked her about her volunteer work. And even if he had, she'd likely have brushed the subject off, so certain he wouldn't be interested. This wasn't the time for wading into the possibilities of what might have been, but a quick dip of her toe to check the temperature couldn't hurt.

"First, it's not a charity, it's a nonprofit, and it's like nothing I've ever done before," she explained as she scrutinized his reaction. Was he truly interested in what she was doing or simply making small talk? Stalling, for reasons only his twisted mind could conceive?

"How so?" Roy asked as he plopped the last of the muffin into his mouth.

Using careful steps, Finley crossed the kitchen and leaned a hip against the counter. "It helps women in transition. I'll be affecting women's lives, making a long-term difference," she said, her excitement mounting. And then as if she couldn't help herself, she went on to explain in tremendous detail the goals of Finley's Garden, and then about the renovation of the slave homes, and how the orchard would help pay for it all. When he continued to seem interested, she pulled out the plans Josh had drawn up along with the logo Royanne had designed for the nonprofit's signature peach brand.

Roy tapped a finger to Royanne's logo. "You could do a lot more with the peach concept than just bottling fruit," he suggested, to which Finley gave him a questioning look. She'd not considered any other possibilities, but then, since the morning she'd first stumbled upon the idea, she'd had more than enough to think about. "Sure, you could design T-shirts and ball caps, make lotions and lip balms, and all in the name of fundraising." He air-quoted the last part.

His suggestions sparked a recollection in Finley's over-tasked brain. "You mean like the lady who started that line of beauty products with her honey?"

Roy turned his palms up. "Why not? And since you have a charity backing yours, consumers will feel like they're helping someone whenever they buy your products *and* feel extra good about spending the money too. It's the most convenient way for folks to feel charitable, and easier than actually doing the work." He tapped his index finger to his temple. "If you're interested, I have a guy over in China who can hook you up, and real cheap too."

An entirely new brand of excitement had Finley tingling all over. Images of her logo silkscreened on hats and T-shirts donned by sassy sorority girls in running shorts and Chacos danced in her head. Then the thought of women slathering peach lotion on their dry skin, and chapstick across their lips added fuel to the untapped potential, growing more vivid by the second in her imagination. "Thanks," she said brightly. "But if I decide to expand my brand, I'd rather use American labor."

Roy shrugged. "Suit yourself. I have a domestic guy I can put you in touch with too."

Evidently, her ex was brimming with contacts. Why hadn't Finley thought to tap his resources sooner? Oh right, because she was keeping away from him, which had seemed like a good idea at the time, but really silly, childish even, when considering the bigger picture.

Roy said, "But you shouldn't sit on this idea too long, the sooner you get products into production, the faster your depleting bank account will refill."

"I'll worry about my money, if you don't mind," she scolded as her brain churned, kicking up new inspiration. "But this does have me thinking. T-shirts, hats, and beauty products along with freshly bottled peaches and maybe a few specialty chocolates *would* make for some real nice gift baskets. We can sell them online, and also donate to other charities for their auctions. Anything to help raise awareness for what we're doing here."

She looked to Roy now, gazing deep into his smiling eyes, and there she saw her life. So much shared history. Sure, she and Roy had never been completely in sync with one another, had never found their groove, but they had raised a family, restored a home, and been a constant in each other's lives for more than two decades. For the first time in a long time, she felt a commonality, a true bond with this man. She wondered again if they could have had this throughout their marriage had she only given him a chance, only tried harder to include him in her life, her interests.

"Now you're thinking like a businesswoman," Roy said, giving her a nod of approval. "I always suspected you had it in you."

"Had what?" Brilliance? Genius? She didn't know what he was talking about, but sensed a compliment coming her way, and a subsequent blush raising on her cheeks.

"A competitive side, a part of you that wants to excel at more than just cooking and gardening. You always tried to pretend like money didn't matter, but it did—it does—even to a do-gooder like you," he said, and just like that, Finley felt as though she'd drawn one too many cards, leaving her holding a losing hand. "Don't look so abashed," he went on. "When it comes right down to it, everyone has a love for a little green"—he rubbed the tips of his thumb and fingers together—"if you know what I mean."

Finley's blush reddened to the shade of offense. "No, I'm sure I do *not.*"

Roy tossed his hands in air. "Fine, keep playing the saint, but you and I both know what a sweet deal this non-profit of yours can become. Of course the first year or so will be lean, but once all your renovations are complete and you're established and the donations start pouring in, you'll be in the black in no time." His gaze found hers with a conspiring glint. "Non-profits, if they're promoted right, can make millions. Take the Shrivers' for example—"

"Making millions is not the point—"

"Hey, how 'bout next year we hold the fundraiser in one of my showrooms?" he suggested like they were still on similar wavelengths. "We can get a country star to perform. Buy a call list. You can have all your residents take a break from the peaches to make phone calls, asking folks to buy tickets to the gala. They can all tell a sob story about how pathetic their life was before Finley's Garden saved them from the streets. It'll be—"

"Stop!" Finley held her hands up. "Just stop."

"What?" Roy questioned, looking affronted. "What did I do?"

*Hmm, where to begin?* "Nothing. Just being yourself, is all." She should have known better than to think he could ever see anything through her eyes, that they could share a vision. They were as different as chalk and cheese, and always would be. "Here, take the Porsche." She tossed the keys onto the counter. "You can drive yourself home."

Roy looked down at the keys as if he'd rather grab a scorpion barehanded. "But, how will I get your car back to you?"

Like Finley cared. "Shep and Royanne will be coming home tomorrow," she said because it was true, and because she didn't have the energy to explain—again—how she was never going to drive that car so he might as well just keep it. "One of them can drive it back."

She turned and started for the shed, hoping he would get her not-so-subtle hint that this conversation, this visit, was over.

"And don't forget your boxes."

Finley was halfway to the shed when she heard the sound of boots gaining on her. She breathed deep, cooling her temper with the crisp air. Of course she didn't think she could get rid of Roy that easily, but a woman could hope, right?

"So are you gonna tell me what I did to make you so mad?" he wanted to know.

Finley spun on her heel and planted her feet firm to the ground. "I don't know, Roy, why don't you tell me?"

"Good golly, woman, I'm not a mind reader." He dragged his fingers through his hair. The curl over his forehead stuck up unicorn-style before slowly falling back into place. "How the heck should I know what set you off?"

Finley spoke through gritted teeth. "Because we were married for over twenty years, that's how."

"Yes, I know," agreed Roy. "And somehow even after all that time, you continue to be a mystery to me." He matched her irritated gaze a beat or so before his began to soften. "That's what I've always loved about you, you know."

Though she was taken aback by his sudden downshift into sentimental mode, something in his voice just now sounded oddly genuine. Still, she'd let her guard down in the kitchen and was determined not to make *that* mistake twice in only a matter of minutes.

"Do you really expect me to believe that you just *love* the fact you don't understand me, that you don't know me—at all?" she questioned, mostly to make sure they were talking about the same thing. "I hate to break it to you, sweetheart, but it's impossible to love a complete stranger."

With an expression she couldn't read—regret, longing maybe?—Roy looked her over a moment or two before saying, "Look, all I know, all I *need* to know, is that every day with you is a new challenge." He smiled at her then, a look of pure admiration. "You're a true one-of-a-kind." He touched his hand to the middle of his chest. "My one-of-a-kind, and the *only* part of my life that was authentic. Something I now know I let go of too easily." With a few strides of his long legs, his boots ate up the gravel separating them. "And that's why, even though I don't always get you, I will always love you."

The ground beneath Finley's feet started to roll, her stomach and heart forming a tangled mess in her chest. After all that had happened, how could he say those things to her and look so sincere while doing so?

"If that's true, then why the other women?" she asked, calling his bluff.

Roy moved closer still, so close she could feel the heat of

his body reaching out to hers. "Over the years, I could feel you slowly slipping away," he said as he tucked a strand of her hair behind her ear. "I was only trying to get your attention. That's all it was, that's all those other women could ever have been to me."

As far back as Finley could recall, she'd never once heard him talk this way. Oh, he'd spoken flattering words to her over the years, but his affection had always felt so . . . hollow. But right here, right now, with him gazing down at her in the silvery moonlight, she felt something pass between them. Almost as if their shared history had formed into a rope, looped around them, and then slipped into a knot, forever tying them to one another. She was unable to imagine a life that didn't include Roy, and at the same time, she couldn't risk going back to him only to find herself trapped in a stagnant marriage all over again. Nor could she risk turning her back on a future wide-open with possibilities.

Straddling a fence with Roy on one side, her newfound freedom on the other, she had no idea which side to place both feet. "I can't . . ." She stepped back.

But Roy wasn't giving up so easily. By all appearances, he knew exactly what side of the fence he belonged on. "Sure you can," he disagreed. "We can." His arms caught her around the waist and pulled her to him. "We can start over," he breathed as his lips came dangerously close to hers.

Her feet itching to run away, it was like she'd mistakenly stepped into quick-drying cement and couldn't manage to move even a centimeter. "No . . ." she whispered, though her resolve grew weaker by the instant. Her lips begged for just a taste of his, hoping that was all it would take to decide, once and for all, if she'd made a mistake, but then a vision of Josh flashed before her eyes. His loyal gaze reminded her of all they'd accomplished together, of the undeniable spark and mutual respect they shared. Roy, so close—too close—and then Josh, both bringing her to a question she hadn't previously thought to ask.

Snapping out of her Roy-induced haze, she pushed with all her might against his chest for distance. "Wait a minute!"

Roy's eyes rounded on her sudden shift in disposition. "What-what's wrong?"

"How did you know I wanted a car for the fundraiser?"

Disregarding her concern, his face softened into a come-hither grin. "What difference does it make?" As if the frosty night air hadn't already swallowed the heat between them, he moved to snake his arms around her again.

Finley put a strong-arm to his chest. "I know you didn't hear about it from anyone at my garden club, and you certainly didn't hear about it from Momma or Skylar. Because if any of them had told you, you'd also know about Josh. So who told you?" she reiterated, though she was starting to have a pretty good idea who'd put him up to this.

Roy sucked in a long breath, then released the air through his nostrils in a fine white mist. "I swore I wouldn't tell, and I don't get what difference it makes anyway."

Finley studied his guarded expression just long enough to see right through it. "It was Cathyanne, wasn't it? And don't you dare lie to me." She jabbed a finger to his chest. "You know I can always tell when you're lying."

He shook his head, his eyes betraying a confidence. "As long as she knows I didn't tell you." He pointed back at her. "You guessed."

"Yeah, I guessed all right," agreed Finley as she took hold of Roy's waistband with one hand and dug into his pocket for her Jeep keys with the other. "Excuse me, but there's someone I need to see."

Then, without another word, she stormed past him, beating a sure path for her garage. She hadn't seen Cathyanne in weeks . . . or was it months? She couldn't recall at the moment. What Finley *did* know was that even though she'd been busy with a new relationship and this non-profit start-up, every time she'd tried to fit in a little time with her best friend, Cathyanne always had a convenient excuse for why they couldn't get together. Well, no more excuses. She'd camp out on Cathyanne's doorstep if she had to. She'd break down the door if it came to that. Either way, they were having a face-to-face conversation about Cathyanne's unwanted interloping whether Cathyanne was willing to have it or not.

"Hey, were are you going?" Roy called after her. "And . . . *who's* Josh?"

## Chapter 17

Jockeying from one foot to the other, Finley danced, trying to keep warm as she beat her knuckles against the cold wood of the door. Without even an awning to protect her from the frigid temperature, the night sky lay over her like a cobalt sheet, poked full of pinholes and stealing every last degree of warmth. She knew it was late, but she was too worked up to go back home. She needed to talk, to make sense of a few things before she could begin to focus again on the yard sale tomorrow, much less catch a few hours of restless sleep.

Her fist poised to begin a new round of knocking; she then pulled back when the door flew open.

"Finnie?"

By way of apology, she held out the plate clutched in her numb fingers. "I know it's late but I brought muffins," she said, her teeth chattering. "Can I come in? I won't stay long. I promise."

Quinton fastened one last button on the wrinkled shirt it appeared he'd grabbed off the floor, closing it over a white tee.

"What's wrong?" he asked as he stepped aside and motioned for Finley to enter.

Finley pressed her lips into a cheerful smile. "What makes you think anything's wrong?"

"Because your right eyebrow always pinches a little when you're upset," he explained as he closed the door behind her. From the recording studio he had set up in the study, she heard the droning of a melancholy tune, which meant he'd been working prior to her intrusion.

"My eyebrow does no such thing," she objected, fully aware, for the first time, of the tiny muscle's pull.

Quinton reached out and took the plate from Finley's shivering hands. "All right, it doesn't." He chuckled as he led her through his mudroom and into the kitchen. "So what brings you to my back doorstep so late on this unseasonably cold holiday night?"

The warmth of Quinton's country kitchen along with his gentle teasing circled Finley like the fluff of a fleece blanket. She took a much-needed breath, then explained, "Hunting down a treacherous, no-good—can't-keep-her-nose-out-of-other-people's-business—offender," as she uncoiled the scarf from around her neck.

Quinton set Finley's plate down on the kitchen peninsula. "What did your momma do now?"

Finley spoke as she unhooked the toggles on her coat. "Not Momma. Cathyanne," she corrected. "But I can't find my ex-best friend anywhere. She's not answering her phone, and her house is as dark as a tomb."

Setting a couple of coffee mugs and a canister of earl gray on the counter, Quinton held out one of the mugs to Finley.

"Yes, thank you," Finley said as she sank down onto one of his stools. "Some tea would be great."

Quinton filled a cast-iron kettle with water and set it on

the stove to heat. "How long has it been since you last saw this *former* best friend of yours?"

Finley exhaled a heavy sigh. "I don't know. A while, I guess," she said, her mind working to recall the exact day she'd last laid eyes on Cathyanne. "I talked to her last week, though. Or was it . . .?" Great, who was the bad friend now? "I can't keep track of time anymore, what with this yard sale and starting up a non-profit . . . But I *do* know we spoke about Finley's Garden and the fundraiser because she sent over some items to donate," she recalled, which also happened to be the same conversation where she'd mentioned asking Roy for a car. "Come to think of it, she sent over some of her most prized possessions, including her complete collection of Chanel handbags, and three of her best cashmere coats—" A few of which Finley had had her eye on. But now that she thought about it, it did seem rather odd that Cathyanne would be so willing to part with items she both used and adored on a regular basis.

And why hadn't she dropped said items off in person?

"Should you be worried?" Quinton asked as he lifted the whistling teapot from the stove and brought it over to the waiting mugs. Steam from the pot rose as he poured, forming a wispy cloud over the scruff on his chin, reaching up to tickle the tousled strands of ochre hair falling over his forehead. Funny how disheveled and sexy can occupy two sides of one very rare coin.

"I don't know, should I be?" Finley considered a moment. "Nah, Cathyanne probably has some new man she doesn't want to tell me about 'cause he's a scoundrel like all the other men she dates. Well, marries, for that matter."

Quinton laughed in agreement as he slid one of the mugs across the counter to Finley. "So what did she do this time to get your underpants all in a wad?"

Finley didn't like it when he referenced her unmention-ables, and he knew it too, but she let it go this time. She had bigger annoyances to contend with at the moment.

Curling her hands around the mug, she allowed the heat permeating the ceramic to further chase her chill away. "Well, for starters," she said, her gaze fixated on the teabag as she began to circle then dip it in and out of the steaming water. Where to begin? All the way back to Tootsie's or should she just skip to Roy?

For reasons currently unknown, she didn't feel comfort-able discussing any of the above with Quinton right now. "I, um, am confused, is all." She dropped her head to the side and shrugged. "It's just that right when I think my life is coming together, and I've figured a few things out, she has to go and . . ." *and make my life more confusing than ever by throwing my ex into the mix?* "Completely trip me up," was the only way she could think to describe her current state of being, and not just with regards to fleshing out her feelings about Josh and Roy.

The look Quinton gave her next conveyed he knew she was holding something back. "Ah, Finnie, I'm sure it's not as bad as all that," he said, then eyed her over the rim of his cup as he sipped.

"Do you think I'm making a huge mistake?" she blurted.

Quinton's eyebrows pulled together. "Mistake?" he echoed. "You might need to be a little more specific."

Finley lifted the mug to her lips but then set it back down without even a taste. "You know, this yard sale and turning my home into a sort of halfway house for divorced women?" she said. "What do I know about running a business, much less one that women will be counting on for survival? Did I *really* take enough time to think it through, to consider what I was getting myself into before leaping with both feet?"

Quinton took a moment to think. "Well, in all the years I've known you, I've never seen you move on something this big, this fast."

A borderline horrified emotion took hold of Finley's heart. "I know," she cried. "What am I thinking?"

He donned the look of a loving older brother attempting to soothe a hysterical younger sister. "Come on now, Finnie." He circled around the island and came to face her. "It's never a mistake to do what you're good at, to do what you were born to do."

Finley blinked up at him through an unexpected onslaught of tears. "I was born to take strangers into my home and take care of them?"

Quinton reached out to finger away a lone tear rolling down Finley's cheek. "Only you know the answer to that question," he said. "What I do know is that people trust you, they look up to you, and why shouldn't they? You're smart, creative, perceptive, and you don't give up on someone even when they're a lost cause." He smiled. "That's what I admire about you. Besides, you've been managing a home, an orchard and garden, all while raising two pretty awesome kids, and doing so with incredible finesse. If anyone can make this non-profit work, it's you."

"But this is a huge financial responsibility," she restated. "And like you said, all I've done my whole adult life is care for others. So now that my kids are grown, shouldn't I go back to college, start a career, do something for myself?" she said, listing all of the usual activities society said a woman in her season of life should reasonably be pursuing.

"Look, Finnie, there are a whole lot of people out there with too many opinions regarding what other people should or should not do with their time. But there's no set course, no ideal that works for everyone. You need to find Finnie's path;

do what works for *you*." He brushed his fingertips across her heart, heightening her awareness of its beating. "And since I was raised in a God-fearing home, I feel compelled to add that you just might have been inspired by a higher power to do this." The left side of his mouth pulled up into an ironic sort-of half smile. "You're doing a good thing, and doing a good thing is by definition . . . well, never a waste of time."

After taking a moment to allow his words to sink in, she considered the possibility that he might be right. She *did* have a talent for nurturing, for loving, and for making things—plants and people alike—grow. And even more important, she loved doing it, loved the feeling that she'd made another person's life better, that she'd made even a tiny slice of the world a more beautiful place. She'd never had a desire to do anything else.

An overwhelming feeling of calm came over her as she took in the twinkle of his gray, tortured-artist eyes, and the adorable way a dimple creased his right cheek when he smiled like that.

"You're a mess, you know that?" she said, and laughed. Well, snorted actually.

He glanced away with a false shyness. "Yeah, I know." He opened his arms to her. "Now get on in here."

Finley didn't have to be asked twice, nor did she hesitate even for an instant before falling into Quinton's embrace. His arms closed around her shoulders and held tight. Pressing her cheek to his chest, she inhaled the pleasing scent of a man who needed no aftershave, a man who sometimes knew her better than she knew herself. How long they'd stood there hugging, she couldn't be sure—far beyond the point of where their closeness should have become awkward, only somehow hadn't—when from the studio, a string of song lyrics caught her attention.

Tuning into the words, she listened . . . *I miss the blue skies.*

*I need a friendly face. I miss the mountains and my friends I left behind. I'll never go back. I burned the bridges that I needed to return to my home . . .*

Finley puzzled, *Why haven't I heard that song before?* Her eyes slid open, her gaze drawn to something across the room. Stacked in neat towers on the coffee table sat a rather large grouping of plastic cases.

Pulling away just enough to get a better look, Finley asked, "Hey, what are those?" and pointed over Quinton's shoulder into the great room that bordered the kitchen.

"Oh, nothing," Quinton dismissed, only there was a pitchiness to his voice that told Finley those little cases were anything but *nothing.* "Just something I've been working on."

Finley dislodged herself from Quinton's arms and stepped quickly around the sofa before he could take hold of her again and slow her up. "Oh my gosh!" she shrieked as her eyes scanned the sepia-washed image of Quinton sitting on a set of weathered brick steps. His guitar rested on his bent knees. Old-fashioned block letters that read, *Yard Sale Memories,* arched over the top of his cowboy hat.

She turned her gaping eyes to face him. "Why didn't you tell me you were putting a new CD together?"

Quinton sauntered over to Finley, a sheepish look in his averted gaze. "I was waiting until tomorrow at the yard sale." He seized the CD from her clutches and carefully replaced it back atop the stack. "I wanted it to be a surprise."

"You know I hate surprises," Finley reminded him as she reached over and snatched the CD for another look.

Quinton reached for it again. "Here, just give it back."

Finley stepped away, holding the CD out of his reach. "So does this mean you're officially going to start touring again?" she asked, both excited and worried for him.

"More or less," he said, bobbing his head from side to side.

"But I'm keeping things low-key this time around with mostly small venues."

He made a move to reclaim the CD.

"I'm so proud of you," Finley gushed as she evaded him by quickly turning away. "But why are you being so secretive?" She pressed the CD to her chest, concealing it beneath both hands.

Quinton must have really wanted that CD bad because he came at her once more, this time wrapping both arms around her from behind and then attempting to grab the case as Finley laughed, squirming like a rogue baby pig.

"Because, if you must know, I'm planning to announce the album's release tomorrow at the yard sale," he explained as he struggled to hold her still long enough to pry his property from her white-knuckled grip. "My publicist lined up a local TV morning show to broadcast the announcement live. I thought it might help bring some more folks out to support your—"

Abruptly, Finley stopped squirming. "What did you say?"

"I'm announcing the release of my CD from your yard sale."

"Tomorrow?"

"Yeah."

"That would mean possibly hundreds of fans showing up to my fundraiser," she mused aloud. Was she prepared for that kind of turnout? Did she have enough food? Enough hot apple cider?

But then . . . with this extra onslaught of Quinton Townes fans, she was sure to make enough money now to get her project started, which would go a long way to stopping up the drain on her dwindling bank account.

"Quinton, you're amazing!" Elated, she threw her arms around his neck. "Thank you, thank you . . ." she was in the process of repeating when she realized something was off. "If all this secrecy is about the announcement tomorrow, then why are you trying so hard to get *this* away from me?" She shook the CD in his face.

Quinton gnawed his lower lip like he wasn't entirely certain how to answer that question. "Because . . ." He reached for the CD, and this time Finley let him take it. "Well, see for yourself." As if made of tissue paper and not plastic, he carefully split the case apart and held it out to her.

Watching as Quinton's nervous gaze refused to meet hers, Finley took the case from his hands. "What's got you looking so weird, all of a sudden?" she wondered aloud as she shifted her focus to the inside of the case. The actual CD mirrored the picture of Quinton on the front fold. But the other side, the stapled paper that concealed all the credits and song lyrics simply showed the name of the album in the same block font as the front. Only here, something had been added.

Written in scrolling letters just beneath *Yard Sale Memories* was the sentiment: *For Finnie, the one person who never gave up on me.*

The air moving through Finley's lungs tripped all over itself. Her already brimming heart felt as though it might burst, causing tears to form, then fall from her eyes. "Q-Quinton, I-I don't know what to say . . ." No one had ever made her feel this appreciated, this loved before. "Y-you didn't have to do this."

Touching a finger to her chin, he lifted her weepy eyes to his. "I know I didn't *have* to," he said, looking down on her as if she were something precious. "I *wanted* to."

What happened next was like a scene straight out of a romance film, the inappropriate sort of scene that Finley generally fast-forwarded through. One second she and Quinton were smiling with mutual adoration. The next they were not so much gazing upon one another with affection as with a strong sense of desire. A kind of yearning that went far beyond anything she'd ever known. Then, she couldn't tell if she'd pressed her lips to Quinton's, or if he'd made the first move. All she knew was that she was kissing him, and he was kissing her back. Not in a brother-sister sort of way either, but more of a sailor-been-lost-at-sea meets desperate-girl-marooned-on-a-deserted-island, eat-drink-and-be-merry-for-tomorrow-we-die variety of kiss. A kiss that brought a whole new definition of delight to Finley's mind, her entire body for that matter, and she knew for certain she'd never—*ever*—been kissed like this before.

That was when, from somewhere in the farthest reaches of her good senses, a voice nudged, saying: *"What about Josh? And that ex-husband you haven't ironed out your feelings for yet?"*

Quinton dropped his hands to her hips and pulled her closer. Like two puzzle pieces, their bodies slid into place, and snapped together—a perfect match.

The urgency between Finley and Quinton soared.

Her head grew light, void, that voice of reason evaporating into nothing but a mangled mass of undecipherable syllables. Before she knew what was happening, hands were touching, feeling, exploring. Fingers fumbled with buttons. Finley's coat slid from her shoulders down to the floor. Quinton's shirt followed close behind. Then Finley's sweater was being tugged over her head, and it hit the floor too, the thin material of her tank top seeming like still too much between them.

"We shouldn't be doing this," Finley half-heartedly objected. Or maybe she just thought she did because at that very instant, Quinton's lips found an X-marks-the-spot kind of place just behind her ear. She gasped, and he kissed the exact place again. The tiny molecules of her skin awoke in celebration, dancing a lively jig—a type of Riverdance to be specific—releasing a sensation that ran all the way to her toes. Hunger, aching, and a total loss of control all cycloned together, consuming her. It felt as though something inside was about to burst forth, an unmanned ship skyrocketing toward a yet-to-be-discovered universe.

"I've wanted you for so long," Quinton mumbled against her lips.

Finley's already racing heart took another victory lap around her chest, but instead of receiving another wave of the checkered flag, her heart was stopped short by that bothersome voice in her head, begging the question: *Meaning because you've loved me from afar all of these years? Or, because you want me the way you "want" all the other women you sleep with and then never see again?*

As if *that* wasn't enough to slow the vortex of raging desire whipping Finley's body, the voice went on to caution, a bit more boldly this time: *If you don't stop this now, there'll be no going back, no time when you and Quinton were just neighbors, and good friends.* No time when Finley hadn't once been an inconsequential face in the parade of women who'd marched into—and then promptly out of—Quinton's bed.

*What self-respecting, Christian mother of two freely places herself into such a tawdry line-up?* the voice accused.

Regrettably, the voice had a point, and so before she'd completely lost the presence of mind to do so, Finley arched back, pushing Quinton away with all of her might.

"What's the matter?" he asked, breathless.

Finley crossed her arms over her heaving chest. "I can't . . ." was all she could manage. It was taking every ounce of willpower to keep her body from flinging itself against him again. Finley had always prided herself as a master of self-control, and though she'd recently come to embrace her spontaneous side, she didn't believe that spontaneity and the forfeit of one's morals went hand in hand.

Forcing in a breath, and then another, she fine-tuned her objection to, "*We* can't do this."

Eyes wide and rimmed in confusion, Quinton stepped through the patch of wood floor she'd put between them. "Why not?" He took her by the waist again and pulled her against him.

Her body still adamantly protesting what her mind had firmly decided, Finley asserted, "Because it's not right, and this isn't me." She shook out of his grip, moving further back. "This isn't us."

Again, Quinton dispelled the air separating them. "Are you sure?" He placed his hands on her shoulders and then slowly traced his fingertips over her collarbones, his thumbs following the line of her jaw. The gentleness of his touch, coupled with the fire in his eyes, laced through Finley like a web of live wires. "It felt pretty right to me. Felt like us."

Though there was no denying that what had just transpired, what was *still* transpiring, between them was beyond amazing, disturbingly so, she couldn't—no, wouldn't—risk losing Quinton's friendship to some cheap one-night stand.

"How can you say that? Nothing about what just happened feels like us," Finley protested. "You're not my boyfriend. We're friends. We don't love each other . . . not like this, anyway."

Quinton's eyes went dark, patronizing. "Come on now, Finnie. Don't you think you're overreacting?"

"Over-re-acting?" she repeated. How could he not see that if they weren't careful, they could ruin a most perfect friendship? And was he mocking her concern as well? "Don't you 'come on now, Finnie' me," she shouted. "Next you're going to say, 'we're both consenting adults.' Or, 'it's just sex.'" She curled her fingers into a set of air-quotes to accompany each platitude. "'What's love got to do with it?'"

Quinton huffed out a humorless laugh. "*No.* I wasn't," he said flatly. "When have you ever know me to be so cliché?"

Was he poking fun now too? "This is not a joke," Finley asserted, and to her complete dismay, felt the burn of angry tears.

Quinton rubbed both palms over the scruff on his cheeks. "Believe me, I know it's no joke," he agreed, though his casual demeanor indicated he didn't feel the same remorse or embarrassment she did. "Look, it's *not* like I—I mean, *we*—planned this. It just sort of happened. Why not relax, see where it goes?"

Finley swallowed back on her flooding array of competing emotions. She'd heard people go on about how wonderful it was to have their lover and best friend be one and the same, but in her experience, those claims were nothing more than fodder for fairytales. Yet, from somewhere deep in her secret heart, she couldn't deny that Cathyanne had been correct in suggesting that Finley had often wondered, *What if Quinton and I . . .*

"To what end?" sped from her mouth before she'd taken the time to fully consider whether or not she wanted to go there.

As if mapping every inch, Quinton's eyes tracked Finley's face. "I don't know," he said, appearing truly perplexed, and a mite frustrated too. "Like I said, I didn't exactly plan for this to happen. But if you're thinking there's a church in our near future, we both know you're yapping up the wrong tree."

The pain of a thousand heartbreaks quaked Finley's chest. What had made her think Quinton might have had even a shred of interest in being her happily-ever-after? What would a man who could have about any woman he desired want with the likes of her?

"First of all, I do not *yap*," she snapped because to show her true feelings, given his, would be completely inappropriate, and because anger was the perfect mask for pain. "Second, I have enough to feel guilty about at the moment without engaging in some sleazy interlude with my playboy neighbor."

Quinton's head snapped back as if she'd slapped him. "Seriously, you're calling *me* a playboy?"

Truth be told, even though Finley rarely saw him with the same woman more than twice, he really didn't keep company with all that many. But still. "When was the last time you had a meaningful relationship with a woman?"

Hurt furrowed his brow. "Finnie, that's not fair," he said and, unfortunately for her temper, she had to agree.

Over the years, he'd vowed more times than Finley cared to mention that he would *never* hurt another person the way he had his wife and family. Just because he'd pledged himself to a life with no emotional ties, what made him think she'd be willing to make the same sacrifice for him? It wasn't fair.

"Exactly," she agreed with gusto. "And I'm not about to become just another face in your string of occasional one-night stands."

Quinton threw his hands in the air. "That's good, because I had no intention of making you one!"

"Fine, then I guess we understand each other," Finley hollered back, immediately realizing she was losing control. She needed to get out of here before she said, or did, anything else she'd come to regret. Digging down deep into her arsenal of good manners, she cooled her temper, turning her words to ice.

"It's time for me to go. I have a big day tomorrow, and I'm not even close to being ready." With shaky hands, she snatched her coat and sweater from the floor, feeling exposed now in just her tank top. "So if you'll excuse me."

Quinton watched in silent contemplation as she stabbed both arms into the sleeves of her coat and closed the toggles over her tank. The sweater, she tucked under her arm.

"Finnie, you can't leave with things all weird and awkward between us," he said, adding an audible breath to his words. "We need to talk."

Finley scanned Quinton from his stormy gaze to the hem of his T-shirt, rumpled and un-tucked from his loosened belt (the work of her desperate fingers, she seemed to remember) and decided he was right.

Summoning up an appeasing smile, she squared her shoulders. "What's there to discuss? Whatever may or may not have happened here tonight is already forgotten," she said with a level of self-control that would have had her mother brimming with pride. "I think we can both agree it was a mistake. Case closed."

Quinton held his response a beat before asking, "Is that the way you want it?"

At the moment, Finley wanted too many things to choose just one. She wanted Quinton's body pressed against hers, his lips on her neck, to feel free to give him whatever he asked. She wanted to not have betrayed Josh with those thoughts. She wanted to go back in time and have stayed at home tonight instead of coming here.

She wanted what she and Quinton would never have again.

Turning for the door, she said decisively, "Of course. It's the right thing to do." And though somewhere in the back of her head a voice screamed *no!* she added, "See you tomorrow then?" as if tonight had been like any other uneventful evening they'd spent together.

In her wake, he mumbled a farewell, equally as civil. "I wouldn't miss it for the world."

## Chapter 18

*E*xhaustion couldn't begin to describe Finley's state of being as she leaned both hands on her kitchen sink for support, taking a quick break before heading back outside to rejoin the swarm of shoppers. From the tension in her neck all the way to the cramp in her baby toe, every muscle in her body ached, twisting into knots she doubted even the massage Josh had promised stood a chance of loosening. It was a good kind of hurt, though. The kind that said, *You've given it your all and deserve to feel proud of your efforts.*

Glancing through her kitchen window, a smile worked its way across her lips. Her garden looked as if it had been overrun by a colony of frenzied ants. Dressed in their winter finest, her guests scurried over a carpet of gold and crimson leaves as if desperate to stock up on last-minute rations before the winter set in. She still wasn't sure whether or not she'd taken on more than she could handle with Finley's Garden, but by the looks of things, the yard sale, at least, appeared to be shaping up quite nicely.

Her eyes slid over to where Josh had parked the car Roy donated. The silent auction had already risen to more than half its retail value. A good thing, to be sure. Next she scanned the tables set up along her garden paths. Once filled with goods, the majority now sat half or completely empty, and it was only a little past noon. As a matter of fact, Ford and Nora had just finished folding the legs on the one that had held Cathyanne's offerings, and were in the process of dragging it out of the way. Too bad Cathyanne wasn't here to see how excited everyone had been over her designer donations. At one point, Finley feared she'd have to break up a fight over a pair of Gucci boots, but the women settled their own dispute with the flip of a coin.

"Cathyanne, where are you?" Finley whispered to the silent walls. After last night's fiasco, she needed her friend more than ever, and not just to yell at this time (well, not *only* to yell at. She was still angry over Roy's unexpected visit) but because she had no one else she trusted to help her make sense of the whole Quinton thing.

Sneaking a peek—as if anyone might see or care—she quickly shifted her gaze to the opposite side of the garden. Underneath the apple arbor, Quinton and his publicist visited with a few of his lingering fans. Images from last night, set on instant replay, had looped relentlessly through her mind all morning, each sequence ending with her walking out and into the cold dark night, alone. In the stark light of a new day, what still hurt more than the fact that she'd felt mortified and rejected, what split her soul like a lightning strike to the chest, was how he hadn't bothered to come after her. What had she been thinking, kissing him like that? Relenting to the secret wishes of her heart?

Then from the corner of her eye, Josh popped into view. His feet had found their way to her doorstep before dawn this morning. From there, he'd not only helped with the heavy lifting and setup but had also been on hand throughout the yard sale to explain the intricate plans for the remodel of Finley's slave homes and outbuildings to any would-be investors.

It had been a long day already for him too, as well as all her other helpers, including her mother and daddy, the rest of her therapy group, and . . . *Skylar*.

Finley's orchard manager appeared at Josh's side. Why she'd shown up, uninvited, was anyone's guess. But by the way she'd been busying around Josh all morning, fetching him coffee, a pen, a snack, whatever his heart desired, her presence had everything to do with stealing whatever time with him she could.

One hand resting on his arm, the curves of her body pressed closer than necessary to his. The notion that the two of them made a lovely couple darted into Finley's head before she could slam a mental door shut against the idea and turn the lock. A wave of jealously washed over her, leaving her drenched in guilt when the feel of Quinton's lips on her neck skittered across her skin. She had no right to be jealous of Skylar. Josh would never be unfaithful to Finley, which, evidentially, was more than she could say for herself. She knew she needed to talk to Josh, to confess all that had transpired between her and Quinton last night and beg for forgiveness—for that matter, she had some explaining to do regarding Roy too—but she hadn't the first idea how to proceed with regards to either one.

What she *did* know, however, was that she couldn't hurt Josh. Even with all the uncertainty she'd been having regarding the longevity of their relationship, she knew she needed him right now, and not just for his skill as a contractor, but because he was the one person who continually pushed her. She never would have come this far, grown this much, without him, and couldn't afford to lose him now.

"There you are." A voice shattered the quiet of her kitchen like a shotgun blast.

Finley whipped around to see Quinton standing mere feet away. As if his presence posed some sort of creditable threat (when it came to her heart, she guessed he did), she gripped the underside of the countertop behind her.

"Good gracious! You like-t'a scared me half to death."

"I'm sorry, I didn't mean . . ." he started to apologize, but then shifted straight to the point. "I want to talk to you about last night."

Finley unlatched her fingers from the counter and smoothed the cashmere sweater she wore along with a plaid skirt, tights, and riding boots. Whether they needed to talk or didn't, right now was not the appropriate time. They'd both acted out of character last night. They'd made a mistake, plain and simple. What would they benefit by reliving a lapse in judgment they both needed to move past?

"Why?" She plucked a nonexistent piece of lint from her skirt. "So you can tell me again, how I'm not good enough for you?" The words seethed from her lips with a calloused edge, and she immediately wished them back. Apparently, the wounds he'd inflicted upon her ego last night ran much deeper than she wanted to admit.

Quinton swung his head from side to side. "That's not what I said." He took a step closer. "The whole thing just caught me off guard, and my words weren't coming out right. That's all."

Refusing to mentally acknowledge how appealing he looked in a turtleneck, wool blazer with elbow patches, and jeans that were worn in all the right places, Finley raised her chin. "Well, whatever you have to say will have to wait. As you can imagine, I'm real busy at the moment." She looked around for the reason she'd come inside in the first place, only now she couldn't remember what it was. "And honestly,

I have no desire to relive any part of last night," she added with certainty—more or less. That kiss would definitely be worth reliving. Thankfully, her flitting gaze landed on a stack of the holiday-themed cups needed to serve the hot cider. *Right!* "So what do you say we just leave last night in the past and move on?" She grabbed a stack of cups in each hand. "Let it go, like they say in my therapy group."

Quinton gave her a serious look. "What if I don't want to . . . let it go?"

Finley started for the door. "Why?" she spared him a glance as she passed. "It was just a silly kiss. A mistake."

Reaching out, he caught her by the arm and pulled her to a stop. "It was a whole lot more than just a kiss, and you know it. And there certainly wasn't anything silly about it."

The feel of his fingers around her arm burned through the layers of clothing separating his flesh from hers, lighting a fire to her cheeks. "Right," she gulped. "B-but we were both under considerable stress. What with me and the yard sale. And you, with the release of your CD. We were just blowing off a little steam. That's all it was."

Quinton eyed her a beat before saying, "And when, *exactly*, have you ever chosen a fit of unbridled passion as a means of blowing off a little steam?"

As usual, his gaze saw straight through her pretense. "That's none of your business." She yanked out of his grip.

Quinton raked his hair into a mass of mangled spikes. "Come on, Finnie," he said, sounding frustrated, "let's not act like I don't know *you* like I would my own—"

"Finley?"

The sound of her name came out of nowhere. She and Quinton shifted their attention across the large island that separated the kitchen from the family room to see Josh standing there, face stricken with chagrin.

*How did he get there without me hearing or seeing? The French doors?* Finley had meant to lock them in order to keep guests from roaming through her house during the yard sale. He must have come in undetected through there. *Stupid! Why didn't I remember to lock those dadgum doors!* But more important than how he came to be standing there was what had he heard or thought he heard?

Panic looped a noose around her throat. "Josh . . ." Finley was barely able to breathe his name as she tossed the cups back to the counter and pushed Quinton out of the way so she could get to him before any improper assumptions could be made.

Josh's suspicious gaze darted between Quinton and Finley. "What were y'all talking about?"

His question started a race between Finley's beating heart and her guilty conscience. Now that she was standing closer, she could see the first etchings of hurt lining his perfect face, and she cursed herself for putting them there. She'd planned on telling him about Quinton, knew the news would be upsetting, but not now, and certainly not like this.

"How long have you been standing there?" She needed to know.

"Long enough."

*Long enough*, Finley repeated in her head. Meaning he'd heard everything from the "whole lot more than a kiss" part, or starting with "unbridled," or maybe just the fact that Quinton knew her like he would his . . . what, exactly? He hadn't finished. A sinking feeling hung heavy on Finley's shoulders. Did it matter what Josh had heard, and what he hadn't? Dissected from every angle, she and Quinton's conversation clearly indicated an alarming degree of inappropriate behavior. There was no easy way to spin kissing or unbridled passion into nothing worth fretting over without sufficient time to choose one's words carefully.

"This isn't as bad as it must have sounded," Finley reassured, the lie slipping from her lips much too easily. "I promise, there's nothing going on between us," she added, which was mostly true. Quinton had turned her away last night, had let her go without a fuss. In all likelihood, today he simply wanted to make sure they could still be friends. "It was just a mistake, a one-time thing, is all . . ." she prattled on.

Josh's eyes rounded on Finley's confession. "When?"

Finley scrambled into backpedal mode. "I don't know. A while ago," she fibbed again. That made two lies in a matter of seconds. She was on a fast track headed straight for hell and still, she couldn't seem to stop the lies from coming. "But like I said, it was nothing."

Quinton joined them in the family room. "I wouldn't consider last night a while ago," he disagreed.

Finley turned to her neighbor to tell him to stay out of this, except a fourth voice, one she knew all too well, joined the fray before she could get a word out.

"Last night?"

In unison, Finley, Josh, and Quinton swiveled toward the kitchen door to see Roy headed straight for them. "You were with *me* last night," he informed the room.

Quinton's mouth fell open. "You were with Roy last night?" he questioned, a frown puckering his lips. "So is that why you were out of sorts when you came to see *me*?"

Josh's befuddled gaze sliced through the other two men, cutting straight to Finley. "Wait a minute," he said, his eyes moving about as if assembling a mental puzzle. "I thought the reason you couldn't hang with me and my friends was because you had *work* to do." He zeroed his focus back in on Finley. "But now it sounds like you had a couple of *hookups* planned instead."

*Ouch!* Finley stepped between Josh and the men who, in this moment, no longer mattered to her. "No, it wasn't like that."

Her eyes pled for understanding. "I-I was working, getting this yard sale ready for today, and then Roy just showed up, unexpected . . . w-with that car. And then he—" He what? Charmed her into thinking they could try again, which was why she'd nearly kissed him? No, she would *not* let that confession slip out. Not without forethought anyway. "He left and then I couldn't find Cathyanne, and I was upset, so I-I went to Quinton's," she said, her sins of omission piling up faster than her outright lies, and both quickly building an unbreachable wall between her and Josh. She pressed her palms together in a show of supplication and added one more stone to the wall. "It was nothing. I promise."

Josh's pained expression hardened to a vacant look. "Let me see if I've got this straight," he began. "Your ex-husband showed up here, out of the blue, with a car he was giving to you, *free*, and somehow that made you *so* upset you were desperate to talk to your best friend. But when you couldn't find her, you ran to your neighbor for comfort instead of calling the man you're supposed to be dating. Then, this morning, you conveniently fail to mention the part where your *ex* dropped the car off in person, alone," he said, exposing each and every unseemly hole in her story.

Finley's panic level rose into the danger zone. "I know that sounds bad, but it wasn't like what you're thinking." She turned to Quinton and Roy for help. "Y'all tell him," she implored, but they both just stood there, eyes rigid, lips locked tight in a mutual refusal to corroborate her denial.

Finley couldn't believe what was happening. The last ten minutes were like living one of those dreams where you suddenly realize you're the only one in the room who forgot to get dressed. Except in this nightmare, you're not just naked, but also desperately trying to communicate, but can't seem to get any words to come out of your mouth. And yet you keep trying, and trying . . .

"Unbelievable!" Josh exclaimed.

Finley spun back around to see that he was in the process of taking a step back. She grabbed both his arms to keep him from walking out. "No, Josh—"

Roy said, "I always knew there was something going on between the two of you." Finley glanced over her shoulder to see him motioning between her and Quinton. "All those years, y'all were carrying on right under my nose. And I'm the one who got labeled the cheating bastard."

Finley let go of Josh with one hand so she could jab a fist to her waist. "Roy, don't be ridiculous," she said. "There was nothing going on between Quinton and me when we were married." She turned back to Josh. "And there's nothing going on between us now." She made mindful eye contact with him before looking to her neighbor. "Quinton, tell him—"

"Momma?" Yet another voice, one she mostly only heard over the phone lines these days, reached out to her in person. "Daddy?" All eyes turned to the kitchen to see that two more bodies had joined the fracas.

Coming through the door, Shep looked handsome, distinguished, with his short, military haircut and pressed slacks, but thinner than usual. The thought that she needed to make sure and feed him well over the remainder of the holiday weekend fluttered across Finley's brain. Royanne followed behind her brother, looking stunning as always. Dressed in an oversized sweater that drooped to expose one milky-white shoulder over a pair of skinny jeans and knee-high boots, her dark hair hung in loose ringlets down her back and around her face, framing that penetrating gaze of hers—the kind of devious glint that implied she knew something no one else did.

Finley's heart turned to stone and dropped to the pit of her stomach. This was not a scene she wanted played out in front of her children. "Shep. Royanne." She forced a motherly smile as she nudged the guys out of the way to get to them. "When did y'all get here?" she asked as she kissed their faces, trying not to think about what *they* might have overheard.

Shep's gaze measured each man in the room. "A minute ago, but we got hung up outside talking with Nana and Papa," he said. "We rode up with Daddy."

"Daddy, huh?" Finley turned to Roy. Now that she thought about it, she couldn't remember having invited *him* here today. "And why *did* you come, exactly?"

Roy's steel-eyed gaze challenged Finley's. "I came to support my wife," he said, emphasizing *wife*. "And to bring you back your car."

"What's he doing with your car?" Josh wanted to know.

Roy's gaze never wavered from Finley's as he said, "I borrowed it *last* night, when I was here, alone, visiting with my wife."

"So, you *were* with your ex last night?" Josh concluded.

With no acceptable answer, given the presence of her children, Finley opened her mouth to say, "How 'bout we finish this conversation later," but Royanne spoke before she could get the first syllable out.

"And who might you be?" she asked as she sashayed over to Josh. Sticking her hand out, she introduced herself, a coy smile curling her pink, glossy lips. "I'm Royanne. I don't believe we've met before."

The pit that had formed in Finley's gut moved into her throat, dragging the contents of her stomach along for the ride. There were no words in the English language—none she could call to mind, anyway—to describe what it felt like to watch one's daughter unwittingly hit on one's boyfriend.

With the help of some precise footwork and a couple of sidesteps, Finley cut her daughter off before any unsupervised handshaking could occur. "I'm sorry. Where are my manners?" she said with a forced politeness. She looked to each of her kids.

"Shep, Royanne, this is . . . Josh." She touched Josh's arm. The familiar feel of his perfectly sculpted muscles called up too many intimate memories, all of which had her unsure of just how to proceed. "He's, um, working with me on this project, on Finley's Garden. He's my contractor, among other . . . *ahem* . . . things."

The look Josh gave Finley next was cold, but he managed a kind smile for Shep and Royanne. "It's nice to finally meet you both." He sent a nod of greeting over to Shep before reaching to shake Royanne's outstretched hand.

"The pleasure's all mine," Royanne demurred.

Josh smiled in return, then promptly dropped Royanne's hand and turned to Finley. "So this is how it's gonna be?" he asked, irritated. "Now, I'm *just* your contractor."

Finley sent him a meaningful look. "Josh, can we please *not* do this right now?" she asked, cringing as she heard what she'd intended to be a decorous request come out sounding more like a bark.

"Momma," Royanne objected. "What's gotten into you?" She bumped Finley out of the way, positioning herself next to Josh. "Why are you being so rude to our guest?"

Subtly, Finley drew in a calming breath before leaning close to whisper in her daughter's ear. "Cut it out, Royanne. He's much too old for you," she quietly cautioned, but not nearly soft enough.

"Are you kidding me?" Josh balked. "If I'm too old for her, what does that make *you* to *me*?"

The pit now lodged in Finley's throat doubled in mass. "It's not the same thing. You and I—" she croaked, but stopped when it became obvious that Josh wasn't interested in entertaining any more of her bogus excuses.

Eyes darting about the kitchen, he took a quick study of Shep and Royanne before moving on to Roy and Quinton. "I see what's going on here," Josh said, his roaming gaze stopping at Finley. "You never told your kids about us. You're embarrassed of me because I'm younger than you. That's why you're running around behind my back with those two." He motioned over to Roy and Quinton.

Josh's flushed cheeks and the humiliation hitching his voice both testified to Finley that she was quickly losing him. A fist full of sand, slipping carelessly through her grasp because she'd mistakenly assumed there was more where that came from. Only as she looked to Quinton first, and then to Roy, she realized that there were no other men like Josh in her life. Loyal. Devoted. Committed. Why had she allowed her doubts, her secret fantasies and second-guesses, to keep her from seeing that she already had the perfect man?

No longer caring who overheard what, she grabbed ahold of his shoulders again. "No, Josh. Believe me," she implored, "I'm not running around with anyone. So could we just drop all this for now? Can we talk later when there's not so many people around? I promise I'll explain everything."

"Wait. A. Minute," Royanne said, drawing out each word. "Are you, and him, you know?" She wagged a finger between her mother and Josh.

Finley's answer came in the form of a guilty look.

"Ew! Momma, but you're, you're like, like . . ." Though she appeared unable to settle on the proper descriptive, what she didn't say was written in the disgust distorting her lovely face. "What's wrong with you?"

"Is it true?" Shep came forward. "Momma, are you dating that man, Josh, and Mr. Quinton, *and* Daddy?" His brow creased, disconcerted. "All at the same time?"

"No," leapt from Finley's mouth before she could stop it.

"No?" Josh, Quinton, and Roy echoed in return.

Finley pulled at the collar of her sweater. Had someone turned up the heat, or had Satan's minions already begun dragging her down to hell? Like she wasn't already there. "Well, yes. I am dating Josh, but there's absolutely nothing going on between me and Mr. Quinton, or me and your daddy." There, she'd come clean, sort of. She'd admitted to her children she was dating a younger man, at least. And honestly, she had no idea how to define her current relationships with either Quinton or Roy, so what more could she have said?

"Seriously?" Quinton hissed, to which Roy chimed in with, "Come on, Finnie, how can you deny what we both felt last night?"

The heat circling Finley surged closer. Her head grew light followed by an incessant ringing in her ears. She pressed the heel of each palm to her temples to still the spinning. *Just breathe.* The ringing abruptly stopped. "This is all just a huge misunderstanding," she was in the process of reiterating when her mother appeared in her periphery.

Her newly remodeled face coupled with the way she'd cinched her alpaca wool coat tight at her trim waist, did, in fact, make her look a good ten years younger.

Gripped between her hands, Adeline held the house phone out to Finley. "Finnie, dear," she sing-songed, "there's a call for you."

Couldn't her mother see that Finley was in the middle of her worst nightmare? "Not now, Momma." She waved her off.

Adeline moved closer, holding the phone out insistent-like. "I'm sorry to interrupt what appears to be a rather untimely discussion, given the public circumstances." She motioned with her eyes over to the French doors. "But you have a phone call."

Finley followed the flutter of her mother's gaze to see Burlie-Jean, Sue, and Nora, along with a vast array of other guests and would-be investors, peering in at the spectacle unfolding on the other side of the glass. A tempest, eerily similar to that of a hissy fit, began to churn, gathering strength inside of Finley. Not only did her children appear appalled by the knowledge that their mother was dating a younger man, but they also assumed she was cheating on that man, and not only with their beloved neighbor and family friend, but with their daddy too. And what was worse, a large part of the people who'd come out on this chilly holiday morning to support her charitable efforts most likely assumed so too!

Saint Finley had fallen from grace again.

"Could you please just take a message?"

"I'm afraid not," Adeline persisted. "You really need to take this call. It's important."

"And what's so important it can't wait for a more *suitable* time?"

"It's Cathyanne," her mother said, gently.

Finley felt a gush of relief. "Finally! Tell her I'll call her back in a minute."

Adeline's head shook slowly from side to side. "No, child. You misunderstand." A grave look clouded her eyes. "This call is not *from* Cathyanne, it's *regarding* Cathyanne."

# Chapter 19

*I'm dying.* Cathyanne had known for the last six months this day was coming. Had thought she'd prepared emotionally, and even spiritually, for the end. Now that her body was slowly shutting down, each breath growing more labored and further from the last, it was evident that no amount of preparation could have made a difference. Alone, she faced a journey into the unknown, one that ended at a destination with no possibility of return. It had been silly, thinking she could have prepared for this. Death wasn't something one could do once, fail at miserably, then dust themselves off and try again. There were no prep classes—not even an instruction book with a title that ended in *for Dummies*—only her list, which looking back had been filled with mostly inconsequential items. The one goal with any real merit regarded Finley, and Cathyanne had yet to place a check mark next to that one.

*Finley.*

Today was the day of Finley's yard sale, and her first real step toward finding happiness. Business had always been Roy's domain while Finley's focus stayed fixed on their home and children, and Cathyanne was proud of her friend for being courageous enough to journey so far outside of her norm. This nonprofit was a huge leap for Finley, and Cathyanne hated that she hadn't been there this morning to cheer her on. Instead she was here where all she could be to Finley was a distraction.

Tethered to her bed by IV drugs on one side and a heart monitor on the other, she'd waited as long as she could before asking the hospice worker to make the call. She wanted so badly to know whether or not Roy had taken the bait she'd dropped him during their impromptu phone conversation a week or so back. Had he gone to see Finley and donated a car? Was Finley still questioning the divorce? Was Josh still in the running for Finley's heart? Lastly, where did Quinton fit into all of this? But all she could do now was wait—and pray that Finley arrived before it was too late.

*Too late . . .*

*I'm ready.* With the fear of the unknown also came the assurance that it was time for Cathyanne to move on. Balance, the one constant thread holding the fractured pieces of this chaotic world together. She was weary and had been for as long as she could remember. Dog-tired at this point from trying to find her place in a society bound by a set of rules that left misfits like herself with nowhere they belonged. She'd endured a life sentence of trudging upstream, every damned day, but had made the best of it. For the most part. Now it was time for her to finally rest. Even if all the religious claims regarding the hereafter were sorely mistaken, if there was nothing beyond this existence, she would, at the very least, ultimately find peace.

Closing her eyes, she sunk deep into the slow, rhythmic *bleep* of the heart monitor, taking comfort in the weight of the pain meds as they coursed a blessed calm through her expiring body.

How long she'd slept before footfalls on the tile floor brought her back from oblivion, she didn't know, but as her eyelids slid up, relief of a more emotional nature poured through her.

Quinton's was the first face she saw, followed by Finley, whom he appeared to be dragging along behind. As expected, the look on Finley's face showed a mixture of disbelief and anger, both of which Cathyanne hoped they could quickly move past. She had some important matters to discuss with Finley before closing her eyes one last time, and given the effort it took to simply pull in one breath, little time to spare.

With a hand resting at either side of Finley's waist, Quinton held her close while muttering what Cathyanne could only guess were words of encouragement against her cheek. Finley gnawed her bottom lip, her fingers gripping the arms of his blazer as if her very existence depended on his. Maybe it was the drugs altering Cathyanne's perspective, but something in the way Finley angled herself toward Quinton, coupled with how his fingers tenderly held her waist, told Cathyanne that there'd been a shift in their relationship.

*Interesting.*

When Quinton turned back to Cathyanne, the smile on his face did nothing to ease the sadness in his eyes as he came close enough to take her hand in his and give it a light squeeze. The calluses on his fingertips from years of guitar playing scraped against her paper-thin skin. She felt as if all her nerve endings had raised to the surface, but no way would she pull back. She wanted to feel while she still could.

"Hey there, beautiful," he said in a reverent tone.

"Hey," she rasped back.

Quinton tossed a glance over his shoulder to where Finley continued to hang back. "We came from the yard sale as soon as we got the call."

"The yard sale," Cathyanne repeated, giving her loopy

mind a moment to reconnect with the here and now. "Right. Was it a success?"

After a slight hesitation, Quinton nodded. "For the most part," he said and then gave her one of his flirtatious winks, the kind that made her stomach tickle. "I believe we sold all of your contributions, at least."

Grateful for a moment of pleasure amidst the pain, Cathyanne smiled. "I hope they went to a good home."

"I'm sure they did," he said, then got real quiet. "How you doin'?"

Tears filled Cathyanne's eyes, flooding her chest with an emotion she couldn't possibly define. How does one describe death? For her, there would be no more sunrises, no new days with hours to fill. No more clients to transform. No marathon shopping trips. She would never again feel the zip of a new boot against her leg, or choose the perfect outfit to go along with them. Never hear the rumble of thunder, or revel in the beauty of an autumn day. No more Christmases. She'd never feel the warmth of a man's chest against her back while he held her through the night. Nor would she feel the cold prick of a snowflake melting on her cheek. She had no legacy to leave behind, no children who bore her name . . .

And yet, somehow it was all okay.

Time to let it go.

She'd loved, laughed, and cried without reservation. She'd made, and kept, one true friend. She'd attacked each new challenge with one hundred percent of her effort. And despite the isolation she'd often felt as a result, she'd never professed anything she didn't believe, hadn't contrived an emotion she couldn't feel. She'd lived life on her own terms.

There was no shame in that. No shame at all.

A smile blossomed through her tears. "No regrets," was her definitive answer.

Quinton grinned back at her with his eyes. "Listen, I'm gonna scoot on outta here. Let you ladies have some time alone."

A tear broke free and rolled across Cathyanne's temple. "Thanks, Quinton."

He squeezed her hand one more time. "My pleasure. You take care now." He leaned in and brushed a kiss across her cheek. "See you on the other side."

Permitting her eyelids to unfold for just a moment, Cathyanne drifted once more into the haze afforded by her pain meds. Dreaming, or possibly not, she looked to heaven with a prayer that this would all be over soon.

Whether it was the drugs or maybe all those claims about seeing a light at the end, she didn't know, but to her complete astonishment, a bright cloud was gathering over her bed. A feeling of unending love and acceptance, of camaraderie and wholeness, spread to the darkest depths of her soul, and she knew she'd finally found the place where she belonged. Turning away from the light, she knew she still had one more thing to do.

When Cathyanne opened her eyes again, she wasn't sure if she'd slept, and if so for how long, but Finley was alone now, and hovering a short distance from the bed.

She gazed at Cathyanne with an unsettling silence.

"Hey, Finnie." Cathyanne did her best to curl her lips into a smile.

"How could you?" was Finley's response.

"What?"

"Don't pretend you don't know what I'm talking about," Finley said, her tone hushed while the undercurrent of her words roared with injustice. "We both know 'innocent' is not a persona you can pull off with any degree of accuracy."

"True," Cathyanne agreed.

"Then why?" Finley reiterated.

"I didn't want everyone telling me I needed to fight," Cathyanne said, which was at least half the reason for her secrecy.

Finley noticeably swallowed. "Since when have you ever backed down from a fight?" she asked, her eyes rimmed in red and shining with emotion.

Tears surged into Cathyanne's eyes too, but she willed them back. "I had one more item on my list, and I needed to be drug-free to accomplish it."

Finley studied Cathyanne a long moment. "I don't suppose that last item had something to do with why my ex-husband showed up on my doorstep the night before the biggest event of my life?" she asked, her voice much too calm for Cathyanne's comfort. "Everything's a mess because of you."

She couldn't begin to imagine what "mess" Finley was referring to, or how it could be all her fault, but then what did it matter? "You were unsure about your feelings for Josh, and rethinking your divorce," Cathyanne explained. "I'm sorry if things got a little . . . messy, but sometimes you have to give life a firm shake so it can resettle into a better place next time."

Slowly, Finley crossed her arms. "So you were somehow doing me a favor?" She turned to gaze out the window.

"Yes."

"You're selfish, Cathyanne," she said, her anger a mere ghost amidst her words. "You always have been and always will be. So don't you dare expect me to believe you kept the truth from me because, in some twisted way, you thought I needed your help. Because of you, Josh is going to break up with me."

The betrayal and sadness in Finley's voice weighed heavy on Cathyanne's struggling heart. "Why?"

"Long story." Finley raised her shoulder. "The only part that matters now is how I'm fairly certain it's over between us." She sounded upset, and then, not so much.

"So, how do you feel about that?"

Finley kept her gaze fixed on the window as she said, "I'm devastated," though she sounded more resigned than ruined.

"Do you think you could ever love him?"

Finley chewed her lip in thought. "I don't know, but I should, shouldn't I?" she said as if she assumed so. "I mean, I'd be crazy not to. Right?"

Fatigue laid itself over Cathyanne. "No, not necessarily, not if he's isn't the right man for you." She struggled to get out each word.

Finley looked to Cathyanne then. "I don't want to talk about this right now," she said, fresh tears collecting in her eyes.

Cathyanne hated herself for dying, for putting her friend through this degree of heartache and loss, but she knew there was no sense in dwelling on what she couldn't change.

"Finnie, I know you have a lot on your mind at the moment, but you have to understand that it will be okay in due time," she said, trying to convey the depth of her faith in all she'd just said, all she was about to say. "All we have is right now. This second. This moment," she said, and for the first time, as Cathyanne stared into the worried eyes of her very best friend, she fully understood what it meant to live this time-honored advice. "We have to live now, Finnie. What do you want, *now*?"

Indignation swam with the tears in Finley's eyes. "For you to get up and walk out of here with me." She pointed at the door.

Cathyanne wanted nothing more than to grant Finley's wish. "We both know that's not possible."

The room fell into a thick silence as Cathyanne struggled to control her breathing under Finley's fretful watch. Then the heart monitor skipped a half-*bleep* followed by a squeezing sensation in her chest, and Cathyanne knew she was running out of time.

"So Quinton, huh?" she said, choking on the words.

Finley's arm dropped back to her side. "I don't want to talk about that either."

Though finding it increasingly difficult to get the words out, Cathyanne wasn't giving up. "Something's different between you two."

Finley turned back toward the window. "It's nothing," she said, gazing off into the afternoon sky. "It was nothing."

Irritation filled Cathyanne with impatience. "It's *not* nothing," she disagreed with as much force as she could muster. "Dish it, Finnie. I'm not getting any less sick." She coughed, and not only for effect. "We're running out of time here."

Finley spun back to Cathyanne. "Don't you dare say that," she demanded with a quiet insistence. "You're going to be just fine."

Cathyanne felt bad for pushing Finley to talk about Quinton at a time like this, but she needed to help her friend while she still could. "What happened, Finnie?"

Finley crossed her arms and turned back to the window. "Things change when friends kiss, I guess."

The bleep of the monitor sped up, a reflection of Cathyanne's racing heart. "You kissed him?"

Finley lifted a shoulder. "That, or he kissed me."

A smile pulled at Cathyanne's lips. "So how was it?"

"What?"

"The kiss."

As if staving off a chill, Finley began to rub her shoulders. Eyes closed, she turned her face to the beam of sun shining through the glass. "Beyond amazing."

Cathyanne wasn't close enough to the window to feel the sun's heat, but her chest warmed all the same. "How so?"

Finley's eyes sparkled with scandal as she uncrossed her arms and came over to the bed. "I've never felt so completely alive in my life," she said—and she had the glow to prove it. "Who knew a kiss could make a woman feel terrified and complete, all at the same time."

A sense of accomplishment soothed Cathyanne's fretful mind. Whether Finley realized it or not, she had found her true love, which meant Cathyanne could finally place a mental checkmark next to the last item on her list.

Peace engulfed her, and Cathyanne wanted more than anything for the light to come back for her, only she knew it couldn't, not quite yet. Her time had come, but she sensed her friend needed her here a little longer.

"I knew Quinton was the one," she said, her voice like sandpaper.

Finley swallowed hard, the movement dragging the elation from her face. "No you didn't," she muttered, "because he's definitely *not* the one."

"Why, what happened?" Cathyanne asked. "I thought you said it was amazing?"

Tears rushed to fill Finley's eyes again. "I did, and kissing Quinton was out of this world, but as it turns out, he doesn't want me."

"Then why is he here, with you, right now?"

Finley laced her fingers together, twisting them one way and then the other. "I guess because Josh is the only person, other than me, with any clue about our plans for Finley's Garden, so he had to stay behind and finish up the yard sale. And Roy needed to stay back to be with Shep and Royanne. They were . . . upset," she said, sniffing as she spoke. "Given the state I was in, no one would let me drive myself, and my nerves would not have held through even a ten-minute car ride with Mother and Daddy. So Quinton was the next logical choice."

Cathyanne placed her cold, shaking hand over Finley's. "Logical choice, or *your* choice?"

Finley's tears formed a prism of confusion over her eyes. "Honestly, I haven't the foggiest idea *what* I want." Turning her palm over, she then pressed her other hand over Cathyanne's, her warmth chasing Cathyanne's chill away.

"And what about Roy?"

Finley rolled her lips together, then let them go. "Jury's still out on that one." She let out a dismal laugh. "One minute I think we could make it work, and the next, I'm thanking my lucky stars I already ended it." She blew out a long breath while consulting the far wall. "I don't know. Maybe this is God's way of telling me I need to be on my own for a while."

"'The brave don't live forever, but the cautious don't live at all,'" Cathyanne recited.

Finley pinched the bridge of her nose between her fingertips. "Cathyanne, I'm in no mood for any of your Zen-master, guru-talk."

The heart monitor hiccupped again. An explosion of fire ripped through Cathyanne's chest. "All right then, but when you think about it, some of our best stories are about things that went terribly wrong," she conceded, barely able to cough up the words.

Finley looked doubtful. "So what you're saying is that, at some point in the future, I'll have a good laugh over this disastrous day?"

"That's what I'm saying," Cathyanne confirmed. "And if not, at least you got to experience true love's first kiss."

Finley touched her fingertips to her lips. "Yeah, I did."

The light that had reached out to Cathyanne earlier began to collect again, gaining strength, suggesting that she didn't have much time left. "Finnie, who's the first person you want to tell when something exciting happens?" she asked, though doing so was using up what little energy she had left. "The one person who has always had a shoulder for you to cry on? Who always has your back?"

One glistening tear tumbled down Finley's cheek. "You."

"Besides me."

Finley shrugged. "Quinton, I guess."

Cathyanne managed a smile. "Amazing kisser and second-best friend."

"But how do you know Quinton's the one?" Finley asked.

"Because I'm dying," was Cathyanne's reply.

A look of helplessness, of desperation, pushed through Finley's tears. "Stop saying that," she cried. "I'm here now. You're going to be just fine."

Cathyanne took one last lingering look at her friend, her sister. She was going to miss Finley more than she could bear, but it was time, and they were both ready to move on. "Yes, you're right, and that's how I know."

The light reached out one final time, threading itself into Cathyanne's soul, conveying to her that she'd done all that had been expected, her friend was no longer in need of her assistance, and that angels had already been dispatched to guide Finley from here.

"Cathyanne? Cathyanne . . ." Finley called out, her words fading to nothing more than a whisper.

Closing her eyes, Cathyanne allowed the light to take her.

"I love you, Finnie . . . Be strong . . ."

# Chapter 20

The gritty smell of dust, mixed with the scent of socks long overdue for a good wash, hit Finley square in the olfactory as she crossed the threshold and then let the gym door ease closed behind her. Normally, the offensive combination would take her a good five minutes to grow accustomed to, but today the odor welcomed her like a pair of worn gardening gloves. Life as she'd known it had been turned on end, the pieces shattered beyond repair, making this room, this group, the only part of her existence she still recognized.

Tucked against the far wall, a fake pine tree had been set up, its bows sparkling with colored lights. She turned away from the merry sight. Like the season had come for everyone but Finley, she didn't have the first inclination to decorate, shop, or even bake.

From the opposite corner, she could hear the echo of Nora's voice. "He wants me to move in with him," she was saying like the idea was crazy, but maybe in a good way. "He thinks he wants to marry me and have babies. Can you guys imagine me living in a house with a white picket fence and a baby on each hip?" When no one responded, she added, "No, really, his house *literally* has a picket fence out front."

Sue spoke up. "Do you love him?"

Nora toyed with her lip ring. "How could I know when I have no idea what real love feels like?" Her gaze glided absently over the group and then beyond, focusing only when she noticed Finley hanging back. The side of her mouth jerked in a devious fashion. "But I bet I know someone who does." She nodded toward the entrance. Bodies and eyes adjusted to follow Nora's gaze. "Since Finley has so many men vying for her affection, I bet *she* can explain what true love feels like."

Careen stood, motioning to the empty chair between her and Burlie-Jean. "Finley, I didn't expect to see you here today," she said, her voice sympathetic.

Finley swallowed against the dry lump in her throat and urged her feet to move forward. *Numb* was the only word she could think of to describe her general state of existence these past few days, her mind deliberately having to instruct even her most visceral movements.

Setting aside the fact that her recovering reputation had suffered another fatal blow, the memory of Cathyanne's face, pale and sullen, her colorless lips cracked and barely able to utter a word, inflicted a pain so unbearable that complete avoidance of all feeling had become Finley's only hope for survival.

Cathyanne was gone and Finley hadn't even known she was sick. Hadn't been there to care for and comfort her friend during her final days. Hadn't had time to prepare for the loss of the closest thing to a sister she'd ever known. Instead, she'd been so focused on her own life that she'd barely given a thought to her friend's persistent absence. Couldn't have been bothered with seeking out the one woman, other than Granny Opaline, who had always been there for her.

How could she ever forgive herself, much less begin to mourn?

As Finley entered the circle, she sent a small smile of recognition over to Sue. She hadn't seen her potting shed's tenant since the day of the yard sale, but there'd been a fresh pot of coffee in the kitchen every morning, and a light meal set out three times a day. Sue's way of letting Finley know she was looking out for her while giving her some much-needed space.

"I honestly had nowhere else to go," Finley openly admitted as she took her seat. "This is the only space in my life right now that doesn't hold any memories of . . ." She didn't say her friend's name, but then she didn't have to, did she? "Now that she's . . . gone, y'all are the only friends I have left."

Immediately upon hearing the news of Cathyanne's passing, all talk of that reputation-annihilating scene at the yard sale had lost its appeal, but Finley knew that once the funeral was over, not only would the conjecture resume, but she would also owe Josh, Roy, and her family some sort of an explanation. At the moment, she couldn't even consider the prospect of repairing all the hurt feelings she'd caused, not to mention restoring her life, her relationships, and her reputation back to normal. Whatever normal looked like these days.

Burlie-Jean placed a plump hand on Finley's knee. "How ya holding up, sweetie?" She too had been an unseen presence on Finley's property over the last few days. By taking it upon herself to begin the allocation of funds from the yard sale to the proper accounts and paying bills, she had given Finley one less thing to worry about.

Finley attempted a smile. "I hardly know." The only thing she knew for sure at the moment was that a full heart hurt a thousand times more when it broke than an empty one could ever imagine. "If it's all right with y'all, I'd rather not talk about the loss of my . . . friend."

Nora perked up. "Hey, how 'bout we discuss that scene in your family room instead? You know, the part where you had three dudes vying for your attention. It was like a love triangle on steroids. Good thing Stephanie Meyer wasn't there to get any bright ideas. A sixth novel with a hunky brooding zombie, or some other forbidden creature, added to the mix would have me puking in my Doc Martins for sure."

"Mmm-m-mm," Burlie-Jean hummed through her full lips. "Why haven't you ever mentioned how mysteriously handsome your ex-husband is?" she asked, quivering as if being tickled. "With those see-all eyes and that gravely voice, every time he uttered a syllable, my lady parts got all tingly."

"Burlie-Jean," Ford cautioned.

"Don't give *me* that look," she scolded with attitude. "Just 'cause I haven't used 'em in a while don't mean they forgot how to work. Besides, I was just tryin' to lighten the mood a little."

Nora's top lip twisted in disgust. "An-y-way," she cut in, "back to Finley and her plethora of men." She wagged her eyebrows at Finley. "Which hunk's shoulder gets the privilege of having you cry all over it?"

The room fell silent as the group's focus turned back to Finley.

"Nora," Careen said, "given all that Finley has been through, I really don't think now is the right time for this particular discussion."

"Why not?" Nora turned her palms up in contrived innocence. "Finley said she didn't want to talk about her friend, so I was just trying to—"

"None of them," Finley said before any further reference to Cathyanne could be made. Her mounting grief, and all the stupefaction that had come along with, was making her brain feel like a pressure cooker set on high and left too long unattended. "I don't even know why any of them were so insistent on wanting me in the first place," she added to further steer the topic away from what she couldn't bear to discuss.

The space between Careen's eyebrows puckered. "What do you mean?"

Did Finley really have to spell it out? "I'm not one of *those* women," she said.

Sue looked confused. "What women?"

Evidentially, Finley did. "You know, glamorous. The kind men fawn over," she explained. "So why me? I don't like to get dressed up. Eight months out of the year I have dirt stains under my fingernails. Sometimes I even wear the same outfit two days in a row, you know, if it's still clean. Why waste time putting together another outfit or washing what's not dirty? Not that I don't appreciate the finer things in life." She glanced down at her two-hundred-dollar Mephisto Odaly handmade loafers. Comfortable and classic, but not flashy, "I'm just not *that* kind of woman."

Nora's eyes spun to the rafters. "Obviously," she disagreed.

But her sarcasm was lost on Finley as she idly continued. "I suspect the only reason Roy and Quinton ever had an interest in me in the first place is because they met me when they were both a nobody—Roy, back in high school, and Quinton after he'd hit rock-bottom," she said, her jumbled thoughts taking advantage of her weakened condition, freeing themselves while they had the chance. "In fact, I'd bet my granny Opaline's antique china that if I were to meet either one of them for the first time tonight that neither of them would give me a second look," she went on, her rambling kicking up the memory of finding Roy's boxes and journal. "And knowing how competitive Roy is, the *only* reason he wants me at all is because he thinks someone else does. For him, it's all about the thrill of the chase, the challenge."

Ford leaned in. "What about Josh?"

Guilt crushed Finley's heart all over again. "Josh likes to fix things. Old things. And obviously I'm old," she sighed, "and broken."

The room went still once more. Finley kept her gaze fixed on her wringing hands. She hadn't come here today to talk about herself. She'd come to get her mind off a loss she couldn't seem to make sense of, hoping, in the very least, that focusing on others for an hour or so might offer her some grounding. But once again, the spotlight had been directed on her. And why not? As pathetic as some of these people's lives were, hers had become pathologically so.

"How 'bout we add a little levity to this pity party," Nora suggested. "Just for fun, let's say that Josh, Roy, and Quinton all *do* want you, and that you're the only one in this gym who thinks they don't?"

"Where are you going with this?" Careen asked, the look on her face one part caution, the other part interest.

Nora hopped up from her seat, giant-stepped over to the chalkboard, and rolled it closer. Eraser in hand, she began smearing the group goals from the top half of the board. "Let's make a pros-cons list," she suggested, a deviant sort of excitement in her voice. She turned back to the group, her sharp gaze scanning the tentative eyes, encouraging everyone to agree. "Oh, come on y'all. It'll be fun."

"Finley?" Careen asked. "It seems to me like you've already begun to process what happened at the yard sale, and that maybe you came here today not only to escape facing the pain of your friend's passing but also to make sense of a few other things. Would it be okay if the group went along with Nora's suggestion? It might help you process a little further."

Normally, something like this would have made Finley beyond uncomfortable, but today, given her general lack of feeling, she simply didn't care. Let Nora have her fun at Finley's expense. A pros-cons list didn't matter either way—and for two reasons. First, when all was said and done, Finley doubted any of those men would still want her. Second, regardless of whether any of them genuinely wanted her or not, she'd already made up her mind to be on her own for a while. Since no one else appeared the least bit interested in discussing his or her own life-dilemmas, better this than dwelling on her grief. If, by chance, this little game of Nora's *did* help her make sense of that yard sale disaster, she might have a prayer at restoring equilibrium to at least one part of her upturned life.

"Fine," Finley conceded. "If you must."

Nora pumped a fist in the air. "Yes!" Then she set to work writing each man's name along the top of the board. Underneath each name, she wrote, "Pro" and "Con."

As she worked, Finley's eyes kept drifting over to Quinton's name, thinking how he, technically, shouldn't be up there. He'd more or less already made his feelings clear the night they'd kissed. Sure, he'd been more than supportive at the hospice center, both prior to and immediately following Cathyanne's passing, but Finley hadn't seen or talked to him since. Only, now that she thought about it, she did have a vague recollection that having the man who'd rejected her the night before holding her in his arms again, safe and protected, had only made her feel worse. Desperately so. Consequently, she'd pushed him away, telling him to stay out of her life, that she didn't need the likes of him, and may have even sworn at him in the process. Yeah, that just might have something to do with his chronic absence.

"Okay," Nora began, a white stick of chalk pinched between her fingertips, "what trait do we want to compare first?"

Sue raised her hand. "Hotness," she offered. "Quinton gets a pro check for that."

"Hotness," Nora repeated as she chalked the word on the left side of the board, and added a check in Quinton's pro column.

Ford cleared his throat. "Am I expected to weigh in on this? Because I'm not really comfortable rating another men on his level of hotness."

Ignoring Ford's concerns, Burlie-Jean leaned around him to send Sue a grimace. "You be trippin' if you think that grungy cowboy gets a check for hotness," she strongly disagreed. "My vote goes to the ex-husband."

Nora placed a check in Roy's pro column while asking, "Anyone going to weigh in on the trainer?" She turned back to the group. "Personally, I'd give him a con. The muscle-man type gives me a twitch, and not in a good way." She pressed the chalk to the board under Josh's con column.

"Well now, that's hardly fair," Ford said. "The trainer is the only one who actually deserves a pro check." All eyes swung to him, blinking in disbelief. "What? He's fit and strong. He's the one mostly likely capable of fending off a credible threat. If that's not 'hot,' I don't know what is."

One of Nora's eyebrows arched at Ford and held a beat. "Okeydokey," she said and moved the chalk from Josh's con column to his pro. "What's next?"

Sue's hand went up again. "Oh, I know," she said in a rush. "Is he rich? That's *real* important. Next time around, I'm looking for a man with money, and lots of it."

"You can say that again," Burlie-Jean chimed in. "Rich *and* handsome. Give that ex of Finley's another pro check."

Careen waved her arms in the air, time-out style. "I'm gonna have to stop y'all right here," she said with a touch of exasperation. "Not that this little exercise isn't giving me some valuable insight into what *additional* topics I need to incorporate into future discussions, but I'm afraid I must intervene before this goes any further."

Nora sent Careen a bored look. "Okay, what qualities do *you* suggest we score them on?"

Careen held up a hand, lifting a tiny finger to go along with each trait. "Well, for starters, how 'bout attraction instead of hotness, and financial stability-slash-hardworking instead of rich. Then there's supportive, shared interests, friendship, sexual chemistry, and love, just to name a few." She eyed each member individually. "And I really think y'all need to give Finley a chance to weigh in on these."

Huffing a subtle groan, Nora spun back to the board and added Careen's options to the list. As the group began to debate the new list, this time occasionally asking for Finley's opinion, she noticed how Josh and Quinton continued to receive one pro checkmark after the other, whereas, Roy appeared to be severely lacking in the supportive, shared interest and friendship categories—no surprise there.

Like Quinton, Josh had received a pro check in the friend category, though Finley wasn't sure if she considered him a friend in the same way she did Quinton. Whether it was because of their age difference and consequential generation gap, she couldn't be sure, but she knew Josh would never understand her the way Quinton always seemed to. And though Josh and Quinton had received mostly pros, neither one of them had given her the two most precious gifts of her life—Shep and Royanne. Her and Roy's shared history, their family, had to count for something beyond what he lacked in other areas . . .

In other words, and hypothetically speaking of course, she was no closer to knowing which man best suited her. Or why any of them had, for lack of a better word, been fighting over her. But if she were pressed to pick the one that stood out from the rest, it would have to be Quinton. Ironically, the only one she knew wouldn't choose her back.

Nora circled the final quality. "Love?" She directed the word to Finley, asking a question Finley was now keenly aware she couldn't answer either. The possibility that she could have three men in her life at one time, clearly indicated she had no idea what the word meant.

Voices from the group began to debate the question while Finley's mind wandered back to Cathyanne. Weak and withering, "Quinton is the one," she'd insisted with her last breath. How could she have said something like that about the one man who clearly didn't want more than friendship from Finley, and then close her eyes forever, leaving Finley with no way of figuring out what to do next?

Cathyanne had secretly meddled in Finley's life, turned everything askew, claiming somehow to have done it all for Finley's own good. What kind of person does something like that to a friend, then abruptly dies? It wasn't fair.

*None* of this was fair!

Finley's enraged gaze narrowed on the board, searing each quality from the top of the board to the bottom, and then further down to where Nora had neglected to erase the last of the goals that had previously been scrawled there.

Below where Nora had written *Love*, step five in the group's progression, *Let-it-go: Leave the past, live the future,* sat undisturbed.

Finley mentally repeated the idiom, each word adding a degree to her fury. "What does 'let-it-go' mean anyway?" she asked, disrupting the steady current of the group's debate. "Shouldn't we hold onto the important things in life? Shouldn't we fight for what we want?" she practically shrieked. "Take living, for example. Isn't it wrong to just let go, to refuse to fight, to die and leave the people who love you behind? What if those people need you?" She clenched her fists hard, turning her knuckles to white. "What then, huh?"

Careen rolled her lips together, steadying Finley with an unblinking stare. "When it comes to let-it-go, there are many different ways of going about it," she said, carefully assuming her calm, collected therapist voice. "Depending on the situation, an individual might need to let go of hurt feelings in order to heal emotionally. Another person might need to let go of thinking they always have to be in control, turning certain outcomes over to God, for example. Then there's letting go of the ones we love, like a child, so they can grow by making their own decisions and learning from consequences." She paused. "What's most important for this particular group is that we learn to leave past mistakes behind and look forward to making better life choices in the future."

Her derisive mind having a difficult time absorbing any of Careen's psycho mumbo-jumbo, Finley shot back with, "But we can't just pitch everything we care about into the wind, not giving a darn where it lands." She swished her hands in the air. "Sometimes we have to hold on to the things that matter. So how are any of us supposed to know what to let go and what to hold tight?"

Careen adjusted in her seat, sitting a bit taller, erect. "I hear what you're saying and I get your confusion, but let me ask you this." She looked square into Finley's eyes. "What is hope?" She held Finley's gaze a moment or two before throwing the question out to the group in general. "I would like everyone to answer," she instructed. "What is hope?"

Nora retook her seat. "Positive energy," she said with a shrug.

Careen nodded, then looked to Ford for his answer.

He tossed a pensive look to the ceiling. "Believing that no matter what, everything will be as it should be, will work out for the best."

Burlie-Jean rushed to add, "Yeah, that's right, because God rules this earth, and *He* would never lead us astray. If we succumb to his will, when this wretched life is over, we'll join Him in paradise."

A shy smile brightened Sue's face. "I think hope is like making a wish."

Pride shined through Careen's pebble-eyed gaze as she took stock of her followers, one at a time, on her way to the last group member. "Finley?"

Part of Finley wanted to offer up an acceptable answer to go along with everyone else's, but when the other part, the bigger part, thought about hope, all she came up with was . . . disappointment.

She'd hoped that by attending these meetings and incorporating the steps into her life—meaning, dating Josh, giving Roy another chance, and risking her financial future on Finley's Garden—her heart would become whole again. And it had, which, as it turned out, wasn't necessarily a good thing.

Because of her full heart, she'd let loose her secret hope regarding Quinton, and that mistake had led to a most embarrassing scene, and more likely than not, had ruined both her chance at obtaining the financial backing she needed and the only real friendship she might have had left after losing Cathyanne.

*Cathyanne.*

Even as she lay struggling for breath, Finley had hoped with every ounce of her being that a miracle would keep her friend on this earth just a little longer. That God wouldn't take the last person Finley could count on, right at the moment she'd needed that person the most.

So what good was *hope* anyway?

Finley shook her head, the eruption of bitterness adding a nip to her words. "In my experience, *hope* is nothing but a big, *fat* waste of time."

Careen narrowed her focus in on Finley. "I'm not surprised with all you've been through here lately that hope is a difficult concept to swallow," she said with genuine empathy. "But I'm sure with time, and healing, you'll come to understand the value of hope, and that hope . . . *is* . . . the ability to let go."

With Finley's life spiraling out of control, how could Careen expect her to just let go? If she did, what would stop the vortex from sucking her all the way down?

*No!*

If there was any chance of restoring her reputation, of mending the relationships that had been ripped apart by her cavalier behavior, she needed to fight, to hold tight to what dignity she had left.

If only she could remember how . . .

# Chapter 21

With the exception of an occasional scratch from a barren tree branch against one of the stained-glass windows, the quaint, gothic-style chapel sat tomb quiet while Finley gathered her notecards from the podium and tucked the stack into her suit pocket. Unshed tears formed a chain around her throat as she made her way back down to the congregation where her mother caught her eye with a nod of approval. Given the disreputable events of her recent past, Finley had donned a mask of contrition this morning, wearing the illusion of appropriate sorrow with precision, making her mother proud.

Many of the same family friends and would-be benefactors who'd attended the yard sale and were thus privy to her second round of public undoing were also in attendance here today. Cathyanne was gone, her friendship with Quinton ruined, but Finley's Garden could still be saved, and to do so, she needed to repair her damaged reputation. Therefore, in the spirit of self-preservation, Finley had kept her words light but eloquent as she'd spoken of Cathyanne's illustrious career, her impeccable dress, and her attention to detail with regards to everything from matching shoes, belts, and purses, to her artfully color-coordinated garden. Highlighting Cathyanne's unique ability to see the world in a way most people could never imagine—exacerbated by a general lack of social filter—Finley had even been so bold as to ask for a show of hands from those whom Cathyanne had unwittingly offended over the years.

Rounding out her eulogy, she'd planned to allow a few tears to fall while thanking all those who had assisted the family during their time of need. Only none had come.

Retaking her seat between Josh and Royanne, Finley sat stick-straight, not wanting to be touched, not wanting to feel. Over the last few days, the numbness that had given way to resentment at her group meeting had now somehow morphed into a surreal-like state. Like the retelling of a dream, her existence made sense only as long as she didn't try to explain it, and so she hadn't. She'd simply kept moving, going through the motions, holding tight to her portrayal of the sympathetic, grieving friend, which in all honesty, she was—or wanted to be. If only she could forgive Cathyanne for keeping the truth from her, for dying without warning, and in doing so, leaving Finley with a trail of fractured relationships in her wake.

Unable or unwilling to clue into Finley's need for distance, Josh circled his strong arm around her shoulders. As if the scene at the yard sale had never occurred, he'd been a constant at her side throughout the planning of the funeral. Seeing to details like chairs and parking, he'd quietly handled what both Finley and Cathyanne's family had found too tedious to bear.

Skylar had conveniently perched herself on Josh's other side. First the yard sale and now Cathyanne's funeral. Finley didn't know if she should admire or begrudge Skylar for her shameless tenacity in pursuit of what she wanted. Next to Royanne sat Shep, followed by a brooding Roy. Roy had asserted his right as husband-once-upon-a-time to be near Finley's side today, but had he been present to lend a hand with the funeral, even a little, as Josh had done? Since Finley's ex had never been one to handle emotionally charged situations with any degree of maturity, the answer to that question, and to why he was sitting two seats removed from Finley, was painfully obvious. With her kids bookended between her ex-husband and one of his ex-mistresses, her new squeeze sandwiched in between, Finley could only imagine the innuendo drifting from ear to ear throughout the sanctuary.

The scandalous whisperings were sure to negate her carefully calculated efforts at rebranding her tattered reputation. Just another sequence in a growing downward trend she was becoming all too familiar with. She was in the process of considering this when a previously undiscovered notion occurred to her. What if, subconsciously, these last few months she'd been undermining her own efforts at recapturing her perfect image? Could it be, deep down, she didn't want to be *that* person anymore?

Except Finley couldn't think about any of this right now.

The pastor had just invited Quinton Townes to the stand.

Since she'd told him to stay away, Quinton hadn't approached Finley, of course, but somewhere during this last week, he'd offered to perform a tribute at the funeral.

Closing out the sight of the man whose kiss she couldn't seem to stop reliving, over and over again, Finley inhaled, breathing in the sweet scent of fresh-cut flowers. Per Cathyanne's request, the turn of the century Episcopal Church had been festooned in white lilies, gardenias, and orbed hydrangeas, with red poppies dotting the sea of white. Against a backdrop of gray stone walls, the contrast created a sight that was truly breathtaking, truly Cathyanne.

Josh tightened his grip on Finley's shoulder. The pressure translated into the probing sting of a thousand needles. Her eyes flew open to see Quinton sliding onto the piano bench. Seeing him—and knowing that nothing would ever be the same between them again—twisted like two strong hands wringing out her heart. She shifted her gaze away, her focus falling on the casket that sat just beneath the stand.

Encased in billows of ivory silk, Cathyanne lay still, her hands stacked atop a chiffon gown made of the palest blue Finley had ever seen. Her blonde hair shined in the mid-morning sunlight, framing her beautiful face in soft, golden waves that rolled over her shoulders before fanning out across her chest and arms. Her skin, subtly tinted to a pale honey brown, and her cheeks and lips highlighted in pink, looked more alive in death than it had the day she'd drawn her last breath. Finley half-expected her friend to sit up and say, "Just kidding. I'm not dead," laughing at how she'd pulled the sickest prank of all, making reality all the more disheartening. How could Finley accept that her friend was gone and never coming back when the empty vessel before her appeared to possess Cathyanne's vibrant spirit, same as always? When so much between them had been left unsaid?

Plunking out a few cords while the fiddle player accompanying him fine-tuned her instrument, Quinton leaned into the mike. "The first time I met Cathyanne, I'd just finished throwing up the sordid array of self-destruction I'd washed down with a pint of tequila the night before," he began. "Finnie was folding me into the backseat of her Wagoneer, taking me back to rehab again, when Cathyanne looks me up and down, and says, 'How long have you been wearing those blue-jeans, cowboy? Cause I haven't seen anyone sporting a pair of five-O-ones with any degree of seriousness since about the early nineties.' Then she slides a business card into the front pocket of my puke-stained shirt and adds, 'How 'bout once they spring you, you and I go shopping, see if we can't fast-forward you into the twenty-first century.'"

He finessed a few more keys and said, "Scout's honor." He chuckled. "Here I am, a pathetic has-been, still drunk and high from a night of doing heaven only knows what, and she's giving me a hard time about my outdated apparel? I shouldn't admit this, especially in church, but that's when I look down at my jeans, and for the life of me, I can't recollect where in the *hell* they came from. All I know is"—he pressed his lips to the mike and lowered his voice—"they aren't mine . . ."

Quinton got real quiet then, his gaze transfixed on the keys as he softly played a melancholy tune. "It's the strangest thing, but that was when I knew, *knew,* I needed to get sober. Once and for all." He noticeably swallowed. "So, I wrote this song for one of the women responsible for helping get me to where I am today." He threw a glance over to Cathyanne's mother and sisters. "She was a true one-of-a-kind."

The rawness of his story hit Finley like a bucket of ice water. Where it had taken her card after card of notes to speak of the woman who had been like a sister to her, he'd captured the true essence of Cathyanne with only a few honest, arguably inappropriate, words. As if it were yesterday, she could remember the retched smell of alcohol and vomit, the dark circles clouding the sparkle from his eyes, and how she'd scolded Cathyanne for her insensitivity. Only now that she was seeing the scene through Quinton's eyes, did she realize that by Cathyanne speaking her mind, making some random comment only she would think to say, Quinton had been able to turn his life around. When all was said and done, was it really all that important to be *so* concerned all of the time with saying and doing the "right" things? How many opportunities to truly impact another person's life had

Finley missed over the years by holding too tight to social correctness?

Shaking his hair away from his face, Quinton's light touch moved the keys, filling the sanctuary with a doleful melody. And then he sang, "Don't it seem like the whole world can change in a minute? Like some tragic old movie but you're starring in it . . . You made plans for someday, just knew that they'd come, your whole world just shattered, they're coming undone. You sit through the funeral, choke back the tears, numb to it all 'til you hear . . ." The fiddle joined in, the bow pulling over the strings in slow, heartrending sweeps as Quinton moved into the chorus. "Live your life with no regrets . . . Seize each day like it's the last one that you'll get. Don't wait for tomorrow or some second chance, to tell her you love her, or cut in and dance. Live your life with no regrets . . ."

The noose of tears around Finley's throat lengthened, tightened, and pulled. He'd taken two of Cathyanne's final words and built a song around them. A song that also mirrored Finley's inner turmoil with such exactness it was like he'd crawled into her head and taken note of her deepest sorrows.

Finley wanted to run, to escape the emotions threatening to unravel her, but as much as she wanted to get away from the song and the pain it was causing, she knew she needed to keep listening.

". . . It's a beautiful spring day but you can't see it," Quinton sang on. "The whole world seems gray because she isn't in it. Then her plans for someday come running on back. You know that your life needs to get back on track. And there she is . . . saying . . . Live your life like I did . . . Live your life with no regrets . . ."

With each word, Quinton took Finley back to that dreadful day, and for the first time made it all real. The surreal veil that had shadowed Finley the last few days began to lift, casting her guilt in a blinding clarity.

Starting with that frightful scene at the yard sale, and then on to the hospice center, and how Finley had been so distraught by all that had happened, by all that *was* happening, she'd reacted to her friend's declining condition with anger instead of compassion. Regardless of what treachery she felt Cathyanne had committed, Finley should have spent her last precious moments with Cathyanne telling her how much she *loved* her, how much she would miss her.

How could she ever forgive herself?

Quinton launched into the bridge, singing the lyrics from what sounded like a broken heart. "*No* regrets for tomorrow. *No* regrets for today. Give a hand when you can . . . if there's a hand that's reaching your way . . ."

Finley rolled her lips together. Biting back tears that wouldn't have come even if she had allowed them, understanding dawned. Cathyanne hadn't needed Finley to tell her something she already knew. With her last breath, Cathyanne had wanted to give Finley an important piece to life's puzzle.

Like Careen, Cathyanne wanted Finley to let go, and just maybe, Finley was starting to understand what that meant.

❧❧❧

Perched atop a rolling hill, the casket holding Cathyanne's body sat amidst headstones dating back to the eighteen hundreds and beyond. A fitting resting spot for an old soul like Cathyanne, she should feel right at home here.

Above abandoned treetops, the sun hid, shamefaced, behind a swath of gauzy clouds. Peeking out only now and again, it was as if it too felt the need to mourn before daring to shine its light on the earth once more.

The funeral had ended, having gone off without a hitch, as did the graveside service. The mourners had left, gone to Finley's house for the luncheon. Finley knew she should have followed too, but she couldn't seem to tear herself away from Cathyanne. Thanks to her mother and the therapy group members, she didn't have to worry that everyone back at the house was being properly cared for without her there to see to it. So now, standing here in the cold afternoon air, Finley found herself alone with her best friend for the very last time.

The wind moved the tree branches, whistling Quinton's homage to Cathyanne into Finley's ears. She'd only heard the song that one time, but already the words had seared themselves into her psyche. *Live your life like I did . . . Live with no regrets . . .* The lyrics lapped over and over in Finley's head, bringing some of Cathyanne's final words back to her, each time opening her mind a little more to what her friend had been trying to say.

Finley had been doing everything right for all of these years, but in the process, had been getting it all, or mostly, wrong. Where she'd assumed she'd find safety in maintaining the status quo, she'd only found stagnation. Sure, she'd taken a few chances here lately. Had dipped in her toe or even waded into the sea of possibilities, which would have been a good start if only she hadn't done so while holding tight to the set of rules she'd always lived by. Cathyanne wanted Finley to let go, to jump, cannon-ball style, into her life. She wanted Finley to search out and find, then have the courage to wholeheartedly go after what she truly needed to be happy.

Of two minds, Finley was starting to understand her friend's reasons, but at the same time was furious with Cathyanne for leaving Finley the way she had—broken and confused, alone. She was too exhausted to keep holding onto a life she didn't know how to live anymore, a life that wasn't working anyway, so what did she really have to lose by giving Cathyanne's dying wish a try? If only she knew how she was supposed to do what Cathyanne had asked, or to even know where to begin? Without her time-honored rules to live by, like a tightrope walker traversing a wire without a net, now that Cathyanne was gone, who would be there to catch Finley if she fell?

"Thanks a lot," she murmured to her friend. "You could have at least stayed around long enough to help me clean up the mess you made of my life."

Placing her gloved hand to the cold wood of the casket, Finley waited for Cathyanne to come to her. How many times had she heard others say they could sense the presence of their deceased loved ones? Hear their whispers? But no matter how badly Finley wanted to say she knew Cathyanne was still here, walking next to her in spirit, she couldn't make herself believe . . .

Couldn't feel a dadgum thing.

Closing her eyes, she cursed life's evasive riddles, waiting for the tears she'd stuffed down to surface, to pour from her eyes and finally relieve the pressure constricting her throat. But none came. The funeral had ended, and thus all of the prying eyes had dispersed, so why couldn't she cry?

Why couldn't she let go?

She felt him an instant before the sound of a twig breaking under the weight of his footfall announced his presence.

Finley didn't turn to him, didn't acknowledge him because she knew why he was here. Like her family and Josh, he worried that she wasn't as pulled together on the inside as she pretended to be on the outside. He was right.

Her aversion to others showing concern for her wellbeing was probably something she should let go of. If only that concern, and the truth it revealed, didn't infuriate her to no end, she might have given allowing him to care a try.

Keeping her gaze firmly planted on the casket, Finley answered his question before he could ask it. "I can't just leave her here, all by herself."

Quinton took a couple steps closer, then stopped. "She's not there anymore," he gently reminded.

Finley sniffed against the cold, dry air. "I know, but it still feels wrong. Putting her . . . or what's left of her, in a box and dropping it into a hole," she said, her voice catching. "How can I leave her here and just walk away like it—like she—doesn't matter?"

"It does seem cruel, doesn't it?" Quinton agreed.

His close proximity and her unfettered desire to reach out to him, to take comfort in the arms of the one man who wouldn't give her what she wanted, burned in the pit of her stomach. Why couldn't she want Josh, or even Roy, the way she wanted Quinton? Something else she needed to let go but hadn't the first clue as to how. How does one make their heart desire what their head knows is best?

So she turned her sights back to her guilt instead. In the very least, a true confession might somehow loosen the restraint on her tears.

"I saw the signs," Finley stated.

"What signs would those be?"

"I knew something was off," she went on. "She was slow, you know, at training sessions, and coming up with lame excuses to avoid me. But I was so consumed with myself, with dating and with what people must be thinking of me. Then I got the idea for the non-profit, and . . . I shouldn't have let her brush me off so easily." Although Finley knew that Cathyanne keeping her at a distance was part of her friend's plan, she still couldn't help but think there had to have been a better way for Cathyanne to accomplish her final task. "I should have been there, encouraging her to fight. If I had, she would have at least died at home instead of in that dreadful hospice center."

Quinton noticeably exhaled. "It was her choice, Finnie. There wasn't a thing you could do about it." He moved closer and their arms touched. "It's not your fault."

The brush of his sleeve against hers sent little fingers of heat threading across her skin. "Then why does it feel like it is?" she asked, choking on a tearless sob.

"Is that why you can't walk away, because you somehow feel like you let her down?"

Finley kept her eyes on the casket, but she could still feel his worried look boring into the side of her face. Again, she wanted to fall into his arms, to let go of all the hurt feelings between them and allow him to hold her. But the bruises he'd left on her ego reopened every time he was near, and her pride kept her firmly in place.

"Maybe," she said, lifting a heavy shoulder. "Or maybe it's because now that she's gone I have nobody."

Quinton huffed out a derisive sound. "How can you say that when there are so many people who love you? People who, right at this moment, know you're hurting and wish they could help you." His insistence shouldn't have enraged her, but it did.

Finley spun to face him now. Immediately, her breath snagged on how handsome he looked dressed in a long wool coat and white shirt with a bolo tie pulled tight at the collar, those unforgettable eyes of his looking deeper, more arduous than ever. She so badly wanted to ask if those "people" included him, and if so, why hadn't he said as much? Why lump himself in with her family and Josh? But she couldn't seem to line the words up properly, couldn't bring herself to let go of her insecurities and directly ask him how he felt about her.

Why did this letting go thing have to be so hard?

"Maybe I just need a little space," she blasted back. "My best friend died. She's gone—forever. And now, ironically, I have no one I can talk to about it!"

Quinton's eyes hardened. "What about that trainer of yours? Even after what you did . . . with me . . . and Roy . . . he seems pretty eager to stand by your side. And from the way you've been clinging to him all week, I'd think he, in the very least, would be someone you could talk to."

The notion that this would be the perfect opportunity to practice letting go by admitting she couldn't talk to Josh the way she could to Cathyanne—the way she'd always been able to talk to Quinton—raced across her brain, but again, the words refused to come.

Turning her gaze back to the casket, she said, "It's complicated."

"Complicated," he repeated like the word possessed a mystery. "I expect that explanation applies to Roy as well, so I won't ask. By the way, when you came to my house on Thanksgiving night, why didn't you mention you'd been with your ex?"

Regret had Finley's tears beating against her eyes, demanding to be released, but even though she gave them permission, they wouldn't fall. She wished she had an answer to that question. All she knew was that if she *had* told him about the near-kiss with Roy, Quinton likely wouldn't have kissed her, and they wouldn't be standing here right now, so close, yet miles apart.

Drowning in her unshed tears, Finley choked on her words. "Quinton, I am not going to talk about any of this with you right now—"

"If you ask me," he charged in, "and you didn't, but I'm gonna say this anyway, I don't see you with either one of them. That trainer's something to look at . . . I suppose . . . but he's not for you. Not long-term anyway. And for the life of me, I never could figure what you *ever* saw in Roy."

Slowly, Finley's eyes tracked back to him. Just as she'd suspected, his stirring of the pot the day at the yard sale had been nothing more than him assuming some sort of role as her protector. One heart-pounding kiss and then like nothing had happened, he'd gone back to being a brother to her, a friend. Well, his misguided attempt at shielding her from heartache was no excuse for all the turmoil he'd caused.

"Is that why you wouldn't back me up at the yard sale?" she accused without waiting to hear his answer. "You nearly ruined everything. Why can't you see that Josh is the best thing that's happened to me in a very long time?"

Jaw clenched, he matched her churlish tone. "If that's the way you truly feel about it, then I apologize for not backing off, for not respecting that *Josh* is the man you want." He tossed his hands in the air. "In fact, if it will make you happy, I'll go over to the house right now, march straight up to him, and tell him that nothing happened between us. And that he has nothing to worry about because nothing ever will. And while I'm at it, just in case you decide to take back that a-hole you divorced, I'll do the same to your ex too." He stopped as his blazing eyes worked over Finley's face. When he spoke again, his voice was only slightly less venomous. "If that's what you really want, I'll set the record straight, once and for all."

His willingness to hand her over to Josh or even to Roy "once and for all" tormented Finley's gut. She wouldn't admit, not even to herself, what his forfeit was doing to her heart. "Great." She turned away. "You do that."

Quinton stood quiet a moment. "You're still angry with me."

Tiring of this conversation, Finley spat back, "What do you care anyway? Your life is just the way you want it. You have a CD coming out. You're going back out on tour. You're free to come and go as you please. To sleep with women, no strings attached. Stop acting like my misery matters to you."

Quinton gaped at her like she'd suddenly grown a second head. "Are you being serious right now? How can you *even* say something like that . . . *to me?*" he asked, but before Finley could formulate a clever response, his look of disbelief quickly morphed into an expression closely resembling the *Ah-hah* variety.

"Wait. I know what this is all about." Shaking his head, his scuffed the ground with the toe of his boot. "This is about that kiss, isn't it?"

Finley's cheeks flamed red. "Please don't bring that up again." Feigning a shiver, she buried her face in the fur collar of her coat. "Why can't you just forget about it and move on?"

"Oh, I don't know," he came back without missing a beat, "why can't you?"

No way was Finley going to dignify his sarcasm with an answer. The fact he would use the lowest form of humor with regards to the intimate moment they'd shared hurt more than his willingness to move past said moment so easily. The longer she allowed this conversation to go on, the more damage it would do to what little there was left of their friendship. Keeping her chin down, her gaze on Cathyanne's casket, she let her silence answer for her.

A few tense moments past before he conceded. "Look, I get that now is not the time, but sooner or later, you and I *are* going to have a discussion about that kiss."

Relieved that he might finally be on his way, Finley raised her head from its makeshift shell. "Great, can't wait." She arched an eyebrow at him. "Anything else?"

"No, we're done." His eyes tracked down to her lips, where they held a long moment before he blinked, his gaze meeting hers again. "For now, anyway."

"Fine."

"Fine." He turned to go, but then stopped. "Oh wait, there *is* something else." He consulted the dormant grass a second or two, then said, "In case you're interested, my kids are coming to my house for Christmas Eve supper."

The barricade encasing Finley's heart started to crumble. "Quinton, that's amazing . . . But how?" she stammered, unable to recall ever having heard him mention he'd been in contact with his children, much less having them over for the holidays. "When did you . . . ?"

"We've been talking more and more lately. They have a band, kind of a Band Perry thing, I guess. I've been to hear them play a few times. They're actually quite good." The cautious look of pride he gave her next was priceless. "Anyway, I invited them over for Christmas Eve. Their mother's spending the evening with her new husband's family, which very likely is the reason our kids agreed to spend it with me," he explained, a distant kind of pain in his eyes. "But if it means seeing them on Christmas for the first time in eight years, I'm willing to be their scapegoat. No questions asked."

A smile scooched its way onto Finley's face. "Quinton, I'm so happy for you." She pressed her hands to her chest. "Really."

Quinton's lips didn't turn up, but the twinkle returned to his eyes. "Thanks. Me too," he said, then scuffed the ground again. "So I was thinking, if the old Finnie is still in there somewhere, and I'm assuming she is, I know her family has other plans, so if she's not busy, I'd love for her to join us." The right side of his mouth lifted, pushing that adorable dimple deep into his cheek. "I would really love for her to meet my kids . . ."

An uncomfortable silence trailed behind his open-ended invitation. With her life all a jumble, she didn't know what she had planned for tomorrow, much less two weeks from now.

"Quinton, I . . ." Desperate not to agree to, nor to decline, another something she might come to regret, Finley faltered. She honestly had no idea what to say next.

Disappointment smudged the sparkle from his eyes. "All right then," he said. "I guess that's all. I'll leave you to it." He turned and started to walk away again.

Her heart left vulnerable from his humble request, Finley found herself torn between knowing she was in no shape, emotionally or otherwise, to tell him she'd come, and wanting more than anything to agree to be there for him.

With no time to deliberate, she offered what she could. "Your song was beautiful," she called after him. "Thank you for that. I know Cathyanne loved it too."

His steps slowed, his feet shifting until he was walking backwards. "Thanks for saying so." He accepted her compliment with a shy grin. "But seriously, if my good friend Finnie does happen to reemerge, and if she decides to attend my holiday supper, I think I can speak for my kids in saying that we'd all much appreciate her bringing one of her famous chocolate pecan pies." He winked, then righted his steps and ambled off.

As Finley watched him go, his usage of the word *friend* to describe her echoed in her head until it took on an offensive, four-letter-word kind of intonation. Obviously she could never simply be his friend, ever again.

He was just too darned cute for his own good, or Finley's.

# Chapter 22

Finley's house was filled to capacity when she finally came trailing home. Putting her kitchen island between herself and the crowd, she turned her back to the rooms full of hungry mourners, trying to forget how many feet were milling about her restored, original white oak floors with plates piled high in food. In her hand, she gripped a sealed legal-sized envelope. Along with a generous check for Finley's Garden, Cathyanne's estate attorney had also handed Finley this letter.

Gliding her thumb across the front, she felt the subtle rise and fall of the ink where "Finnie" had been penned in Cathyanne's looping handwriting. She'd dotted the "i" with a pair of puckered lips. The angry half of Finley wanted to rip the envelope to shreds. She didn't want a letter. She wanted Cathyanne back so she could help Finley reassemble her life. Unless this envelope held step-by-step instructions as to how Finley was to go about this . . . letting go thing, and she seriously doubted it did, she was leery of reading the words of a woman who, in the end, had only brought grief and destruction to Finley's life. The other half wanted to understand why Cathyanne had meddled the way she had, to make sense of why she'd thoughtlessly kept her illness a secret.

"Miss Finley . . ."

Startled, Finley spun around, pressing the envelope to her beating chest. "Good gracious, Skylar. You can't sneak up on folks like that."

Skylar set a stack of dirty plates next to the sink. "I didn't mean to frighten you." She gave Finley a remorseful smile. "I just wanted to say how sorry I am for your loss."

Folding the envelope in half, Finley tucked it into the pocket of her suit. "Thank you, Skylar, that means a lot." On the inside, her reply was a lot less civil, but she wasn't going to make a scene.

"I haven't had a chance to tell you this, but for what it's worth, I think the non-profit you're starting is a noble cause," Skylar continued. "If there'd been something like Finley's Garden around when my daddy took off, my momma and I wouldn't have ended up living in her car."

The rod of fury holding Finley's back stick-straight buckled under the weight of Skylar's confession. "I'm so sorry," she said. "I had no idea."

Skylar waved Finley's sympathy away. "It's all right," she said as if she didn't wish to be bothered anymore with the past. "My momma found another husband pretty quick. He didn't treat her much better than Daddy did, but at least we had a roof over our heads," she explained, then quickly changed the subject. "Listen, the orchard is pretty well buttoned-up for the winter, so I guess I won't be around much for the next couple of months, but, with your friend's passing and renovations getting underway, and the holidays and whatnot coming up, if you need anything—anything at all—please don't hesitate to give me a call." The smile she gave Finley next seemed genuine. "I'd be happy to help. No charge."

Finley eyed Skylar's little black dress (showing a tad too much cleavage for a funeral), sheer pantyhose, and four-inch heels, rounding out her appraisal at the innocent look on the young woman's face, searching for evidence of an ulterior motive. It didn't take a PhD in psychology to see that the attention of a certain man whose name didn't need mentioning likely had everything to do with Skylar's charitable offer. *Unless* . . . Skylar did say that she'd had a rough childhood, which would make her sympathetic to Finley's cause, and Josh did seem as committed to Finley as ever, even with Skylar's persistent presence, so Skylar likely wasn't throwing herself at him. Could it be that Finley was mistaken and Skylar's ever-increasing presence *did* happen to have at least a little to do with sincerely wanting to help out? Would it be too much of a stretch for Finley to show Skylar a little indulgence? Give her the benefit of the doubt? For Finley to let loose some of her anger toward this woman?

"Thanks, Skylar, I'll do that." Finley sent her an appreciative smile. "I'm sure we'll be needing an extra pair of hands before this project is over." She was surprised at how much she actually meant it, and how light she suddenly felt. Pride overshadowed the bitterness in her heart. Finley had skated through her first experiment in letting go with flying colors.

"And," Skylar said with hesitance, "I'm sorry about the other thing too."

Finley had assumed this conversation was over, and found herself just a tad annoyed that Skylar wasn't moving on. "What other thing would that be?" Finley asked, impatient. Apparently, there was letting go, and then there was *letting go*.

Where Skylar was concerned, it appeared Finley was having trouble with the second.

Skylar took in a couple of breaths as if steadying herself. "I am *so, so* sorry I slept with your husband," she said, her eyes zipping between Finley and the floor. "And, well, for being a real . . . you know, b-word, sometimes."

Not entirely comfortable discussing her husband's indiscretions and with one of the very women with which he'd committed his various offences, and on the day of her best friend's funeral no less, Finley felt it best to gloss over the past as quickly as possible.

Forcing her lips into a smile of sorts, she managed to say, "Thanks for saying so. I appreciate it." Honestly, somewhere deep inside, she was shocked to find she did.

But Skylar wasn't ready to drop the subject just yet. "I really thought you wouldn't mind, you know, me and Roy," she went on, a reluctant look crossing her eyes. "I was under the impression that because of how Roy had a habit of, well, running around with other ladies, and given the *thing* you had with Mr. Townes, and all, that y'all had one of those"—she finger-quoted—"'open marriages,' or something."

The words *open* and *marriage* used consecutively, *and* in reference to Finley, turned her stomach. The very thought that she would agree to Roy's affairs as long as she had his permission to carry on with the man next door was incomprehensible. "Um, no," she adamantly disagreed. "Quinton and I have never had, and still don't have, any sort of 'thing' between us."

Skylar studied Finley a moment. "Yeah, you keep saying that," she mumbled before quickly getting back to what she'd been saying. "Anyway, for whatever reason, I just want you to know that it was hard for me to see where the lines were for sure." An endearing shade of pink colored her cheeks. "And you know Roy, and how he's so charming-like. I know it's no excuse for what I did, but I'd never had a handsome, powerful man like him show me that kind of attention before."

Finley had never seen this side of Skylar: young, naive, just wanting to be loved, desired, and therefore vulnerable to a man with Roy's charisma. Underneath that low-cut dress was an insecure woman who loved plants and children, and perhaps even dreamed of having a family someday. In other words, one not all that dissimilar to the young woman Finley had once been. How could she fault Skylar for being drawn in by the same man's spell that she, as a grown adult, had found herself falling victim to just the other night? If what Skylar said was true and she *did* believe Finley *had* condoned her affair with Roy, then Finley must have been the one acting like a real b-word to Skylar. Had she sorely misjudged her orchard manager all this time? Finley was in the process of puzzling when somewhere between her grief and perplexity, like Doc Seuss's Grinch, she felt the frost around her heart thawing, the resentment she'd harbored for this young woman melting completely away.

The beginnings of a smile worked its way onto Finley's lips. "I find that hard to believe. You're very beautiful, and diversely talented too."

Skylar's blush deepened. "Thanks," she was saying when the sight of Josh coming in through the French doors caught her attention. "You're real lucky to have him, you know." A faraway look gave her a moment of pause. "He's the best kind of man—loyal and hardworking. He's gonna make some lucky woman a damn fine husband one day. And be a real good daddy, too."

Finley's gaze alternated between Josh and Skylar. "Yeah, I think you might be right."

❧❧❧

Finley stared with purpose out her kitchen window into her faded garden, trying to organize the crazy mixed-up notions occupying her current train of thought. She wouldn't have believed it possible, but her world had just gotten more distorted than it had been only a few moments earlier.

First, she had no idea what to make of Skylar or how a few simple words of explanation could erase more than a year's worth of animosity and blame. Second, would it be too terribly disloyal to all of the other victims of a cheating spouse to break the code of bitterness and allow one of the women who'd slept with her husband to have her boyfriend too? Third, what in heaven's name was happening to her? Was she going stark, raving mad? Or was this what letting go felt like? Curse Cathyanne for not being here, if only in spirit, to help her through this.

Josh's hands slipped onto her shoulders from behind. "Hey, babe," he said, his voice low, empathetic. "How you holding up?"

Finley cringed under his touch. "I'm fine."

Leaning close, his breath brushed her ear as he said, "You don't have to be so brave, you know." He stepped up next to her. "It's okay to cry."

The feel of his kind heart beating strong against her back should have brought comfort, but instead his close proximity only made her want to squirm.

Finley wiggled out of his grip. "Don't you think I'd cry if I could?" she snapped before she could stop herself. "I'm sorry; I'm not myself today."

"It's okay, I understand," Josh said, then got real quiet, thoughtful. "Your neighbor was here a while ago," he said, running his fingernail along the corner of the countertop. "He pulled me aside and assured me there was nothing romantic going on between you two."

Finley assessed his guarded gaze. "But you don't believe him?"

Josh shrugged. "He seemed more put-out than sincere, which leads me to believe he was only saying it because you put him up to it, which would also mean that whatever may or may not have happened between you two doesn't really matter because you ultimately chose me." He snuck a look at Finley as if to make sure his assumption was correct. She nodded. "So I guess I'm just a little confused as to why you keep freezing me out?" he asked, gazing back at her through wounded eyes. "Why you flinch every time I touch you."

The pain in his voice made it nearly impossible for Finley to do what she knew she had to, what she wasn't entirely sure she wanted to do. What she didn't, technically, even have to do. She'd already successfully let go of one thing today—her anger toward Skylar—so with all she'd already lost, would it be too terribly selfish of her to keep Josh all to herself just a little longer?

"Josh, I don't think now is right the time for this discussion—"

"Really?" he cut her off, frustration steamrolling the hurt from his face. "And when would be the right time? Or would you rather discuss your feelings with that neighbor of yours . . . or your husband, maybe?"

Finley shut her eyes, blocking out the sight of his malcontent. "Josh, don't."

"Don't what?" he challenged. "Talk about what's really going on here?"

"I don't know what you're talking about," Finley lied in hopes that he wouldn't push her to go where neither of them was in any shape to go right now.

The green of his eyes darkened to defiance. "Don't you?"

His persistence was like a whisk to her guilty conscience, churning up what need not be disturbed. "All right, if you're so sure," she said, turning his question back on him, "why don't you tell me?"

Josh's nostrils flared. "You're never going to love me, are you?"

Finley gaped at his candor as Cathyanne's voice rang inside her head, asking, "Do you think you could ever love him?" A question Finley should have been able to definitively answer, but she couldn't—and truthfully, she knew she never would. How long was she going to keep stringing this wonderful man along, despising herself a little more each day for the additional hurt her indecision would eventually cause him? Except, hadn't she heard somewhere that it was unwise to make life-slash-love decisions during a time of immense grief? Probably, but then she wasn't about to speak out loud anything she hadn't already entertained in her head a thousand times before today.

Finley couldn't believe she was about to say this, about to let go of the one man who'd facilitated so much change in her, but she'd never been a selfish person, and she wasn't about to start now.

"Honestly," she said with equal directness as he'd given her, "I'll never be able to love you the way you want me to."

An instant of disbelief was quickly overshadowed by a pooling of tears filled Josh's eyes, and Finley hurried to soften the blow. "Look, you're a great guy—the best, in fact. I've never been with a man who's more sweet and attentive, and at the same time able to physically challenge me in ways I'd never imagined." She took his handsome face in her hands. "You've made me a better person by helping me step outside of my normal to see that there's a whole world out there I never knew existed." Rolling up onto her toes, she brushed her lips across his. "You've been such a blessing to my life."

"Then what's the problem?" he whispered.

Finley's lips began to quiver, but as with Cathyanne, her tears for Josh would refuse to fall too. "I can't be the woman you need me to be." Falling back onto her heels, she threw a blatant glance over to where Skylar stood talking with Shep and Royanne. "You need someone who will happily climb a mountain with you. Someone who wants to build a family with you, and will give you children of your own someday," she said, and to her dismay, felt the urge to selfishly take it all back. She rushed to finish. "You deserve more than I can give you."

Josh dropped his forehead to hers. "Finley . . ."

"I would hold you back," she pressed on, "and we both know it."

Josh swallowed hard, deliberate, his gaze taking a peek toward Skylar. "What does a man do when what his head is telling him to do and what his heart wants are two very different things?"

Finley had asked herself that very question earlier today, and now she finally had an answer. Laying a finger on his chin, she steered his gaze back to hers. "He does everything in his power to bring his head and his heart together, to make them one and the same," she said with no idea where the words were coming from. All she knew was that they felt good sliding over her tongue, so who was she to question the source? This letting go thing was hard and . . . enlightening. "I believe that when all is said and done, our hearts and minds want the same things. Compromise brings change. And change makes us grow, which is good for not only the heart and the mind, but for the soul too."

A single tear popped from Josh's eye and rolled down his tanned cheek. "I'm gonna miss you."

A sudden impulse to kiss his perfect lips one more time took hold of Finley, but she wouldn't allow herself the pleasure. It wasn't fair for her to do anything that might keep either one of them from moving on, from letting go.

Stepping back, she pretending to be appalled. "What do you mean? You wouldn't ditch out on Finley's Garden, would you?"

The look of dismay on Josh's face flipped to determination.

"You know I'd never leave a job half-finished." He smiled, and in that smile, Finley thought she spied a speck of relief.

"I know," she teased, "of course you wouldn't . . ."

ole ole ole

The fire crackled, lapping flames high into the chimney as Finley held her hands out to the warmth. Her gaze roamed over her formal living room, noticing how empty it felt now that all the guests from the funeral were gone.

The first week of December had nearly come to a close and she hadn't listened to a single Christmas song, bought a gift, or hung an evergreen swag. In years past, there would already be a tree here, tucked in the corner between the front window and the hearth. Thanks to Cathyanne's abrupt passing, for the first December Finley could recollect, she had absolutely no holiday spirit, no desire to cover the front of her home in white twinkle lights, bake cookies, or drink hot chocolate by the fire pit out back.

Easing the envelope from her pocket, she ran her finger under the seal, daring to hope that reading what Cathyanne had left for her might bring the closure she needed to endure this season. With her children coming home for the Christmas break, she needed to salvage what holiday traditions hadn't already been obliterated by the divorce or her mother and daddy's impending absence.

Her fingertips had barely touched the stationary folded inside when a *thunking* grabbed her attention. She jerked toward the noise to see that Roy had entered the room and apparently dropped a stack of boxes to the floor.

"Roy, what in the world?"

He shook his head. "My boxes," he explained. "Burlie-Jean said if I forgot to take them home again she was going to turn me over her knee and give me a good spanking." The look he gave her next was part disturbed, part amused. "I think she meant it too."

Finley held her lips tight to conceal her smile. "I bet she did," she said, then looked at his stack of boxes, remembering how she'd found them the evening before the yard sale in the potting shed (currently being converted into Burlie-Jean's office) and how she'd told him to take them home that night. The next morning they'd been right where she'd dropped them in the driveway, covered in frost.

"What are they still doing here anyway?"

Roy gave the stack a doleful glance. "I don't know what to do with this stuff." He raked his black hair with his fingers. "What good is any of it without you? Might as well have just sold it all at the yard sale."

Following his gaze, Finley considered the boxes and their contents, her mind settling on his journal and the way his athletic stats had given way to actual thoughts and feelings the day they'd met. Meeting her must have really meant something to him, something even more important than sports. Could it be that in some roundabout way, his reluctance to hold on to memories related to their relationship, now that their marriage had ended, meant that she was just as important to him now as she had been back then?

"Where's Lover Boy?" Roy asked, pulling Finley from her thoughts.

"By 'Lover Boy,' I'm assuming you mean Josh," she said with a sigh. "He left a while ago . . . with Skylar."

Roy's eyes narrowed, then rounded. "Really?" He laughed. "That's ironic."

"You're telling me." Finley found herself laughing right along with him. To her complete surprise, the laughter felt good, really good.

Roy sniffed back on his amusement. "And Quinton?"

Finley bristled. "What about him?"

Roy adjusted his stance to one leg and rested his hands low on his hips. "Finnie, let's not play games." His steel-eyed gaze probed deep into hers.

Her heart weak from grief, Finley encased her chest tight beneath her arms. "I'm not," she said because nothing that had happened to her lately felt anything like a game. "There's nothing but friendship between Quinton and me. Never has been." Loss moistened her eyes as she returned his intense stare with one that was wide open. "I mean it, Roy."

"And what about us?"

"Wish I knew."

"Me too."

They both fell quiet, listening to the pop of the fire, thinking. Finley's mind scrolled back through all the times her mother had pounded home the belief that God did not look kindly on those who broke their wedding vows, then forward to the night before the yard sale and how Roy had offered up some inspired marketing ideas for Finley's Garden. If only his brilliance hadn't been quickly overshadowed by the obvious differences in their core motivations. Could the two of them ever truly be partners? Friends? Could they really start again as he'd suggested? Did these questions factor into God's judgment? And if they did, knowing what they knew now, could they do better a second time around? Was their shared past, and mutual desire to not lose all they'd built that was good, enough to sustain a marriage that could feasibly last another forty years?

"Do you think we *really* tried?" she threw out. "You know, to make our marriage work?"

Roy gnawed at his bottom lip. "Hell if I know," he said, the devious spark returning to his eyes. "All I know is that I loved you like crazy. I always will."

His declaration of love fluttered about inside Finley's chest. "I know." A faint blush warmed her cheeks. "That's why I feel like maybe I gave up on you too easily."

Roy shuffled a few steps closer. "I wouldn't say that," he said, a smirk pulling up one side of his mouth. "You stayed with my cheatin' ass for over twenty years."

"And you put up with my silent disapproval," Finley countered.

Roy took both Finley's hands in his. "Then I expect we were trying the best way we knew how."

The feel of his palms against hers stirred her need to grab hold of one of the few things from her former life that still felt familiar. "What if we could find a new way to try? Work harder this time to better understand each other?" Her heart went crazy, beating manically against her rib cage with with she said next. "Then, do you think we could make our marriage work—"

"Sunk cost," a third voice called out from the doorway.

The statement tore Roy's gaze from Finley's. "What?"

Across the room, Shep and Royanne stood just inside the threshold. On the floor next to his foot, Shep's packed duffle bag sat, reminding Finley that he was due back at the naval academy first thing in the morning.

"Sunk cost," Shep repeated as he came closer. "In economic terms it means money that has already been spent can never be recovered," he explained, calm, collected. "Logic dictates that because sunk cost will not change, no matter what actions are taken, whatever changes are made, these changes should not play a role in future decision-making."

Roy dropped Finley's hands. "Son, I know what sunk cost means," he said, impatient. "What's your point?"

Royanne stepped around her brother. "His point is that, no matter how hard y'all try to make your marriage work, it's not going to, so you should just stop sinking time and energy into it, and move on, once and for all."

Finley felt that surreal feeling sinking around her again. "What are you two saying? You don't want your daddy and me to be together?" Didn't all children want their parents to stay married? To work things out, if possible? "But we're a family."

"I'm sorry, Momma, but we were never really a family," Shep said, his confident eyes rimmed in sadness. "We went through the motions, but there was always this . . . space between us."

Exaggerating her eye-roll, Royanne elbowed her brother. "What he's trying to say is that just because you and Daddy don't live in the same house anymore, doesn't make us any less of a family than we were before."

Disbelief quickly accompanied by a strong sense of failure speared Finley to the core. Hadn't she been careful all these years to shield her children from her and Roy's disconnect? Hadn't she covered her disappointment with enough love steeped in family tradition to hide the lack of true substance in her marriage? Yet another casualty to Cathyanne's infernal meddling, the answer to those questions was written in the resolve on Shep and Royanne's faces. Finley's one saving grace—the belief that even if she'd failed at everything else, she'd at least been a good mother—drifted away like dandelion shafts on a strong summer breeze. What a waste, all those years of pretending, and she hadn't even fooled the only two people who mattered.

But she—no, they—could do better. She and Roy could get it right this time.

"What if we tried again?" Finley offered. "Your daddy and I—"

"Sunk cost, Momma," Royanne cut her off. "Sunk cost."

Finley's desperate gaze alternated between her son and daughter's unwavering expressions, noting that they'd both obviously given this a lot of thought. "So that's it then?" she asked, her guilt turning to tears that brimmed against her eyes with an unbearable pressure. "This is what you want our family to be from now on? Switching off holidays, weekend visits split between my house and your daddy's?"

Royanne rolled up a shoulder. "That's up to y'all," she said as if issuing a challenge. "I think we might could combine some of those holidays and visits. Other divorced families get along, spend time together, so Shep and I don't see why we can't do the same. Besides, would it really be that bad to take a break from the pressures of family holidays every now and then? You're going to be crazy busy starting this non-profit." She raised a hand toward Roy. "And Daddy is always busy with his businesses and, well, being . . . Daddy," she added, which needed no further explanation.

Finley crossed the floor to her children. "But y'all know, no matter how busy I am, I always make time for you," she said, the tears that still refused to fall clogging her throat. "You're my babies."

Shep rested his gentle hands on his mother's shoulders. "Yes, Momma, but we're adults now. Someday we'll have jobs and families of our own. It's time you did some things *you* want to do, for a change." He gave her a loving smile that broke her heart in a way she'd never imagined possible.

Royanne spoke next. "You and Daddy can't see it, but we can, and y'all are happier now," she added. "Daddy finally has that media room you wouldn't let him build when he lived here, and he bought the boat you said you never had time to go out on with him." A flicker of pride lit her grown-up gaze. "And Momma, just look at you. You're all in shape and rock climbing, dating a super hot guy, or you were at least, and what you're doing here with Finley's Garden is truly amazing."

"Look, kids," Roy sternly interjected, "your momma and I appreciate all y'all's input and everything, but we're still the adults in this family. We're perfectly able to handle things between us. We know what's best . . ."

As Roy admonished their children, Finley's eyes were drawn to his boxes once more. All he'd saved of their twenty-one years together were distant memories. Nothing after the first five years or so. Like Finley, was Roy holding on to her because he'd already invested too much time to move on, because she was his "familiar" too? His sunk cost?

Finley touched her ex-husband's arm. "Roy?" she said, her voice cautious. "Why *did* you let me go?"

Roy's brow pulled together, irritated. "What?"

Finley adjusted her position so they were eye to eye. "You moved out, signed the divorce papers without even the tiniest of resistance," she reminded him. "That's not like you. You always get what you want. In fact, you insist on it."

"That I do," he agreed.

"So if you wanted me, wanted our marriage, then why did you give up so easily?"

Roy's Adam's apple noticeably moved up then down his neck. "Truthfully, I didn't think you'd go through with the divorce. And given your silently stubborn ways, I figured that if I didn't put up too much of a fuss, you'd come to your senses and ask me back home."

"But I didn't, did I?" Finley reminisced aloud.

"No, I guess you didn't," Roy said, his gaze not so much looking at Finley as through her.

"And you didn't come after me either," Finley added.

Roy gave his head one slow swing. "No, not until," he paused, "well, until Cathyanne . . ."

Finley searched the face of the man she'd spent half her life thus far loving—or working to love anyway—the man who had given Finley her two most prized possessions, perplexed as to what to do now. Did letting go mean she needed to let go of past hurt and betrayal, of dysfunctional behavior, in order to put her family back together? Or did it mean letting go of what hadn't worked the first time around and moving on? Would a just God expect two people who'd foolishly married too young, who had no chance of attaining true love and understanding, to stay together when their children, the very individuals who should want them together, didn't think it was a good idea?

Her fingers reaffirmed their grip on Cathyanne's letter, wishing she could read it before allowing her next logical thought to surface, but then nothing Cathyanne could have written would change what Finley already knew in her heart she had to do. If she was being truly honest with herself, she wasn't really all that sad, nor did she feel a speck of regret. Her only regret lay in not having the courage to end what had been making both her and Roy miserable sooner. But just because she knew this was for the best didn't mean it wasn't going to hurt, that closing the last chapter on her marriage, her love affair with this man, wouldn't be hard.

Bracing herself for the unbearable finality of irrevocable loss, Finley took in a deep breath, then let the air go, and in the process, released her emotional grip on Roy for good.

"So I guess that means the kids are right then?" she decided. "We're all better off if you and I stay divorced?"

Tears filled Roy's eyes. "Yeah, I suppose it's for the best."

# Chapter 23

*A*lone.

The one word Finley never would have imagined she'd use to describe her state of being on Christmas Eve. But with Shep and Royanne spending the first half of the holiday with Roy and his family, her mother and daddy preparing to leave for their cruise, and Quinton maintaining a safe distance, here she was, standing in her living room, gazing at her beautifully decorated tree while listening to the crackle of the fire, alone.

"So what now?" she asked herself the same question she'd been asking for the last few weeks. A question that encompassed not only this very moment, but one that also extended to the remainder of her life. Since the loss of all three men in her life, plus the realization that her children were growing up and would never need her the way they always had, other than her work on Finley's Garden, Finley hadn't been able to figure out what she wanted for herself. Until she could answer this, in lieu of curling up in a ball and sleeping until the New Year, she'd done what she always had at this time of year. She'd baked, she'd decorated, and she'd shopped, and in the normalcy of it all, had begun to heal, or more specifically, to accept.

Rolling the ottoman up to the hearth, Finley then settled close to the fire's warmth. With Cathyanne's letter splayed across her open palms, she noticed that the edges were becoming frayed, the creases splitting from the many times she'd read and re-read these words.

After sending up a silent prayer for understanding, she whispered, "Amen," and began to read.

*Finnie,*

*If you're reading this, then I'm already dead (sorry, couldn't resist the cliché) and I hope the mortician didn't make me look like a china doll. You know, all rougie and pink lipped with some god-awful 1980s blue eye shadow. Remember when my Aunt Pearl died? Yeah, that's what I'm talking about. News flash, people, just because it's retro doesn't make it chic. If he did, I hope you brought a compact and were able to set my face straight. If not, I'll have to hide on resurrection day 'til everyone else has risen and moved on before slinking from my casket. I thought about asking to be buried with my cosmetic case, but I didn't want God to know how vain I really am. Like He doesn't already know.*

*But then, I digress . . .*

*Finnie, I'm sure you're furious with me right now for keeping my declining condition a secret. Knowing you the way I do, you're even finding a way to blame yourself for my unscheduled death.*

*Well, don't.*

*Dying this way was my choice, and there wasn't a thing you could have done to change my mind. I'm actually proud of you for being so distracted with your own life that I was able to hide my illness for so long. It's about time you put yourself first. There's nothing wrong with caring for oneself every now and again. Just like the flight attendants say, "Secure your oxygen mask before assisting others," Finnie, you have to take care of your own needs before you can properly meet the needs of anyone else.*

*Besides, you know how it was the last time I had cancer. Folks I barely knew were coming out of the woodwork to be of assistance. And my family was the worst. My momma, my sisters, they'd never once taken the time to visit me since they moved away, and suddenly they were dropping everything to drive over and stay with me. I just couldn't stomach another round of guilt trips.*

*I know you're angry with me for not fighting. Hurt that I didn't love you enough to do everything in my power to live, to stay with you when your life was finally starting to get . . . um, how should I put this . . . interesting? My final prayer is that somehow this letter will help you get some closure, to understand why it had to be this way.*

*When the doctors told me I was sick again and laid out my chances for survival—in other words, no one beats ovarian cancer twice—they said my only hope was to start treatments immediately. The first thought that popped into my mind was,* No, I can't go through that again, *but I couldn't see any other choice. So I went home and cried through the night, cursing God the entire time. Once I'd used up all my tears, I sat with my eyes fixed on the stars, my heart wide open and pleading for mercy. Ironically, that was also the first time I'd prayed. Boy, was I surprised when I got an answer. It hadn't come in the form of a voice exactly, but more of an impression. A very vivid, insistent, impression. I don't have the words to describe what I heard or felt that night, but what I can tell you is that I knew without a doubt I didn't have the power to save myself, no one does, and neither did the doctors.*

*In other words, believing you can battle a fatal disease is the same as betting all the money you have left on a hand at poker and expecting to win, even though your opponent knows what cards you're holding.*

*It's God's decision who lives and who dies.*

*End of discussion.*

*So you see, with cancer there is no battle, no heroes, no winners or losers. There's only God's will. And whether I chose traditional or alternative treatment it wouldn't have mattered. I was going to live only as long as God wanted me to. But even though I had no control over how many days I had left on this earth, what I could control was how I spent those days. And I didn't want to waste what time I had bald and sick in a treatment center with a machine pumping chemical poison through my heart and into my veins. Poison, that when all was said and done, had no chance of saving me.*

    *I hope you can understand.*

    *And please don't think I didn't want you with me, holding my hand, watching movies, telling me that everything was going to be okay. The last two months have been the loneliest I've ever spent. All those hours holed up in my tomb of a house, my body slowly eating itself away. Who would have guessed that isolation could defy the universal laws of time, stretching a minute into an hour, an hour into a day?*

    *But don't you see, that's why I couldn't tell you. I wanted to be the one to focus on you for a change. And look at all you've accomplished. You're dating and starting a non-profit. Breaking out of the old Finnie-mold. I did it for you.*

    *And don't you dare begrudge me my one selfless act. Doing this for you has opened my eyes to how good it feels to put another person first. In other words, to be like you, Finnie. I'm blessed to have died, passing into the next life with the peace of knowing I put someone else's needs before my own at least once in my lifetime. Hopefully now, and with all the time I've spent on my knees, I'll be able to recognize my Lord and Savior when He calls me home (fingers crossed).*

    *I love you, Finnie, my friend, the only real sister I ever had. I'm going to miss you more than I can bear. Live your life while you still can. Take chances every single day. Don't think so much about what's missing. Just enjoy what you have each second. Do it for the both of us. I'm counting on you . . .*

    *TTFN because I know we'll be together again some day.*

*All my love, always and forever,*

*Cathyanne*

*Ta-ta for now.* Finley squeezed her eyes closed, trying to relieve the burden of those pesky, all-talk-and-no-action tears, but they refused to fall. Though part of her was beginning to accept why Cathyanne had kept her condition a secret, and thus ready to let her resentment toward her friend go, the other part was terrified of the hurt that would rush to fill the vacancy left by her retreating anger. With her two sides engaged in a never-ending game of tug-of-war, the one thing her whole self could agree on was that she wanted to live her life while she still could, to do like Quinton's song and live with no regrets. If only she knew what either of those things really meant.

*What would Cathyanne do?*

Wasn't Finley living? Wasn't she breathing, moving from task to task, filling her hours with good things like family and service to others? And in doing so, taking a huge risk on the success or failure of Finley's Garden? But then, wasn't there more to living than simply breathing and persevering the very same gamble day in and day out?

How does one live life with no regrets?

Sure, she'd let go of the regret regarding the men in her life, was in the process of letting go of her anger toward Cathyanne for dying and of the guilt over breaking her wedding vows and splitting up her family. But as she released more and more of her former life and the old concerns, she found she had no idea what should take its place.

Releasing Josh and Roy had been for the best, and Finley felt good about those decisions. Still, catching sight of Skylar stealing the occasional kiss from Josh while working with him in the construction site out back had been . . . well, strange, while not entirely unsettling. As far as Roy was concerned, after he'd offered to help Finley put up the outside Christmas lights, which had been nice and not at all as awkward as she'd expected, they'd spent hours bundled up, sitting in the driveway, sipping hot chocolate while talking about everything, and nothing at all. Turned out, with the pressure and expectation of marriage removed, she and Roy could be friends after all. And while both realizations were a good start to her goal of learning to let go, neither held the capacity to make her feel any less alone.

Nevertheless, cinnamon, pine, and cloves scented the air. Her home, inside and out, swaged in evergreen and accented in classic tartan plaid, twinkled merrily with white light. A crisp winter wind made the fire all the more inviting. What traditionally would have been a bustling holiday morning sat quiet.

*Don't think so much about what's missing. Just enjoy what you have each second,* Finley repeated Cathyanne's words until, like a calming salve to her frayed soul, the peace promised by this season began to seep in, to wrap her soundly in its saving grace. Even with all she'd lost, she couldn't help but somehow feel hopeful, and in this moment she realized that alone wasn't all that bad.

Pulling in a deep breath, she let it go, slowly . . .

Today, alone was all right.

Three *dongs* from the clock in the hall startled Finley from her thoughts, warning her that she needed to get moving. Her folks were due at the airport early this evening, and Finley's mother had asked to borrow one of Finley's Lily Pulitzer sundresses for the cruise. A serial packer, it took Adeline at least three days, and numerous packs and re-packs, before she felt ready to take on the world outside of her meticulously ordered home, and was likely cursing her daughter for not having dropped the dress off sooner.

Duty calling Finley's name, she would have to put her quest for answers on hold—for now, anyway.

The Porsche roared to a screeching halt in the circular drive in front of Finley's parents' sprawling, French-style home. Her heart humming a vigorous melody, she inhaled a long breath to slow the adrenaline shooting through her veins. Forget about scaling a boring old faux rock cliff. Drag racing kicked climbing's butt any day.

Maybe she was taking Quinton's song a little too literally, but since her pondering had left her begging the question, what would Cathyanne do, she'd found herself struck with the brilliant idea of asking herself just that. Hence, when she'd opened her garage doors, intent on hopping into her Jeep and speeding off to her mother's rescue, the Porsche had caught her eye, and she'd known exactly what Cathyanne would do.

Two hours and numerous traffic and speed law violations later, Finley was kicking herself for not having driven this car sooner, for being stubborn and vindictive, trying to teach Roy a lesson he never had a chance of learning.

Talk about regret. Well, not anymore.

The sun had just fallen below the tree line as Finley grabbed her folded dress from the passenger seat and slid from the car. She knocked the door closed with her hip and looked up, her breath stumbling on the beautiful sight before her. Lying over the twilit sky, bundles of thin clouds, stained a vivid salmon-pink by the sunset, spread across the darkening horizon. Though she'd seen the Tennessee sky bursting with color more times than she could count, today the sight stepped in front of her, demanding that she slow down for once and enjoy the view.

Already beyond late, she chose to defy practicality and heed the sky's summon by edging herself up and onto the hood of the car.

In the grand scheme of things, what harm could another minute or two do?

Heat from the engine radiated up, warming her from the inside out as she tucked her knees to her chest and took in the miracle of nature's splendor. The cold winter air stung as she pulled it through her nose to fill her lungs. Given the wondrous sight before her, how could anyone doubt the existence of an all-knowing God in heaven? Holding her breath until it burned, she released the trapped air in a slow stream of white, letting what was left of her anger toward Cathyanne go once and for all along with it. Her heart swelled, a witness that Cathyanne was indeed right where she belonged. Even though so many things had changed, had been lost forever, she now understood that God was in charge and everything was exactly as it should be.

So she sat, a unique blend of love and acceptance creeping in where her anger had been, and watched the sky as the pink faded to gray, the indigo night closing over the heavens.

Finley hadn't even realized she was crying until a single tear dropped from her chin to form a smear on the knee of her jeans. She swiped at the moist trail on her cheek and then held her hand out for a closer look, rubbing the wetness between her fingers. Joy and relief quickly turned into an eruption of laughter, causing more and more tears to squeeze from her eyes. The juxtaposition of mirth and tears; no emotion had ever felt so good. A Christmas miracle.

❧❧❧

Once inside, the peace that had lightened Finley's load only minutes earlier started to crumble under the burden of the gloom that welcomed her.

Her folks' home was dark.

Besides a twelve-foot tree that been meticulously strung with lights and hung in imported ornaments, her mother hadn't put out a single holiday decoration. Not a bow on the sweeping staircase, not even a nutcracker on the table.

Stopping in the center of the marble-floored entry, Finley looked up at the tree and her heart sank. No one had even bothered to plug it in. What was it about a darkened Christmas tree that made a body feel so dismal?

From the study, the crackle of newspaper grabbed Finley's attention. Her winter boots made a hollow sucking sound as she moved into the next room. In his usual spot, her father sat behind his desk with his feet resting on the corner, the back fold of the local paper obscuring his face.

"Hey, Daddy," Finley greeted him.

Preston lowered the paper and offered her a smile. "Evening, sugar beet," he said and then checked his watch. "Tell that momma of yours to shake her tail feathers. We're two hours from missing our flight."

Though Finley knew her mother was not one to be rushed, she accepted the challenge and turned for the stairs. "I'll do my best."

"Finnie, heaven above!" Adeline called out, exasperated as Finley entered her parent's room. "Where have you been?"

Finley thought about admitting she'd been out driving. That's probably what Cathyanne would do, but unlike Cathyanne, Finley had never been so brash in her rebellion as to openly admit that her own needs far outweighed the needs of one who might have been counting on her. She wasn't about to start, and on a holiday centered on giving, no less.

"I've been busy getting ready for Christmas," Finley half-lied, "unlike *some* people." She crossed the vast expanse of the room and tossed the dress onto the bed next to her mother's open suitcase. "And it's not like that dress was just hanging in my closet. I had to dig through boxes of summer clothes to find it. Besides, it's only one little dress. Just slide it in and you're ready to go," she minimized, her voice tripping on the word *go* as the recognition that her folks were actually leaving her alone for the holidays *really* sunk in.

Adeline frowned. "I'm sorry, honey," she gushed her apology. "I didn't mean to be ugly." She circled the bed and took Finley in her arms. "Bless your heart. How ya holding up?"

Finley stiffened under Adeline's atypical show of motherly affection. "Actually, I'm doing all right," she said, gently easing from her mother's grip. "But it's not like I've ever spent a holiday without you and Daddy before." She fingered away a tear. "And now, without Cathyanne or my husband and kids . . ." She added Quinton to the list, but only in her head. "I guess I'm feeling a touch emotional."

Adeline's eyes dampened. "I know, sweetheart, and I'm sorry." She gestured to her fastidiously packed suitcase. "The cruise seemed like a good idea a few months ago, but, well, with everything that's happened . . . If the tickets were refundable . . . and if your daddy and I weren't in need of some time away together." Crossing her arms at the waist, she opened her mouth and then closed it a few times as if struggling with two unacceptable dilemmas. "What are your plans for tonight?" she asked, pleadingly so. "Please tell me you have some."

A good daughter would have conjured a quick lie, but suddenly Finley wasn't feeling all that charitable. "I dunno," she started, but when her mother's eyes further saddened, Finley's heart turned to mush, and she couldn't help but show Adeline some mercy. "I have . . . options."

Adeline grinned. "With that trainer?" she asked, hopeful.

Finley sent her mother a bothered look. "No, Momma," she groaned out the words. "You know we broke up. Josh is with Skylar now."

"Right," Adeline said as she turned back to her packing. "Just thought maybe you'd changed your mind." She paused to steal a quick look at Finley. "Something tells me he'd take you back in a heartbeat."

"I thought you didn't approve?"

Adeline lifted a shoulder. "Maybe not at first, but he's such a lovely young man." A dreamy smile played with her lips. "So polite and he treated you well." She turned her palms up. "What's not to like?"

"Momma, he wants kids." Finley pursed her lips. "Need I say more?"

A horrified look wiped the smile from Adeline's face. "Um, no." She shook her head as she placed a few final items into her suitcase. "So what about Roy? I'm sure he'd be happy to have you too," she said, failing at her attempt to sound nonchalant.

"He and the kids are going to his momma's house." Finley shared a look of mutual understanding with her mother. "Again, need I say more?"

Adeline raised a hand in a stopping motion. "That woman," she muttered, referring to Roy's mother and how she never felt Finley was good enough for her precious son. Then without another word, Adeline quickly got back to rearranging her suitcase, her sharp movements telling Finley that there was more her mother wanted to say, but for reasons unknown, was holding back. Since Finley had never known her mother to hold back when speaking ill of Finley's former in-laws, she was left to assume that something else was eating her mother, and was pretty sure she knew what.

Some of the guilt Finley thought she'd moved past caught up to her again. "I know you're disappointed in me for breaking my wedding vows, for not forgiving Roy's indiscretions the way you did Daddy's," Finley apologized, "but, well . . ." *What's the point in trying to explain what she refuses to hear?* "I guess it doesn't matter. You wouldn't understand."

Straightening, Adeline put her hands to her hips with finality. "I understand more than you think." She flipped her suitcase closed. "Mine and your daddy's love runs far deeper than any hurt we could ever think to inflict on one another." The zipper hissed as she pulled it around. "But your and Roy's love was always more, I don't know, on the surface, I guess."

Shock and confusion braided the muscles between Finley's shoulders into an aching knot. "Then why do you keep trying to push us back together?"

Adeline shook her head as if having no idea. "It's just what mothers do, I guess." She looked at Finley through a perplexed gaze. "You can't possibly expect me to explain it."

Finley laughed. "Momma, you're impossible."

Adeline rebuked her daughter with a stiff look. "So, what about your tenant? Sue, is it?" she asked. "Or the other people from your therapy group? Can't you spend the evening with one of them?"

Tiring of this subject, Finley exhaled. "Sue's celebrating the holiday with Burlie-Jean and all her extended family. They invited me, but," the ache in her back pulled tighter, "I don't know, it sounds like a lot of people, and I'm in no mood to make small talk with a gaggle of strangers."

Adeline nodded her agreement. "And that neighbor of yours?" she asked, almost too carefully.

Finley's heart danced around inside her chest. "Quinton," she breathed out his name. "He invited me to his house, but he's having his kids over for the first time in eight years, and . . ." *And what?* She'd love to go, to meet them, to support Quinton, but she could hardly look at him without reliving their kiss and the heartache that had preceded their very brief tryst. *Lord, I'm pathetic.*

Adeline seared her daughter with a penetrating look. "He wants to introduce you to his kids?"

"That's what he said," Finley confirmed, squirming under her mother's all-knowing gaze. "But things have been weird between us ever since—"

"Finnie, I don't know what happened with you two," Adeline rushed in before adamantly adding, "and I really don't want to know." She gave her daughter a discussion-over look. "But what I *do* know is that a man doesn't want to introduce a woman to his children unless he cares for her. *Deeply.*"

The pressure in Finley's back dropped to her stomach. "It's not like that between Quinton and me," she said, and could hear the misery in her own voice.

Adeline raised an eyebrow and flung it at Finley. "Oh, really?"

"Momma, stop."

Adeline's censured look softened to a patronizing smile. "Look, baby girl, you gotta start seeing the silver lining, the lesson in each mistake." She moved over to Finley and took her daughter's hands in hers. "Good or bad, everything happens for a reason."

Tears re-assembled in Finley's eyes. "I know, Momma, and I'm trying," she said, choking on the part of her indecision she was starting to realize scared her the most. "Part of me is terrified I'll end up like the old man in one of Quinton's songs. Sitting alone with nothing but my memories packed in a bunch of yard sale boxes, not knowing what to do with all my regret."

"Memories are only good for as long as it takes us to learn from them," her father interrupted. Finley dropped her mother's hands and turned to see him entering through the open doorway. "Only then can the past direct us to make better decisions in the future." The smile he gave her next was small and sad, but held the enormity of a father's love. "Look, sugar beet, we can't change what we did yesterday. All we can do is decide what we're going to do about it today," he said and held Finley's gaze long enough for his meaning to sink in.

As Finley searched her father's loving eyes, she felt his wisdom and that of her mother's taking hold. She didn't have to fear her past mistakes, nor did she have to carry them with her, or even find a place to store them. She simply needed to make good use of them by making better choices in the future. To look inside her mistakes for the lesson that needed learning. She could do that, right? She could take the isolation from her stifled upbringing, from her years of pretending, from her failed marriage, and all the disasters that had befallen her since, and turn every experience into something positive for the future. Right? After all, she'd already gotten pretty good at letting go. What she needed to learn now was how to move on.

To his wife, Preston said, "As for you, you better move that cute little butt of yours so I can parade my trophy wife"—he bounced his eyebrows—"in front of all the other old geezers on that godforsaken boat you're forcing me on."

Adeline's face colored. "Oh, Preston, you're such a mess." She flicked his flattery away. "Take these bags to the car. I'm right behind you," she instructed, to which Preston gave his wife another come-hither look. Holding back a bashful smile, Adeline motioned toward to the door. "Go on, now," she insisted, "you crazy old coot . . ."

As Finley watched her parents flirt, and after forty-five years of marriage, the idea that she'd finally settled on what *she* truly wanted in life popped into her head before she could consider the probability of such a notion. How many people really ever connected with the love of their life, then went on to form a bond secure enough to weather every storm? And where did one go in search of such a man?

"Lord help me, if that man wasn't the first person I wanted to see every morning . . ." Adeline was saying, her words severing Finley from her thoughts. Returning her attention to her mother, she saw that her father had disappeared along with Adeline's suitcases. "Your daddy's right, you know. It's time you figured out what *you* want," Adeline went on, sounding a whole lot like Cathyanne. "Whether or not you attain it is not what matters. What's important is that you had the courage to try." She brushed the back of her hand down Finley's cheek. "That way, come what may, you won't have any regret."

Her mother's touch, so gentle and loving, had Finley longing to be a child again. "So isn't this the part where you tell me what I want?" she asked, her words beseeching.

Adeline tucked a strand of Finley's hair behind her ear. "When you were a little girl I used to worry because you were so much like your granny Opaline. All sassy, and with your panties always in a wad about one thing or another and not giving a good-gosh-darn who knew it. But I wanted you to be more like me, to grow into a proper Southern lady," she said, a single tear dropping from her eye. "And baby girl, I am so proud of you. You've grown into a beautiful, caring woman that people respect. But even I can see that you're not happy, and probably never have been—"

"Momma, don't . . ."

"Hush now. It's rude to interrupt," Adeline scolded, and more out of curiosity than any sort of proper upbringing, Finley obeyed. "As I was saying, I think it's time I stop trying to live your life for you, which means you're going to have to answer that question for yourself."

Finley smiled through her befuddlement. Her mother had admitted to being wrong *and* had refused to meddle—both at the same time. While not in the least bit helpful to Finley at the moment, this was another Christmas miracle indeed.

"But this time, I'm asking for your opinion."

Adeline gave her daughter one last smile before turning to lift her coat from the bed. "Well, like I said, it's your choice." She shrugged her arms into the sleeves and then cut Finley a firm look as she started for the door. "But if I were you, I'd take that Quinton up on his offer."

## Chapter 24

Finley slipped the simple black dress over her head and turned toward the mirror. She hadn't seen this much cleavage looking back at her since . . . well, the last time she'd worn this dress, a good five years back on New Year's Eve, if memory served, when she was still trying to catch Roy's attention. Only that night, Roy had deigned to charm every woman in the room but Finley, a common strategy of his she now understood had been meant to capture *her* attention. Tragic really, how they'd both wanted the same thing but were incapable of conveying their desires with any degree of efficiency, much less mutual affection or even love.

Turning from side to side, she asked herself, what would Cathyanne do? Obviously, Cathyanne would wear the dress. Even so, did Quinton's song mean that Finley literally had to do everything Cathyanne would do, or just that Finley needed to, like Cathyanne, start asking herself what she wanted? The second interpretation seemed much more likely.

So, "What would Finley do?" she asked the mirror.

Appraising her reflection again, she noticed the way the velvet fabric fit to her body without clinging, the hemline falling just short enough to show off her newly toned thighs. Though she didn't generally wear revealing clothes, she *did* want Quinton to see her as more than a friend, and this dress should do the trick.

Yes! Finley would definitely wear it. Decision made.

With her hair wanded into loose curls she'd then pinned up with rhinestone clips, the freshly baked chocolate pecan pie warmed her hands as her heels crunched the frosty ground that separated her drive from Quinton's.

Stopping at the steps that led the way to his front porch, she looked back toward her home and smiled at the sight of the lit-up sign Josh had recently installed for Finley's Garden. Everything she'd been looking for, all she'd thought her life was missing, had been right here the entire time—at home. Turning her focus back to Quinton, she glanced up, her gaze running over the sleeping rose bushes she'd been pruning the first time they'd met. Her smiled stretched as she noted that he'd done as she'd advised and kept the bushes trimmed over the years, and now had them draped, along with the other hedges that lined his home, in colorful net lights. His windows and eaves were also outlined in light, giving the home that gingerbread house look.

Her legs shaking, and not from the cold, she managed the wooden steps. Afraid to risk the possibility that she might chicken out, she rapped on the glass of the storm door the very instant her toes met his welcome mat. A minute or so—and about a hundred heartbeats—later, the interior door swung open, and a woman in her early twenties, bearing a striking resemblance to the man Finley had come in search of, greeted her with a hesitant look.

Finley froze. Why had she assumed Quinton would be the one to answer the door? What should she say now? Had

Quinton even mentioned to his daughter that Finley might be joining them? Or did her unexpected appearance on his doorstep, with a pie in hand, scream of desperate-lonely-divorcée seeking last-minute-holiday-hook-up?

The young woman pushed the glass open a few inches. "Can I help you?"

Finley struggled against her angst to recall the young woman's name. *Amy? No, not Amy* . . . "Um, well . . ." *Annie? Yes, Annie!* "Hi Annie, I'm your daddy's neighbor, Finley Harrison." She sheepishly held out the pie. "He invited me, a few weeks ago, so he may have forgotten, but here I am anyway . . ."

Annie's eyes slid in the direction of the house next door, then back to Finley, and finally down to the pie in her hands. Recognition slowly crept across her face. "Oh, right, Finnie, isn't it?" She opened the door to capacity and stood back, motioning for Finley to enter. "My dad's mentioned you, once or twice," she said, a smile twisting the corners of a pair of lips she'd obviously inherited from her father.

The glass door banged shut behind Finley, and she was immediately overcome by the smell of brisket and rolls mixed with hints of pine, and yes, maybe even ginger. A tree decorated in ceramic cowboy boots and blue tin stars peeked around the corner that led into Quinton's great room. From the stereo speakers, Hank Williams Jr. droned the lyrics to "The Little Drummer Boy."

Annie closed the inside door and reached for the pie. "Here, let me take that so you can hang up your coat," she offered, her smile further yanking at her mouth.

Finley relented the pie. "Thank you," she said as she removed her coat and hung it on the coat rack. "Careful. The pie's still warm, so it might not be fully set yet," she was in the process of saying when a pair of boots clattered into the entry.

"Finnie?" Quinton said as if he couldn't have been more surprised to find the ghost of Christmas past standing in his entryway. "I'm s-so glad you could make it."

What felt like a team of Santa's elves chose that very moment to start cartwheeling through Finley's stomach. "Thanks, me too," she said, her voice all wobbly.

Quinton held a hand out to his daughter. "Finnie, this is my . . . um," he began, but as his eyes scrolled from Finley's shoulders to her toes, his words appeared to get lost somewhere along the way. "Um, my daughter. Annie."

Finley smiled through her blush. "Yes, we met."

Quinton's eyes took another turn over Finley's dress before landing on her face. "You look beautiful," he said, the words coming out all throaty, like he was having trouble catching his breath.

"Thanks," Finley replied, her voice more breath than substance too. "You don't look so bad yourself," she returned the compliment with every bit of heat Quinton had put into the one he'd given her. And he did look strikingly handsome in that pair of jeans he wore so well coupled with a dark, forest-green sweater that accentuated the twinkle in his gray eyes even more than usual.

"Ahem!"

Finley tore her eyes from Quinton's to see that Annie was having a very difficult time holding back that knowing smile she'd been struggling with. Finley had forgotten the girl was there. "Oh, um, right," she stuttered as she snuck another peek at Quinton to see that he was blushing too. Though things between her and Quinton seemed to be off to a good start and she didn't want to do anything to ruin what had the potential of being an interesting evening, she knew she'd come here tonight looking for more than company and a mutual flirtation.

After first giving Annie an apologetic look, she turned back to Quinton with earnest. "Hey, I was wondering if we could talk. Privately?"

A flash of surprise, or maybe worry, Finley couldn't tell which, flashed across Quinton's eyes. "Can it wait? We're about to eat." He stole a glance at his daughter before sending an anxious look over to Finley.

Finley considered retracting her request, but then Quinton's daughter spoke up, saying, "It's okay, Dad." She pointed toward the kitchen where Finley could hear what sounded like Quinton's teenaged sons teasing each other over something to do with a girl. "We'll set another place and finish up with supper." She gave her dad a shrewd smirk that she also shared with Finley. "Y'all take your time."

Quinton led Finley into the small office that bordered the entry and pulled the door closed, leaving it open a crack. "So, what's up?" he asked, his focus sidetracked to Finley's neckline again. His intent gaze, like ten playful fingers, tickled her skin. "You look amazing, by the way."

"Yes." Finley chuckled a little. "You already said that."

"Did I?"

"Uh-huh." The dress had definitely caught his attention, but what Finley needed now was for him to focus on more important matters. "An-y-way . . ."

Quinton gave his head a little shake. "Right, so there was something you wanted to discuss?" he asked, planting his eyes firmly on her face.

Finley's heart revved, preparing to race. "Remember when you said we should talk about . . . the kiss, and I cut you off, both times?" she said, rushing the words through her lips. "Well, now I want to hear it. I want to hear what you have to say about it . . . the kiss, I mean."

Quinton drew his eyebrows together. "What, right now?"

Finley crossed her arms over her chest, both to keep her heartbeat in check and to give the impression she wasn't budging until he spilled his thoughts. "Well, I don't see how we can sit down to a nice Christmas Eve supper with all this awkwardness between us." She lifted an eyebrow. "Do you?"

Quinton's gaze flitted over his shoulder in the direction of the door, and the muffled voices of his kids just beyond. "I guess it might be a good idea to clear the air." He stepped back and pushed the door all the way closed.

When he turned back to her, he simply puffed out his cheeks and then blew the air through his lips, but seemed to have nothing to say.

"So?" she questioned.

Shaking his head, Quinton began, "I'm not really sure where to start. I guess it's just that all these years I've been watching you, falling a little more for you each day while forcing myself to keep a safe distance. And it was easy too. You were married, and I knew you would never be disloyal to your husband or family." He smiled a sullen smile. "But then, you caught Roy cheating, and I could hardly believe it but you threw him out. Since he left, it's become harder and harder for me to hide my feelings." He stopped, his gaze drifting off to the far wall. "I never should have kissed you, though. I knew it was wrong, but I'd always wondered what it would feel like." A touch of the spark returned to his eyes as he focused back in on Finley. "And I was ready to go all the way, to take you upstairs and make love to you. But then you pulled back, and I saw the concern in your eyes, the mistrust, and I knew that sooner or later you'd come to your senses, figure out you'd made a big mistake."

The part of Finley's heart he'd broken that night tentatively started to mend. "Is that why you let me go so easily?"

Nodding, Quinton confirmed. "After you left I couldn't sleep, and that was even after a few very cold showers." He laughed dryly. "Anyway, all I could think was how perfect it would be if you and I could actually be together. Besides this insane attraction I have for you, you're my best friend, Finnie."

Finley smiled. "I know, and I feel the same the way about you."

"Do you?" he asked, but the dismal way in which he'd said it had Finley suddenly feeling uncertain.

"Y-yes," she stammered.

He eyed her a moment before continuing, "That's why I came to talk to you in the kitchen the day of the yard sale, to see if you'd felt something too. Only you were so intent on denying what had happened between us, and then there was that business with Roy . . . I started to question whether you could ever care for me that way. After Cathyanne . . ." he said, leaving her fate unspoken, "when you pushed me away—told me to stay away to be exact—I figured that whatever may have happened between us didn't really matter. You wanted that trainer, or Roy maybe, I couldn't tell for sure." He gave her a look of pure misery. "What would a woman like you want with a man like me anyway?"

"Funny, I've been asking myself the same thing about you."

Quinton huffed out a humorless laugh. "Finnie, no. You and I are nowhere near the same playing field." He held a hand out to Finley. "You're a good person. You always do the right things." He touched the same hand to his chest. "And I'm . . . well, I break the hearts of the people I love."

"You've come a long way since the day we first met, the day I was clipping rosebuds," Finley reminded him.

Shaking his head, Quinton's gaze avoided hers. "Finnie, you've seen my demons," he said. "Had a front row seat to the horror, so to speak."

It was true, she had seen the worst in him. "Quinton, everyone has demons."

Quinton hung his head. "Yes, but some people's are more destructive than others'."

Sure, reason dictated that once an addict, always an addict, which meant he could relapse at any time, but Finley couldn't let a maybe keep them apart. She'd seen him through recovery before, and heaven help her, she could do it again.

"You don't think I know that?" she asked.

Quinton's eyes lifted to hers and held a long moment. "What do you want, Finnie? Why did you come here tonight?" The way he was looking at her, through her, put her on edge. She felt exposed, vulnerable, uncertain. *You know what to do, Finley,* a voice, one that sounded eerily similar to that of her best friend's, whispered. *The answers you're looking for are inside of you, a part of who you are.* Cathyanne? Finley released the breath she hadn't known she'd been holding. *Finally . . .*

Shifting her focus inward, Finley flipped through memories, both good and bad, from her childhood to her marriage and then divorce, dating Josh, and losing both her best friend, and in some ways her children too. What did it all mean to her now? What was the lesson to be learned? As she searched deeper, she found that it all added up to one thing: if she was ever going to be happy, she needed to take responsibility for her own life, and to do so, she had to ask for what she wanted.

*Very good.*

Before she could take that leap, however, she needed to make sure Quinton was, in fact, a risk she wanted to take. And to do so, she was going to have to do something so uncharacteristically Finley, she had trouble believing the inkling had originated from her own head. Then again, maybe it hadn't . . .

On timid feet, Finley crossed the floor until she was standing toe-to-toe with Quinton. Slowly, she raised her eyes to his, and there she saw confusion and possibly something else. Fear? Desire?

"Okay, well, it's just that . . ." Finley pressed her hands to his chest. She could feel his heartbeat keeping pace with hers. Sliding her hands up, over his shoulders, and around his neck, she threaded her fingers together and pulled his mouth close to hers. "I need to check something first," she said as she rolled up onto her toes.

Bringing her lips to his, she was welcomed by the warm softness she remembered. The simple feel of his lips against hers sent the blood coursing through her veins, pumping at a dangerous speed. If she hadn't been the only one doing the kissing, the rate of her heartbeat would have been a good indication that she was on the right track.

Disappointment trailed by embarrassment had her dropping her heels back to the ground, but before her lips had fully cleared his, Quinton's arms came around her, one hand circling her waist, the other cupping the back of her head. Gently, he held her close, kissing her softly, like she was something delicate he didn't want to break. The subtle force of his intention whipped the strength from her legs. If it hadn't been for the grip he had on her, she had no doubt she'd have fallen abruptly to the floor.

Quinton pulled her closer still. Finley responded by loosening her grip. She fell into him, allowing his body to consume hers until they were one—one body, one soul, soaring to heights that both terrified and inspired. How could she have ever doubted that this man was the one she wanted—no, needed—to spend the rest of her life with?

Then, much too quickly, Quinton broke away. With both hands at her waist now, he created a safe distance and dropped his forehead to hers. "What was that for?" His breath hit her face in short, sporadic bursts.

The space he'd put between them bespoke of doubt, but when it came to Quinton, doubt was no longer in Finley's vocabulary.

She lifted her gaze to his. "You're right," she said. "I do know what I want."

"What about that trainer of yours?"

"He's with Skylar now."

Quinton's brow rose. "Really?" He grinned. "And Roy?" His smile faded. "His truck has been in your driveway quite a bit here lately."

"We're friends, that's all."

Quinton licked his lips. "I still don't know, Finnie." He stepped back, dragging his heady gaze over her again. "I want you. Man, how I want you, but at the same time, I'm afraid." He ripped his eyes away, casting them down. "No way can I allow you to get hurt the way I hurt my family."

Impatience pushed Finley forward. "Quinton." She gripped him by both his arms. "I know better than anyone what I'm getting into with you, and I'm not afraid." She gave him a steady, reassuring smile. "I think it's time we both leave the past where it belongs and start moving forward. No more regrets, like your song says."

He smiled, sad but amused. "No more regrets, huh?"

"None."

"And you're sure about this?"

Finley stared him directly in the eye. "Positive."

"You saved my life," he said fondly. "For some reason God brought you to me, and by doing so has given me a second chance at life." Admiration swam amidst the tears, collecting in his eyes. "At being a father too."

Finley circled her hands around his neck again. "I know." She brushed another kiss across his lips. "But He didn't just bring me to you, He brought you to me too," she said, and then hesitated, gathering courage. *Steady, Finnie, you're almost there.* "And because of that, I would regret every second, from here on, if I didn't tell you that I love you." Tears bathed her eyes. "I denied my feelings for you all these years, buried them deep, but from the instant you first kissed me, I was yours. I love you Quinton Townes, and nothing you say is gonna make me stop. I want what we can have together," she said, surprising herself with how decisive she both sounded and felt. "I want to be in love with my best friend, and I refuse to settle for anything less."

Quinton smiled, and for the first time since he'd shut the office door, hope touched his glistening eyes. "So you're saying you want for us to be together," he restated, "as in dating, and a whole lot more kissing?"

Finley pressed her lips to his long and hard. "Yes," she said, to which something indecent but playful snuck into Quinton's dark gaze.

"I bet we'd be pretty good at a few other things too," he said.

The very thought awakened places in Finley she'd forgotten existed. "I can't wait to find out."

Quinton slipped his hands around her waist and pressed a soft kiss to her lips. "So you're saying"—he kissed each cheek—"we're going to do this"—his lips nibbled at her neck—"we're going to"—he dragged his mouth across her collarbone next—"be a couple?"

Finley knew it was physically impossible, but her heart felt like it was fixin' to beat its way right out of her chest. "Yes, that's what I'm saying."

Quinton dropped one last kiss over Finley's pounding heart. "So when you meet my sons"—he nodded toward the door—"should I introduce you as my neighbor or my girlfriend?"

Finley pretended to mull the question. "Definitely, your girlfriend," she said as visions of a spring wedding under a blossoming apple arbor danced in her head. "That title should do," she added along with a wry smile, "for now anyway."

As if he too could see their future, Quinton pulled Finley closer. "I like the sound of that." He kissed her again, slow and deep.

"Do you now?" Finley teased once he'd allowed her to breathe again.

Then Quinton got real quiet, reflective. "So, I guess this is the part where I say that I love you too?"

A speck of doubt snuck in. "That'd be nice," Finley confirmed even as the voice inside her head whispered that she didn't need him to. *Why wouldn't I need him to?* Finley was in the process of questioning when the answer along with what Cathyanne had been trying to say struck her all at once.

For the bulk of her life, Finley had been trudging from one goal to another, thinking that once she had achieved this or that, jumped this hurtle or dodged that bullet, *then* she would finally be happy. What she didn't know until this moment was that happiness wasn't found at the crest of the mountain, it was in each foothold of the climb. In each stumble, each fall, and in the determination to get back up and keep going. Happiness meant having the courage and perseverance to get over yourself and go after what you wanted, accept the outcome, and then move on without fretting over what might have been. And in knowing that for better or worse, life would always turn out the way it was meant to be.

*Thank you,* Finley told the voice in her head. *I finally get it.*

A sense of finality settled in as the voice retreated. *You're so very welcome my friend.*

Quinton ran his tongue over his bottom lip. His mouth

parted, readying to spill what Finley assumed were the words she'd been longing to hear.

Laying her finger to his lips, she shushed him because it didn't matter anymore if Quinton said he loved her. She now knew that she didn't need his love to be happy, and wanted to relish in this moment of enlightenment, of pure joy, a bit longer.

"But, Finnie, I—"

Finley pressed her mouth to his with a lingering kiss. "You don't need to say a thing," she purred against his lips.

"I was simply going to tell you, Merry Christmas."

"Merry Christmas to you too, Quinton."

"I love you," he said.

"Yes, I thought you might."

$\mathcal{A}$ graduate from San Diego State University with a BA in Political Science, Julie N. Ford also earned a Masters in Social Work from the University of Alabama, which has only made her better able to recognize the unhealthy, codependent relationship she has with writing. Professionally, she has worked in teaching and as a marriage and family counselor. She is the author of six women's fiction novels, including *Count Down to Love,* a 2011 Whitney Award finalist. When she's not writing, she entertains delusions of being a master gardener, that is, when she's not killing the unsuspecting plants in her yard with her good intentions. She lives outside of Nashville, Tennessee, with her husband, two daughters, and the cutest Scottish fold cat you've ever seen. She loves to chat with readers. Visit her at JulieNFord.com, Facebook, Twitter and Instagram.

CPSIA information can be obtained
at www.ICGtesting.com
Printed in the USA
LVOW04s1546160816

500619LV00021B/1375/P